The
SPIRIT
GUIDE

BRIDGET WALSH

Pushkin Press
Somerset House, Strand
London WC2R 1LA

First published by Pushkin Press in 2026

ISBN 13: 978-1-80533-583-2

A CIP catalogue record for this title is available from the British Library

The authorised representative in the EEA is eucomply OÜ,
Pärnu mnt. 139b-14, 11317, Tallinn, Estonia,
hello@eucompliancepartner.com, +33757690241

Typeset by Tetragon, London
Printed and bound in the United Kingdom by Clays Ltd, Elcograf S.p.A.

Pushkin Press is committed to a sustainable future for our
business, our readers and our planet. This book is made from
paper from forests that support responsible forestry.

www.pushkinpress.com

1 3 5 7 9 8 6 4 2

BRIDGET WALSH was born in London to Irish immigrant parents. She studied English literature at university and later acquired both a PhD in Victorian domestic murder and an obsessive interest in the weirder elements of nineteenth-century life. Bridget lives in Norwich with her husband, Micky, and her two dogs. Her debut and the first book in the Variety Palace Mysteries, *The Tumbling Girl*, won the Historical Writers Association Debut Crown and was shortlisted for the CWA John Creasey Dagger. *The Innocents* was longlisted for the CWA Gold Dagger for best crime novel of the year. Both are available from Pushkin Vertigo.

This book is dedicated
to the sisterhood

'Well then, it now appears you need my help'

WILLIAM SHAKESPEARE
The Merchant of Venice

ONE

'So you see, Mrs Willoughby, the evidence is what we might call damning.'

Minnie glanced down at her wedding ring. It was a touch on the small side, had been from the first moment she'd put it on. On a hot day like this her fingers swelled, the flesh curling over the edges of the ring. It'd be a bugger to get off.

She'd had to remind herself on more than one occasion that she was Mrs Willoughby now. She imagined someone respectable, conventional. Perhaps with a substantial bosom and a recipe for the perfect scones.

'Mrs Willoughby?' the man prompted her.

In the normal run of things, you'd be forgiven for thinking Wendall Potts was quite an attractive fella. Tall, with striking blue eyes. Nice smile, although he only used it when he was making you squirm. 'Am I keeping you from something?'

'Nothing,' she said, shaking her head to clear her thoughts. 'You were about to tell me what the new price is gonna be. And I'm guessing you won't be offering me a discount.'

He named a figure. More than twice what he'd originally told her. She'd been expecting him to ask for more, but the increase was so audacious that it still came as a surprise.

'I don't have anything like that money,' she said.

'Well, you'll have to find it, won't you? You can give me what you have now and the rest later.'

She scrutinised the piece of paper on the table. A typewritten list of meetings with dates and brief, damning descriptions. 'Mrs X witnessed in intimate situation with Mr Y, heads inclined toward each other. Mrs X holding hands with Mr Y. Mr Y's arm round waist of Mrs X.'

Minnie raised her eyes and looked round Brown's tea room. Saturday lunchtime and it was bristling with customers, perfectly presented waitresses weaving their way between tables with pots of tea, delicate china crockery and plates of elegant sandwiches and cake. She and Potts were seated at a table tucked away in the corner. No one was close enough to read the list of meetings – *the evidence*, as she was now coming to think of it – but still she felt uncomfortable. She'd always liked it in here. Felt it was a second home. She didn't want the waitresses, the other customers, to think ill of her, whatever the circumstances.

She looked down again at the typewritten sheet. She was Mrs X. Mr Y was Albert. Of course. Who else could it be other than Albert? As she read the sterile list of their assignations, she once again recalled the moment when his arm had slipped round her waist, his hand broad and strong, the fingers warm, so warm she swore she could feel their heat right through her clothes, on her skin. He had held her hand; they had laughed about how it was like holding hands with a bear, her slender paw enveloped in his. They had walked together like that, talking nonsense as their heads inclined towards each other.

Wendall Potts had been watching them the whole time, lurking in the shadows, writing down precise details of exactly where they'd been, what they'd done. And now he was going to present the evidence to her husband unless she found the money to pay him.

Potts gestured to the waitress across the crowded tea room and mimed writing on his hand. A few minutes later the waitress, a slip of a thing no more than fourteen, appeared with the bill. She looked at Minnie, a flicker of concern crossing her face. 'No cake today, Min?'

she asked, looking down at the two cups of tea, the one in front of Minnie untouched. 'You feeling all right?'

Minnie nodded and smiled weakly. 'I'm fine, Nora,' she said. 'Had a big breakfast.'

Nora cleared the cups and left Minnie and Potts alone again. Minnie reached into her bag and removed an envelope stuffed with banknotes. She pushed it across the table towards Potts, the tips of her fingers staying in contact with the buff envelope until the last moment. It was a lot of money, and she was very sorry to see it passing into Potts's nasty little flappers.

Potts snatched the envelope, peered inside and riffled through the notes with his thumb, mentally adding up the amount.

'It's what we agreed,' Minnie said. 'And you're gonna have to wait if you want any more. I don't have anything like the sum you're asking for.'

'Well, best you find it. And quick smart. I imagine Mr Willoughby won't take too kindly to hearing about your little – friendship.'

He slipped the money into an inside pocket of his jacket, then pushed back his chair, the feet scraping on the wooden floor, and rose slowly. At the last minute, he took the typewritten sheet, folded it carefully and slipped it into the same pocket.

'Pleasure doing business with you, Mrs Willoughby. We'll meet again in' – he gazed upwards, as if inspiration lay on the ceiling of the tea room, and then seemed to randomly pluck a date from the air – 'two days. Same time, same place. And I'll be expecting the rest of my money.'

He'd spoken loudly enough for a dark-haired man on the nearest table to look up from his newspaper. Minnie turned away, trying to hide her face. Potts laughed and tossed the bill at her. 'Your treat, Mrs Willoughby.'

He was nearly at the door when it happened. The dark-haired man seated nearby who, on closer inspection, bore more than a passing resemblance to Inspector John Price of the Metropolitan Police, threw aside his newspaper, leapt from his seat and lunged towards Potts. Before Potts had time to understand what was happening, John had slapped a pair of handcuffs on him.

'You, my lad,' John said, 'are coming with me.'

'I ain't done nothing,' Potts said, his voice pitched high in protest. 'I was just sharing a cup of tea with my lady friend.' He gave her a pointed look. 'We was sharing a few quiet moments, weren't we, Mrs Willoughby?'

'You've got me confused with someone else,' she said. 'My name's Minnie Ward. And you've just accepted blackmail money from me. That fella you saw me with – Mr Y? He's my partner. You might have heard of us. Easterbrook and Ward? Private detectives? And there ain't no Mr Willoughby.' She tried to wrestle the ring from her finger as a final dramatic gesture, but it wouldn't shift. She cursed under her breath and turned to Nora, who was standing, slack-jawed, taking in the whole proceedings.

'You ain't got a pat of butter going begging, have you, love?' Minnie said.

Ten minutes later, Potts was on his way to John's police station. Minnie had paid the bill at Brown's, leaving Nora a generous tip, and left the tea room. The wedding ring, however, was stuck fast.

She wove her way through the crowds of tourists and day-trippers taking in the delights of the Strand, and headed towards the Variety Palace Music Hall. Before she'd gone too far, a tall, well-built man fell into step beside her. She turned and grinned at him.

'I take it everything went smoothly, Mrs Willoughby?' Albert Easterbrook said. A woman passing close by threw him a quizzical glance. The elegance of his well-rounded vowels stood in stark contrast to his pugilist's nose and hands. Minnie was used to the apparent contradiction, although she remembered her surprise when she'd first met him. He'd been sporting a black eye at the time, which made it all the more confusing when he opened his mouth and sounded like he'd stepped straight off the playing fields of Eton.

'Couldn't have gone better, Mr Y,' she said. 'It'll be a while before Potts is up to his tricks again.'

'Miss Barnes will be delighted.'

Eustacia Barnes had sought their help a month ago. Her fiancé, a suspicious-minded individual named Wilbur Renton, had hired Potts to investigate Eustacia's past. When Potts had uncovered evidence of a former liaison, rather than inform Renton of his findings, he'd approached Eustacia herself and tried to extort money from her, in return for his silence.

'What he found was nothing to be ashamed of,' she'd told Minnie and Albert, 'just some fella I walked out with a few times. But Wilbur might think differently.'

On closer examination, Minnie and Albert discovered Potts was making a tidy living through blackmail and extortion. Minnie had created the character of Mrs Willoughby, with Tom Neville, Albert's former assistant, acting as her suspicious husband, seeking proof of his concerns from Potts.

'Too late for the wedding, though,' Minnie said. Eustacia's fiancé had reacted with horror to the news that he was not the first man she had kissed. The wedding had been called off. 'She had a lucky escape, if you ask me.'

She noticed Albert shortening his stride so she could keep up and realised he did this every time they walked anywhere. Funny how she'd never noticed it before. 'You coming to the Palace?' she asked.

'I am.'

'And that wouldn't have nothing to do with the fact a certain Madame Ivanova is currently rehearsing for tonight's performance?'

'It might.'

Minnie and Albert entered the Palace by the stage door. The music hall was strangely quiet, which never boded well. They walked down the backstage corridor, glancing into changing rooms with costumes thrown over the backs of chairs and tables littered with stage make-up and remnants of food. No one. Minnie exchanged a look with Albert.

'Out the front?' he suggested.

They took the door into the auditorium and were greeted with the strangest sight Minnie thought she'd ever seen at the Palace. Everyone was there – Tansie, Kippy, Bernard, the stagehands, front of house, all the performers, most of whom weren't due in for a few hours yet. Tables and chairs were stacked against the walls and no one had bothered to grab themselves a seat. There were close to a hundred people, all standing in complete silence, all facing the stage.

Tansie, the manager of the Variety Palace, gestured frantically for Minnie and Albert to join him. Known for his sartorial choices, Tansie had made an extra effort today, sporting a dark mustard suit, a teal-and-mustard checked waistcoat and a very nice pair of highly polished Oxfords. Minnie's mother had always said you could judge a man by his shoes. Which was worrying, 'cos Tansie wore the nicest shoes Minnie had ever seen on a man, and he was not a fella you'd want to hang up the ladle for. Or at least Minnie wouldn't want to. Other women seemed to find him irresistible.

'She's just about to start rehearsals,' Tansie hissed, nodding towards the stage.

'And you didn't think to give her a bit of peace and quiet?' Minnie hissed back.

Tansie gave her an old-fashioned look. 'It's Madame Ivanova,' he said needlessly. 'Here. At the Palace. What, we were all gonna pop out for a bite to eat and leave her to it?'

Minnie turned towards the stage. Madame Ivanova had positioned herself at what looked like the exact centre point. She was small, unprepossessing. Her dark hair was parted severely in the middle and pulled back into a simple bun at the nape of her neck. Her eyes were dark, with a slightly mischievous glint, her mouth set in a firm line.

She wore a black dress, cut simply, not a single flounce or furbelow. Nothing to draw the eye or mark her out as different in any way.

Then she opened her mouth and the whole world changed.

Her voice was achingly pure, a single note held for an impossible length of time. And then, when it seemed as if there was nothing else, as if perhaps this was all she had to give, Madame Ivanova's voice soared, growing in volume, looping and weaving in unimaginable ways. Ways that seemed impossible for a human voice to behave.

Minnie didn't know enough about opera to recognise the song. Didn't even know what language Madame Ivanova was singing, although she guessed it was Italian. Couldn't understand a word. But none of that mattered. She'd never stood this close to an opera singer in full flow, and she swore she could feel the woman's voice reverberating through her own chest. The whole auditorium was transformed by the sound. Lamps sprang alight. The very quality of the air was changed.

And then it was over. As the last, lingering memories of the notes faded, Minnie realised the lamps were still unlit and the shimmer in the air had left with the last note.

Around her, Minnie heard what sounded like a collective sigh and noticed that she, too, had been holding her breath for at least part of the performance. She also found, somewhat to her surprise, that she was holding Albert's hand. Swiftly, she disentangled herself and wiped the tears from her face. No one said a word for what felt like the longest time. The clatter of balls from the bowling alley adjoining the Palace broke the silence following Madame Ivanova's performance. And then, as if on cue, everyone broke into applause, though applause seemed insufficient for what they had just witnessed.

Minnie still couldn't quite believe their luck. Madame Ivanova, the pre-eminent soprano of her day, could sell out Covent Garden and the Royal Opera House within a few hours and could charge any figure she liked for private performances. Which made it all the more remarkable that she was performing at the Variety Palace for three nights, entirely free of charge.

Madame Ivanova gave a little shrug. 'So,' she said as the applause died away, her voice heavily accented from her native Russia, 'now we rehearse. We work. We improve. Tonight will be better, yes?'

Back in Tansie's office, Minnie scanned the columns of numbers, although she wasn't entirely sure she knew what she was looking at. Bookkeeping was not one of her strong points and she'd been heartily relieved when Tansie had taken back control of the more boring side of running the Palace. After what felt like an acceptable amount of time, she looked at the total and winced.

'You told me things were going well, Tanse,' she said. 'Don't look much like that to me.'

'That,' Tansie said, pointing to the figure at the bottom of the page, 'is how much we're in profit, Min.'

Minnie looked again at the total. 'That's a very big number, Tanse. Sure you ain't been doing a little – creative accounting?'

'Just 'cos you nearly ran us into the ground when you were in charge of the Palace, don't mean the same applies to me. It might surprise you to learn I do know what I'm doing. Plus, Madame I's three appearances are gonna set us up for the rest of the year.' He nodded towards Albert. 'Ta very much, by the way.'

Madame Ivanova had sought Albert's help two months previously. She'd had a suspicion that a member of her staff was stealing from her, but had been unable to determine who. Albert had enlisted the help of Dorothy Lawrence, the Palace's bookkeeper, who found within a matter of days that Madame Ivanova's manager had been appropriating a large amount of her earnings to feed his habits. On closer investigation, Albert discovered one of those habits was a woman secreted in a luxury apartment in St John's Wood, a woman with very expensive taste. When she received the news from Albert,

Madame Ivanova promptly sacked her manager and offered to double Albert's fee by way of thanks. It had been his suggestion that she might perform at the Palace in lieu of payment. He had suggested a single night. Madame Ivanova, with theatrical generosity, had insisted on three.

'Why'd you do it?' Minnie asked. 'I mean, the Palace ain't exactly known for its operatic leanings.'

Albert smiled to himself and shot Tansie a conspiratorial glance.

'He did it for you, you cod,' Tansie said.

Minnie looked confused.

'You love it, don't you?' Tansie said. 'All them arias and whatnot.'

'How'd you know that?' Minnie asked suspiciously. Tansie was right. She adored opera but she couldn't remember ever sharing the information with anyone. Opera was for toffs, everyone knew that.

'Bernard spotted you one night, coming out of Covent Garden,' Tansie said. 'Then I dropped a few little hints here and there about Verdi and Puccini and a few other fellas whose names end in "i". Every time your little face lit up. It weren't difficult to figure it out.'

'It seemed the obvious choice,' Albert said. 'And judging by your reaction when Madame Ivanova was singing just now, it was the right one.'

'You've gotta stop doing that,' Minnie said, her eyes narrowing.

'Doing what?' Albert said.

'Watching me when I don't know you're doing it.'

'I didn't know it was a habit of mine.'

'Well, it is. That, and sneaking up on me unannounced. It could give a girl the collywobbles, y'know.'

He smiled and shrugged his shoulders in a gesture of surrender. 'It was worth it,' he said. 'Particularly when you held my hand.'

'Yeah, well don't go getting any funny ideas,' Minnie said. 'I was swept up in the moment. It could have been anyone's hand.'

'Weren't though, was it?' Tansie murmured, his face buried in a cupboard from which he extracted a tin of sardines. He opened the tin and started to feed the contents to a small black-and-white monkey seated on the desk in a miniature deckchair.

A draught whipped round their ankles. It was the same every time someone opened the stage door, and no one seemed able to solve the problem. A minute later Dorothy Lawrence swept into the room. With Tansie back managing the Palace, Minnie had less to do with Dorothy these days, and she hadn't seen her for a few weeks. She was struck anew by the sheer physical presence of the woman. Tall, all hair and curves, the envy of every girl in the chorus. Always beautifully attired, today Dorothy was sporting a rather simple day dress thrown into sharp relief by a feather-trimmed velvet dolman. On anyone else the dolman might have looked brash. On Dorothy it looked sensational. Minnie looked down at her own outfit. She always felt a little drab beside Dorothy. Invisible, even.

Tansie and Albert turned to look at Dorothy with undisguised admiration.

'Gentlemen. Minnie,' Dorothy said, nodding and smiling at each of them in turn. 'Have you finished cooking the books, Tansie?'

'I have indeed. And they make magnificent reading, might I add.' He shot Minnie a loaded look. 'Ain't you and Albert got somewhere to be?'

'No,' Albert said. 'We're done for today.'

Minnie wondered if Albert hadn't spotted Tansie's hint or had simply chosen not to take it. Obtuse, that's what Bernard called him.

'Actually,' she said, grabbing Albert's arm and guiding him towards the door, 'I need a quick word about our invoice for the Eustacia Barnes case. Out the front.'

'What was all that about?' Albert said as they made their way out into the auditorium, where the waiters were already laying tables and placing chairs. They'd started preparations earlier than usual because Tansie had doubled the number of tables, knowing there'd be no difficulty selling tickets for Madame Ivanova. And he'd been right. They could have sold ten times the number and still turned people away. 'Why were you in such a hurry to leave?'

'For such a clever man, you are remarkably beef-headed at times, Albert. Tansie likes Dorothy. In a special way.'

'Good God! And does she return his interest?'

'That I ain't so sure about. It seems a bit unlikely, given that she looks like she could be carved onto the front of a ship and he's more like something you'd scrape off the bottom. Last time he had his heart broken I ended up running the Palace, and that weren't good for anyone. If she ain't interested I might need to have a gentle word with Tanse. Although, judging by the spoony looks she keeps chucking his way, I'd say she's smitten. Either that, or soft in the head. Possibly both.'

Albert pulled out a seat for Minnie. She took it, and gazed round the auditorium. It was one of her favourite times of day at the Palace; although, to be fair, she loved it pretty much any time of day or night. But in these late-afternoon hours the place was stirred by a gentle industry and a mild anticipation mixed with nerves, even from the most seasoned of performers. Soon the lamplighters would get to work and the hundreds of gas burners, the candles in the elaborate chandeliers, would spring to life. The place would be transformed, all the grubby corners and tatty paintwork cast into shadow. When the audience came through the doors, they'd only see the magic.

The calm was pierced by a rich and sonorous voice, each vowel stretched to breaking point. Minnie suppressed a sigh. Bernard Reynolds had a habit of appearing when he was least wanted.

'Minnie, my love, your services are required in the ladies' dressing room. If you can tear yourself away from the lovely Albert, that is.'

'I think I can just about manage it,' Minnie said. 'What's the problem?'

'Some contretemps between Jemima and Alice. An affair of the heart, I suspect.'

'And you couldn't sort it, I suppose?' Minnie said.

'Good God, no!'

These days Bernard no longer trod the boards, having decided to retire from the stage after the death of his brother nearly two years ago. He'd created a role for himself as Tansie's right-hand man which he'd proved surprisingly good at, particularly when it came to informing performers that they needed to buck up or their services would no longer be required. Despite his own notoriously thin skin, he was ruthless when it came to delivering bad news to other people.

Bernard gave a theatrical shudder. 'I have a strict policy never to involve myself with ladies and romantic matters.'

Ten minutes later Minnie had convinced both women they could do a darn sight better than Elmer Wilkins, who spent his nights courting a succession of women and his days collecting the inappropriately named 'pure' for the local tanning factories. Jemima had conceded that Elmer did, indeed, most of the time stink of the dog shit he picked up, 'but he's got all his own teeth, Minnie, and that's more than can be said for a lot of fellas'.

Minnie was on her way back to the auditorium when someone burst through the stage door. A cottage loaf of a woman, somewhere in her forties. She was out of breath and noticeably distressed.

'You all right?' Minnie asked. 'Looking for someone?'

'I was told I'd find Mrs Lawrence here,' the woman said, catching her breath. 'Mrs Dorothy Lawrence?'

Minnie knew Dorothy went by Mrs Lawrence to avoid unnecessary interest from men, though it didn't always have the desired effect.

The door to Tansie's office opened and Dorothy appeared.

'Mrs Albemarle?' she said. 'What on earth are you doing here?'

'Your assistant at your office said I'd find you here. You need to come,' Mrs Albemarle said. 'It's awful, Mrs Lawrence. Just awful. He's—' She broke off.

'Henry?' Dorothy said, a noticeable tremor in her voice.

Mrs Albemarle nodded her head, tears spilling down her cheeks. 'He's dead, Mrs Lawrence. Dead. I can't – I can't talk about it in front of these—' She gestured wordlessly at the crowd that had now gathered backstage, Albert included. 'You just need to come.'

Dorothy had already grabbed her things and was halfway out the door.

'Wait,' Tansie said, 'don't you want someone with you?'

'You can't, Tansie,' Dorothy said distractedly. 'You've got the performance tonight. You need to be here.'

'We'll come,' Minnie said, 'me and Albert.'

Mrs Albemarle flinched at the suggestion. 'It's not – you shouldn't – it's not something you should see, miss. Trust me.'

Paying no heed to the warning, Minnie checked Albert was behind her, took hold of Dorothy's hand and the four of them headed out of the stage door.

TWO

Six o'clock in the evening and it felt as though the entire city was making its way home. The pavements were dense with black-jacketed men brushing off the dust of their office jobs only to have it replaced by the dust on the streets, and the roads were almost at a standstill with cabs and omnibuses, carriages and bicycles.

'Where does this man – Henry? – where does he live?' Albert asked.

'Devonshire Street,' Dorothy said, frantically scanning the Strand for an available cab.

'It'll be quicker to walk,' Minnie said. 'Even if you can find a cab at this hour, it'll take forever to get through the traffic.'

The four of them turned in the direction of Devonshire Street. Minnie had a hundred questions she wanted to ask but Dorothy was striding along at such a pace it was all Minnie could do to keep up with her.

'It's just here,' Dorothy said eventually, indicating a house close to the end of a small terrace.

As they approached the front door, Minnie spotted a young woman waiting on the front step – some sort of maid by the look of her. She gave Dorothy a fleeting smile and then seemed to realise it was no time for smiling. She ushered them into the house, then stood to one side, as if afraid to venture any further.

'He's in the morning room,' Mrs Albemarle said.

Dorothy led the way to a room at the rear of the house. Minnie braced herself for the sickly-sweet smell of decay as Dorothy opened the door, but thankfully there was nothing. Which meant the man – whoever he was – hadn't been long dead.

Minnie's first instinct was always to look away, to allow the deceased some dignity. But she knew it was important to examine the scene of death, that it often held clues as to what had taken place. In the case of murder, an answer, perhaps, to who had committed the crime. So she turned her eyes reluctantly towards the man, inwardly apologising for what felt like the ultimate invasion of privacy.

He was probably somewhere in his thirties, with a thatch of dark hair and a full beard. He lay on the floor, dressed in a pale grey pair of trousers and a white shirt. There was no sign of a jacket. The left sleeve of his shirt was rolled up. Hanging from his arm, bizarre and incongruous in this comfortable domestic space, was a syringe. Splayed on the rug next to him were a handful of photographs. Young women in various states of undress. Each of the photographs looked as if it had been positioned carefully, like some bewildering game of cards with rules Minnie didn't understand.

Mrs Albemarle's warning had led Minnie to expect a scene of violence. But this was worse, somehow. A moment of intimacy that nobody should have witnessed.

Albert crossed to the body and felt for a pulse, although it was obvious to everyone in the room the man was dead.

'Have you alerted a police officer?' Albert asked Mrs Albemarle.

She shook her head. 'I didn't know what to do. I just found him, and the first person I thought of was—' She turned towards Dorothy, who was staring at the body, transfixed. She swayed ominously. Minnie caught her in time and led her to a chair.

'Head between your knees,' Minnie said quietly. 'Deep breaths. It'll pass.'

After a few moments, Dorothy sat upright again. Her face was leached of all colour, her eyes staring vacantly into the distance.

'Forgive me for asking, but who are you, exactly?' Albert said to Mrs Albemarle.

'I'm the housekeeper and cook. Peggy' – here she glanced round her, noticing for the first time that the woman who had greeted them wasn't in the room – 'Peggy's the maid-of-all-work.'

'Any other staff?' Albert said.

'No. Just Mr Gregg the gardener. He doesn't live in.'

Albert nodded and left the room. Moments later they heard the front door slam. He'd gone for the police.

'When did you find him?' Minnie asked.

'An hour or so ago. Peggy and I had the day off yesterday. It was my son's wedding and Mr—' She struggled to continue.

'Henry,' Dorothy murmured.

Mrs Albemarle nodded, on the verge of tears. 'He insisted I take the day off – Peggy too. He was so generous like that. The wedding was in Oxford, so we stayed overnight and got back this morning. The house was quiet when we arrived, but we just figured maybe he'd gone to his club, or to see a friend. It wasn't until later we started to think it was odd he hadn't appeared. It must have been somewhere around half past four, five o'clock I decided to check the rooms. That's when I—' She broke off, her eyes drawn back to the body.

'Was this room locked?' Minnie asked.

Mrs Albemarle shook her head.

'And he was exactly like this when you found him?' Minnie asked. 'You haven't moved anything?'

'Nothing. Although I felt I should – tidy up somehow,' she gestured towards the photographs, an expression of distaste flickering across her face. 'But my cousin's a copper and he says you should never touch anything.'

'Why didn't you go for the police?'

'I didn't know what to do. Like I said, the only person I could think of was—' She nodded at Dorothy, who was gazing at some fixed point in the distance, saying nothing, reacting to nothing. 'I went to her office and her assistant said she'd gone to the Variety Palace. Which is where I found her. Obviously.'

'Do you think you could make us some tea, Mrs Albemarle?' Minnie asked. 'Lots of sugar.'

'Of course,' the housekeeper said, visibly relieved to have something to do.

Minnie looked round the room, desperate to distract herself from the body. Full-length French doors led out to the garden. The sky had darkened dramatically since their arrival, and it looked as though a storm was on the way. The glass reflected them back: Dorothy seated on a chair, Minnie standing awkwardly, like actors waiting for direction. And the body. Always the body. Demanding their attention even as every instinct told them to look away. To leave the man in peace.

Minnie shifted her gaze to the walls lined with bookshelves and two comfortable armchairs, positioned at an angle to the French doors. Henry had been an eclectic reader, with a leaning towards sensation novels. Sprinkled amongst the books were a number of studio photographs: an elderly couple who were presumably Henry's parents; a young woman – sister? sweetheart? – and then one which drew her eye. A wedding portrait, the groom bearing more than a passing resemblance to the man lying dead on the floor. And the bride. Minnie gasped. It had been taken several years ago, but the bride's hair was unmistakeable, her figure all curves.

'Dorothy?' Minnie said, 'That's you, ain't it? In that wedding photograph?'

Dorothy pulled her gaze away from the wall and followed Minnie's pointing finger. Her eyes narrowed as she focused on the photograph, as if she were struggling to make sense of what she was seeing.

'Yes,' she said. 'That's me.'

'So – Henry—?'

'Henry Lawrence is – was – my husband. Yes.'

THREE

Albert returned with two policemen in tow. The younger of them took one look at the scene and stumbled out of the room, his hand to his mouth, his footsteps tripping down the hallway and out the front door. Minnie wondered if it was his first dead body and wished she could say the same.

The older police officer bent down to examine the body more closely. The room seemed to shrink in his presence, and they all waited in silence, as if needing his permission to be told what to think, how to feel.

He straightened up and looked slowly round the room. He had a kind face, Minnie thought, gentle blue eyes and a brow permanently furrowed in thought.

'I'm Inspector Waters,' he said. 'Is there somewhere else we can talk?'

'Of course,' Mrs Albemarle said, leading them into the kitchen.

The younger officer returned, still looking decidedly green about the gills. Waters asked each of them to introduce themselves.

'Does anyone else live here?' he asked. 'Any other staff?'

'Just Mr Gregg, the gardener, but he don't live in,' Mrs Albemarle said. 'He comes twice a week. Or he did, at least.'

'Did?' Waters said.

'He lost his position last Monday.'

'Why?'

'Couldn't tell you. There was some sort of falling-out between him and Mr Lawrence. I heard raised voices down the end of the garden but couldn't hear what they said. Come Thursday, which is Mr Gregg's other day, no Mr Gregg. Mr Lawrence said there'd been a mutual parting of the ways, but no mention of who was gonna take care of the garden. Which don't make any sense. You can't see it so well now it's getting dark but believe me, that garden is a full-time job all on its own. And I'm certainly not getting on my hands and knees out there. I've got enough to do—'

'So,' Waters said, cutting off the flow of talk that threatened to overwhelm them all, 'Gregg was last seen on Monday.'

'That's correct,' Mrs Albermarle said.

'And who found the body?' Waters asked.

'That was me,' Mrs Albemarle said, recounting what she had already told Minnie and Albert.

'Had anything unusual happened in the days leading up to Mr Lawrence's death?'

'Nothing,' she said. 'At least—'

'Yes?' Waters prompted.

'He did seem a little distracted these past few days. Like he had something on his mind.'

'Mrs Lawrence?' Waters asked, turning towards Dorothy. 'Did you notice any change in your husband's behaviour?'

Dorothy raised her head, her eyes barely registering the presence of these strangers. Minnie knew she was reliving the horror of what she'd seen, playing it over and over in her head. She took Dorothy's hand and spoke to her softly. 'These police officers need to ask you some questions, Dorothy. Do you think you can manage that?'

Dorothy nodded but Minnie was unsure she'd even heard, never mind understood Minnie's words.

Waters moved forward, pulling up a chair so he was on a level with Dorothy. 'My name's Inspector Waters,' he repeated. 'Can you tell me how your husband might have died?'

Dorothy stared at him, no recognition of his question on her face.

Though it had been less than half an hour since they'd discovered Henry's body, Dorothy looked like she'd shrunk. As if somehow the life had drained out of her, as it had done with poor Henry.

'Mrs Lawrence?' Inspector Waters prompted.

'She's in shock,' Albert said. 'Surely this can wait?'

'And remind me again who you are?' Inspector Waters said.

'Albert Easterbrook. Formerly Sergeant Easterbrook. Marylebone Station. I worked closely with Inspector Price.'

Waters looked at Albert again, more closely this time. 'Inspector Price has mentioned you,' he said. 'You're a private detective now?'

'That's right. If you'll release Mrs Lawrence into my care, I can promise she'll be available for questioning tomorrow. For now,' and here he gestured towards Dorothy, 'there seems little point, wouldn't you say?'

Dorothy had sunk back into the chair, and it looked like it might envelop her completely. This was a woman who commanded attention under normal circumstances. But now you might not even have noticed she was in the room.

Waters nodded. 'Tomorrow morning should be satisfactory. We'll finish up here.'

'What about Mrs Albemarle?' Minnie asked. 'And Peggy? It don't feel right just leaving them here.'

Mrs Albemarle pulled herself upright. 'We'll be fine, won't we, Peggy? Although you won't get nothing out of her, Inspector Waters, I'll warn you now. She don't say much. Works like a little Trojan, mind. I'll answer any questions you have, but we don't want to be here when you take Mr Lawrence away.'

'Of course not,' Waters murmured.

Albert took Dorothy's arm, and the three of them left the house. The threat of rain seemed to have passed, for now at least. Allowing Dorothy to walk ahead, Minnie pulled Albert back beside her.

'Where are we taking her?' she whispered. 'I mean, this is where she lives. My rooms? Your house?'

'My rooms,' Dorothy said, turning back. 'I don't live here.'

❦

Dorothy's rooms were above her bookkeeping business in Lombard Street. After the noise and movement at Henry's house, Minnie was struck by how cold and empty the space felt, even after Dorothy's housekeeper had lit the fire and all the lamps and made tea.

Slowly, as if the heat of the fire were gradually returning her to life, Dorothy became more aware of her surroundings and what had brought her there.

'I keep thinking maybe it's not him,' she said carefully, measuring out each word as if speech were unfamiliar to her. 'But I know it is. I keep – seeing him.'

'That'll pass,' Minnie said, not convincing herself with the words. Her closest friend, Rose, had been murdered. She still had nightmares about identifying Rose's body in the mortuary, nightmares she suspected would not fade with time.

'I'm afraid to go to sleep,' Dorothy said. 'That moment when you wake up and for a moment you've forgotten and you think everything is how it always was. And then you remember.'

'We can be here in the morning, when you wake,' Minnie said. 'It might make it a little easier.'

'Do you have anything to help you sleep?' Albert asked.

Dorothy shook her head.

'We passed a pharmacy on the corner,' Albert said. 'I could get you some laudanum? Just a small dose to help you through these first few nights?'

'Please,' Dorothy said, reaching for her bag.

Albert held up a hand, refusing her money. 'I'll be back shortly,' he said.

The front door closed behind him and a hush descended on the room. Minnie had learned from Albert the value of sitting out a silence, but she was never entirely comfortable with it.

'How did you and Henry meet?' she said eventually.

'We've known each other since we were children. My father managed the finances for Henry's family and he'd often bring me with him when he made business calls on Henry's father. Henry and I first met when I was seven, he was nine. For much of my childhood and well into adulthood, I would say Henry was my closest friend.' She paused, took a sip of tea and placed the cup back on the saucer with unnecessary deliberation. 'Go on, then,' she said. 'Ask me.'

'About what?'

'My marriage. I know you've been itching to ask me since I told you Henry and I were together.'

Dorothy wasn't wrong. Minnie had a hundred questions to ask, but she'd decided they could wait, given they'd only just found Henry's body. Still, grief and shock did strange things to a person. Minnie had known people who'd become voluble, giddy even, minutes after being given the worst news in the world. Dorothy seemed happy to talk now, and Minnie was happy to ask the questions.

'Well, I did wonder, now you mention it,' she said. 'I mean, I've known you well over a year and you never once mentioned a husband. I know you go by Mrs Lawrence, but I just figured that was for respectability and to keep the fellas off your back.'

Dorothy inhaled sharply, as if bracing herself. 'It's complicated, you won't be surprised to learn. Although, in another way, very simple. On my eighteenth birthday, my parents spoke to me of marriage, the advantages it offered, the imperative to make a beneficial match. My father was the most unconventional of men in some matters but, when it came to marriage, he was as traditional as they come. He wanted me to find an appropriate partner, and soon.'

'But that weren't what you wanted?'

Dorothy shook her head. 'I wanted to make my own way in the world. Achieve a degree of independence. I had a good mind and an excellent head for numbers. I saw no place in my future for marriage. Fortunately for me, Henry felt the same.'

'Why?' Minnie said. 'I mean, I get why *you* didn't want marriage. But why would a fella turn it down? It seems to me he gets all the advantages and keeps all of his freedom. Why wouldn't Henry want to marry?'

Dorothy blinked rapidly. 'I don't think he was against it in principle. Just maybe later in life. And to someone of his own choosing.'

Dorothy was holding something back, Minnie was certain of it. The blinking had given her away, but she'd had her suspicions from the moment Dorothy started talking about the marriage.

'So, who popped the question?' Minnie said.

'I did,' Dorothy said, blushing slightly at the memory of her audacity. 'From the speed with which he said yes, I think it had been on Henry's mind, but he was too cautious to broach the subject. It seemed the perfect solution. It would give me respectability, and Henry even offered me money to help me set up in business. He also sent many clients my way over the years. He was a journalist, he specialised in writing about banking and other financial matters, so he inevitably got to know some people with money to invest.'

'Did you share the same house?'

'Never. I have my own rooms, but I made myself visible at Henry's house at the weekend when the neighbours were most likely to be at home and would see me. Sometimes in the week as well. On occasion, we would have some of the neighbours over for supper.'

'When did you last visit?'

'Wednesday.'

'And he was fine?'

'Knowing what we now know, I'd say not entirely. He seemed a little out of sorts. Like he had something on his mind. His aunt Lucy passed away a few months ago and Henry took it hard. I thought it might be that and I tried talking to him, but he said he didn't want to discuss it. Said I'd know soon enough.'

The front door opened and Albert entered the room, bringing the chilly night air with him. He handed Dorothy a small bottle. 'It's a low dose,' he said, 'but if you're not used to taking it, three drops should suffice. Better to take a small amount and see if it works.'

Dorothy stood and swept down her skirts. 'Thank you, Albert. Now, it's time for you both to go. It's been a very long day, and I suspect tomorrow will be even longer.'

Minnie glanced at the sofa. 'I'm happy to stay,' she said.

'No, really,' Dorothy said briskly, spreading wide her arms and ferrying them towards the door. 'I need to face this on my own at some point. I might as well start sooner rather than later. I'll see you in the morning.'

After they'd turned out of Dorothy's street, Minnie shared with Albert her conversation with Dorothy, and her conviction the woman was keeping something from them.

'Aside from the fact she was married and she never mentioned a husband?' Albert said. 'I have to confess, I didn't see that one coming.'

'No one did. Even if it was one of them—'

'—marriages of convenience?' Albert offered.

'Exactly. Even if it was that, you still think she might have mentioned him once or twice in all the time we've known her. And I reckon there's more to it than she's letting on. She ain't telling us the whole story, Albert, I'm sure of it.'

'You don't like her, do you?' Albert asked abruptly.

'Who? Dorothy? I like her well enough.'

'Try telling your face that.'

'Meaning?'

'Meaning you get this slightly pinched look when she enters a room. Like you've just sniffed sour milk. You don't think you're a little ... jealous?' As he said the final word, Albert gave an exaggerated flinch, as if anticipating a blow from Minnie at the mere idea she might be jealous of another woman.

'You're not wrong, as a matter of fact.'

'What? Why on earth would you be jealous?'

'Well, you've seen her. All curves and eyelashes. Every man in the room tripping over his tongue as soon as he lays eyes on her.'

'And that bothers you?' Albert said. He sounded genuinely puzzled.

'Well, yeah.'

'Why?'

She sighed. 'Because, just occasionally, I would like men to notice me in the way they notice Dorothy.'

Albert came to an abrupt halt and turned towards her. 'But they do.'

'No, Albert, they don't. I'm the funny one. The clever one, although Dorothy's probably got me beaten on that front as well. Just every now and then I'd like to be the pretty one.'

'But you are. You're the prettiest girl in any room.'

Minnie was thankful that the cover of night hid her blushes. 'Well,' she said eventually, 'you might try telling *your* face that, next time Dorothy sashays into the Palace.'

FOUR

Early the next morning Albert had just finished breakfast when there was a loud knock on the front door. Mrs Byrne entered the drawing room a few minutes later.

'Someone to see you, Albert,' she said. 'Business.'

'I don't have the time, Mrs B. Dorothy's due here shortly. Can't you put them off?'

'She's young. And nervous, despite pretending to be otherwise. I think you should see her.'

Albert sighed. 'Show her in. But if she's not out of here in half an hour, interrupt us with an urgent message.'

A few moments later Mrs Byrne showed the potential client into the room. She was a sweet-faced young woman. Or child, perhaps. Albert couldn't be certain. She wore her hair down but there was a maturity about her that suggested someone older. Pretty, rosebud lips and large eyes which turned down at the corners, giving her rather a mournful air when her face was at rest.

She held out her hand. Another thing that seemed at odds with her youthful appearance.

'Miss Grace Hardy,' she said, her voice high-pitched and slightly breathy. 'Very pleased to make your acquaintance, I'm sure. Although we have already met, informally, like.' She was trying hard to sound refined but her humbler origins were evident in her voice.

Albert shook her hand and offered her a seat. She eyed him carefully. 'You don't recognise me, do you?'

Albert shook his head. He had a pretty good memory for faces, and he was certain he'd never met this woman before.

'Little Gracie?' she prompted, leaning forward and tilting her head coquettishly to one side. 'I go by Grace these days, now I'm so much older, but you might remember me as the Pocket Chanteuse?' She pronounced it Shon-toose.

A memory flickered at the back of Albert's mind. A young child with the voice of a grown woman.

'You've … grown,' Albert said. He could remember nothing of the girl's earlier career.

A frown creased her brow and then she shook herself and smoothed down her dress, as if the physical action could eliminate her concerns.

'Yes – well – I was a mere five years old when I started out in the business, Mr Easterbrook. I'm twenty now.' She might as well have declared she was ninety-five, her voice sounded so weighted with gravity and maturity.

'And still performing?' Albert asked. Twenty-year-old singers were ten-a-penny in the halls.

Grace looked puzzled. 'You ain't got much of a memory for faces, have you? Which is a little worrying in a private detective, if you don't mind my saying. I was at the Palace the other day when Madame Ivanova was rehearsing. Don't you remember?'

'There were a lot of people—' Albert tailed off, having learned the wisest action when finding yourself in a hole was to stop digging.

'My career has taken a new direction,' she said, tilting her chin up and adopting a loftier demeanour. 'I am training for the opera and Madame Ivanova has taken me under her wing. That's how I got your name. I heard you was proper helpful with Madame Ivanova's fella.'

The girl had abandoned all efforts at a more sophisticated way of speaking. Albert acknowledged her kind words. He wasn't sure how successful she'd be in her new career. It was odd for a performer to progress from music hall to opera. Why not just stay in the halls?

'I must say, you ain't what I was expecting,' Grace continued. 'I heard you was a bit of a toff, but I weren't expecting the—' she waved her hand vaguely in the area in front of her nose.

'A boxing accident,' Albert said. 'You should have seen the other chap.'

'Should I? Why?'

'It's just a saying, Miss Hardy. A boxing joke.'

She looked blank.

'So, what may I help you with?' Albert said.

'I'm guessing you read about what happened to me a few weeks ago?'

Albert had a vague recollection of reading something. 'Remind me of the details,' he said.

She gave another little frown as if surprised that, whatever the incident, it wasn't firmly engraved on his memory. 'Two weeks ago? I was found lying on the banks of the Thames? Opposite side of the river from the Embankment? I believe it was in all the newspapers. I can't think how you missed it.'

Another memory nudged at the back of Albert's mind, but he invited her to continue.

'A fortnight yesterday, it was. I went to bed as usual. Next thing I remember is waking up soaking wet, freezing cold, with a bleedin' great policeman looming over me. It was half past four in the morning.'

'You've no memory of leaving your house? Going to the river?'

She shook her head firmly.

'Do you suffer from sleepwalking?'

'That's what the coppers asked me. Not meaning to be too intimate, Mr Easterbrook, but once I'm tucked up in bed there's no stirring me until Ma brings me a cuppa in the morning.'

'What did the police think happened?'

'They reckoned I'd tried to take my own life and it didn't work.'

'I take it that wasn't the case.'

'No, Mr Easterbrook, it most definitely *weren't* the case.'

'So, how did you get there?'

She leaned in closer, dropping her voice, although there was no one else to hear her words. 'I reckon somebody slipped me something, Mr Easterbrook. They took me from my bed in a – wotchacallit – soporific state,' she sounded out each syllable carefully as if it was likely to explode in her mouth. 'And then, whoever it was done it, I reckon they took me to the river and tried to drown me. Somebody or something must have disturbed them before they could finish the job.'

'Did you tell this to the police?'

'I did. But they weren't having none of it. Said my mind was altered and I tried to take my own life, only I changed my mind and swam to safety. Which is nonsense. For starters, I can't swim. And anyone'll tell you I'm as happy as a sandboy, me.'

Albert thought carefully, working out how best to phrase his next question. 'Please don't take this the wrong way, Miss Hardy, but what you've described does seem rather an elaborate way of trying to kill you. If someone got into your bedroom – which they must have done if you were taken from there – why not just kill you in that room?'

She thought for a moment, a tiny frown creasing her brow. Albert could almost hear the cogs turning.

'Maybe they didn't want to kill me. Maybe they just wanted to embarrass me. I was found in my' – she paused, a blush colouring her cheeks as she lowered her voice to a conspiratorial level – 'in my night attire, Mr Easterbrook.'

'Do you have any idea who might have wanted to harm you in any way? You enjoyed a considerable degree of success when you were a young child. Might that have given rise to any professional rivalry?'

She preened at the mention of her former fame. 'There is always rivalry, Mr Easterbrook. Always jealousy. That is – I fear – one of the sad consequences of a fame such as mine.'

'Anyone in particular?'

She shook her head. 'That's where you come in. I ain't got a clue who could have done this to me. But I do know one thing. Someone's been following me.'

'For how long?'

'A month. Maybe two.'

'Description?'

'Of what?'

'The person. The one you think has been following you.'

'Tall fella. Dark coat and hat. Keeps his face covered.'

Albert suppressed a sigh. Yet another useless description that could be applied to half of London. 'When you say tall?'

She stood and held a hand a few inches higher than the top of her own head. So, not tall, then. Distinctly average height.

'And how do you know it was a man?' Albert asked.

'Well, what else would it be?'

'A woman?'

'Oh,' she said, nodding her head slowly as understanding dawned. 'Well – I don't know it was a fella. Not for sure. But he dresses like a man. Walks like a man. As my ma always says, if it walks like a duck and quacks like a duck—'

'—it's probably a duck.'

She gave him a knowing look, as if they had shared some profound insight.

'So, this mystery man. Where have you seen him?'

'Outside my house. He stands on the corner opposite, staring at the living room window. I've seen him in shops, too. And walking behind me sometimes in crowds.'

'Have you reported it to the police?'

'Tried to. They weren't having none of it. Said I was seeing things. Which is why I'm here. If the fella following me is the same person who left me by the river, what's to say he ain't gonna try something else? I want you to find him. Find out what it is he's after.'

'I can try, Miss Hardy. But to be fair, you haven't given me a great deal to work with. It would help if you could supply me with a list of anyone – anyone at all – who might wish you harm.'

She frowned again. 'When you say *harm*—?'

'Maybe someone who was jealous of your former success? Or had been rude to you? Someone you might have had a falling-out with?'

She nodded her head vigorously, as if it had been entirely unnecessary for Albert to explain what he meant. 'I can do that. Let you have it tomorrow. And you should have a chat with Artie Buckley, my manager.'

'Forgive my asking, but are you sure you can afford me?'

She fumbled in her bag and pulled out a handful of sovereigns, laying them down on the table. 'You find the fella, and that's all yours.'

'That's not quite how it works, Miss Hardy. Regardless of whether or not I find this mysterious stranger you have to pay me.'

'You sure you've got that right? In my world, there'd be murder if a punter paid their shilling and no one took to the stage.'

'It's my time you're paying for, Miss Hardy. Results are sometimes unpredictable.'

He explained his fees to her, but she seemed unfazed.

'I made a tidy sum in my youth, Mr Easterbrook,' she said, the irony of her words entirely lost on her. 'You don't need to worry about getting paid. Just find the fella what's been following me.'

FIVE

After Grace Hardy's departure, Albert stood at the drawing room window. Minnie had just come into view, turning the corner into his street. As he often did when standing in this exact position, he recalled the first time he had seen her, standing on his front path, nudging Ida Watkins into knocking on the door. He wondered what his life would have been like if he'd been out that day, if Minnie and Ida had sought the help of some other private detective, or if he'd simply turned down the case. And, not for the first time, he remembered the precise moment he'd fallen in love with her. After one awful night, when he'd woken to find her asleep in a chair next to his bed, the morning light catching glints of copper in her hair, he'd reached for her hand, his fingers resting on her wrist, her pulse slow and steady. If he'd known that nearly three years later he'd still be waiting for her, would he have given up hope sooner? Found some other, more straightforward woman to marry? He pushed the thought from his mind, telling himself that thinking of a future with Minnie was an exercise in pain and futility. And yet he couldn't walk away from her.

As Minnie got nearer, he was struck by the difference between her and Dorothy. Minnie, animated, purposeful, her face a rolling map of emotions, her body inhabited by a restless energy that he'd found unnerving at first and now wondered how he'd ever lived without. He could appreciate that Dorothy was a beautiful woman, but somehow Minnie drew all the light in the room towards her.

He heard the key turn in the lock. Albert had given Minnie a key long ago, and she'd somehow managed to devise an informal arrangement with Mrs Byrne where a bed was always made up for her in the back bedroom. Not that she'd ever used it, but still. Mrs Byrne objected if Albert wore the wrong tie to a formal event, yet somehow sanctioned the idea of an unmarried young woman sleeping under the same roof. She'd told him once that all he needed to do was give Minnie some time; he wondered now if even Mrs Byrne had accepted there was no future for them.

Minnie entered the drawing room, bringing a chilly blast of air with her that put Albert in mind of the stage door at the Palace.

'Jesus,' she said, walking quickly to the fire to warm herself, 'you don't know whether you're coming or going with this weather. Beautiful day yesterday, now it's cold enough out there to freeze the rudder off a brass monkey, not just its nuggins.'

'So delicately phrased,' Albert murmured, crossing to the fire and shovelling on some more coal.

Minnie shot him a broad grin. 'There's a lot more where that came from,' she said.

'No doubt.' He went to ring the bell, but Mrs Byrne was already pushing open the door, a tray heavy with teacups and plates held in front of her. She placed it on a small table near the fire, then handed Minnie a slab of cake that looked like it would feed a family of four, but which Albert knew Minnie would dispense with in moments.

'Try that,' Mrs Byrne said. 'A new recipe I'm trying out. I thought the walnuts made a nice addition.'

Minnie took a huge mouthful, then rolled her eyes in pleasure and gave a gentle groan, which Albert found rather unsettling.

'Mrs B, you've surpassed yourself,' Minnie said, reaching for another slice.

'Leave enough for Dorothy,' Mrs Byrne warned her. 'In my experience, there's nothing stokes an appetite like grief.'

'Speaking of which,' Minnie said, 'you ain't got any way of getting this thing off, have you?' She held out her left hand and gestured towards the wedding ring she'd sported as Mrs Willoughby. 'I thought maybe we should try to remove it before Dorothy gets here, given that she's just found her husband dead and all. And my hands are freezing, which should help.'

Mrs Byrne left the room, returning a few moments later with a tub of goose fat, which she handed to Albert. 'Big hands,' she said in response to his perplexed look. 'Strong fingers.'

Albert wasn't entirely convinced of the logic, but dipped his finger in the fat and rubbed it around the ring. Minnie was right: her hand was frozen, but the ring remained stubbornly in place. He twisted it, pulling gently at the same time, but it wouldn't move past the knuckle.

'It won't shift,' he said. 'And I don't want to hurt you.'

'Maybe you're doing it the wrong way,' Mrs Byrne said.

'How can I be doing it the wrong way?' Albert said. 'There's only one way to remove a ring, surely.'

'You know what I mean, Albert Easterbrook.'

Albert looked at Minnie, a blush gently colouring her cheeks. Or maybe it was just the heat of the fire.

'Here,' she said, 'let me have a go.' With one determined twist the ring came free. She wrapped it in a handkerchief and slipped it into her bag, all the while firmly avoiding Albert's eye.

A brisk rap on the door saved them from any further embarrassment. Mrs Byrne scurried off and returned within a minute, Dorothy behind her.

'Now, you sit yourself there,' Mrs Byrne said, ushering Dorothy towards the fire and the seat next to Minnie, 'and there's a nice cup of tea for you, and some cake.'

Dorothy shook her head and gave a gentle smile. 'No appetite,' she said quietly.

Her words brought the presence of Henry Lawrence into the room, and the awful discovery of the previous day. Minnie placed her cake on the table in front of her and took one of Dorothy's hands.

'When you feel up to it,' Albert said, 'we'll take you to the police station.'

'I've already been,' Dorothy said. 'Inspector Waters brought Gregg, the gardener, in last night for questioning. He had an alibi. Although I could have told them it wasn't him. And now it's like Waters has given up. Or, no – that's not fair – he hasn't given up, exactly. But he seems to be favouring the idea that it was an accidental overdose. He says he'll have to wait for the post-mortem, but it's like he's already decided what the outcome will be. He seemed very busy. Preoccupied with other cases, I'm assuming.'

'But you don't agree about it being an accident?' Albert asked. 'Did Henry take anything for medicinal purposes?'

Dorothy shook her head firmly. 'Never. He didn't take a pipe, he didn't touch alcohol and lately he'd sworn off meat. He was obsessive about what he put in his body. Whatever was in that syringe he'd never have touched it, no matter what the alleged health benefits.'

'And you shared these thoughts with Waters?' Albert asked.

'I did. And I told him the syringe was in the wrong arm.'

'How d'you mean?' Minnie asked.

'Henry was left-handed. Why would he inject the syringe into his left arm? It makes no sense. Waters hasn't said as much, but I got the strong impression that, unless the post-mortem throws up a surprise, he has no interest in pursuing the matter any further.' She sighed, wrapping her arms tighter around her body as if she couldn't get warm, despite the fire blazing beside her. 'So I need your help. To find out what happened.'

Albert shared a sceptical glance with Minnie. The police might have got it right. Everything about what they'd seen the day before suggested a private moment gone tragically wrong.

'You mentioned the death of his aunt,' Minnie said. 'Henry took it hard? Might that have affected his mind? Grief can do funny things to people.'

Dorothy shook her head. 'He was upset, as you would be. He was very close to Lucy. And her daughter, Rebecca, died only a few months earlier. It was a lot to deal with. But – no.'

'What do *you* think happened?' Albert asked.

'Well, if it's not suicide and it's not an accident that only leaves one alternative. Someone murdered him.' Dorothy seemed to have woken up with a fire in her belly, all the shock and despair of yesterday transformed into determination. Albert recognised the behaviour, the belief that taking action could somehow make sense of tragedy. But he wasn't sure if Dorothy's determination was aimed in the right direction.

'Do you know of anyone who'd have wished him harm?' Minnie asked.

Dorothy shook her head. 'No one. He is – was – a lovely man.'

'Which makes me question whether it's murder, Dorothy,' Minnie said gently. 'If he'd been knocked down in the street, or got caught up in a fight, maybe interrupted a burglary, it might make more sense. But he was at home with no sign of any disturbance. He let the person into his house, so he either knew them or he was expecting them. If he had no enemies, why would someone come into his house and kill him? And what about the photographs? If they killed him, why leave the mucky photographs?'

'To make it look like it was self-administered,' Dorothy said. 'The syringe, the photographs. It all looks like an accident, but I think it's the opposite. And that's where you come in. I want you to look into it. Find out exactly what happened.'

'We can do as you ask,' Albert said carefully. 'But it might be the police have got it right this time.'

'In which case, at least I'll know it's been thoroughly investigated.'

'We'll need to speak to his family,' Albert said. 'Mother and a sister, I think you mentioned?'

Dorothy nodded.

'Anyone else you can think of – friends, work colleagues, anyone – let me know.'

Dorothy nodded and stood up, the meeting clearly at an end. 'I'll have a list with you by the end of the day,' she said. 'I'll see myself out.'

Albert waited for the sound of the front door closing, then turned to Minnie. 'We may have a problem,' he said, explaining the Grace Hardy case to her.

'And that's a problem, why?'

'If we're now investigating a possible murder too, that's going to leave us stretched very thin.'

'Tom ain't got any free time, has he?' Minnie said.

Tom had proved helpful with the Wendall Potts case, but these days he had his hands full running a rescue centre for dogs and horses.

'I can ask, but it's unlikely. He's getting new dogs into the home every week, and not all of them can be safely rehomed. If you ask me, the kindest thing would be to put some of them out of their misery.'

'I'm guessing you ain't shared that sentiment with Tom.'

'Indeed not,' Albert said.

'What about Bobby?' Minnie suggested. Bobby was a young lad who mainly helped Kippy at the Palace but had assisted Albert on occasion.

'Good idea. Could you have a word?'

'I will. And we'll manage,' Minnie said, rising from her seat. 'We usually do. There's something about Dorothy's marriage, though, that she ain't telling us.'

A thought seemed to flicker across her face.

'What?' Albert said.

'I'm just wondering if Dorothy is fond of a tipple. Might be able to get a few port and lemons down her neck and see if she'll let the cat out of the bag. And maybe you could have a word—'

'—with John? I'm meeting him tonight. Perhaps he'll know why Waters is so keen to view this as an accident.'

SIX

Albert paid the barman and took the two pints over to the table where John Price was sitting. Both men took a long draught of their beer, then settled themselves back against the wooden benches. Across from them a man was reading a newspaper, and Albert wondered how long it would be before news of Henry's death made the headlines.

'So,' Albert said, shaking his head at the proffered cigarette, 'what can you tell me about the Henry Lawrence case?'

John smiled. 'So that's what it is. I figured it must be something to do with work, you wanting to see me so suddenly. It ain't my case, Albert.'

'No, but I'm guessing you know more about the police investigation than I do. Has Waters had the post-mortem results yet?'

'They came in this afternoon. There was evidence of an unknown substance in Henry Lawrence's bloodstream. The empty syringe contained traces of the same thing.'

'Unknown? Not arsenic?'

'Why're you thinking arsenic?' John asked.

Albert shrugged. 'Just an idea. Waters seems to be working on the theory that Henry accidentally overdosed. Every time I open the newspaper there are advertisements extolling the virtues of arsenic. It can cure everything from asthma to a lack of performance in the bedroom – allegedly. The problem is, it can also kill you.'

John shook his head. 'Not arsenic. Not strychnine. Not anything the police doctor had come across before. Waters is still convinced it was an accident. Henry was enjoying one off the wrist, took a little something to heighten the pleasure, and accidentally took too much. Heart attack. Case closed.'

'Not for Dorothy Lawrence. She's hired Minnie and myself to look into it. She's convinced it was murder.'

'Why?'

Albert shrugged. 'Gut feeling. She swears blind Henry never took any drugs.'

'And she knew everything about him, did she? Nah,' John said, puffing vigorously to coax his cigarette back into life, 'there's nothing there, Albert. Tell the woman to save her money. You ain't telling me you agree with her?'

'I didn't. Not at first. But the more time I've had to think about it, that scene of death just doesn't add up.'

'In what way?'

'Firstly, Henry was left-handed, but the syringe was in his left arm.'

'Maybe he was – whaddaya call it?'

'Ambidextrous?'

'That's the one. Or maybe he'd injected himself once too often in the right arm and the vein was a bit weak, so he swapped to the other arm. It's not impossible to do it with the wrong hand.'

'Did the police doctor find evidence that he'd injected himself before?'

'Dunno. Not sure he was even looking for that.'

'And why was he on the floor? If he'd injected himself with something, why not just sit in a chair? Or lie on a sofa?'

'Maybe he was in a chair, and he just slid onto the floor.'

'You're far more likely to fall over to one side, surely? And the pornographic photographs, there's something not right about them. They were fanned out on the floor near him. If he'd been holding them, looking at them while he injected himself, even saying he slides off the chair, the photographs would have landed any old how, wouldn't they? But it was like each of them had been placed near him. The more I think about it, the whole scene feels – staged. As if somebody were trying to discredit him, humiliate him. And if he was, as you so delicately phrase it, enjoying one off the wrist, why on earth didn't he lock the door?'

'Didn't need to. The servants were away for the night. He had the house to himself.'

John said nothing further for a few moments, quietly supping his pint. Then he inhaled sharply on his cigarette. 'Look, Waters ain't the best copper I've ever worked with. But he certainly ain't the worst. If he's not pursuing it, there'll be a reason. And it strikes me you should be grateful Waters ain't treating it as suspicious, 'cos if he was, Dorothy'd be the first person he'd be looking at. Assuming this unknown substance was a poison, it's a woman's game, ain't it?'

'Not always,' Albert said slowly, 'and I know her – so do you, John – I just don't see it.'

'Like you didn't see it with Maisie Young?'

Albert gave John a weary look. 'Do you have to trot that one out every time?'

Maisie Young had been a case Albert worked on when he was still a police officer. She'd been an elderly lady. Sweet and tiny, with a dusting of powder over her cheeks so her face looked like a withered peach. Her neighbour, Thomas Connors, had died from arsenic poisoning. Closer investigation had found that Connors' dog had died the week before. Maisie Young proved an extremely helpful witness, apparently unwittingly sharing information that pointed the finger at Connors's nephew, who was due to inherit his uncle's wealth. Albert had been on the verge of arresting the nephew when he paid Maisie one last visit to ask a few more questions. Maisie had clearly thought Albert was on to her, because he caught her trying to slip enough arsenic into his tea to kill an elephant. She died two years into her prison sentence.

'The only time,' Albert said, stressing his words in a way that showed this was a well-worn litany, 'the only time I got it so wrong, and you never stop reminding me of it.'

John gave a broad grin. 'Only 'cos you rise to the bait every single time,' he said. 'Anyway, my point is that we both know people can be very different from the face they show to the world. That's all I'm saying. And Dorothy's got a motive.'

'Which is?'

'She was married to this Henry fella, weren't she, even though it weren't exactly what you'd call conventional. Maybe she wanted out, and he weren't willing. What's her alibi for the night of his death?'

Albert frowned. 'Good point. We haven't asked her.'

John tutted and shook his head with exaggerated disappointment. 'You're losing your touch, my son. First thing you do is determine the alibi. You're sure you ain't a little swayed by the lovely Dorothy's charms? Does Min need to worry?'

'No one needs to worry, believe me. And why hire us to look into a death that the police aren't even investigating, if it's going to lead us straight to her? Besides, it's Dorothy we're talking about. You can't really think she's capable of this, John?'

'The longer I stay in this job, the more convinced I am that anyone is capable of anything. But, no, I don't reckon it was Dorothy. But I don't reckon it was murder, neither.'

He gestured towards Albert's empty glass. Albert nodded and John went to the bar. As he watched his friend waiting to be served, Albert was convinced of one thing. Despite John's assertions to the contrary, Henry Lawrence's death was looking decidedly suspicious.

SEVEN

The following morning, Minnie trotted up the steps to Dorothy's office on Lombard Street. She'd never visited Dorothy at work, but she'd heard about the taxidermy displayed in the office and was eager to see if it was as bizarre as Albert had described. Before she had a chance to examine any of her surroundings, she was caught short by a familiar figure facing Dorothy across her desk. And something about his manner told her he wasn't just here for business.

'Tansie?' she said.

He leapt up at the mention of his name, as if he'd been caught with his hands in the biscuit tin.

'Minnie,' he said. 'How lovely to see you.'

Now she knew something was up. He was only ever nice to her when he wanted something, or when he was feeling guilty.

'I didn't expect to find you here,' Minnie said, removing her coat and scarf and placing them on a nearby chair. 'Didn't Dorothy look at the books only the other day?'

Tansie coughed. 'Other matters, Min,' he said. 'Financial stuff. Nothing you need to worry your head about.'

'What, me with my tiny woman's brain the size of a pea? If there's anything going on at the Palace that involves "financial stuff", I need to know about it, Tanse. I am the majority owner, remember?'

'As if you ever allow me to forget,' Tansie said.

'It's nothing, Minnie,' Dorothy intervened. 'Tansie was just kindly seeing how I was after poor Henry's demise.'

'Made any progress yet?' Tansie asked.

Minnie was about to retort that it had only been two days since they'd found the body, and she and Albert weren't miracle workers. Then she saw Dorothy's face, her skin sallow, her eyes looking imploringly at Minnie, desperate for an answer.

'Nothing yet,' Minnie said. 'But we're working on it, I swear. I couldn't tempt you to a swift half at the Dog and Duck, could I, Dorothy?'

Dorothy looked vaguely alarmed.

'Port and lemon?' Minnie offered. 'Sherry?'

'Two women?' Dorothy said. 'In a public house? Are you mad?'

'I'm happy to escort you ladies,' Tansie said.

'That'd be lovely, Tanse,' Minnie said. 'I'll warn you, though, we're gonna be talking about womanly stuff.'

The colour drained from Tansie's face. Any mention of matters relating specifically to the fairer sex usually saw him walking firmly in the opposite direction.

'Why not the Palace bar?' he offered. 'It's still early. You can have a quiet chat. I promise I'll leave you alone. And the drinks are on the house,' he offered magnanimously, forgetting once again that Minnie was now the majority owner of the Palace, so any free drinks were more on her tab than Tansie's. Nonetheless, the offer had caused him some pain, Minnie guessed. The number of times he'd offered her a free drink could be counted on the fingers of one hand. By a fella with no hands. He must be keen on Dorothy if he was offering free fizz.

'Or, if you don't fancy the pub,' Minnie said, reaching into her bag and withdrawing two bottles of what Tansie optimistically sold as champagne at the Palace, 'we could stay here and drink these. When I lost my ma what really helped was getting drunk as a boiled owl and bawling my eyes out.'

'Best I leave you ladies to it,' Tansie said, as if he were doing them an enormous favour.

'Before you go, Tanse, I just wanted to check I can borrow Bobby tomorrow night? Maybe Wednesday as well? Surveillance job with Albert.'

'If it's all right with Kippy, I ain't got a problem with it.' He grabbed his hat and coat and was gone.

Minnie wandered over to the fireplace. There it was. A glass case with half a dozen stuffed rabbits sitting on little benches, grasping tiny pencils and tiny exercise books. Minnie drew closer. Albert had been right. They were doing mathematics. Complicated mathematics that was way beyond Minnie's capabilities. An angry-looking rabbit at the rear of the classroom had thrown down his pencil in despair. Minnie couldn't blame him.

Half an hour later, they had consumed the best part of a bottle of what Minnie was increasingly convinced *was* actually champagne. Minnie had been careful to ensure that Dorothy drank the lion's share, but she was still feeling the effects.

'Champagne always makes me feel like I should be celebrating,' Dorothy said, draining her glass, and nodding as Minnie offered her a top-up. 'Which is the exact opposite of how I feel at the moment.'

'It was awful,' Minnie acknowledged. 'Seeing him like that. I found it a shock and I didn't even know him.'

She watched as Dorothy emptied the glass in one go. If she left it much longer, Dorothy would be too buffy to string a sentence together. Her instinct was to leap right in and interrogate Dorothy about her marriage, but she'd learned that the direct approach wasn't always the best. So she went for a more gentle opener.

'What are your happiest memories of Henry?' she said.

A rather dippy smile spread across Dorothy's face, but Minnie let that pass. 'When we were little, we used to play with Father's taxidermy.'

Minnie recoiled in horror and pointed at the rabbits in the classroom. 'You *played*? With *that*? You mean, you *touched* them?'

'Touched them. Gave them names. Made up stories about them. Look,' Dorothy rose from her seat and stumbled. 'Whoops. Stood up a bit quickly.' She walked over to the taxidermy display with exaggerated carefulness, lifted the glass lid and removed one of the tiny rabbits. 'See?' she said, holding out her hand for Minnie to take the creature. 'They're rather lovely.'

'If you bring that thing one inch closer to me, Dorothy, I won't be responsible for what I'll do.'

'D'you not like rabbits?'

'I've got no feelings about rabbits one way or the other. What I don't like are dead things stuffed with God knows what and then made to do maths.'

'Oh, if that's what's bothering you, I've got them doing other things.'

Dorothy opened the double doors at the rear of the office, which led into a small cupboard lined with shelves. Most of the shelves bore ledgers and dusty old tomes, confirming Minnie's belief that book-keeping wasn't the most thrilling of occupations. Dorothy reached for the highest shelf. With an effort, she got hold of another glass case and brought it over to her desk. No rabbits this time. Squirrels having some sort of party. One was entering the room with a tray laden with glasses and a bottle of wine. Two others were already on the sauce, one of them with his leg raised up on a chair, gesticulating towards a book on the table. And, to one side of the display, two more sat at a table playing a game of cribbage while one of them smoked a pipe.

Dorothy went to remove the glass lid.

'No!' Minnie shrieked. 'Do not remove anything from that box.'

'You don't like squirrels either? Well, what do you like? I've got cats playing croquet and a whole mouse orchestra if you'd prefer.'

'Dorothy, you are a brilliant bookkeeper, and you have clothes that are so beautiful they make me want to cry. But you are, without a shadow of a doubt, a very strange woman.'

Dorothy gave a decidedly lopsided smile and reached for her glass. She looked puzzled to find it was empty, and Minnie quickly opened the second bottle and refilled her glass.

'I am,' Dorothy said, her voice growing in volume with each mouthful of champagne, 'a strange woman, as you say. Henry was a strange man.'

'In what way?'

'Well, maybe not strange, but ... different.'

Dorothy eyed Minnie carefully, as if weighing up how much to reveal. Or, at least, she tried to eye her, but she was clearly having a little difficulty focusing. Minnie tipped a little more fizz into both their glasses – just enough to loosen Dorothy's tongue but not enough to knock her out.

'What I'm about to say can go no further than this room,' Dorothy said, throwing her arms wider than was strictly necessary to illustrate her point. 'Reputations can still be damaged after death.'

Minnie nodded and waited for Dorothy to speak again.

'Henry liked men,' Dorothy said, and came to an abrupt full stop, as if she had shocked herself with this revelation. She also seemed to sober up in an instant, and Minnie guessed this was a secret she had never intended to share.

'Is that all?' Minnie said. 'I thought you were gonna tell me he was a goat botherer.'

Dorothy looked blank.

Minnie patted her hand reassuringly. 'I work in the halls, Dorothy. Fellas liking fellas in that special way? It ain't nothing new to me.'

'Oh my God,' Dorothy said, dropping her head into her hands. 'I can't believe I told you. You must swear – swear to me, Minnie – you won't tell anyone. Although I suppose it doesn't matter, does it? I mean, they can't throw him in prison now, can they?'

'Well, I think I'm gonna have to tell Albert. It might have a bearing on why Henry was killed – *if* he was killed. But Albert won't say a word, I promise.' Minnie looked at Dorothy's glass but refrained from pouring any more. 'If Henry liked fellas so much, why'd you marry him?'

'He was such a lovely man, Minnie. I wish you'd have known him. And we can't be the only couple in London who married for that reason. It makes perfect sense, after all. I got to live a life of independence; Henry carried on his transactions discreetly.'

'These transactions – anyone in particular?'

Dorothy frowned. 'Do you think one of those men could have caused him harm?'

'We have to pursue every line of enquiry, Dorothy,' Minnie said, mimicking a phrase she'd heard Albert use a hundred times. 'Speaking of which, and please don't get the hump, but what were you doing last Friday night?'

'You want an alibi? From *me*?'

''Fraid so. Standard procedure, so Albert tells me.'

'I was here until late in the evening. And then – I went home.'

'Can anyone back that up? Your assistant here? Your housekeeper?'

'Stella went home at five o'clock, as usual. And it was my house-keeper's half day.'

'And you didn't speak to anyone else?'

Dorothy shook her head. She should never play poker, Minnie thought. The blinking gave her away every time.

'So, if Henry had a loose tongue,' Minnie said, deliberately steering the conversation back onto its original course, 'that could mean prison – even worse – for someone. That's reason enough to kill.'

Dorothy thought for a moment. 'To be honest, Henry was very discreet, but I could always tell when he was – it feels strange to say "courting", but that's what it was. He lit up.' She smiled at the memory, but there was a sadness in her eyes. 'Some of the dalliances were fleeting, I think. But there were others of a more lasting nature. Unfortunately, Henry never spoke of them by their real names. He named them after Greek gods and goddesses, would you believe?'

'Were there any individuals he seemed particularly fond of?'

'There was one he named Hermes. Another – Demeter, I think – for whom he seemed to have real affection. But more than that, I can't tell you.'

'And was there any significance in what he named these men? Some link between the god or goddess and what the man did for a living, say?'

'Not that I know of. I never asked him, to be honest. I felt it was his business and nothing to do with me. And now it's too late, of course.'

'D'you reckon the police got wind of Henry's preferences? And that's why they weren't interested in investigating his death? 'Cos he liked fellas?'

Dorothy frowned. 'How would they know? Henry was very discreet.'

Minnie shrugged. 'He might have been, but you can't necessarily say the same for the fellas he saw, can you?'

Dorothy paused. 'Now I think about it, Inspector Waters used the word "deviance" about three times when I spoke to him. I thought he was talking about the – you know, the photographs – but maybe you're right.'

'The photographs,' Minnie said slowly. 'Albert and I felt there was something odd about them, and now they make even less sense. If Henry liked fellas, why on earth would he have been looking at saucy photos of women?'

'I don't even remember the photos,' Dorothy said. 'I don't remember much about that evening, to be perfectly honest.'

'That's to be expected, Dorothy. You had a terrible shock.'

Minnie went to refill Dorothy's glass but the other woman placed her hand over the top and shook her head.

'So, this arrangement with Henry,' Minnie said, 'it's all well and good, but what if you'd fallen in love with someone? What was gonna happen then? And children? Seems like rather a lonely life

to me. You with your accounts and your stuffed rabbits and no one
to go home to at night.'

'Well, how do *you* find it?'

Minnie frowned. 'It's different for me.'

'Is it? You've got a busy life but you still go home alone, Minnie.
Does it feel lonely to you?'

Minnie thought for a moment. 'Sometimes, yeah,' she admitted
finally. 'But if I wanna do something about that, I can. I ain't already
married to someone else.'

'We'd agreed that if that were to happen, Henry would grant
me a divorce.'

'And has it happened?' Minnie probed, recalling the way Tansie's
face lit up whenever Dorothy entered the room.

Dorothy blushed and said nothing.

'So – Friday night,' Minnie said. 'You and Tansie—' She tailed
off, reluctant to dwell on what Dorothy and Tansie got up to when
they were alone.

'It's not what you're thinking,' Dorothy said. 'He came to my
house for supper and we stayed up talking until the early hours. Do
you have a problem with that?'

'I ain't got any kind of problem with it, just so long as you're
square with him. He's had a tough time of it, Dorothy. I don't reckon
he could take another heartbreak.'

'Well, I have no intention of breaking his heart.'

And neither had Cora, Minnie thought. But sometimes life took
over in ways you hadn't anticipated.

'I hope you don't mind me asking,' Minnie said, 'but what do
you see in him?'

Dorothy laughed. 'I take it his charms are wasted on you.'

'Too bloody right.'

Dorothy paused for a moment, a faraway look entering her eyes
as she considered Tansie's charms. 'He's kind,' she said eventually,
'and honest. You know where you stand with him. If he likes you, he

lets you know. He doesn't mind that I'm clever. In fact, he positively likes it. He makes me laugh. I don't think he'd ever hurt me. That's a lot in a man. But then, you'd know that, having Albert.'

'I don't "have" Albert,' Minnie protested.

'Which begs *my* question: why not? He's a lovely chap, he's clearly very keen on you and you get on like a house on fire. What on earth are you waiting for?'

A memory tore through Minnie's mind: a bloodstained hansom cab, the doctor Ida had scraped the money together to pay, a gentle-faced chap who looked a little broken as he told Minnie she'd never have children. The months of trying to track down the man who'd seduced her, with the dawning realisation that he'd lied to her right from the start. And the slow, painful journey that had led her to where she was now: independent, safe, secure.

She shook her head to dispel the images. 'Nah, all that love and marriage nonsense? Not for me.'

'Why not? You must have thought about it – you and Albert?'

'Once, maybe.' Minnie was surprised to find herself opening up to Dorothy. The fizz definitely wasn't watered down. 'But Albert and me, we've seen some pretty awful things since we started working together. Terrible things that people do to each other. And we've seen how easily a life can be snatched away.' Memories threatened to overwhelm her, but she pushed them away.

'So you think you can protect yourself by not allowing anyone to get too close to you?' Dorothy asked. 'In my experience, it doesn't work like that. If you'd told me two years ago I was going to fall for a short, foul-mouthed music hall owner I'd have said it was more likely those stuffed rabbits in my office would spring back to life. And I'd pay good money to see your face if that happened.'

She pushed back her chair and stood up, then staggered, grabbing hold of the table just in time. 'I need to go and lie down,' she said. 'Before you wrestle any more secrets out of me.'

EIGHT

Minnie had just filled Albert in on her conversation with Dorothy and the revelation about Henry.

'I wondered if that was the case,' Albert said. 'And that might explain Waters's reluctance to pursue Henry's death any further,' Albert said.

'Does it? Just 'cos Henry liked to sling a slobber on a fella every now and then, don't mean he wasn't murdered.'

'When I was on the force we stayed well clear of anything to do with men like that. They're often involved in more – insalubrious activities.'

Minnie stopped abruptly. '"Men like that"?' she said. '"Insalubrious activities"? You went to boarding school, didn't you? Ain't it part of the timetable at places like that? And you do know Bernard is one of those "men like that"? And Pedro? And Leo? And half a dozen other fellas at the Palace?'

'I'm well aware of that,' Albert said.

'So if something happened to one of them, you wouldn't bother investigating it?'

'I'm not saying anything of the sort, and you know that very well. All I'm saying is that the police tend to avoid cases involving men of a Uranian persuasion.'

'Why? 'Cos fancying a fella inevitably means you're gonna end up at Abney Park?' She registered the blank look on his face and sighed. Having to translate for him was interfering with her righteous anger. 'Abney Park. Cemetery in the East End. Going to Abney Park means you're dead.'

'No, Minnie, I'm not saying that,' he said with exaggerated slowness, as if she were a tiny child who needed something explaining to her. 'I'm just saying that there are problems with investigating crimes of that nature. Not least that those men have often placed themselves in harm's way – sometimes intentionally – and it makes it more difficult to solve the case. Add in the fact that no one wants to admit any involvement on any level and the police, overstretched at the best of times, tend to pass on those kinds of death.'

'But Henry was poisoned. He weren't found in Vauxhall Gardens with his trousers round his ankles. Him liking fellas might have nothing to do with his death, and if it looks suspicious it should be treated as suspicious.'

Albert sighed. 'I think we're going to have to agree to disagree on this one, Minnie. The long and the short of it is, the police are not investigating Henry's death as suspicious. So we are.'

'And him being what he was, it ain't gonna get in the way of us doing our job?'

He looked genuinely hurt. 'Of course not. You know me better than that, Minnie. I'm astonished you could even say it.'

'Well,' she said grudgingly, 'better I say it than it becomes a problem later on. The point is, with Henry liking the fellas, that scene of death makes even less sense.'

'The photographs,' Albert mused. 'Exactly.'

Henry Lawrence's neighbours were, as far as Minnie could tell from her limited experience, no more or less useful as eyewitnesses than most people. Which was to say, utterly clueless. Still, it was worth interviewing them. Sometimes people had seen something significant without even realising.

To the left of Henry's house was a young couple with more children than seemed wise. The children spent most of the interview climbing the furniture and hollering at each other from opposite ends of the house. The parents, Mr and Mrs Grey, were oblivious to the chaos. Or maybe they'd just realised the futility of trying to do anything about it.

No, they hadn't noticed anything unusual in the days leading up to Henry's death. If Henry's wife was 'the handsome woman', as Mr Grey referred to her, much to his wife's irritation, then he hadn't seen her since the weekend before Henry was found dead.

'I hardly ever see her in the week, but then I'm at work all day. Saturday evenings or Sundays she usually says hallo,' he offered, matching Dorothy's account of the subterfuge she and Henry had undertaken.

Mrs Grey looked like she would happily swap a major organ for a good night's sleep and confessed she had no memory of seeing anyone on any particular day. 'The children ...' she murmured, her hand waving vaguely in their direction, as if this were sufficient explanation for everything.

To the right of Henry's house was Miss Crisp, an elderly woman who was almost blind. She was excessively eager to help, despite being of no use at all. She remembered speaking to Dorothy on the Saturday before Henry was found.

'She brought me over some Victoria sandwich,' Miss Crisp said. 'I have the most shocking sweet tooth, and Dorothy brings me a little something most weekends.'

'Only at the weekend?' Albert asked.

Miss Crisp paused for a moment. 'Now you come to mention it – yes, only ever at the weekend. I expect Saturday's her baking day.'

Nothing about Dorothy suggested to Minnie that she knew her way round a kitchen, much less that she had a baking day. But Dorothy and Henry's ruse of having her be very visible at weekends clearly worked with Henry's immediate neighbours. Neither side had noticed she was rarely present in the week.

They did the rounds of the other houses, but no one offered anything useful. It was a street where people kept themselves to themselves, and Minnie wondered if that was why Henry had chosen to live there. No one other than Dorothy or Henry had been seen entering or leaving the property. John was right: if the police had been investigating Henry's death as suspicious, Dorothy would have been firmly in the frame.

Finally, they turned towards number 17, the home of Mr Stephenson, a former police officer and a 'loathsome individual' according to Dorothy. The man's curtains had started twitching when they first arrived, and he'd found some vital work to do in his front garden which involved leaning on a rake every time Minnie and Albert emerged from one of the neighbours' houses. Minnie had suggested they speak to him first, as he looked eager to talk. Albert disagreed.

'Let him wait,' he'd said grimly. 'I've met his kind before. Want to let you know how important they are. And I'd like to see how his memory tallies with everyone else's.'

Stephenson was, Minnie guessed, somewhere in his fifties. Everything about him was neat and trim, from his moustache to his fingernails. Before Minnie and Albert had done much more than introduce themselves, Stephenson waved that morning's copy of *The Tribune* under their noses. News of Henry's death had made the papers, with the inevitable focus on the more salacious details.

'I am appalled,' Stephenson hissed. 'Appalled and disgusted.' Although he looked anything but.

'Appalled by Mr Lawrence's death?' Albert asked calmly. 'Or by the reporting of it?'

'Both,' Stephenson barked. 'Such goings-on, a matter of feet from my front door. This is a respectable neighbourhood, Mr Easterbrook.

And now we've got every ink-slinger in the city accosting us on the doorsteps, eager for details. The more revolting the better.'

Albert frowned. 'We didn't see any journalists.'

'They were here earlier. I gave them short shrift, I can tell you.'

Minnie suspected none of this was true, although she thought Stephenson probably had spoken to the press. The *Tribune* article carried details about Henry's marriage that the journalist must have got from somewhere. She bit her tongue, knowing it was wisest to let Albert take the lead with men like Stephenson.

Stephenson's house was entirely devoid of ornamentation, and looked like nobody actually lived there. He noticed Minnie glancing at the bare walls, the unadorned surfaces.

'Not to a lady's liking, I'm sure,' he said, offering her a patronising leer. 'The fairer sex favours the knick-knacks and the gimcracks. Dust gatherers, I call 'em. I keep a clean ship, Miss Ward.'

He set a tea tray in front of them. 'You'll be mother,' he said to Minnie, not offering her a choice. She bridled but forced a smile. 'Of course,' she murmured.

While Minnie poured the tea, Albert kicked off the questioning, asking Stephenson first if he'd seen anything on the days leading up to the discovery of Henry's body.

'Nothing. No visitors that I saw, other than Mrs Lawrence, who arrived on the Wednesday at precisely 5.03 postmeridian.'

Albert coughed. 'That's very – exact.'

Stephenson smiled to himself, as if Albert had congratulated him. 'I wind my carriage clock every Wednesday at five o'clock. I had just completed the task when I saw Mrs Lawrence enter number 20. She appeared distracted.'

'In what way?' Albert asked.

'She was fiddling with her hair, tucking it under her hat – needlessly in my opinion, but then you ladies do love to play with your hair, don't you?' This last comment was addressed to Minnie. 'She removed her gloves before letting herself into the house.'

'And that was a sign of her being distracted?' Minnie asked.

'My mother taught me that a lady should never remove her gloves until she is firmly inside the front door,' Stephenson said.

Minnie decided it was best not to honour that comment with any response.

'Did you see her leave?' she asked.

Stephenson glanced at her then fixed his attention on Albert again, as if it were he who had asked the question.

'At approximately seven o'clock she left. I'm sorry I can't be more precise than that.'

'Clock didn't need winding, I take it?' Minnie said, earning herself a sharp look from Albert.

'Having wound the clock at five, it would hardly need winding again at seven, would it?' Stephenson said. 'They thought they were fooling everyone, having her around in the evenings or on Sundays, but it was obvious to me that the marriage was a sham. If, indeed, they were actually married.'

'Meaning?' Albert asked.

'A young woman visits a man every week for a few hours. I don't think you need me to explain what might have been taking place, Mr Easterbrook.'

'Mr and Mrs Lawrence were married,' Minnie said.

'Seen the marriage certificate, have you?'

'We have, as a matter of fact, yes,' Minnie lied.

Stephenson looked momentarily nonplussed, then regained his bluster. 'Well, whatever was going on between them, she wanted people to think she lived there, so she made sure to show her face once, maybe twice a week. But she never stayed overnight, I can assure you.'

They didn't bother asking him how he could be so certain. The man probably had a pair of binoculars permanently trained on number 20. There was something about his manner when he mentioned Dorothy's name. Something that suggested he had no fondness for her. A snub, perhaps? A failure to acknowledge his importance?

'The night of Friday the ninth,' Albert said, 'did you notice anything then, or in the early hours of Saturday morning?'

'I visit my sister every Friday night and stay over,' Stephenson said. 'I wasn't home until midday on Saturday.'

'What a terrible shame,' Minnie said. 'Your meticulous powers of observation might have solved the case for us.'

Albert coughed loudly and gave Minnie a pointed look. 'Would you say you were good friends with Mr Lawrence?' he asked.

'No more than acquaintances. I keep myself to myself' – Minnie nearly choked on her tea – 'as did Mr Lawrence.'

'Did he have any regular visitors?'

Stephenson made a show of remembering, but Minnie suspected he had a little notebook secreted about his person with details of every visitor to every house on the street. 'His mother used to visit fairly regularly. And a sister, I believe.'

Albert nodded. Minnie was due to interview Henry's family later.

'Mr Stephenson, you've been most helpful,' Albert said, kicking Minnie under the table pre-emptively. 'One final question, if I may. Can you think of anyone who might have wished harm to Mr Lawrence?'

Stephenson smirked, as if he'd been expecting the question and was disappointed in Albert for having taken this long to ask him. 'Other than Mrs Lawrence? No one.'

'And why do you believe Mrs Lawrence wished him harm?'

'I imagine she wanted her freedom. Women like that often do, don't they?' – here he shot Minnie a look. 'Or money. Henry was comfortably off, I imagine. She would stand to gain if he died.'

Minnie held her tongue, although it took a monumental effort to do so. Albert thanked Mr Stephenson and they left the house. Once outside, Minnie took a deep breath of air.

'Well done,' Albert said, as they walked to the end of the street. 'There were several moments in there when I thought you were going to explode.'

'It ain't like I ain't heard it before. But that don't make it any easier to swallow. Particularly when he changed his tune. One minute he reckons Dorothy weren't even married to Henry, the next he figures she's after her freedom or desperate to line her own pockets and would kill Henry for it.'

'What about a large piece of cake as a reward for your forbearance?'

She smiled and took his arm as they turned towards the Strand and Brown's tea rooms.

After a satisfying hour at Brown's Minnie and Albert separated, Albert to interview Henry's business contacts while Minnie paid a visit to his family and then on to Jimmy Gregg, the gardener.

It was difficult to know what Henry Lawrence's mother and his sister, Kate, looked like normally. Deep grooves were etched into their foreheads, and both of them had dark smudges around their eyes and a look of permanent exhaustion. Minnie knew grief when she saw it. Remembered what they were feeling all too well. Quietly, she took the tea they offered her and gazed round the drawing room. The house was small but well-kept, with every item looking like it had earned its place there. A handful of photographs in silver frames on top of a piano. Some watercolours that looked like they might have been painted by someone close to the family, by Henry perhaps. A worn Persian rug that must once have been magnificent in colour. It was a warm, comforting room. And now it had been visited by unbearable grief.

With her first few questions Minnie established that Kate and Mrs Lawrence had last seen Henry three days before he died. No, there had been no indication that anything was wrong. He seemed happy and his usual self.

'And is there anyone who might have wished him harm?' Minnie said, bracing herself for an attack on Dorothy similar to that delivered by Mr Stephenson.

The two women looked at each other, shook their heads and turned back to Minnie. 'No one,' Mrs Lawrence said. 'Everybody loved my son.' She wrestled a handkerchief from her sleeve and turned away.

'Dorothy would know more than us about Henry's day-to-day life,' Kate ventured. 'No one knows a man better than his wife. Has she mentioned anyone?'

Just like Henry's neighbours, his mother and sister seemed unaware that Henry's marriage to Dorothy was one in name only. They spoke of Dorothy with great affection, said they'd seen her only the day before and were working closely with her to arrange Henry's funeral.

Minnie asked a few more questions, but it was obvious that Henry's mother and sister could offer no help. She took her leave, Kate walking her to the front door.

'I'm not sure how much longer I can keep the newspapers hidden from my mother,' Kate said quietly as she opened the door.

'They'll find something new to write about soon enough,' Minnie said. 'Although I appreciate that ain't much consolation right now.'

'The things they're saying. The photographs, the syringe. Is all of that true?'

Minnie nodded. 'It is. But we're thinking that maybe not everything's quite as it seems. If your brother was harmed by someone, they most likely left those items to make it look like he did it to himself.'

Kate took hold of Minnie's hand. 'Get to the bottom of this, Miss Ward. My mother is not blessed with good health and she's already grieving the loss of her sister. If word reaches her of what the press are saying, I'm not sure she'll survive the shock.'

Jimmy Gregg lived in a small terraced house. A sign on the front door informed visitors that he could be found in the garden, and Minnie took the side gate. The garden was impressive to say the least, spanning only the narrow width of the house but stretching a long way into the distance. It was impossible to see the end of it, shrubs and trees blocking out the far fence, and a winding path leading the eye in different directions.

A young man looked up as Minnie closed the gate behind her. He was halfway through digging over a border; tall and lean, but with an implied strength in his wiry frame. He was built like a piece of whipcord.

'Jimmy Gregg?' Minnie asked.

A smile lit up his features. 'That'll be me.'

He was in his late twenties, Minnie reckoned, close to her own age. Somehow she'd been imagining someone much more avuncular, perhaps with a pipe permanently between his lips. Nothing like Jimmy Gregg.

'I'm surprised you wanna do more of the same when you get home,' she said, gesturing towards the garden.

Jimmy smiled. 'Doing your own ain't the same as doing other people's. What I do in the day, that's a job. This out here? It's pleasure, relaxation, whatever you want to call it. Here, come and have a look at this,' he said, gesturing for her to follow him to the far end of the garden.

Hidden behind a group of shrubs that Minnie wouldn't have been able to name in a million years was a large expanse of the strangest plant she had ever seen. A green so vivid it almost hurt the eyes, tall pillars of flowers with a dark-red eye at the heart of each one.

'Euphorbia,' Jimmy said, grinning at her reaction. 'Amazing, ain't they? And worth every bit of effort.'

Minnie had never had a garden, and never really understood the point of it. Just one more chore. But this was different. It felt like a space you'd want to wander into, get lost in. She could see the appeal of a garden like this. No regimental borders, no closely clipped grass. This garden felt like it had simply sprung out of the earth. She sighed contentedly, then reminded herself why she was there.

At the mention of Henry Lawrence's name, Jimmy gave a bitter laugh. 'Should've known it was too good to be true. Pretty girl come looking for me. So,' he said, wiping his hand with a dirty rag and stuffing it in his back pocket as he walked back to the bed he'd been working on, 'what is it you want to know?'

'Why'd he sack you?'

He laughed. 'You don't beat about the bush, do you? Wanna know my inside leg measurement while you're about it? He didn't *sack* me, as it happens. We had what I believe they call "a mutual parting of the ways".'

'Why?'

He eyed her carefully, then turned away. 'It ain't none of your business. You clearly ain't a copper, and I've already answered all their questions and they let me go. All I will say is that I didn't have nothing to do with his death.'

'Know anyone who might have done?'

Jimmy shook his head. 'I kept my head down. Didn't have much to do with him, to be honest. Certainly couldn't tell you anything about anyone wanting him dead.'

He turned away, making a show of raking over the soil he'd dug. To Minnie's eye, it didn't look like it needed such close attention. It was evident he wasn't going to say anything more. At least not yet. Not for the first time she wished she actually was a policeman, with the power to force people to talk to her and offer up their secrets. Albert might have more luck with Jimmy. Either way they'd be back and, eventually, Jimmy would tell them why he'd argued with Henry.

Minnie thanked him for his time and wound her way back through the garden, flowers on both sides of the path brushing against her skirts.

NINE

Henry's club, the Bonaventura, was located on St James's Street, in a quietly impressive building with a columned entrance porch and floor-to-ceiling windows on both storeys. Nothing about the exterior of the building suggested its purpose.

The doorman welcomed Albert and indicated for him to wait in the entrance area. An array of leather wing chairs were clustered at the bottom of a magnificent staircase which split into two at the midway point. After a few minutes, footsteps clipped across the tiled floor, and a portly man in his sixties held out his hand.

'Michael Conway, club secretary,' he said. 'I understand you're here about our dear friend, Henry. Such a tragic loss.'

'Indeed. I'm wondering if he was here at all in the past week.'

Conway crossed to an alcove and retrieved a large leather-bound ledger. 'All our members sign in,' he explained, flicking back a few pages and running his finger down the column of signatures. 'Look,' he said, showing the ledger to Albert, 'Henry was last here on Wednesday. A week ago.'

Two days after Henry argued with his gardener, Albert thought. And Dorothy had seen him later on the Wednesday. He'd seemed distracted, she'd said.

'Anything unusual about his visit on Wednesday?'

Conway thought for a moment. 'Now you come to mention it, he wasn't quite himself. He arrived here shortly after lunch, which was unusual. He normally only visited us in the evenings.'

'How was he not himself?'

'Did you know Henry?' Conway said.

Albert shook his head.

'He was a remarkably serene man,' Conway continued. 'Softly spoken. I've never heard him raise his voice. A very calming presence in the club.'

'And he was different when you saw him last week?' Albert asked.

'He was. Nothing extreme, no shouting or belligerence. But he seemed – agitated. Like I said, not quite himself.'

'Did he talk to anyone while he was here?'

'No one but me, and all I did was welcome him. It was three o'clock on a Wednesday afternoon. There was hardly anyone here. Henry stayed for half an hour. Had a brandy as I remember it, and then left.'

'And nothing out of the ordinary occurred?'

'Nothing. I'm sorry I can't be of more help, Mr Easterbrook.'

'Not to worry. But if anything comes to mind, you can reach me here,' Albert said, handing Conway his card.

Albert's next appointment related to Grace Hardy. He'd arranged to speak to her manager, a man by the name of Arthur Buckley but 'known to everyone', according to Grace, as Artie. Buckley's office was tucked away down a side street near Leicester Square, on the third floor of a narrow building that housed a tobacconist, a seamstress and a birdcage-maker on the floors beneath.

When Albert entered Buckley's office, the man peered up from his desk, squinting at him appraisingly. 'I can get you nothing as a strongman,' he said, scanning Albert with every word, 'but the Adelphi are seeking a substantial individual to play Frankenstein's monster. The remuneration is rather pleasing and not a single line to con. How might that strike you?'

'I'm not in search of work, Mr Buckley. I'm Albert Easterbrook. I made an appointment to speak to you about Grace Hardy?'

A smile had transformed Buckley's features the moment Albert opened his mouth. 'Are you certain you are not seeking employment, my son? With a voice like that and a build like Hercules I am confident we could find you something very niche. And the pay is always better for niche. Feel free to address me as Artie, by the way.'

He rose from behind the desk: no more than five feet tall and almost as wide. And not a single hair on his body, if his face and scalp were anything to go by. Albert wondered if this would qualify as niche.

Artie made heavy weather of crossing the room to take Albert's hand, then gestured him towards a chair. 'Are you positive I cannot find you a little something? Just as a sideline?'

Albert shook his head, finding himself smiling. The man had just compared him to Frankenstein's monster but there was something very likeable about him.

'It's a generous offer, but no. I really just want to talk to you about Grace Hardy.'

'Ah, Little Gracie. I thought I'd be able to retire early the day I signed her onto my books. Did you ever see her, Mr Easterbrook? In her heyday? Remarkable she was,' he continued, not waiting for Albert's reply. 'Little dot of a thing, you needed binoculars to see her even if you were sat in the front row. Out she'd come, like a tiny doll. Then she'd open that mouth and get those lungs working. I once saw her blow a man's hat right off his head with her rendition of "Summer Serenade". Not a word of a lie, Mr Easterbrook. Not a word of a lie.'

He trimmed the end of two fat cigars, offering one to Albert, which he accepted.

'If she'd only stayed like that, Mr Easterbrook. But they grow, don't they?'

'Children?'

'Yes, of course, children.'

'They do have a habit of growing, yes.'

'We tried piling books on her head for a while, see if that'd stop her. Gave her only milk to drink. Then no milk at all. Diet of largely Brussels sprouts for a while. I shan't go into the consequences of that idea, but we abandoned it fairly rapidly. Someone said eating a lot of corn might work. But it was all no good. She turned eleven and she just shot up.'

'But her voice was the same, surely?'

Artie raised his hands, as if to indicate the fickle nature of the audience. 'What can I say? Tiny girl with a big voice? Dynamite. Ordinary-sized girl with a big voice? Ten a penny. Now she reckons she's turning her hand to opera, would you believe it? She'll never make good money out of it, but what can you do? Mother Nature is a cruel mistress, Mr Easterbrook. A very cruel mistress. We might just have got away with it, mind, her voice was that good, if it hadn't been for the night at the Swan.'

He shot Albert a quick glance then smiled to himself. 'Much as I thought. The lovely Gracie failed to inform you about that small but crucial detail in the demise of her career.'

'What happened?'

'She died, Mr Easterbrook. Went on stage, top billing as usual, stood there like a rabbit in the path of an oncoming carriage, her mouth open but not a sound coming out. Like a carp, she was. Management had to yank her off stage. She then went on the missing list, although we all knew she was hiding out at her ma and pa's. After a month or so, she turns up at the Swan, bold as brass, asking for her job back. But she'd proved herself unreliable, see, and there's nobody a music hall manager hates more than an unreliable performer. So, no more work for the lovely Gracie, what with that and her having shot up about a foot in the intervening weeks. Funny she didn't tell you that little detail. Speaking of which, why are you here, exactly?'

Albert explained why Grace had hired him, Artie nodding his head all the way through the details of the abduction, the discovery of Grace on the banks of the Thames and the appearances of the nondescript stranger.

'And you're hoping I can provide you with a nice neat list of all the people who might want to hurt Gracie, one of whom happens to sport a dark coat and hat and was seen in the environs of the river on the night in question?'

'It would be very convenient.'

'Indeed it would, but such is not the way of the world, Mr Easterbrook. You know much about theatrical folk?'

'A little.'

'Rivalry is what drives them all. Rivalry. Envy. Comparison, the thief of joy. Miss Smith has secured herself top billing and is the envy of all her fellow performers. But Miss Smith knows that Miss Jones has nabbed the top spot at the theatre up the road, a much more salubrious establishment. So Miss Smith takes no joy in her position, just wishes herself in the shoes of Miss Jones. And Miss Jones?'

'Is jealous of Miss Brown?' Albert suggested.

'Exactly, my boy. Exactly. The industry is fuelled by rivalry, envy and comparison.'

'Which is your way of telling me that Grace Hardy has enemies.'

'Not enemies, as such. Merely those who might wish her just enough harm to put her out of action for a few weeks. Long enough for someone to fill her slot and earn themselves a similar celebrity. And we're talking strictly in the past tense, here. Her current situation is unlikely to stir the green-eyed monster.'

'I don't suppose you can give me the names of any of these former rivals?'

'Half of them are my clients, Mr Easterbrook. That would, as they say, be cutting off my nose to spite my face. And besides, I seriously doubt that any of them would go to the trouble the mysterious stranger has gone to. Hauling the lovely Gracie from her slumbers and abandoning her on the banks of the river? And on the Surrey side, as if it weren't bad enough already? There are much easier ways to bring about the downfall of a fellow thespian, Mr Easterbrook. Particularly one whose star is, shall we say, already on the wane.'

'So, in essence, you can't tell me anything?'

'In essence, that is the case.' And he gave Albert a broad smile, as if he had provided him with the solution Albert had been seeking all along.

'Now, to other matters. I have been observing you closely, Mr Easterbrook, during this charming exchange. And I am increasingly of the mind to see you in a character role. Your snorting organ, fine as it is, prohibits you from playing the hero, given that it's spread all over your phizog, but an aristocratic villain, perhaps? The dastardly landowner with designs on the sweet-faced young heroine? There's a new production of *The Red Barn* starting at the Britannia in a month's time. You'd make a bang-up William Corder. No? Well, here's my card. If you change your mind, you know where to find me.'

Albert offered his thanks for what had been a largely pointless but strangely enjoyable half hour.

TEN

Albert wrapped his scarf round his chin and pulled it tight, then buried his hands deep in his pockets. Even though it was now May, the nights felt bitterly cold, and this one seemed like the coldest in quite some time. And yet it was the night he had chosen to surveil the house in Stepney where Grace Hardy lived with her parents.

'Nothing to report, Mr Easterbrook,' Bobby said.

'But there was definitely someone here last night?'

Bobby nodded. Grace had said the mysterious man often appeared two or three nights in a row. So there was a reasonable chance he'd be there tonight.

'You should go home,' Albert said. 'I'm here now. It doesn't need two of us.'

Bobby gave a diffident smile. 'S'alright. I'm happy to help. Really.'

'And why is that, Bobby?' Albert asked. 'It's a very cold night.'

Bobby dropped his head and scraped a shoe on the pavement.

'You'd sooner not go home right now?' Albert asked.

Bobby nodded but kept his gaze downwards.

'Would you care to say why?' Albert said.

'I'd rather not, Mr Easterbrook, if it's all the same to you.'

The light glowed warmly through the living room window of the Hardy residence, and smoke filtered from the chimney. Meanwhile, Nelson Street remained resolutely empty of enigmatic strangers. Anyone passing had either turned at the end of the road or entered one of the other houses. Albert glanced at his watch. He'd give it another half an hour and then call it a night.

A figure emerged from the end of the street and walked slowly towards them. Albert gripped Bobby's arm and the pair of them slipped further into the shadows. Albert was certain they couldn't be seen by anyone approaching. The gait of the figure, the long, confident strides, told him it was a man. Like Albert, he was wrapped up tight against the cold, hat pulled low over his head, a scarf enveloping the lower half of his face, hands thrust into his pockets. Probably just another weary worker wending his way home.

The man paused and pulled something from his pocket. The fleeting spark of a match briefly illuminated his face as he lit a cigarette. Then he stopped diagonally across from the Hardy house, underneath a gas lamp. It provided a small circle of illumination, as if the man were on stage. Albert waited, still and alert, Bobby breathing heavily beside him. The man calmly smoked his cigarette. Despite the glow of the streetlight, the brim of the man's hat cast his face into shadow and Albert could make out nothing of his features.

His cigarette finished, the man flicked it away, then leaned back against the garden wall and trained his gaze firmly on the Hardy house.

Albert had had his doubts about Grace Hardy and her mysterious stranger. The story about being taken from her bed and deposited on the banks of the Thames, all of it without rousing her from sleep, seemed a little far-fetched, even given her suggestion that she might have been drugged. And there was no reason why anyone would wish her harm. Yet here he was. A man of average height and build, clearly watching Grace's house.

Albert held out his hand, palm facing towards Bobby. Bobby nodded, understanding he was to stay where he was. Moving slowly and taking care where he placed his feet so as to make as little noise as possible, Albert crept from the shadows. The man was fiddling with his matches and was paying no mind to anything going on around him. Taking advantage of the situation, Albert ran towards the man and had him by the shoulder before he even realised Albert was there.

The stranger might have been surprised by Albert's presence, but he was quick to react. In the blink of an eye, he'd wriggled out of his coat and was off.

Albert shouted for Bobby, but there was no need. The lad was already in pursuit. Even so, the stranger had the advantage of a good thirty or so feet on them. Cursing under his breath, Albert took off after them.

The stranger took a sharp left at the end of Grace's road, and then almost immediately a right turn. He had the air of someone who knew these streets very well, which put Albert and Bobby at a distinct disadvantage. But the road they'd turned into was long and straight, lined on either side by terraced houses. No alleyways to duck into, no hidden gaps between buildings.

Albert was a powerful runner over short distances, but the stranger was like a whippet. Thankfully, Bobby was a greyhound, and he started to gain on the man. As the stranger passed each streetlamp he was temporarily illuminated in a brief circle of light and then plunged back into darkness. But his footsteps were audible in the evening quiet. And Bobby was definitely getting closer. Given enough time, he'd have him.

At the end of the road, the man took a left. This new road was busier, carriages clipping past, omnibuses pulling into stops and discharging passengers. Albert was slowing, but he could see Bobby weaving in and out of the crowds, gaining on his quarry with every step. He was within a couple of feet of him when, swiftly sidestepping a woman with a pram who was taking up half the pavement and seemed lost in thought, the stranger suddenly turned back towards Bobby and pushed him hard. Bobby stumbled backwards, landing awkwardly on his arm, and a sharp cry of pain cut through the air. Albert reached the lad in time to drag him out of the road, narrowly avoiding a dray laden with beer barrels. The stranger turned back in the direction he'd been running, made a flying leap onto the deck of an omnibus and disappeared into the night.

An hour later, Albert was at the Hardys' house. He'd left Bobby at home with Mrs Byrne, wrapped up in so many blankets he looked like an Egyptian mummy, and sipping a huge mug of chocolate. A doctor had visited and confirmed it was, thankfully, just a sprain.

Now Albert was firmly ensconced in the Hardy living room, a large glass of brandy warming him from the inside, a blazing fire doing the same job from the outside. Mr and Mrs Hardy – Reginald and Martha, as they'd insisted he call them – were seated opposite him. Reginald was a short, stout man with an avuncular air about him. Grace had inherited her mother's looks entirely, the same rosebud lips, the same large eyes turned down at the corners. Albert had recounted details of the chase three times already, but Martha Hardy in particular was pressing him to repeat it all one more time.

'That's enough, Martha,' Reginald Hardy said. 'He's told us everything he knows. The young lad – Bobby, weren't it? – he didn't get a decent look at the fella. And neither did Mr Easterbrook.'

'And you're sure there's nothing in that coat of his?' Martha said, nodding towards the overcoat Albert had grabbed from the man.

'Christ, Martha,' Reginald growled. 'We've gone over it enough. There was nothing in the coat.'

'Well, excuse me for asking,' Martha said, visibly riled. 'It's only Gracie's safety we're talking about, after all.'

'But you're just covering the same ground over and over,' Reginald said. 'It ain't like he's suddenly gonna remember some crucial new detail, is it?'

Although that was what sometimes happened when people gave an eyewitness account, Albert thought. But mentioning it now wasn't going to help matters. Besides, Reginald was right. He'd told them everything he knew.

He turned towards Grace, who was seated in the corner of the room, curled into a tight ball as if trying to make herself invisible. She looked much younger than her twenty years, like a child awaiting instruction, watching the dialogue between the adults play out in front of her.

'Grace?' Albert prompted. 'Are you all right?'

She lifted her head slowly at the mention of her name, as if she'd been lost in her thoughts, and turned towards him.

'Not really,' she said quietly.

Albert nodded. 'I'll inform the police of what happened tonight,' he said. 'I have a friend at Marylebone Station, a former colleague. He might be able to throw some light on the matter.'

'He won't though, will he?' Grace said, her voice not much above a whisper. 'We ain't gonna catch him, are we?'

'Now, don't say that, Gracie,' her mother urged. 'Mr Easterbrook has been very successful with his other cases. That's why we chose him, remember? He'll find this fella, I'm sure of it.'

'Well, *I* ain't sure,' Grace said. 'Albert had the best chance possible of catching him tonight, but it didn't work, did it? This fella – whoever he is – we don't know what he looks like, where he lives. He came in the house for God's sake – took me from my bed with no one noticing and then disappeared just as quickly as he came. It's like he lives in the shadows.'

'He's not a ghost, Grace,' Albert said, 'or a demon. He's a man. He'll make a mistake at some point. And that's when we'll catch him.'

'If you say so, Albert,' Grace murmured, giving a weak smile that fooled no one.

ELEVEN

Minnie knew it was a long shot, but sometimes long shots worked. The mysterious substance in the syringe left in Henry's arm hadn't been identified by the police doctor, but from what John had said, maybe the doctor hadn't been looking too closely. He'd probably ruled out arsenic and strychnine and then not looked any further. There were plenty of other things that, taken in sufficient quantities, could kill a man. And there was still the possibility that Henry's death was just what the police thought it was – a tragic accident.

Taking Henry Lawrence's home as her centre point, she was slowly working outwards in a circle, visiting every pharmacist along the way. So far she'd had no luck, and she was getting further from Henry's house with every step. Her feet were aching, she was starving and desperate for a cuppa. She'd try this last one and then call it a day.

The bell above the door brought the pharmacist out from behind a row of tall shelves at the rear of the shop. He swept some crumbs from his waistcoat and Minnie realised with a pang that he'd been eating his lunch. Probably with a nice cuppa.

He was tall, with round glasses and a shock of dark hair that had resisted all his efforts to tame it. Somewhere in his thirties, which was good: Minnie found that older men were far more resistant to accepting her in her role as a detective, often flat out refusing to help in any way.

She showed him her card and explained she was investigating a death in the neighbourhood. 'So I was wondering if I could take a look at your poison register.'

The pharmacist frowned. 'How's that going to help?' he asked. 'Surely anyone who was planning on poisoning someone would just leave a false name?'

'You'd be surprised,' Minnie said. 'People often automatically leave their own name without thinking. Or they figure they can come up with some story about rats and that'll explain it all away. This gentleman whose death we're investigating, there's a possibility – slim, mind you – that it might just have been a terrible accident and he took the stuff by mistake, or took too much. His servants say he never keeps any arsenic in the house, but that might not be the case. I've drawn a blank so far, and you're the last pharmacist I'm trying before I get myself a very well-earned cup of tea. Parched, I am.'

The hint was lost on him, despite Minnie fluttering her eyelashes in a way that had worked well on fellas in the past. Maybe she was losing her touch.

'Very well,' the pharmacist said, reaching underneath the counter for a large leather-bound book. He looked behind her at the quiet street. 'You don't mind if I finish my lunch, do you? It usually gets busy in about half an hour, and if I don't grab something now, I won't have another chance until I lock up.'

'Don't let me stop you,' Minnie said, relieved that he wouldn't be standing over her shoulder, breathing down her neck like the last two pharmacists had done.

She opened the book at the most recent entries and flipped back to the date of Henry's death, her finger running quickly up the page as she tracked back in time. No sign of Henry's name.

She'd reached the entries from a week before Henry's death when she saw it. An elegant copperplate that her eye had almost slid over. It was the surname that did it.

Dorothy Lawrence, Devonshire Street. Two ounces of arsenic mixed with soot. Purchased two days before Henry was last seen alive. The day Dorothy had visited him.

Minnie called out to the pharmacist, who re-emerged from the rear of the shop. She pointed out the entry in the poison register. 'There's no witness to the purchase,' she said. 'Do you know Dorothy Lawrence?'

You'd have to be quick to spot it, but Minnie was quick. And Albert had taught her to look closely at someone's face when you asked them a question. The pharmacist was about to tell her a lie.

He sniffed and made a performance of looking closer at the entry. 'Ah yes, Mrs Lawrence. I know her well enough not to need a witness. She's been in here more than once.'

'To purchase arsenic?'

'Not to my memory. More general items. Nothing of note.' He stopped, looking at Minnie properly for the first time since she'd entered the shop. 'Is there a problem?' he asked.

'No,' Minnie said calmly. 'No problem at all.'

'Interesting,' Albert said, topping up Minnie's cup with tea and gesturing to the waitress at Brown's for more milk. 'Although it doesn't necessarily prove anything. There was no arsenic found in Henry's body.'

'But we didn't know that before the autopsy. You thought it might be arsenic, so did I. Why didn't Dorothy say she'd bought some? And why give the address on Devonshire Street? She doesn't even live there, Albert.'

'There could be a perfectly reasonable explanation. She bought arsenic for the rats. Or as a cosmetic for herself. She gave the address on Devonshire Street because it was easier, or because she was known there as a married woman. If the pharmacist had got uncomfortable about selling arsenic to a woman, she'd have Henry there as insurance. But you're right. I'm curious as to why she didn't mention anything about it.'

'Well, there's one easy way to find out. We're meeting her tomorrow at Henry's house.'

Albert nodded, a frown creasing his brow.

'What?' Minnie asked.

'It's not exactly professional, but I'm hoping she has a valid explanation. I like her.'

'So do I,' Minnie said, 'but she's got a motive.'

'Which is?'

'She wanted out of that marriage. Judging by the sappy way her and Tansie look at each other, they're a heartbeat away from a blanket hornpipe. If it ain't already happened.'

'But she also told you she and Henry had agreed they'd divorce if ever the need arose.' Albert smiled at the waitress who'd bought the extra milk and refilled his own cup.

Minnie herded the crumbs on her plate into a tiny pile, then licked her finger and dabbed it up. 'True,' she said, brushing any remaining crumbs off her hands, 'but either way we need to find out why Dorothy bought arsenic two days before Henry died and neglected to mention it.'

TWELVE

Albert had arranged to meet Dorothy and Minnie the following day at Henry's house, in the hope that closer scrutiny of the dead man's belongings might turn up something useful. Or anything at all. They were hitting a dead end with every line of enquiry.

Minnie was running late. Albert took advantage of her absence to ask Dorothy about the arsenic.

'You're right,' she said. 'I bought two ounces a few days before Henry died. Henry asked me to pick some up on my way to visit him. He'd sacked Gregg, his gardener, and Gregg kept a check on the rats. Henry was worried it might take him a while to find someone new, and he had concerns about what might happen with the rats in the meantime.'

'The pharmacist didn't get anyone to witness the transaction.'

'It was very busy, as I remember. I think he just wanted to get through everyone as quickly as possible.'

'So he didn't know you?' Albert asked.

'I've never been in that pharmacist's before,' Dorothy said.

Minnie had said she thought the man was lying. If he didn't know Dorothy but he'd let her sign the poison register without a witness, he wouldn't be happy to share that information.

'What's this all about, Albert? There was no arsenic in Henry's body, so it's of no relevance whether I bought any or not, surely?'

'You're right, it's not relevant. It's just you didn't mention it earlier, and Minnie spotted your name on the poison register. We have to follow up everything.'

A sharp rap at the door interrupted their conversation and a few moments later Mrs Albemarle showed Minnie into the morning room.

Dorothy seemed uncomfortable at Minnie's arrival.

'Is there a problem?' Albert asked.

'I'm finding this more difficult than I anticipated,' Dorothy said, her eyes constantly flicking towards the spot where they'd found Henry's body. 'It's—'

'Of course,' Albert interrupted, inwardly chastising himself for not anticipating her distress. 'There's no need for you to stay, Dorothy. If you can just let us know where Henry kept his correspondence?'

'In his study. First floor. I'll show you and then – if you have no objection …'

'Of course not,' Albert said.

'What are you hoping to find?' Dorothy asked as she led them upstairs.

'Most murders are motivated by love or money, one way or the other,' Albert said. 'Henry left everything to you, so you're the only one with a financial motive—'

'Had I killed him,' Dorothy interrupted, 'which I didn't.'

Albert nodded. 'In which case there's a strong possibility we're looking at love. If we can find out who Henry was involved with, we might be able to determine someone with a motive to want him dead.'

The study was small, tucked away at the rear of the house. Every available inch of wall space was covered in books, their jackets often torn, or faded from the sunlight. Each of these books had been carefully chosen and read more than once. Nothing here was for show.

Albert walked to the window and looked down at the garden. It was one of the most beautiful he'd ever seen. The abundance of flowers and foliage filled every inch of space. Albert guessed it must be at least a hundred feet, which was unusual in this part of

London. It was a sea of colour, from whites so pure the petals were almost translucent, right the way up to a dark, delicious purple that was verging on black.

'It's magnificent, isn't it?' Dorothy murmured, following Albert's gaze out of the window. 'Henry's pride and joy. You should see it in June when the roses come out. However often I come here, I never get used to it.'

'I can see why he chose this room,' Minnie said. 'Must be the best view in the house.'

Dorothy smiled. 'It is. And he positioned his chair so he could look out whenever he chose.'

'I'm surprised he ever got anything done,' Minnie said.

The desk was completely bare of ornament. Just a blotter and inkstand.

'Was it always like this?' Albert asked. 'Has anything been tidied away?'

Dorothy shook her head. 'Henry was an extremely tidy man, everything in its place.'

'Like Stephenson at number 17,' Minnie murmured.

'Except without the pompous bigotry,' Dorothy said.

'He don't like you much, neither,' Minnie said. 'What's that all about?'

'Stephenson decided early on that Henry and I were not married. From which he immediately jumped to the assumption that I was a lady of the night. He propositioned me once and I slapped his face so hard he sported a bruise for at least a week. I'm guessing that's why he's not overly fond of me.'

Albert opened the desk drawers but found only writing paper, envelopes and a handful of new nibs.

Dorothy reached up to the top of the bookshelves that lined the room and retrieved a large box inlaid with marquetry. 'Do you mind if I—?' she said, with uncustomary hesitation. 'It's just, there may be items from myself in here that I'd rather keep private.'

'I thought your marriage to Henry was just for show?' Minnie said.

Albert detected the hint of suspicion in her voice, and wondered if Dorothy spotted it too.

'It was,' Dorothy said. 'But there was a short time, when I was sixteen, seventeen, when I believed myself in love with Henry. I'm afraid I wrote him some rather unfortunate poems and I'm not entirely sure he threw them away.'

Albert suppressed a smile and nodded at the box.

Dorothy rifled through it and gave an audible sigh of relief.

'Wouldn't you be curious to re-read them?' Minnie asked.

'Heavens, no,' Dorothy said with a shudder. 'I'm an excellent bookkeeper, but I have no facility with poetry. From memory, I believe one of my more successful rhymes was "Henry" and "when we". And the concept of scanning was entirely lost on me.'

She passed Albert the box. 'I'll be downstairs if you need me,' she said. 'Oh, I forgot to ask. Did you have any luck at Henry's club?'

'Nothing,' Albert said. 'He was last seen there two days before his death, the day you saw him. He seemed distracted, just like you said, but no more than that.'

Dorothy nodded, as if she'd been expecting the answer. 'We're not making any headway, are we?'

'It can feel like that,' Albert said. 'Lines of enquiry that lead nowhere. And then, suddenly, the whole thing falls into place.'

'And I know it feels like a lifetime, but it's only been a week,' Minnie added. 'These interviews that look like they're leading nowhere, they're helping to narrow the focus. Stop us wasting time on dead ends.'

Dorothy sighed and left them to it, clearly unconvinced.

Albert took a seat and leafed through the contents of the box. There were some legal documents, Henry's birth certificate, his marriage certificate to Dorothy. Several sheets of paper were pinned together, covered in a scrawling, barely legible script. Albert peered

more closely. Numbers, possibly bank accounts or financial transactions? Henry had been a financial journalist; maybe this was part
of a story he'd been working on. The numbers were followed by a
series of what might be names. Hopefully Dorothy would be able
to decipher her husband's handwriting.

Then, buried beneath the official documents, a small bundle of
letters tied with red ribbon.

Albert opened the first, dated a year earlier. No letterhead to
helpfully reveal the sender's identity, and the letter was simply
signed 'D'. The handwriting was sprawling and effusive; it looked
like it had been written in a hurry. But the content was intimate
and measured. It told of the writer's joy at spending the night
with Henry for the first time. The quiet intimacy of waking in
the morning, turning his head on the pillow to see his loved one
beside him.

Minnie had drawn closer. He could feel the warmth of her body
as she pressed up against him, leaning in to read the letters.

The second letter, dated some months later, spoke of a function
both Henry and the writer had attended, where they had circled each
other all evening, unable to speak or show their love for each other.
The writer talked of a moment when he had stood next to Henry in a
crowded room and shyly extended his little finger, brushing it against
Henry's leg and then finding his hand. For one fleeting moment they
had been alone in that crowded room.

Albert read on and his immediate surroundings seemed to dis-
appear. As he finished each letter, he handed it to Minnie for her to
read. But soon he forgot she was even present, mechanically passing
her each page, eager to move on to the next, to understand how this
story had progressed.

The final letters were painful. The relationship – no, Albert
corrected himself, the love affair, for that was what it was – had
deteriorated.

My dearest Henry

It is with a heavy heart that I write this but there is no point any longer in maintaining the façade that things are good between us. To that end, I am seeking an amicable parting of the ways. I would be grateful if you could return any correspondence you have received from me.

D.

Dear Henry

Last night was difficult, was it not? I understand your feelings, trust me, I do. I once felt the same and believed we might grow old together. But I no longer share those sentiments and it would be wrong of me to pretend otherwise. Let us be civilised about this and acknowledge that love, once lost, cannot be rekindled. I would prefer that our final memories of each other were generous ones, not marred by acrimony and pain.

D.

Henry

You tell me you have accepted our parting and yet you refuse to relinquish my correspondence to you. It is such a small thing to ask, I fail to see why you will not agree to my request.

D.

Henry

Is it some exercise of power on your part? You cannot, surely, wish to revisit the correspondence of one who no longer feels the sentiments expressed so plainly therein? What can this cause you but pain?

D.

Albert laid down this last letter and turned his gaze to the magnificent garden through the window. Already, he noted, it was showing signs of neglect. The grass needed cutting. Some of the flowers had started to go over.

With a sigh, Minnie placed the final letter back inside its envelope.

'They loved each other,' Albert said.

'You sound surprised.'

'I am, I think.'

'What did you expect? A quick fumble down the Cremorne on a Saturday night?'

He turned to her, his answer evident on his face. Minnie's mouth softened. 'Oh, Albert.' She rested her hand gently, fleetingly, on his arm and the two remained in silence for a moment, the ticking of the clock on the mantelpiece punctuating the quiet.

'There's a motive there,' Albert said eventually. 'This "D" wanted his correspondence returned and Henry seemed to be refusing to comply.'

'Dorothy said Henry named one of his lovers Demeter,' Minnie said.

Albert nodded. 'I thought the same. The writer of these letters could be using the shared nickname. It doesn't get us any closer though, does it?'

He cast his mind back to his classics education. Demeter's daughter, Persephone, was condemned to Hades for half of every year. Demeter was the goddess of the harvest, he seemed to remember. Agriculture as well?

'Albert,' Minnie said, drawing his attention back to the box. At the bottom, hidden within the marquetry patterning, was a slender drawer without a handle. Minnie reached underneath the box and moved her hand. With a click, a drawer was released. Inside it, beneath some scraps of paper, lay a single letter in a different hand, the writing scratched and cramped, as if each individual letter had had to be extracted with force from the writer.

Dear Henry

I've waited so long, I can't wait any longer. I used to think you'd change your mind, but I was wrong, wasn't I? Only an idiot would

*carry on hoping. And I have been an idiot, but not any more. I've
wasted what feels like half my life on you, hoping you'd love me
in the way I love you. May God help me to continue the rest of
my life without you.*

For the last time, I sign myself with the name you gave me.

Hermes

'Hermes was the god of travel and trade,' Albert said. 'Could the
god or goddess reference somehow relate to the line of work for
these two men?'

'Maybe,' Minnie said. 'In which case, maybe Demeter was a
farmer, Hermes worked for Thomas Cook?'

'Or maybe the names have no significance at all, and we're in
danger of leading ourselves up a blind alley.'

Albert looked again at the correspondence from the mysterious
D. The person was intent on retrieving their messages to Henry. If
the letters disclosed his real identity, the man's desperation would
be understandable. Had he worried that Henry might blackmail him
with that knowledge? It would be reason enough to kill a man, to save
yourself from the noose. And Hermes? The man sounded heartbro-
ken, desperate. Love could make a man commit all sorts of follies.

Minnie scanned the scraps of paper that were in the hidden drawer.
'Look,' she said, passing one of them to Albert. It was a ticket stub
for the overnight train from London to Edinburgh. Written in pencil
along one edge, the writing so small as to be barely discernible, was
a message: *I finish at 6. Meet Waverley lost luggage. Stephen.*

'Hermes?' Minnie queried. 'He works on the railway?'

'Maybe,' Albert said.

'And these,' Minnie said, showing him a handful of newspaper
clippings. Each of them made reference to Sir Toby Menzies, Minister
for Agriculture.

Demeter.

THIRTEEN

Sir Toby Menzies refused Albert's first request for an interview to discuss the recent demise of Henry Lawrence. With his second request, Albert included mention of Demeter and certain letters. The reply was swift and positive. Menzies would see him at his home in Grosvenor Square at five o'clock that evening.

The clock in a nearby church was tolling the hour when Albert was admitted to Menzies's study, a room larger than Albert's entire ground floor. The rest of the house was large, palatial even, furnished with impeccable, quiet good taste.

Menzies stood awkwardly by the fireplace and turned quickly as Albert was announced. He was somewhere in his late forties, Albert surmised. A nondescript face, apart from piercing green eyes. His demeanour was unassuming, as if this were Albert's home, not his. More like a bank clerk than a knight of the realm. It took Albert a minute or two to realise that Menzies was almost paralysed with fear.

Menzies gestured to one of the armchairs flanking the fireplace and seated himself opposite, perching on the edge of the seat as if ready to take flight at any moment.

'Please let us dispose of the formalities,' he said, not meeting Albert's eyes. 'Name your price.'

'I think you may have misunderstood the reason for my visit, Sir Toby,' Albert said.

Menzies's head shot up at the sound of Albert's cut-glass vowels and he made no attempt to hide his confusion.

'I'm not here to blackmail you,' Albert continued. 'I'm a private detective investigating the death of Henry Lawrence. I have no interest in your personal life, unless it has some impact on Mr Lawrence's death.'

At the mention of Henry's name, a flicker of acute pain crossed Menzies's face. 'I heard it was a most unfortunate accident,' he murmured.

'Not according to his wife. She thinks it was murder.'

All the colour drained from Menzies's face. 'Murder? But who on earth—? No one could have wished Henry harm. No one. He was the kindest, sweetest—' He broke off, turning his face away from Albert.

After a few moments he resumed speaking. 'Am I a suspect?'

Albert ignored the question. 'You wanted your letters to Henry returned to you, I understand?'

'I did. And, assuming you've read them, you must understand why. I have a wife, children. If those letters had fallen into the wrong hands—' He broke off again, visibly shuddering at the prospect.

'Some might call that a motive,' Albert said quietly.

Menzies's eyes grew wide with fear. 'I didn't kill him, Mr Easterbrook, you must believe that. I wouldn't have hurt a hair on that man's head.'

'Can you tell me your whereabouts on May the ninth?'

Menzies rose and crossed to a large mahogany desk positioned near the window. He opened the drawer and produced a diary. 'I was at Covent Garden,' he said. '*La Traviata*. With my wife and a married couple of our acquaintance. I was with them all evening.'

'And later that night? There's rather a large period of time during which Mr Lawrence might have been murdered.'

Menzies looked bewildered. 'I came home. Went to bed.'

'Do you share a bedroom with your wife?'

'No. My wife is a very light sleeper and has her own room.'

Which meant that Menzies could have kissed his wife goodnight, crept out of the house to Henry's, poisoned him and returned home in time for his manservant to bring him his early morning cup of tea. With no one any the wiser.

'We're trying to track down Henry's other lovers,' Albert said, deliberately changing tack to unsettle Menzies and hopefully trick him into saying more than he realised. 'I don't suppose you know any of them?'

'If I did, Mr Easterbrook, I wouldn't be revealing their names to you. Or anyone else, for that matter.'

'Not even if it moved the finger of suspicion away from you?'

Albert could almost hear Menzies's brain working, desperately seeing if he could trawl up a name or two from his memory, pin the blame on someone else, but then he slumped down in his seat. 'I don't know any of them. Henry never talked about any other men. He made me feel as if I was the only person who existed—' He broke off, caught up in his memories.

'We found correspondence from an individual named Hermes. Did Henry ever mention someone going by that name?'

Menzies shook his head, then ran a hand through his hair compulsively. 'This Hermes character,' he said eventually, 'did his involvement with Henry pre-date mine? Or was it afterwards?'

The man's loss was palpable. A loss he could make no mention of to anyone, one which he was having to bear alone.

'By all appearances Hermes' affection for Henry was not requited,' Albert said, thankful he could give Menzies some form of consolation, however sparse. 'And Henry kept no other letters. Only yours.'

Menzies gave Albert a look of such gratitude, his eyes filled with tears, that Albert found himself equally moved. Rising quickly to hide his emotions, he thanked Menzies for his time and showed himself out.

For once, luck was on Albert's side. He asked around at King's Cross station and learned of a Stephen Woodhead who regularly worked on the London to Edinburgh overnight train.

Woodhead lived in a much more modest dwelling than Sir Toby, a terraced house near Liverpool Street station. His rooms were on the first floor and an obliging landlady directed Albert up the stairs. Stephen had agreed to meet Albert, but he looked no happier about it than Menzies had done. The room was sparsely furnished, but clean and tidy. Stephen was a handsome man, neat and dapper with a quiet grace about his movements. His voice had a West Country burr, and Albert wondered what had brought him so far from home.

Albert explained that he was interested solely in matters pertaining to Henry's death and Stephen visibly relaxed.

At the mention of his letter to Henry, Stephen looked shocked. 'He kept it? Why on earth would he have kept it?'

'I was rather hoping you might be able to answer that question,' Albert said.

'Sorry, I can't help you. Unless—' The thought flickered across his face. Maybe he had been loved after all.

'I appreciate this is a very sensitive matter,' Albert said, 'but why did your relationship with Henry not work out?'

'Strikes me you're being generous to call it a relationship, Mr Easterbrook. I were in love with Henry. He didn't feel the same. Told me I were too needy. Loved him too much, I reckon. He were easy to love, mind. Such a kind man.' Stephen wiped his eyes on his sleeve and turned away for a few moments. Albert gave him time to grieve.

'If you want to know where I was when he died – murdered, you think? – I were on the overnight to Edinburgh. Plenty of folk can confirm I were there. We left King's Cross at six o'clock on the Friday evening, travelled through the night to Scotland. Short stay over, then we refuelled, turned round and came back again. Got back into London around eight o'clock Saturday night.'

By which time Henry's body had been discovered. So Stephen was out of the picture, but Albert had felt as much from the moment he first met him. You needed hate or anger or fear inside you to kill someone you'd once loved. And Stephen Woodhead had none of those. Albert would check out his alibi, but he suspected it would hold true.

Menzies, though, he was a different matter. He had everything to lose if those letters had got into the public domain.

'Did you notice any change in Henry in the weeks leading up to his death?' Albert asked. 'Anything on his mind?'

'Aside from the spiritualism thing, nothing.'

'Spiritualism thing?'

'Got himself involved with spiritualist groups,' Stephen said, clearly surprised that this was news to Albert.

'He believed in all that?'

'No, quite the opposite. He'd got a bee in his bonnet about debunking them all. Showing them up as frauds.'

'Why?'

'It were his aunt. Lucy, her name was. Henry were very close to her. Lucy's daughter died last year. Only twenty-five but she had something growing inside her. By the time they found it, it were too late. Henry's aunt Lucy spent a small fortune on séances, table-tappers, anything she could think of that might offer her some consolation. They all promised her the moon and delivered nothing. Henry watched her fade away in front of him. In the end, she took her own life.'

'And that's when Henry started looking into these individuals?' Albert asked.

'Not the ones his aunt Lucy saw. He never knew who they were. But Henry figured one bunch was as bad as another and the fewer of them around the better.'

'I don't suppose you know who any of them were?'

Stephen exhaled sharply. 'There were two sisters, I remember that much. And an old fella calling himself the Psychic Professor. The last time Henry mentioned it, he was looking into a new group he'd come across – very strange. All women, except for some fella who was in charge of the whole set-up. They did séances once or twice a week, Lambeth way usually, but they all lived together in some big house out in Suffolk. And before you ask – no, I can't remember their name.'

Albert thought for a moment. 'You're the first person who's mentioned Henry had an interest in these groups. Not even his family knew about it.'

'Henry had quite a reputation as a journalist. He were worried this might appear … frivolous. So he published his findings under a pen name, in *The Recorder*.'

Which would explain why Dorothy knew nothing about it.

'I don't suppose you can remember his pen name?'

Stephen shook his head. 'He did tell me, but I've forgotten. Something Latin, I think.'

'And Henry was investigating this Suffolk group when he died?'

'I think so. I last saw him about two weeks before he died, and that's when he said he was looking into them.'

Albert rose from his seat, thanking Stephen for his help. 'It strikes me,' Albert said, 'that Henry may have cared for you more than you think. He kept your letter, and the ticket stub from when you first met.'

A shadow of something crossed Stephen's face. 'Thank you,' he said. 'I never knew that.'

Albert took his leave, reassuring Stephen that the details of his private life would remain a secret, and slowly made his way home. He thought about the two men he'd interviewed, both of them having to hide who they really were, living a life in the shadows. He imagined how that must feel: knowing that your love for someone might end with you hanging from a noose. His father believed that homosexuality, or any form of 'deviance', as he called it, could be beaten out of a child at its first showing. 'It's a choice,' Albert had once overheard him saying, 'and, with correct handling, anyone can be convinced to make a better choice.' But why would anyone choose that life, knowing it could end in imprisonment or death? Albert suspected it was a little more complicated than that. It was true what he'd told Minnie: when he was on the force, he'd avoided any crime involving men like that. And she was right, he'd thought relations between two men something unsavoury, taking place in furtive, out-of-the-way locations. Something to be ashamed of. But Menzies and Woodhead, their love for Henry, it was no different from his for Minnie, was it? If someone told him that loving Minnie in the way he did was wrong, no number of beatings could make him think or feel differently.

He thought again about Stephen Woodhead's words, that he'd loved Henry 'too much'. Was the same not true of his love for Minnie? Was he 'needy', sacrificing any thoughts of a future life with some-one else, running around after Minnie? He'd given up mentioning it, given up hinting at his availability.

He remembered a day when he'd known Minnie a few months. He'd been meeting her at Brown's. When he arrived, she was already inside and he'd stood at the window, watching her chatting to one of the waitresses. It looked as if they were sharing a joke. Then the waitress moved on to another table. Albert stood outside, amongst the noise and bustle of the Strand, and thought, 'In a minute, she'll look up and see me. She'll smile and I'll go inside and we'll spend time together.' And in that moment, it seemed enough. More than enough.

He'd stayed true to her for nearly three years. She'd seen that he wasn't going anywhere, that he wasn't going to betray her like others had done before. They'd become friends – true friends. But never had she given the slightest hint that she might be interested in something more. And here he was, almost three years older than when he'd first met her, no closer to the life he dreamed of.

FOURTEEN

The following morning Albert paid a visit to Jimmy Gregg. He had to agree with Minnie: Gregg's garden was a sight to behold. Albert had followed the sign left on the front door and found him on his knees, weeding a border.

Gregg leapt to his feet and extended a hand, then realised it was black with mud and quickly withdrew it.

'Mr Gregg?' Albert asked.

'At your service,' Gregg said. 'You in need of a gardener?'

'I'm not. Although looking at this,' Albert gestured towards the borders filled with brightly coloured flowers, 'I might be persuaded to change my mind.'

'My rates are fair,' Gregg said. 'And you won't find better in London.'

'I'm sure that's the case. However, I'm here to talk to you about Henry Lawrence's death. And your reasons for leaving his employment.'

The broad grin was wiped off Gregg's face in an instant. 'You something to do with that woman who was here the other day?'

'I am.'

'Well, I told her it was none of her business. And it's none of yours neither. So, unless you're serious about offering me work, I'd suggest you be on your way.'

'It's not that simple, I'm afraid. We believe Henry Lawrence was murdered, and the easiest way for you to prove it was nothing to do with you is by answering my questions. Which we can do here, or I can get my close friend Inspector John Price to arrest you and the questioning will be conducted at Marylebone police station.'

'On what grounds would he arrest me? They've already tried that and got nowhere,' Gregg said belligerently.

'Oh, I'm sure he'd find something. You've got a nasty collection of poisons in that shed I passed on the way in and no lock on the door. I suspect most of your work is cash in hand and the Inland Revenue might not be fully informed of all your earnings. I could go on. Inspector Price is a tenacious beast once he gets his teeth into something.'

'What do you want to know?' Gregg said.

'Why you left Henry Lawrence's employment. His cook, Mrs Albemarle, said you had a falling-out. I think you should know we're aware of Mr Lawrence's – preferences.'

Gregg did a very poor job of hiding his surprise.

'We have no interest in pursuing that line of enquiry,' Albert said. 'We just want to know what happened to Henry.'

Gregg nudged a few clods of earth from the path back into the border, clearly playing for time. 'Look,' he said eventually, 'I could feed you some line about him not paying me enough or not being happy with my work. Truth is, Henry Lawrence became a little too interested. In me.'

'Was his interest reciprocated?'

'I've got a sweetheart,' Gregg said. 'We're planning to be married next year.'

'That doesn't exactly answer my question.'

Gregg sighed heavily. 'Look, I liked him. He was a nice man. Kind, considerate, funny. Working on his garden? It was my favourite job of the week. But when he made it clear he'd be interested in – something else – I couldn't risk that. What if word had got out? That'd be my livelihood gone in an instant. A prison sentence, most likely. Maybe worse.'

'Could you not have stayed working for him?' Albert asked.

Gregg shook his head. 'I liked him. A lot,' he said, raising his eyes to look at Albert. 'I don't need to explain it any further, do I?'

'No,' Albert said. 'Thank you for your time, Mr Gregg. And if I ever need a gardener, I'll know where to come.'

It was a manageable walk from Gregg's house to the offices of *The Recorder*. The newspaper's archivist was a young woman by the name of Miss Cunningham, a neat, self-contained person sporting round spectacles and an air of brisk competence. Albert explained that he wished to look at the recent series of articles about spiritualists.

'Henry,' Miss Cunningham said, investing the two brief syllables with her loss.

'You knew his real name?' Albert asked.

'The newspaper world is a small one, Mr Easterbrook. I'd known Henry for years. When he told me about the loss of his aunt, and his desire to do something to unmask those frauds, I suggested he might find a home at *The Recorder*. Regrettably, he only wrote three articles for us before his passing. Might I ask why you want to look at them?'

'Henry's wife believes his death was suspicious and has hired me and my partner to investigate.'

'You believe her?'

'I do, increasingly so. We're wondering if the answer might lie in his involvement with the spiritualist world.'

Miss Cunningham nodded and invited him to take a seat in an anteroom while she found the necessary items. Albert looked around him, enjoying the quiet calm of the space, in sharp contrast he guessed to the activity elsewhere in the building. This small room reminded him of a library, dust motes hovering in the air and the vague smell of paper.

Miss Cunningham returned with three newspapers, each opened to the correct page. 'Henry wrote under the name "Veritas", a subtlety lost on some of our readers. The number of letters we had addressed to Miss Verity, you wouldn't believe.'

The articles followed a format. Henry opened with the claims made by the different spiritualists, then gave an account of his visit to each of them and the trickery they'd indulged in. His tone was matter of fact and almost scientific in its approach. He'd written about a Mrs Enid Turnbull, sisters Maggie and Emmeline Bird, and a Professor Augustus Macintyre. No mention of a group of women operating out of Lambeth.

'Did the newspaper receive any backlash about what Henry wrote? From the spiritualists themselves, or their followers?'

'Some outraged letters,' Miss Cunningham said. 'But we receive outraged letters about anything we publish. People with too much time on their hands.'

Fleetingly Albert remembered Stephenson, Henry's neighbour. He'd be the type to write an angry letter about which direction the wind was blowing.

'Henry was wondering if his writings were having any beneficial impact at all,' Miss Cunningham. 'For every letter he received in support of his work, he received half a dozen berating him.'

'But nothing that caused him or the newspaper concern?'

'Nothing.'

Albert thanked Miss Cunningham and took his leave.

Later that same day, Albert and Minnie were back at Henry's house, examining the papers in his study a little more intently. Albert had filled Minnie in on his meeting with Gregg.

'And you believed him,' Minnie said.

Albert noted that it wasn't phrased as a question. 'I did.'

'Me too,' Minnie said. 'So that's another dead end.' She turned her attention back to the sheets of paper covered with Henry's scrawl. 'These are his notes on each of the articles he wrote. See? Turnbull, Bird, Macintyre. Nothing else, though.'

'No,' Albert mused, 'just these numbers that we found before and something illegible.'

'Do you think these people he wrote about might have wanted revenge for what he did?'

'Miss Cunningham thought not. If anything, Henry's work had the opposite effect, stoking a staunch defence of these people.'

'Look,' Minnie passed him another sheet, 'there's the name Ernest. Weren't there an Ernest on that list Dorothy gave you of Henry's associates? Fella you've left messages with who ain't responded?'

'That's right,' Albert said. 'And here it is again. And again.'

'Time we paid Ernest a visit I reckon.'

FIFTEEN

The following morning Albert had just returned from the newsagents when Mrs Byrne appeared at his side. 'You've got a visitor,' she said. 'Ernest Gaunt, his name is. He says you've been looking for him in connection with Henry Lawrence's death. He got here five minutes ago and I've put him in the drawing room with a nice cup of tea.'

Ernest Gaunt suited his name. He was probably somewhere in his thirties but seemed a lot older, with a stooped demeanour and a way of craning forth his neck and squinting as if he were trying to see into the very heart of existence. Either that, or he just needed new spectacles. His dark hair was thinning on top and was already liberally speckled with grey. Albert wondered if perhaps he'd had a particularly challenging life, but decided now was not the time to ask.

'You're a difficult man to get hold of,' Albert said, refusing Ernest's offer of a cigarette.

Ernest sniffed. 'And you're a difficult man to shake,' he said.

'Why didn't you come and see me when I left my first message?'

'I'm here now, ain't I? I've been busy. Some of us have a living to make.' He lit his cigarette and looked slowly round the room. 'And from what I read in the newspapers, you're making a darn sight better one than I am. You said in the messages you left that this was something to do with Henry Lawrence's death?'

'Mrs Lawrence, Henry's wife, has hired me to investigate his death,' Albert said, inviting Ernest to sit. 'She believes it may have been murder.'

'Murder? I ain't heard nothing about it being murder.'

'That's because the police believe it was accidental.'

Ernest frowned. 'What sort of accident?'

Albert explained the police theory that Henry had self-administered the unidentified poison.

Ernest shook his head vigorously. 'No way. Henry never touched nothing.'

'A sentiment shared by his wife. Hence my investigation. Mrs Lawrence provided me with a list of Henry's associates. Your name was on that list. And you're mentioned several times in Henry's papers.'

'So?'

'What was your association with Henry Lawrence?'

'We worked together.'

Albert frowned. 'You're a journalist?'

'Not me,' Ernest said. 'I'm in your line of work, as it happens.' He fished around in his pocket and produced a somewhat grubby business card. *Gaunt & Sallow, Consulting Detectives.*

'Who's Sallow?'

'He don't exist. I just thought it sounded more impressive with two of us.'

'So what were you investigating for Henry Lawrence?'

'Spiritualist groups. Henry was investigating them for – what was the word he liked to use? – authenticity, that's it. Debunking is what I'd call it. He wanted someone impartial to help him, someone with an eye to notice things. At a séance, for example, it's handy to have two people looking at different parts of the room. Which is where I came in.'

'Go on,' Albert said.

Ernest sniffed again. 'Henry'd identify a medium or a group. We'd go along to a séance or similar. Work out what trick they were pulling. Then Henry'd expose them and write about it in the paper.'

Albert nodded. 'In *The Recorder*. I read his articles. How did he figure out their tricks?'

'Depended on what they were offering. If it was spirit visions, for example, Henry'd insist on the meeting being held in broad daylight, all participants with their eyes open. That sort of thing.'

'It doesn't sound terribly rigorous, if you don't mind my saying.'

'Oh, there was other stuff.'

'Such as?'

'Table-turners were the ones we'd been looking at mostly. Y'know, everyone joins hands in a circle and the table rises up, apparently lifted by the spirits.'

'And what did you find?'

'All sorts of gadgets,' Ernest said, warming to his subject and leaning forward in his chair. 'Some of the tables have a small pin stuck in the middle. The medium is wearing a ring with a little slot in it that fits over the shank of the pin. She passes her hands over the table, slots the ring into the pin and lifts the table, but her hands are flat, see? So it looks like magic. Other times the medium might have a hook attached to a piece of metal which fits under his sleeve. The hook catches the underside of the table, and the medium has a chum on the opposite side doing the same thing. They ask everyone to stand up and the table rises. We saw that done a few times.'

'So everyone you investigated was using trickery like this?'

Ernest nodded. 'To be fair, you'd only have to be five minutes with them to know they were charlatans; no need to carry out any tests. But Henry adopted a scientific approach. Wanted to *prove* they were cheats and liars, as opposed to just knowing they were.'

'Could you get me a list of all the individuals you investigated?' Albert said.

Ernest nodded. 'I can tell you now if you want. It ain't a long list 'cos we'd only been investigating for a few months. There was a Mrs Enid Turnbull who lived in Whitechapel. Bent as a flash note.

Professor Augustus Macintyre, Islington way. If he was a professor I'm a monkey's uncle. Two sisters, Maggie and Emmeline Bird. Pretty things they were.'

'But frauds?'

Ernest nodded. 'Welshers, the pair of 'em.'

'An acquaintance of Henry's mentioned a rather unusual group of spiritualists. They hold séances in Lambeth but live somewhere out in Suffolk. I've looked through Henry's notes but there's no mention of them and he didn't publish an article about them.'

'The Spirit Sisterhood,' Ernest said. 'They were different.'

'In what way?'

'Henry often got letters sent to him via *The Recorder*. Some supportive ones, applauding him for what he was doing. Others full of vitriol. Like he was personally attacking the writer of the letter, just for saying these spiritualist groups were a load of pony. Either way, Henry ignored them on the whole. But this one woman, Lady Harriet West, she wrote to him about the daughter of her best friend. Gwendolen Harper was the young woman's name. Died under suspicious circumstances while staying with the Spirit Sisterhood out in their house in Suffolk. Nothing wrong with her, and suddenly she's dead from heart failure. Lady Harriet wanted Henry to focus on the Sisterhood for his next investigation, with a view to finding out the truth behind Gwendolen's death.'

'What did he find?'

'We attended a few of their séances in London but we didn't spot anything other than the usual. More than that, I couldn't tell you. He was planning on speaking to the doctor who'd signed her death certificate. But before I got word of what happened, Henry was dead.'

'I don't suppose you have an address for this Harriet West?'

'Not her home address. She wrote to Henry from something called the Society for Lady Explorers. Can you believe it? Lady explorers.' He gave a half laugh. 'I reckon you'll find her there.'

Albert stood and retrieved one of the empty clay pipes he kept in a small dish on the mantelpiece. Gaunt offered him a cigarette for a second time, but Albert shook his head.

'It would have been helpful if you'd replied to my messages a bit sooner, Mr Gaunt.'

Gaunt winced. 'Fair point. But I didn't know who you were, exactly, and I've had a bit of previous with the constabulary. You wouldn't think it to look at me now, but I was a treacle-man.'

Albert looked blank.

'Burglary. I'd sweet-talk the housemaid, get the layout of the house, the owners' comings and goings. Feed all that back to my nefarious chums and away they'd go.'

'And you did time for that?'

Gaunt nodded. 'And the one thing I'm certain of in this life is that I ain't going back inside. So I steer well clear of anything that might involve any conversation with the crushers. Around the time Henry died, I had another job on that was taking up a lot of my time. Me and Henry was supposed to be meeting up a few days after he spoke to this doctor fella. Then I heard he'd died. No further investigation and I'm back looking for missing cats and catching thieving servants.'

A shadow crossed Gaunt's face, and he struggled to speak for a few moments. 'I liked Henry a lot,' he said eventually. 'He was kind and honest and fair. If he was murdered, I'd like to help you find who did it.'

SIXTEEN

Minnie and Albert had both agreed that the Society of Lady Explorers might respond more positively to a woman than a man. Which is how Minnie found herself alighting from the omnibus in Kensington and walking down a tree-lined road. Albert would know the name of the trees, Minnie thought. His head was full of that kind of useless knowledge. Minnie looked up. Trees. Nice tall, sturdy trees. She sneezed three times in rapid succession.

Her route should have taken her down the road where Teddy and Edie once lived, but she took a detour. Even so, the memory of that house and the horrors they had uncovered there sent a chill down her spine. She assumed the new owners had no knowledge of the house's history. Or maybe they did, and that had been the attraction of the place. People's fascination with the dark and depraved never failed to astonish her.

The headquarters for the Society of Lady Explorers was housed in rather a plain red-brick building: nothing to mark it out, other than the addition of a round tower which seemed a little fanciful to Minnie's thinking. The entrance hall was a surprise, covered in tiny blue-and-white tiles depicting birds in flight, fruit and flowers. Minnie gave her name, explaining that she was here to see Lady Harriet West, and was shown into the most remarkable room she thought she'd ever seen. The ceiling was studded with tiny mirrors and the walls were lined with glazed tiles of aquamarine and a green so deep it was almost black. Three deeply recessed arched windows punctuated with stained glass looked out onto the rear garden. A billiard table stood in the centre of the room, cues and balls racked against the wall. The centrepiece was the most astonishing fireplace, with mermaids and sea serpents carved into the marble. The wall above the fireplace was taken up with an elaborate wooden sculpture featuring unicorns and other mythical creatures.

'I call it the Grotto of Whimsy,' a woman said, just as Minnie was leaning in to take a closer look at the marble carvings. 'Fanciful nonsense, to my mind, but some of the other members find them charming. And these,' she pointed to the tiny mirrors that covered the ceiling, 'are designed to reflect candlelight. They just give me the most terrible headache, but there you go. You must be Miss Ward.' She held out her hand. Her handshake was firm, dry and brisk. 'I am Lady West, but you may call me Harriet. No standing on formality.'

Minnie found herself warming instantly to the woman. She was tall and slender – all knees and elbows, as Minnie's ma would have said. She had a generous mouth and an aquiline nose. Most notably, she was wearing trousers and a man's jacket. Her eyes quickly surveyed Minnie, as if she were a horse Harriet was considering laying a wager on.

'I can give you the tour later,' Harriet said. 'Most people want to have a poke around once they get inside here. Particularly as we don't encourage visitors. But we should talk first. I take it you like tea.'

Harriet had a way of phrasing questions as statements, making assumptions on the part of her guest that would normally get Minnie's back right up. But she liked the woman's breezy efficiency. And besides, she did like tea.

A minute or so later a servant appeared with a tray bearing a silver teapot and two delicate china cups. No cake. Not even a biscuit. The two women seated themselves in one of the deep recesses looking out on the garden. Not quite as impressive as Henry Lawrence's or Jimmy Gregg's, but nice enough.

'Your letter said you wished to speak to me about Henry Lawrence,' Harriet said, passing a cup of tea to Minnie.

Minnie explained Dorothy's decision to hire her and Albert to investigate Henry's death.

'A lady detective, eh?' Harriet said, a wry smile playing across her face which was instantly removed as she returned to the business in hand. 'When I heard of Henry's passing, I went straight to the police to voice my concerns. I'm not sure they took me seriously.'

'But you had concerns?'

'I did. In my experience, Miss Ward, there is no such thing as coincidence. And Henry's death seemed a little too convenient for my liking.'

'Ernest Gaunt, Henry's assistant, told us you'd been in contact with Henry. He remembered the name Gwendolen Harper, but very little beyond that.'

'Gwen was the daughter of my closest friend, Emily Harper. Both of them are now dead. Gwen was what I would call a lost soul. Adrift, unsure of where she belonged. Perfect fodder for the likes of the Spirit Sisterhood.'

'She attended their séances?' Minnie asked.

'More than that. She became enamoured, went to live with them out in the middle of nowhere in Suffolk. She told Emily that she planned to stay with them for a few days. Six months later she had not returned home.'

'Did her mother not visit her? Speak to her?'

Harriet gave a grim smile. 'She tried both of those things but was told that any interference was not tolerated by the organisation. Gwen was on a spiritual journey and was not to be disturbed. Spiritual journey? What a load of hogwash. Emily couldn't even speak to her own daughter. You need to know, Miss Ward, that Gwen was due to inherit a substantial sum of money when she turned twenty-five. She was two months shy of that when she died.'

'Did her mother get the police involved?'

Here Harriet paused for a moment, refilling their teacups and clearly playing for time. 'Emily was my dearest friend, Miss Ward, and I am loath to speak ill of the dead. But she was weak. A lack of backbone. She had an almost clinical fear of what she termed "making a fuss". As if anything would ever change in the world if women didn't make a fuss. But so be it. And she was very unwell. A wasting illness that the doctors were never able to diagnose. That, combined with her timid nature, meant she did nothing more to get Gwen out of their clutches. She simply waited, wrote to Gwen regularly – although I suspect the girl never got the letters – and hoped that her daughter would come to her senses.'

'You strike me as the opposite of timid. You didn't think to go out to that house in Suffolk, bring Gwendolen home?'

'Believe me, I would have done, had I been here. But I was travelling in the Far East at the time. I knew none of this until I returned home. By which time, Emily and Gwen were both dead.'

'What did Gwendolen die of?'

'Well, here's the thing. Emily received word from the Spirit Sisterhood that Gwen had died of heart failure. Which even Emily raised an eyebrow at, given that her daughter was hale and hearty with no history of a heart condition.'

'Did her mother receive a death certificate?'

'She did.'

'I don't suppose you have a copy of it?'

Harriet rooted through the voluminous handbag she had with her, an unlikely pairing with the man's suit. 'With Gwen dead, Emily's estate passed to me. I inherited everything, including all her papers. Ah, here it is.' She handed an envelope to Minnie. Inside was a death certificate for Gwendolen Harper. Cause of death was heart failure, and the certificate had been signed by a Dr Venables. It all looked legitimate.

'Gwen died in early March,' Harriet continued, 'Emily a few days later. I returned to England at the end of March. Emily left a letter for me in her belongings, explaining what had happened and asking me to investigate further. Like Emily, I had no success gaining access to the house. I tried attending the séances, raising merry hell and demanding answers, but they soon got wind of what I was up to and I was refused admittance.'

'Did you go to the police?'

'The police said everything was above board. Gwen's death might have been a shock, but the presence of the death certificate gave them no reason to suspect foul play. Which is where I found it necessary to pull a few strings, my late father having been very good friends with the commissioner.' Here she paused for a moment. 'I had Gwen's body disinterred, Miss Ward. A gruesome business, but a necessary one.'

'And what did they find?'

'Nothing. The autopsy was completed and there was nothing untoward or suspicious.'

'But you weren't buying that?'

'I wasn't. I'm still not. I am of a scientific bent, so the autopsy should have quelled my concerns, but something in my gut told me Gwen's death was not normal. Which is where Henry came in. I read his articles in *The Recorder* about these so-called spiritualists and I asked him to look into the Spirit Sisterhood.'

'What did Henry find?' Minnie asked.

'His attendance at their séances revealed nothing more than the usual guff. And like me, like poor Emily, he couldn't gain admittance to the house in Suffolk. But he did speak to the doctor who signed Gwendolen's death certificate.'

'And?'

'He said the man is a drunkard, Miss Ward. As my father used to say, he couldn't see a hole in a forty-foot ladder, never mind determine a cause of death with any accuracy. Despite that, Henry said the doctor had answers to all his questions about the death certificate and the circumstances of poor Gwen's death. Good answers, but delivered poorly, like the first rehearsal of a play, was Henry's description.'

'He thought the Spirit Sisterhood bought off the doctor?'

'He did.'

'Do you agree with him?'

'I do.'

'When did he speak to this doctor exactly?'

'May the sixth.'

Lady West leaned back in her chair. She knew the significance of her words had hit home.

'May the sixth,' Minnie echoed. 'Four days before Henry was found dead.'

SEVENTEEN

Dr Venables had been surprisingly easy to find, although Albert wasn't entirely sure he hadn't broken the law in doing so. After consulting a register of medical practitioners that Albert felt certain John shouldn't have shared with him, he'd located the address in Sudbury of Venables' practice. The surgery was closed by the time he got there. Given Lady Harriet's declaration that the man was a drunkard, Albert figured the nearest pub might be as good a place as any to find him. And he'd not been wrong. The landlord of the Sorrel Horse had identified Venables, a sorry-looking individual propping up the far end of the bar. Albert had fallen into easy conversation with the man after he'd stood him a pint. That pint was now exhausted, and Albert nodded at the landlord for a replacement.

'There's more where that came from,' Albert said to Venables, 'if you're willing to answer a few questions.'

'What about?' Venables said, his eyes fixed on the pint glass in front of him.

'A death that occurred a few months ago. Young woman by the name of Gwendolen Harper. You signed the death certificate.'

'You're the second person who's come asking after that young woman.'

'The first being Henry Lawrence?'

'That's right,' Venables said warily. 'Mind telling me what all this is about?'

'Henry Lawrence was found dead two weeks ago. The circumstances of his death are suspicious and I've been hired to investigate.'

'Well, he was alive and well when I last saw him.'

'I don't doubt it,' Albert said. 'This Gwendolen Harper, was
there anything unusual about her passing? The cause of death was
given by you as heart failure, but those closest to her say there was
no history of heart complaints.'

'Well, that doesn't mean anything. People can be walking round
all their life with a dodgy ticker and have no idea until they drop
dead. Not a bad way to go, if you ask me. Quick.'

'Were you present when Miss Harper died?'

"Course not. I was sent for after she died.'

'So, how do you know it was her heart?' Albert asked, gesturing
to the landlord to bring two shots of whisky.

'Chap told me,' Venables continued, nodding his thanks for the
whisky and downing it. Albert quietly pushed the second glass towards
the man. He wasn't comfortable plying Venables with alcohol and he
had to be careful not to give him too much, but he needed answers
and he didn't imagine Venables would willingly admit there'd been
something negligent about his involvement in Gwendolen's death.

'What chap?' Albert asked.

'Tall fella. Skinny. Rather a domineering way about him. It was
him who sent for me.'

'Did you get his name?'

Venables shrugged. 'Can't remember now.'

'How did this man know it was her heart?'

'Said she had a heart condition. I wanted to check her medical
records but he told me she'd recently returned from a long spell overseas and her records hadn't yet arrived. I wasn't entirely convinced
by that tale, I must say.'

Neither was Albert. Lady Harriet hadn't mentioned anything
about Gwendolen having been overseas. She'd been staying with
the Spirit Sisterhood for several months before she died.

'Did you voice your concerns?' Albert asked.

'I did,' Venables said, downing the second whisky and turning away from Albert, as if unwilling to meet his eye. 'But there were no signs of violence or anything untoward.'

Albert wasn't a betting man, but he'd wager his house that Venables had received some sort of bribe from the tall man. Money or alcohol. Maybe both.

'Was there anyone else present when you examined the body?'

'Servant girl let me in. She stayed in the room while I carried out the examination, which I thought was a little – off.'

'Can you remember what she looked like?'

Venables snorted. 'Like I said, servant girl. Why would I pay her any mind?'

'And there was no one else present?'

Venables shook his head a little too vigorously and almost lost his balance. 'Got the feeling other people in the house, though. Tall fella kept glancing up at the ceiling. Listening out for someone. Chance of another?' he said, touching the whisky glass with one finger and a studied show of indifference.

'No, that's me done,' Albert said. 'Might be best if you headed home as well.'

As Albert passed the landlord he slipped him some coins to ensure Venables got home safely.

EIGHTEEN

The following night Minnie and Albert were on their way to the Lambeth home of Mrs Margaret Turner for a Spirit Sisterhood séance.

'So, Lady Harriet thinks the Spirit Sisterhood target wealthy young women?' Albert said. 'And Gwendolen Harper was due to inherit a substantial sum of money when she turned twenty-five?'

'She was. But she died two months shy of her birthday. Which is where Lady H's theory falls to pieces. If they were after her money, why have her killed before she inherits?'

'An accident, maybe?' Albert theorised.

'Then why not say as much? Why cover up the death by paying off Venables to sign a death certificate?'

'The publicity they'd attract – even if it were an accident – would be disastrous for an organisation like theirs.'

Minnie shrugged, pulling her coat tighter around her. 'Maybe. It ain't all adding up at the moment, but I'm with Lady H. There's something dodgy about this bunch. And I don't reckon it's a coincidence that Henry spoke to that Dr Venables about Gwendolen's death and four days later Henry's dead.'

Any further discussion was terminated by their arrival at a modest house on King Street. The door was opened by a middle-aged woman. She had a gentle face, as if all her features had been rubbed out at the edges, but her eyes were alert and knowing and there was a steeliness about her that suggested she'd be a tough nut to crack.

She gave Minnie a cursory glance before allowing her entry, but Albert was more of a problem.

'The psychic flow does not always respond well in the presence of male energy,' the woman said, eyeing Albert carefully. 'What brings you here tonight?'

Thankfully, they'd rehearsed this before leaving Albert's house that evening.

'Our mother,' Albert said, placing a tentative hand on Minnie's arm. 'Departed for the spirit realm three months ago.'

'We've tried everything,' Minnie said, adopting a more refined accent to match Albert's. 'We seek guidance from our dear mother for the most beneficial disposal of her legacy—'

'Mary, dearest,' Albert interrupted, his voice lowered as if speaking in confidence, but clearly loud enough for the woman on the door to hear him, 'we did agree to make no mention of the inheritance.'

'Oh, yes, indeed,' Minnie said, visibly flustered, 'I'm so sorry, Jonathan, I completely forgot.' She turned towards the woman on the door. 'Our mother passed recently. We miss her terribly and wish to make contact. However, I understand the contentious nature of male energy and we have no desire to impinge on the evening's proceedings.'

She turned to leave, but the woman placed a hand on her arm. Her face had softened but she looked again at Albert. 'Should you disrupt the flow of the spirits, sir, you will be asked to leave.'

'Of course,' murmured Albert, lowering his head in agreement.

The woman took their money and allowed them past.

'Where did all that stuff about contentious male energy come from?' Albert whispered as they got out of earshot of the woman on the door. 'Very impressive.'

'Ida got into spiritualism for a little while, after Rose died,' Minnie said. 'I never went with her, but I'd been to a séance or two before then, learned a bit of the lingo.' She didn't tell him her reason for not going with Ida: not because she thought it wasn't genuine, more because she was afraid it might be. The thought of communicating with her dead friend from beyond the grave had filled her with horror at the time, particularly given the way Rose had died.

The room they found themselves in was large, with a circle of mismatched chairs – enough to seat about twenty people. In the corner of the room was what Minnie guessed was the spirit cabinet, where the medium would sit and commune with the spirits. It was a very rough and ready affair, little more than a chair with a heavy curtain pinned to one side. Minnie wondered if the makeshift nature of it was designed to make events seem more authentic, or whether the Spirit Sisterhood were just very short of money.

The seats nearest the spirit cabinet were already filled, even though Albert and Minnie had arrived early. The audience was predominantly women, although there were two men whose male energy was presumably not too disruptive for the spirits. They looked like they were regulars. There weren't two seats together, so Albert and Minnie sat apart. They'd agreed beforehand that this would be a useful approach if they wanted to get a good view of proceedings.

The room somehow felt like a church. Most people were silent, apparently lost in their own thoughts. Those who were speaking did so in whispers. Minnie looked at her watch. Five minutes to go. The remaining seats were filled by a group of three young women dressed in deep mourning who looked strikingly similar to each other. No guesses as to why they were there.

The woman seated on Minnie's left turned towards her. She was somewhere in her sixties, with a lived-in face, her sorrows etched in hard lines on her forehead and around her mouth. 'A new friend,' the woman said, so quietly Minnie had to lean in to hear her. 'Have you witnessed Miss Spinks's manifestations before?'

Minnie shook her head. 'This is my first séance,' she said.

The woman's face lit up. 'Oh, you are in for such a treat, my dear. Particularly if Pooky joins us.'

'Pooky?'

'Miss Spinks's spirit guide,' she said, then registered the blank look on Minnie's face. 'Oh my, you are a novice, aren't you? A spirit guide is one who has gone before us to the other side and serves as a helper for the medium, enabling her to get in touch with our dearly departed.'

'And this one's called *Pooky*?' Minnie could barely keep the incredulity out of her voice.

The woman laughed to herself. 'I know. Unusual, to say the least. I believe his name was Edmund Pook in the earthly realm, but he's acquired a more irreverent attitude since passing. He can be quite the scamp if he's in one of his more playful moods. However, he doesn't always join us.'

'What happens if he doesn't?' Minnie asked, wondering if she'd just wasted a shilling.

'Oh, Miss Spinks usually channels messages from beyond. But it's never quite the same without Pooky.'

Minnie wasn't sure how she felt about a playful spirit called Pooky, and she was just about to prise more information out of the woman when the clock on the mantelpiece struck seven and a nervous-looking woman rose from one of the seats near the spirit cabinet.

'For those of you who do not know me, I am Mrs Margaret Turner. Welcome to my home,' she said, repeatedly clasping and unclasping her hands. 'As my dear friends in the audience will know, I am not fond of thrusting myself into the spotlight, so I will now hand over proceedings to Mr William Wentworth.'

William Wentworth was very tall, well over six feet, and he dominated the room the moment he entered. Venables had said he was called out to Gwendolen's death by a very tall man. Skinny too, and this Wentworth was as thin as a barber's cat, with a shock of grey hair but dark eyebrows and beard. His voice, when he spoke, was nothing remarkable, but his gaze was intense, focusing on one individual at a time for a protracted spell before moving on to someone else.

'Sisters, brothers, I welcome you to this meeting hosted by the Spirit Sisterhood. May I extend my thanks to Mrs Turner for the generous offer of her home this evening. There are some familiar faces here, I see, and some new friends' – here he looked at Minnie, holding her gaze for an uncomfortable length of time until she broke eye contact. 'Whatever circumstances have brought us here today, whatever personal loss, we are all seekers after communion with those who have gone ahead. I can make no guarantees, my friends. No promises. The spirits can be capricious. Wilful, even. Those of you who have spent time with us before may know that Pooky, should he appear, is never predictable. So, as I have said, no guarantees, no promises. Just approach this evening with an open mind and a willing heart and who knows? We may witness wonders. But first, for those of you new to our gatherings, may I introduce Miss Elizabeth Spinks, who will serve as the conduit for the spirits, should they seek to bless us with their presence tonight.'

He turned towards the door and a woman walked through. She was young, maybe no more than eighteen, and unexceptional looking: a high, wide forehead, grey eyes and thin lips, as if permanently pursed in concentration. She wore a simple brown serge dress. The only notable thing about her was her hair, so fair as to be almost white, worn in a single, thick braid that hung over one shoulder and reached almost to her waist, like something Rapunzel might have used to gain her freedom from the tower. Every eye had turned towards her, but she seemed unfazed by the attention. In fact, she gave off an air of extraordinary calm and self-possession.

She took Wentworth's hand and he led her to the seat in the corner of the room, the curtain pinned back beside her. Wentworth produced several lengths of rope.

'Sisters, brothers,' he said reverently, as if he were indeed in a church and starting a prayer, 'I invite you to come forth to restrain our dear sister, so there can be no accusations of falsehood or chicanery. You, sir,' he said, handing two lengths of rope to a robust-looking man who gave off a faint odour of meat, 'her arms, please. And you, madam' – he turned to one of the women dressed in deep mourning – 'her legs, if you would be so kind. Finally' – and here he extended a length of rope to Minnie – 'her neck.'

Minnie hesitated, reluctant to take the rope from Wentworth's hand. 'Please,' he said, dropping his voice even lower, 'it is necessary in case we have any non-believers in our midst. And Elizabeth will feel no pain, I assure you.'

Minnie rose slowly and approached the girl. For that was what she was, close up: little more than a child. Maybe as young as fourteen? Sixteen? As Minnie drew closer, she detected a faint aroma of jasmine. Elizabeth gave her a gentle smile and nodded at the rope in her hand. Minnie placed it around the girl's neck and tied it behind her. Wentworth then invited a fourth member of the audience to test the strength of all the knots. Satisfied they could not be untied by Elizabeth, he lowered the curtain in front of her.

'May I remind you,' Wentworth said, scanning the room slowly as if to give extra weight to his words, 'if we are fortunate enough to be joined by a manifestation tonight, you must not – under any circumstances – touch the apparition. It is formed from the essence of Miss Spinks's corporeal form; the slightest human touch will cause the essence to flood back into Miss Spinks's body, and that movement is so violent it could kill her. Similarly, once the lamps have been lowered no one, under any circumstances, is to turn up the light until the apparition has firmly returned to Miss Spinks's form inside the cabinet.'

Convenient, Minnie thought.

'Now,' murmured Wentworth, after he had led the group in prayer, 'if we might all join hands to create an uninterrupted flow of energy.'

The group did as they were instructed. The man to Minnie's right had a pleasantly cool and dry hand, but the woman she had spoken to earlier was sweating. A cold breeze passed over Minnie's hands. She lifted her head and looked pointedly at Albert, who gave an almost imperceptible nod. He'd noticed it too. An open window?

'I will now lower the lamps,' Wentworth said, 'and we will join in a rendition of "The Day Thou Gavest, Lord, Is Ended". And remember, the spirits love a rousing song, so as loud as you can, please.'

The lamps now lowered, Wentworth took a seat some distance from the spirit cabinet and blew out the candle that had guided him. The room was in complete darkness. Had Minnie been able to disengage her hands from her neighbours', she could have held them in front of her face and not seen a thing.

The singing started and Minnie was reminded of the dreadful Temperance meeting she'd attended once. Thankfully, the spiritualist community seemed better able to hold a tune. After repeated exhortations from Wentworth to sing ever louder, she was surprised the police weren't called out, they were making such a racket. It was unsettling to be sitting in complete darkness, singing so loudly.

The hymn finally came to an end and the group waited, the only sounds occasional sighs or the shifting of bodies on seats. They sat in silence for what seemed an interminable length of time. And then suddenly, from somewhere in the room that Minnie couldn't quite determine, a loud rapping. The woman next to Minnie started and inhaled audibly.

'The spirits are with us,' Wentworth intoned. 'Who has joined us tonight? Pooky?'

There was a single rap. The woman beside Minnie started again and then murmured 'Oh, he's joined us! Dearest Pooky!'

Wentworth urged silence on the group and then proceeded to ask Pooky a series of questions. Minnie was surprised to learn that the afterlife was decidedly dull. Pooky seemed to spend his days fielding questions from the living and undertaking what sounded like light housekeeping. No harps. No clouds. No blissful days spent eating cake and doing nothing.

Then Minnie heard what sounded like the curtain on the spirit cabinet being drawn back, and a figure emerged. It was draped in several feet of white, flowing fabric that glowed radiantly in the darkness. No head was visible, just the shape of a graceful form. Beside her, she heard a sigh. 'Pooky,' the woman whispered almost reverently.

Pooky moved amongst them. Minnie thought it was most likely Elizabeth Spinks in some sort of costume, but it was impossible to tell in the darkness if it was her or somebody else. At one point, Minnie felt a tug on her earlobe from what seemed like decidedly human fingers.

As Pooky did the rounds, Wentworth directed questions at him, which were answered by the loud raps that had heralded the spirit's arrival: one for yes, two for no.

'Is there anyone who wishes to communicate with us?' Wentworth asked.

A single rap.

'A man?'

Two raps.

'Someone's mother?' Wentworth asked.

Two raps.

'A child?'

One rap. From the other side of the room, Minnie heard an audible gasp from someone in the audience. A lengthy series of questions followed, with Wentworth eventually learning from Pooky that a six-year-old girl had recently crossed over to the other side; she was happy and didn't want her parents to grieve. The child was then joined by an elderly man who had recently crossed over to the other side, was happy, and didn't want his wife or children to grieve. Everyone was happy. No one was to grieve.

The evening's proceedings drew to a close with another rousing hymn, after which the lights were raised. Everyone stood and started to leave the room. As Minnie walked past Wentworth, who had positioned himself near the door, he spoke to her. 'You are new to us, sister. Might I ask your name?'

'Miss Butler. Mary Butler.'

'And you seek communication with your mother, Mary?'

Minnie nodded. He'd almost certainly got that information from the woman who'd first greeted them.

'Do not despair that she did not speak to us tonight,' Wentworth continued. 'Elizabeth felt there was someone very close. Someone who had crossed over only recently. Elizabeth was getting a letter in the first half of the alphabet? Would that be correct?'

'My mother's name was Susan,' Minnie said, wondering how Wentworth would react.

'A middle name? Sometimes the spirits go by other names once they have passed over.'

'Wilhelmina,' Minnie said. 'Susan Wilhelmina.' She made a show of suppressing a sob and dabbed at her eyes with her handkerchief.

Wentworth gave a beneficent smile. 'Of course, of course,' he nodded. 'Your mother is sending you a message. The world expects you to grieve, but she is telling you to be joyful. To do the opposite of what is expected. Hence her telling Elizabeth that her name came from the first half of the alphabet.'

It seemed a very complicated way of conveying a message. Minnie raised a hand to her chest. 'Thank you, Mr Wentworth. That is of enormous help. You meet here again——?'

'Tomorrow. Can I expect to see you then?'

'Oh, most definitely.'

He placed a hand on her shoulder. 'An open heart, that is all we ask.'

'Thoughts?' Albert said, as they made their way out into the chilly May evening, a fine drizzle just starting to fall.

'Wentworth's the tall, skinny man who dealt with Venables?' Minnie said, opening her umbrella.

Albert slowly nodded his head. 'Not that "tall and skinny" is a particularly distinctive description but, yes, I'm guessing that's him.'

'And the woman who let the doctor into the house but stuck around? Elizabeth Spinks? Or our friend on the door?'

'Or someone else,' Albert said. 'Either way, Wentworth seemed interested in you.'

'He did, didn't he? Might be better if I come back tomorrow without you and your contentious male energy. I'll drop a few more hints about my substantial inheritance and see if that doesn't earn me an invite out to their earthly paradise in Suffolk.'

'Did you find the performance convincing?' Albert asked.

'If you were of a mind to believe that kind of stuff, you'd be convinced by it, I reckon. And let's face it, everyone there was of a mind to believe. Apart from you and me. No huge surprise that the seats nearest the spirit cabinet were already filled when we got there.'

Albert nodded. 'Either Wentworth's accomplices, or ardent followers who can be relied on not to investigate too closely. And the singing was obviously to drown out the sound of Miss Spinks changing into her outfit as Pooky, although I'm not sure where all that material came from. Wentworth was too far away from the spirit cabinet to be passing her anything.'

'You'd be amazed what a woman can fit under her skirt, Albert. Did you figure out how they made the material glow?'

Albert shook his head.

'Oil of phosphorous, I reckon,' Minnie said. 'Magicians use it all the time in the halls.'

Albert nodded. 'Of course,' he said, sounding annoyed that he hadn't figured this out for himself. 'And the rapping?'

'It could have been Wentworth,' Minnie surmised. 'Or Elizabeth. With the material draped over her, it would leave her hands free. Did Pooky touch you?'

'He did. Ruffled my hair and very briefly sat on my lap.'

'Oh. All I got was a tweak on my ear. Maybe Pooky's fond of the fellas.' She punched him playfully on the arm.

Albert rubbed the spot and winced theatrically. 'Remind me never to get in the boxing ring with you.'

'Everything else,' Minnie said, returning to the evening's performance, 'was pretty much what you'd see from a mediocre mind-reader in the halls. All that fishing for answers. Getting the audience to fill in the gaps.'

'You sound disappointed.'

'Not really. Just surprised they weren't—' She broke off.

'What? Genuine?' Albert gave a short laugh.

'Maybe, yeah.'

'You're not telling me you believe in any of that nonsense?'

'I dunno. Imagine if you really could talk to those you'd lost. Wouldn't you want to?'

'Of course I would. But we can't. They've gone, Minnie. However much we might want to think otherwise.'

Minnie said nothing more, merely lowering her umbrella against the rain.

NINETEEN

The séance at Mrs Turner's house the following night offered no surprises. The singing, the rapping to signal Pooky's arrival, his movement amongst the group, the exhortations for everyone not to grieve – it was all much as it had been the night before. Minnie even recognised some of the faces in the audience and shared a nod or a few words.

After the final hymn and the raising of the lights, Minnie made sure to hang back a little. As she approached the door, Wentworth clasped his hands to his chest, as if the mere sight of her had transported him to a higher realm.

'Miss Butler,' he said, 'how graced we are by your presence.'

'I said I'd come back,' Minnie said.

'And how did you find tonight's offering?'

'Most comforting, Mr Wentworth. For others, at least. I must confess I am a little disappointed that my mother has not yet spoken.'

'Come with me,' he said, placing a hand on her upper back and leading her back into the room. 'There are some friends I should like you to meet.'

He offered her a chair and a few moments later Elizabeth Spinks emerged from another room, followed by Mrs Margaret Turner, the owner of the house, and lastly the woman who had offered admittance.

'You know Lizzie and our dear host, Margaret,' Wentworth said. 'And this is Ruth Warren, a senior figure in our sisterhood.'

Ruth Warren's frostiness had melted a little, but she wasn't exactly what Minnie would call welcoming, pulling up a chair some distance away. Lizzie and Margaret took seats either side of Minnie.

'We are so glad you returned,' Margaret said, her voice high and fluttery. She reached out a tentative hand and placed it over Minnie's. 'It is always such a joy to welcome someone new into our little family.'

Minnie murmured her thanks.

'I understand you have recently lost your mother?' Margaret said. 'Such a difficult time. Did you receive any consolation tonight?'

'I took strength from witnessing the delight of others,' Minnie said. 'But – no – my dear mother did not speak to me.' She turned towards Lizzie. 'Did you feel she was near?'

'Very near,' Lizzie said. 'And she has much to tell you. There is a barrier, though.'

'Not – my brother?' Minnie offered, injecting her voice with just the right amount of concern. 'I know Miss Warren expressed concern about his presence, which is why I came alone tonight.'

'Your brother is – resistant to our work, is he not?' Lizzie said.

'A little,' Minnie said. 'He attended the séance last night at my urging. To "indulge my whims" was how he phrased it.'

Lizzie shared a glance with Ruth. 'It is as I thought,' Lizzie said. 'Your mother is keen to speak to you, but she wishes for a more harmonious setting.'

'But where would we find such a place?' Minnie asked. 'If she will not speak to me here, amongst believers such as yourselves, where *would* she speak?'

'Our home,' Ruth said. 'In Suffolk. We are a very small, select group. Many have wished to join us, but few have proved suitable.'

'And I – I am – suitable?' Minnie faltered.

'You are,' Lizzie said, her face aglow with a quiet fervour as she gazed into Minnie's eyes. 'The energy flow from you, Miss Butler, is most powerful. If you could join us – even for just a short time – I believe you will hear much to give you joy from your dear mother.'

'How long are you thinking?' Minnie asked.

'It's difficult to say. Possibly a day, although it may take a little longer,' Lizzie said.

Minnie placed a hand to the chest. 'I should be honoured,' she said.

'Good,' Ruth said. Her matter-of-fact manner formed a sharp contrast with Lizzie and Margaret, who were staring at Minnie, eyes wide with wonder. 'If you send me word in advance and catch the ten o'clock train to Sudbury, we can have someone there to meet you and take you to the house.'

They all rose from their seats, Lizzie and Margaret ushering Minnie out of the room, each one holding her lightly by an elbow, as if she were precious cargo that required careful handling. As they reached the front door, Minnie noticed a collection of photographs decorating the wall. At first glance they looked like any other group of family portraits: couples seated stiffly beside each other; individuals staring down the lens as if deep in thought; a family group, young children posed carefully on their parents' laps. But, as Minnie looked closer, she detected faint, shadowy images standing or hovering nearby in all the photographs. In one, a veiled woman. A man in another. A child inserting itself into the family group, positioned between the parents, extending a hand towards each of the children.

'You know what they are?' Wentworth asked Minnie.

'Spirit photographs,' Minnie said. 'I've heard of them, but never seen any.'

'Margaret is fortunate enough to have quite the collection.'

'To think we can actually capture the images of our lost loved ones,' Margaret said. 'And yet there are those who still doubt that those same loved ones can communicate with us from beyond the grave.'

Beside Minnie, Lizzie reached forward to adjust one of the photographs that had gone askew. 'You see, Ruth, it's moved again. That's the third time tonight. And half a dozen times last night.'

Minnie found her eyes drawn to the photograph Lizzie had readjusted. It was an elderly couple, the woman seated and the man standing behind her, one hand resting on the back of her chair. Beside the man, a ghostly apparition of a young woman in a loose-flowing gown, her hair down, her head encircled by a coronet of flowers. Minnie leaned in closer, her breath catching in her throat. She held up a tentative finger, traced the outline of the ghostly young woman. Her eyes pricked with tears. It couldn't be.

And yet it was.

Captured by some miracle, preserved behind glass in the hallway of a terraced house in Lambeth, the image of her dear, dead friend.

Rose.

TWENTY

'I'm telling you, Albert, it was Rose.'

'I'm not doubting it was Rose,' Albert said, passing Minnie a large brandy and ushering her to the sofa. 'But the image was taken while Rose was alive and then, by whatever trickery these things are achieved, she was made to look like a ghost. You can't seriously tell me you think *any* of those photographs are genuine?'

'I didn't. Until I saw Rose in one of them.'

Albert gave an exasperated sigh. 'Minnie, you are a highly intelligent woman. You cannot, in all conscience, believe in any of this nonsense.'

'You didn't see the photograph, Albert.'

'No. And I don't need to. Because seeing, in this instance, is not believing. Next you'll be saying you believe the photograph realigned itself numerous times, accidentally coinciding with your two visits to Mrs Turner's house, as if a ghostly hand were moving it.'

'Maybe—'

'*Minnie*—' He broke off, throwing his hands up in the air in exasperation.

'Look, I ain't saying it's all true. I ain't saying we can talk to our dead loved ones. But what if we could, Albert? What if we *could*? What if I could talk to Rose again, just one last time? Tell her how much she meant to me. Or talk to my ma. Take her to Brown's for a cuppa and a slice of cake and a natter about nonsense. Say sorry for being such a gobby little madam when I was a kid. Tell her how often I think to tell her something and then have to remind myself all over again that she's gone. What if we could say those things that we left unsaid while they were alive?'

'It would be wonderful, Minnie. Of course it would—'

'And what if,' she interrupted, knowing what he was about to say, 'somehow, no matter how unlikely it seems, someone found a way to do just that. Wouldn't you take that chance?'

'I would,' Albert admitted. 'But if it were genuinely possible, don't you think someone would have proved it by now?'

'Maybe they will. Any day now. We're reading in the newspapers about all the amazing things people can do that they couldn't even have dreamt of ten, twenty years ago. Maybe you'll open up *The Times* tomorrow morning and there'll be scientific proof that we can speak to the dead. Wouldn't that be something?'

'And if that ever occurs, I owe you an enormous apology. But, until it does, we are not going to see eye to eye on this matter. What concerns me – and should be concerning you – about the photograph is that it's no coincidence.'

'How d'you mean?'

'You're in that house, going by the name of Mary Butler, and there just happens to be a photograph featuring the dead best friend of Minnie Ward hanging in the hallway?'

'Well, if they know who I really am, why did they invite me out to their house in Suffolk?'

'I don't know, but you shouldn't go.'

'How else are we going to find out what they're up to? Gwendolen Harper died in that house. Henry Lawrence was sniffing around and he ended up dead. We need to get to the bottom of what they're up to, and I've been offered an invitation to get closer to them.'

'You don't think you're a little – blinded by what you saw in Margaret Turner's hallway?'

'I'm curious, Albert, I won't deny it. But I'm also more than a little nervous about taking up their invitation. For a start-off, where the hell is Suffolk? I get twitchy going south of the river, never mind out into the wilds of the countryside. Secondly, their little persuasive chat tonight gave me the creeps. Lizzie and Margaret staring at me like I'd sprouted wings. And Wentworth? That way he has of peering at you, not breaking his gaze.' She shivered and took another swig of brandy. 'But what other option have we got?'

'We could send Ernest Gaunt,' Albert said. 'He's already offered to help. He's done time as a treacle-man so I'm assuming he has a way about him with the young ladies.'

'Well, they ain't gonna let him inside the house.'

'No, but he could try sweet-talking the servants? At the very least, we'll get a better idea of what you might be walking into.'

Two days later, Gaunt sent word that he'd report back to Minnie and Albert at the Palace.

'Why here?' Minnie had asked.

'He has romantic notions about being backstage at a music hall,' Albert said.

'And you couldn't disabuse him of those notions?'

'Believe me, I tried. I'm assuming five minutes back here will set him right.'

The customary draught from the stage door whipped past them, and Gaunt appeared at the doorway of Tansie's office. He was like a puppy, all wide eyes and eagerness. Minnie wondered how long it would take to crush his dreams. It seemed a shame really, particularly given her own love affair with the Palace. But backstage was not a place to nurture romantic expectations.

Gaunt took a seat, gazing all round him as if fairy dust were sprinkled on every surface. 'I love the Palace, me,' he said, his cadaverous features lit up by a smile. 'Been coming here since I was a nipper. Never thought I'd get to see backstage.'

'I'll take you on a tour later,' Minnie said. 'But, for now, we need to know what happened in Suffolk.'

Gaunt nodded. ''Course. The Sisterhood are notorious. Everyone seems to have heard of them, but no one knows much about them. I got chatting to a sweet little thing called Bessie. She worked at the house for a while. Said it was all women, except for Wentworth, and he was in charge. All the women, with the exception of one – and I quote, "with a face like a slapped backside" – were young. And, more importantly, rich. Or with the prospect of money sometime soon when they reach their majority.'

'Much as we thought,' Albert asked.

'Bessie said the place is more secure than the Queen's gaff. Once the women go inside the grounds, they ain't seen again until they leave. If they leave. Some of them have been there months.'

'Did Bessie know anything about Gwendolen Harper's death?'

'No, she didn't know nothing about her. But she only worked there a couple of months, after Gwendolen had died, I'm assuming. Left a few weeks ago—'

Gaunt gave a yelp of surprise. Tansie's monkey had appeared from nowhere, flying onto Gaunt's lap. 'Who's this little fella?'

'Monkey,' Minnie said. The creature removed its tiny fez and gave a small bow.

'Well, would you look at that!' Gaunt exclaimed. 'Ain't he just the sweetest thing!'

Minnie looked at Albert. Maybe, just this once.

'Oi, what's he up to?' Gaunt said. 'He ain't—'

'He is,' Minnie said.

Gaunt shrieked and leapt to his feet. Monkey dropped to the floor, ran to the corner of the room and resumed his activities with barely a break in his flow.

'You still want the tour?' Minnie said.

After Gaunt had taken his leave, Minnie and Albert returned to Tansie's office.

'I'm gonna have to go to that house, ain't I?' Minnie said.

'It's looking that way,' Albert said reluctantly.

'It's only for a day, Albert. What can happen in a day?' The irony was intended. They both knew how quickly life could change beyond all recognition.

'Promise me – promise me, Minnie – you won't stay any longer. No matter how enticing the prospect.'

'I promise. Now, ain't you got a mysterious stranger to find for the Pocket Shon-toose?'

'I have. You make contact with Wentworth and arrange a visit. I'll see you later.'

A few minutes after Albert's departure Dorothy popped her head round the door. She had a very comfortable look about her, Minnie thought, as if she were part of the fixtures and fittings these days.

'You all right?' Minnie asked.

'I'm having trouble sleeping,' Dorothy said, running her hand along the back of Tansie's chair. On closer examination, Minnie noticed the dark circles under her eyes. 'Any cures?'

'Time,' Minnie said. 'It does get easier.'

'But it doesn't go away, does it?'

'No. It just becomes part of you. When Rose died, I used to dread going to sleep 'cos when I woke up, for a tiny moment, I'd forgotten. And then I'd remember and it was like it was happening all over again.'

'And that passes?'

'It does. Every morning now, I wake up and I know she's gone. I know my ma's gone too. Most of the time.'

'Sounds like a sad start to the day.'

Minnie said nothing.

'I passed a very agitated man in the corridor just now,' Dorothy said. 'I take it Monkey's been up to his usual tricks?'

'He has. I'm thinking of getting back in touch with the fellas that kidnapped him last year, asking if they'd like another go.'

Dorothy laughed. 'Tansie loves that creature, I can't imagine why.'

'That fella you saw, he's helping us find out what happened with Henry. We're getting closer, Dorothy.'

'I know. Albert's been keeping me updated. Be careful, Minnie. Whoever did that to Henry, they're not someone I want you going anywhere near.'

'I'm always careful, me.'

'We both know that is very far from the truth,' Dorothy said. 'Fancy a drink at the bar later, before curtain up?'

Minnie nodded. 'I would.'

Dorothy left and Minnie remained seated. She thought of Rose, the way her terrible singing voice used to echo through the backstage corridors. Sometimes she swore she still heard it. Late at night, after most people had gone home. She used to dread it, but she welcomed it now. Welcomed any reminder, no matter how small, of the friend she once had.

It was true, what she'd told Dorothy. It did get easier. You carried the grief more lightly, but you never put it down. She thought again of the spirit photograph. If there was a chance, however unlikely, what wouldn't she give to talk to Rose again?

But she was nervous about going to that house in Suffolk. Scared, truth be told. Scared of going there without Albert close by. Then she recalled Dorothy's face, the dark shadows, the lines that hadn't been there a few weeks ago. And Harriet West. She hadn't said as much, but Minnie could tell she blamed herself for Gwendolen's death. If Minnie could help it, no one would ever again feel the way Dorothy and Harriet did.

TWENTY-ONE

The carriage waiting for Minnie at Sudbury train station was in need of a lick of paint, but the horse looked reasonably sprightly. The driver was a tall young woman with a face reddened by time spent outdoors.

The woman gave Minnie a vigorous handshake. 'Aggie Meadows,' she said. 'Hop in, we'll be there in half an hour.'

The horse clipped jauntily along narrow country lanes, fields either side. Minnie knew she was supposed to like the countryside, but she didn't. Give her the noise and bustle of the Strand any day of the week. This was all too quiet. And she was convinced the cows kept giving her dodgy looks.

'Are you a member of the Sisterhood?' she asked Aggie after they'd been travelling for about ten minutes.

'Not likely!'

'Why not?'

'No money for a start-off,' Aggie said. 'And, no offence intended, but they're an odd bunch out there. All smiley and blissful, but I'm not convinced. No one's that happy that much of the time. No, I just do occasional jobs for them. Drive them to the station so they can catch the train to London for a séance, that kind of thing.'

True to Aggie's word, after half an hour they pulled up in front of an impressive building nestled within substantial grounds. The house was handsome, with high porticos and large Georgian windows. Arranged in a row just in front of the door were four women, all in identical white dresses. Minnie wondered how long they'd been waiting. What if the train had been delayed, would they have maintained the welcoming committee as it grew later and the light slowly faded?

As Minnie alighted from the carriage, the women moved towards her as one. Minnie took a step backwards, the alarm evident on her face. The women laughed.

'Sister, we are not here to harm you,' said the shortest of them. 'We only wish to welcome you.'

Minnie reminded herself that she was supposed to be joining this group willingly and forced a smile. 'Of course,' she murmured, remembering just in time to adopt her more upper-class accent. 'It's just I am a little fatigued from the journey.'

There was a flurry of movement and Minnie was hustled inside the house. It was a lovely place: spacious, high-ceilinged and filled with light. The furniture and carpets were a little worn and shabby but that only added to the feeling of ease and comfort.

Ruth Warren emerged from the kitchen. In stark contrast to the effusive welcome when the carriage had pulled up, Ruth was unsmiling, casting an appraising eye over Minnie as she came towards her.

'Miss Butler,' she said, and Minnie had to remind herself she was going by the name of Mary Butler. The other woman's voice was low and mellifluous, something Minnie hadn't noticed at their previous meetings. 'It's good to see you again. I serve as the administrator for the Spirit Sisterhood. If you have any questions about how we live here, any concerns, I am happy to help.'

'Mr Wentworth——?' Minnie asked.

Ruth wiped her hands on a tea towel pinned at her waist. 'Mr Wentworth was called upon by the spirits this morning. They keep their own hours, so we do not know when he will rejoin us. Jessica will show you where to freshen up' – here she gestured towards the small woman who had first spoken to Minnie and who was hovering expectantly behind her – 'and then we shall eat.'

Jessica tripped up the stairs ahead of Minnie, turning every few seconds to cast excited glances at her.

'Do you get many visitors here?' Minnie asked.

'Not many,' Jessica said. 'Mr Wentworth is very particular about who gets invited. It's so lovely to welcome someone new into the fold.'

'And how long have you been here?'

'Six – no, seven months. Possibly.' She smiled. 'Do you know, I'm not entirely sure? Time means nothing here, you'll find. It's such a wonderful place.'

'In what way exactly?'

Jessica seemed lost for words for a moment. 'Empowering,' she plumped for eventually. 'We're encouraged, as women, to think beyond the constraints society imposes on us at every turn. There is a freedom here – of thought, of action – that is sadly lacking in the wider world. You'll see.' She gestured towards a door on her right. 'I'll wait here,' she said, 'and then take you back to the dining room.'

If Jessica was anything to go by, the women were there willingly. And happy to stay for some considerable time.

Lunch was a simple affair of bread, cheese and hardboiled eggs. Wentworth was notable by his absence, as was Lizzie Spinks. Minnie asked after her.

'Lizzie's work is quite exhausting and she sleeps for large parts of the day,' Ruth said. 'The spirits tend to be most lively at night and they are less than willing to take no for an answer. She knows you are here, however, and will endeavour to speak with you later today.'

Minnie nodded sagely, as if she were well acquainted with the liveliness of the spirits and their night-time habits.

After lunch the women dispersed to complete chores, and Ruth took Minnie on a tour of the house and grounds. It was certainly impressive, set in forty acres with a smallholding, a tennis court and numerous outbuildings.

'Mr Wentworth believes firmly in the value of physical exercise,' Ruth said, pointing towards the tennis court, 'which is more feasible with the mode of dress some of us have adopted.' She gestured towards her waist and Minnie realised the woman wasn't wearing a corset, her dress loose and free flowing.

'I am an adherent of the dress reform movement,' Ruth said. 'Some of the women here have followed my lead; others remain tied to this particular constraint. I believe it was Voltaire who said it is difficult to free fools from the chains they revere. Not that I'm calling the women "fools", mind you, but some of them are inordinately fond of a tiny waist, at whatever cost. Such vanities will pass, we hope, with a prolonged stay here.'

Minnie thought of her relief every night when she loosened her stays and could move more freely. What liberty there could be in doing this all the time.

Ruth led her from the grounds back to the house and into the library, oak panelled with bookshelves running from floor to ceiling on three sides of the room, the fourth dominated by large French doors looking out onto the grounds.

Minnie wondered where the money for all this had come from and, as if she could read her mind, Ruth said, 'Mr Wentworth inherited this house when his uncle passed away. He spent many happy summers here in his childhood.'

'How did you meet?' Minnie asked.

'My brother died in the Indian Rebellion,' Ruth said, her voice clipped, as if even after all this time, she still struggled to control her grief. 'I was only nineteen and I loved him dearly. For many years following his death I drifted, unable to settle, unable to really move on from my loss. Then I attended a meeting led by Mr Wentworth and my life changed.'

'You communicated with your brother?'

Ruth nodded, her eyes fixed on Minnie but her mind clearly back on that séance, and the belief that her dead brother was talking to her. 'I did. He spoke to me – through Lizzie, of course – for some time.'

'Do you mind my asking you what he said?'

'Not at all. He told me he was at peace, that I was to move on with my life. Find a purpose.'

The kind of advice that could apply to anyone suffering a bereavement, Minnie thought. And exactly what she'd heard at the two séances she'd attended.

'And you found that purpose——?'

'Here, yes. Well, initially with the Spirit Sisterhood in London, and then Mr Wentworth invited me to head up our community here at Summerland.'

'Summerland?' Minnie looked blank.

'Summerland,' Ruth said insistently, as if the repetition of the word would trigger Minnie's understanding. When she received no response she frowned and then gave a small, tight smile. 'Of course, you are relatively new to this world. Summerland is what the spiritualist community call the afterlife. For those of us who live here, this is the closest thing to paradise.' Ruth gave another tight smile, as if she were rationing her pleasure. 'And you?' she asked.

'I'm sorry?'

'What brought you to the Spirit Sisterhood? There must be hundreds of spiritualist groups in London. Why us?'

Minnie couldn't be certain but she thought she saw a flicker of suspicion crossing Ruth's face. Or maybe it was just the light.

'My friend, Gwendolen – Gwendolen Harper – spoke most favourably of you.'

'Ah yes, Gwendolen,' Ruth said, a frown creasing her brow. 'She did not find with us what she was seeking. She stayed here a short while but then returned home to London. It's pleasing, though, to hear that she spoke well of us.'

Ruth didn't look like she was lying. But Gwendolen was definitely dead. So why didn't Ruth know about it?

'I've been searching for some time,' Minnie continued. 'For consolation. Guidance. My dear mother passed a few months ago, and I feel … adrift. I sought the comfort of contact with her, but the first man I went to was a charlatan. The second was no better. You can understand why some people are so keen to debunk the whole nature of spiritualism. Those articles in *The Recorder*?'

Ruth looked blank.

'A man who visits spiritualists, uncovers their "tricks" and writes about it in the newspaper,' Minnie explained. 'There are undoubtedly some fraudulent individuals out there, although one wonders why this man doesn't have the courage to put his own name to the articles. He goes by the name of Veritas.'

Again, no reaction from Ruth. 'There will always be those who seek to undermine what they do not understand,' she said. 'Lizzie is, however, the genuine article. And I know she is eager to speak to you. I'll see if she is sufficiently rested.'

Ruth departed the room, leaving Minnie alone in the library. She scanned the bookshelves, telling herself it was unlikely she'd find anything incriminating – a handy ledger labelled 'Swindled Heiresses', perhaps – but she looked nonetheless. Nothing. The books looked as though they'd been bought by the yard, and she suspected most of their pages were still uncut. Fleetingly, she thought of Henry Lawrence's study with its shelves of well-thumbed volumes.

The door opened and she turned, expecting to see Lizzie. Instead it was one of the young women she'd met at lunchtime.

'It's Charlotte, isn't it?' Minnie asked.

The woman nodded, glancing nervously behind her. She was a pretty thing, Minnie thought. Porcelain skin, delicate features and hair with just a hint of copper. Young, like all the women at Summerland apart from Ruth. There was something vaguely familiar about her, but Minnie couldn't put her finger on it. She moved quickly towards Minnie, holding out an envelope. 'Please,' she whispered, forcing it into Minnie's hand. 'Get this to my mother.'

Minnie held the envelope, confused. 'Can't you—'

'Ssh,' Charlotte interrupted, looking fearfully behind her again, as if expecting to be barged in on at any moment. 'Give it to my mother. Tell her—'

She broke off abruptly at the sound of footsteps tapping down the corridor towards the room. Minnie thrust the envelope into her pocket and ushered Charlotte towards the French doors, almost pushing her through and quickly closing them behind her.

The library door opened. This time it was Lizzie. The young woman, in the simplicity of her appearance, had seemed incongruous at the séances in a busy part of London, but here she seemed of a piece, exuding a serenity and calm of which Minnie felt slightly envious. She wasn't sure she'd ever felt as calm as Lizzie looked, even in sleep. The young woman wore the same white dress as the other women. Her hair, as before, was in the single long plait, draped over her left shoulder.

'Miss Butler,' she said, moving towards Minnie with her arms outstretched in welcome. 'May I call you Mary?'

'Of course,' Minnie said.

'And you shall call me Lizzie.' She was taller than Minnie had thought, with at least two or three inches on her. 'Might we talk outside? The natural world clears my head. Silences the voices.'

'And that's good?' Minnie asked.

Lizzie gave a half-smile. 'Oh, very good. I welcome the spirits' communication but they can be a little – insistent – at times. And they have a habit of talking over each other.'

'I thought it was mainly Pooky you spoke to?' Minnie said, putting on her coat and bonnet.

'Oh, no. Pooky is one of many spirit guides who come to me.'

Lizzie opened the French doors and they made their way out into the grounds. The sun had now disappeared behind a cloud, and the air felt much colder.

'Have you heard anything from my mother?' Minnie prompted, as they circled the tennis court.

'Not clearly, but I feel her presence nearby. It can take time, Mary. The spirits do not always respond in the way we hope.'

There was a firmness, a confidence in the way Lizzie spoke that made Minnie wonder how old she was, exactly. At the séances, Minnie had figured her as young as fourteen, but now she couldn't be sure.

'Other spirits, however, have been very agitated since they learned of your visit to us here,' Lizzie continued. 'One in particular is most eager to pass on a message.'

She stopped, her eyes now focused on some point in the distance, as if she were watching something unfold on a stage. Her voice changed, dropped in timbre and became more fragmented; individual words seemed to rip out of her. 'Blood,' she said. 'So much blood. And pain. A man is shouting. At you, Mary.'

Minnie's heart lurched in her chest. She told herself to calm down. This didn't mean anything. It could just be a fishing exercise to get her onside.

'A child,' Lizzie continued. 'And then – no child.'

Bile rose in Minnie's throat. In an instant, as had happened so easily before, she was flung back in her memory to a hansom cab, a belligerent driver, Ida and Rose helping her into their home, Ida's shouts at the cab driver.

'No child,' Lizzie repeated, clutching hold of one of Minnie's hands so tightly Minnie wondered if she might break some bones.

Minnie tried to wrestle her hand free, spoke Lizzie's name loudly, hoping to pull her out of whatever had taken hold of her. Hoping to stop Lizzie reliving the worst part of Minnie's life. But Lizzie was beyond her reach.

'You – you are not to blame. You must forgive yourself.'

And then, as suddenly as it had all started, Lizzie seemed to return to herself. She let go of Minnie's hand, her eyes refocusing on the landscape around her. She smiled tentatively at Minnie.

'Who told you?' Minnie said. Anyone who knew her would have been suspicious of the calmness with which she asked the question.

'I'm sorry?' Lizzie said, confused.

'Who told you about my past?'

'The spirits,' Lizzie said, as if the answer were self-evident. 'One in particular has been insistent on speaking to you.'

'Oh yeah,' Minnie said, the anger rising within her. 'And who would that be?'

Lizzie gave her another gentle half-smile and took her hand. 'Rose,' she said. 'Her name is Rose.'

TWENTY-TWO

The train back into London was delayed. After being stuck in a tunnel for half an hour, they were finally on the move again. Which was probably a good thing because it gave Minnie time to think.

As they approached the city, Minnie looked out at the rows of terraces and their backyards. This was normally her favourite thing about train travel, nosing in on other people's lives. Passing houses where someone had taken care with their backyard, planting flowers that valiantly bloomed despite the relentless smoke and smog. Trying on houses for size, wondering what it would be like to live there, what kind of person she might be with pretty curtains at the window, flowers in the yard and a tabby cat weaving its way round her ankles. But now the houses and gardens swept past her, unnoticed, as she replayed the conversation with Lizzie in her head.

Two people knew about her past. One of those people was Ida, Rose's mum, who'd been there to pick up the pieces. Ida had never said a word to anyone over all the intervening years. Why would she say anything now? And – if she had – how on earth had it got back to Lizzie Spinks?

The other person was Albert. And the same applied to him. Why would he betray her secret? And, even if he had, how had Lizzie Spinks got hold of that information?

Which left the second option. Lizzie was a genuine psychic and Rose had communicated with her from beyond the grave.

The train finally pulled into Liverpool Street. Minnie flagged down a cab and was at Albert's house in less than half an hour, letting herself in with the key he had given her.

Albert was sitting by the fire, reading. His face lit up when he saw it was Minnie, then he noticed her expression and his own darkened in response. 'What is it?' he said, throwing the book aside and rising to his feet.

Minnie shook her head swiftly, letting him know there was no immediate peril. Suddenly she found herself lost for words, unsure of how to start.

'Minnie?' he prompted, then crossed to the sideboard and poured them both a large brandy.

The alcohol loosened her tongue. 'I went to Summerland today,' she said.

'I know,' Albert said, bemused. 'We discussed it beforehand, remember? Do they know your real identity? Did something happen?'

'I ain't exactly sure.'

She started with the letter Charlotte had asked her to pass on. 'She was more nervous than a pig in a bacon factory, Albert. There's something going on there, I'm sure of it. I just can't see what it's got to do with Henry Lawrence.'

'If, indeed, it's got anything to do with him at all. Hopefully this girl's mother will provide some answers.' He refilled her glass. 'Should we open the letter, do you think?'

'I thought that too,' Minnie said. 'But it don't seem right, somehow.'

'Well, make sure you arrange to see the mother as soon as possible.'

Minnie nodded. She was distracted.

'What else happened?' Albert asked. 'You're not yourself.'

She told him, briefly, what Lizzie Spinks had revealed to her. When she'd finished Albert said nothing.

'So?' she said.

'It's puzzling, certainly. And worrying.'

'Puzzling? *Puzzling?* It's a bit more than bleedin' puzzling, wouldn't you say?'

'You're not seriously entertaining the notion that Rose spoke to Lizzie Spinks from beyond the grave, revealing the details of your past?'

'Well, how else did she know? It was so specific, Albert. None of that "be happy, move on" guff we heard the other night at the séance. She knew about the pregnancy. She knew about the abortion. And she weren't fishing around for a name, throwing out letters of the alphabet hoping I'd land on one. She specifically said the information had come from someone called Rose.'

'Oh, Minnie, please. You can't tell me you believe in any of that nonsense. It's nothing more than exploitation of people when they're at their most vulnerable.'

'I dunno,' Minnie said cautiously. 'I went to a séance not long after Ma died. The medium told me stuff they couldn't possibly have known about her.'

'Such as?' Albert said.

'What she'd done for a living. Where we lived.'

'Let me guess. Somewhere close to where the séance was being held, because you'd be unlikely to have travelled far, given your age at the time and obvious lack of money. And your mother was a laundress, wasn't she? Hardly the most unusual occupation in the world.'

Minnie bridled. 'There's no need to get the spike, Albert. So what if people are happy to hand over a few coins and get a little consolation? It ain't doing you no harm.'

'When I was on the force, Minnie, I knew women who let their children go hungry while they handed over every last farthing to some charlatan who'd tell them their grandfather was desperate to get in touch with them, but needed just a little more time to break through the spirit wall, or whatever blarney they were calling it. It might not do me any personal harm, but it certainly hurts others.'

'So you don't think any of it could be true? I'll grant you that most spiritualists are con artists. But what if, just occasionally, one of them was genuine?'

Albert shook his head, a half-smile playing about his lips, as if she were just a foolish child whose opinions barely counted. 'None of them are genuine, Minnie. I don't know what happens when we die but I know for certain that we don't come back and have a chat with the living.'

'Well, in that case, how does Lizzie Spinks know what she knows? I've told two people, Albert. You and Ida. I'd bet my life on neither of you saying a word to anyone.'

Albert crossed to the fireplace and made a show of stirring the fire back into life.

'What?' Minnie said. 'What ain't you saying, Albert?'

He turned back towards her. 'I did tell someone. About your past.'

Minnie felt as if the ground had gone from beneath her feet, all the air sucked out of her lungs. She staggered and Albert caught her, leading her to a chair near the fire.

'You did *what*?' Minnie said, not entirely sure she'd hadn't misheard him.

'I talked to Mrs Byrne about what had happened to you—'

'After I specifically told you not to say a word to a single soul?'

'I know, I know. I'm not proud of it. But you'd trusted me with this huge secret, this terrible thing that happened to you that was stopping us having the future together I hoped for. I tried to talk to you about it several times – do you remember? – and each time you shut me down like there was nothing to say. Like it was old news. But it wasn't old news to me, Minnie. I needed to get to grips with what you'd told me, try to find a way to help you move forward—'

'So you had a little chat with your *housekeeper*?'

Albert flinched at the disdain in Minnie's voice. 'Don't say it like that, Minnie. Mrs B is much more than a housekeeper, and you know that. She knew what my feelings were for you. She knew something was keeping us apart.'

'And who else did *she* tell?'

'No one,' Albert said. 'I swore her to secrecy.'

'Yeah, just like I did with you. And look where that's got us.'

Minnie jumped up from her seat and rang the bell by the fireplace. A few moments later Mrs Byrne entered the room.

'Minnie,' she said, 'I'm so glad you're here. I've got a little of that – what is it?' Mrs Byrne broke off, reading Minnie's expression.

'Albert here's just told me he's been sharing my secrets with you,' Minnie said, struggling to keep the tears out of her voice. 'And I'm wondering who else you've told.'

'Minnie's past—' Albert said, by way of explanation.

'No one,' Mrs Byrne said. 'I swear to you Minnie, I've never said a single word to anyone else. Albert told me about what happened to you, we talked about it and we've never discussed it again. Why are you asking?'

'Lizzie Spinks, the medium with the Spirit Sisterhood, has knowledge of Minnie's history,' Albert murmured.

'Well, I can assure you it didn't come from me,' Mrs Byrne said.

'Well, that leaves us in something of a pickle, don't it?' Minnie said, affecting an air of nonchalance that couldn't have been further from her true feelings. 'You're saying it weren't one of you two, and I'm telling you it weren't Ida. Who else does that leave?'

'Beresford himself?' Albert suggested. 'The doctor who performed the operation? The other doctor who saw you afterwards?'

'I gave both those doctors a false name. And Beresford? I can't imagine it's something he'd be bragging about. Plus, he didn't know anything about what happened after the abortion. He weren't there.'

'There's one other person who *was* there,' Mrs Byrne said, her voice low and quiet.

'Rose? Never,' Minnie said defiantly.

'How can you be so sure?' Albert asked.

'Because I knew her, Albert. Because she was straight as a die. She'd never have said anything.'

Albert swirled the liquid in his glass. It didn't fool Minnie. He was playing for time.

'Minnie,' he said eventually, clearly measuring his words carefully. 'I'm sure Rose was a wonderful young woman. I have no doubt about that, knowing how much she was loved by both you and Ida. But there is a tendency when someone dies—'

'—to turn them into some kind of saint?' Minnie interrupted. 'She weren't no saint, Albert. She was forgetful and clumsy and always running about twenty minutes late. She could be cruel some-times – not deliberately, just 'cos she didn't think before she opened her mouth. But she was loyal and true. And she'd never have said a word about Beresford. Unlike you.'

'Even if I had told anyone other than Mrs B – which I haven't – who would I tell? And how would it have got back to Lizzie Spinks?'

'I dunno. Maybe you let it slip to John one night when you were in your cups. John mentions it to someone, who mentions it to someone else, and so on, until somehow it ends up with Lizzie Spinks.'

'That's ridiculous, and you know it.'

'Do I?' Minnie knew it was ridiculous; she even understood his reasons for sharing her secret with Mrs B, that desire to confide in someone and lighten the burden. But the argument was escalating now, and she couldn't find a way to back down, to take it back to a rational discussion about how Lizzie knew so much about her life.

Albert said nothing for a moment, clearly trying to control his emotions. 'Yes, you do,' he said finally, firmly, as if drawing a line under the argument. 'The point we *should* be discussing – the issue you seem to have completely overlooked – is that Lizzie Spinks knows about your past. Which means she knows who you really are. Not Mary Butler. Minnie Ward. And if she knows who you really are, you are in danger.'

Minnie waved a hand dismissively.

'Don't,' Albert said. 'Don't do that. Don't play fast and loose with your safety. We know where that's got us in the past.'

Minnie went to say something in her defence and then it felt as if the weight of all she had been carrying, all the thoughts of Rose that had consumed her suddenly became too much to bear. Her voice broke and she started to cry. In her mind, she felt Albert's arms around her, because that's what he always did when she cried. She felt his broad chest beneath her head as she leaned in, smelled that curious blend of sandalwood and maybe just a hint of lemon. She felt the warmth of his hands on her back as he held her.

Except she felt none of those things, because Albert did not pull her to him. He stood back from her, his face a mask.

'I understand you feel betrayed by my telling Mrs Byrne,' he said. 'But I have sworn to you that your secret went no further than that. And if you won't believe me, there's not much point in our discussing it any further, is there?'

There were a hundred things Minnie wanted to say, to justify her reasoning, to explain herself. Most of all, to rewind the clock before the conversation escalated into this terrible argument. But one look at Albert's face told her it would be pointless.

She turned and left without another word.

TWENTY-THREE

Albert waited a few minutes to ensure he wouldn't run into Minnie, then grabbed his coat, hat and a leather holdall and left the house, ignoring Mrs Byrne's desire to talk further. He needed to let off steam, not sit pondering and turning over the meaning of Minnie's words in his mind. There was one place he could go where no one would ask anything of him.

Marylebone Boxing Club was tucked away down a side street, but you'd have to know it was there to find it. A narrow doorway nestled between two shops with a simple sign on the front, then down a long corridor which opened into a large space running along the back of several shops. It was dominated by a central boxing ring but away to one side were punchbags, suspended from heavy rings in the ceiling. This was what Albert had come for.

The previous night had been fight night, so it was quiet, which was exactly what Albert wanted. He emerged from the changing rooms, nodded at some regulars whom he recognised but couldn't put a name to and headed for the punchbags. After ten minutes, he unlaced his gloves and threw them to the ground in frustration. Normally, he could shrug off any worries with some sparring or training, but this time it wasn't working.

In his heart, he felt guilty for ever having discussed Minnie's past with Mrs Byrne, but he'd been truthful in what he'd said. He'd needed to share the burden, and he knew Mrs Byrne would take it no further. And now Minnie had made this ridiculous suggestion that he'd shared her secret thoughtlessly with whoever happened to be listening at the time.

'Going bare knuckle, are you?' a familiar voice said. 'You'll spoil those pretty hands!'

Albert turned. John had arrived for some practice. The smile died on John's face as he took in Albert's bad mood. 'What's up with you? You look like you lost a finny and found a flatch.'

'Not that fortunate, I'm afraid,' Albert said, retrieving his gloves from the floor.

'Fancy a pint?' John asked.

'You've only just got here.'

John exhaled. 'To be honest, Albert, I only came here for a bit of peace and quiet. Lily's teething and she's raising merry hell.'

'And Mary doesn't mind you sloping off?' Albert asked.

John gave a sly smile. 'She don't exactly know this is where I am. Told her I had some urgent paperwork to finish at the station.'

'In which case, you don't want to go home stinking of beer. Mary's got the nose of a greyhound. What about the baths?'

John's face lit up. The Argyll Baths were opulent and spacious, with the added luxury of plenty of hot water, towels and soap. Nothing like the public baths John was used to and a real favourite of his, although a treat he could rarely afford.

A cab deposited them outside the baths near Liverpool Street station. 'This one's on me,' Albert said, as John searched in his pocket for the three-shilling entrance fee. 'Although I'll be needing some advice in return.'

'Not a problem.'

Once they'd changed and made their way to the bath, with its warm springs, marble floors and rich mosaics, Albert remembered that John knew nothing about Minnie's past. *See?* He said to her in his mind, *I didn't tell John, and he's my closest friend.* In a fleeting moment of spite he considered telling John everything, but no matter how angry he was with Minnie, he would never betray her trust.

'Something happened to Minnie a long time ago,' he said. 'Something she told me about in confidence.'

John nodded. He knew Albert well enough not to press for details. Albert went on to recount the argument with Minnie.

'And you didn't tell anyone other than Mrs B,' John said. Albert was gratified to hear it was a statement, not a question.

'I didn't, but she won't believe that. It strikes me it's all of a piece, John. Ever since we've met, despite everything we've been through, she still doesn't fully trust me.'

'Does she trust anyone? Properly trust them.'

Albert considered it for a moment. 'Tansie, maybe? Ida?'

John slowly shook his head. 'I ain't so sure about that. She likes them, loves them even – although how anyone can find it in their heart to love Edward Tansford is beyond me – but you always get the feeling with Min that she's happier relying on herself to get things done.'

Albert nodded.

'There's more to this though, ain't there?' John said. 'I mean, you've had arguments before, but this seems more—'

'—worrying?' Albert offered.

'Yeah. So why's it different?'

Albert thought for a moment. 'Well, she's never accused me of anything this bad before. And it just feels like an accumulation. One more thing – the final thing, maybe – that convinces me we don't have a future together.'

John leaned back further into the water. 'Well, there's plenty of women who'd tip their cap at you, Albert. You'd have no shortage of offers if you set your stall out. Although I ain't never met anyone quite like Min.'

And that was the problem, Albert thought. No one quite like her.

Minutes passed, with John clearly remaining silent so that Albert could discuss things further if he chose. But what was the point?

'I checked out Woodhead's and Menzies's alibis,' Albert said eventually. 'Henry Lawrence's lovers.'

John looked relieved to be moving on from the tricky area of feelings to the safer ground of interviews and alibis. 'And?'

'I never had much doubt about Woodhead's, and half a dozen colleagues confirmed he was on the overnight to Edinburgh. Menzies's alibi had a few holes in it that warranted a probe. He doesn't share a bedroom with his wife, and there was time for him to leave the house, kill Henry and get back without anyone noticing.'

'So, did he?'

Albert shook his head. 'I interviewed his servants. It turns out the butler had a raging toothache that night. He said he didn't sleep a wink, sat in the kitchen all night with a bottle of clove oil. He'd have heard if anyone left the house.'

'So, where does that leave you?' John said.

'Nowhere,' Albert said. 'Worse than nowhere. If Lizzie Spinks knows about Minnie's past – however she found it out – it follows that she knows Minnie isn't Mary Butler.'

'Which means Minnie's cover's blown and your chances of finding Henry Lawrence's killer have gone from slim to non-existent.'

Despite John's attempts at persuasion, Albert hadn't felt in the mood for a pint, and the two men had parted ways outside the baths. As he entered his house, Mrs Byrne appeared.

'It's Miss Hardy,' she said. 'She's been here since just after you went out. I've put her in the drawing room.'

Albert removed his hat and coat and joined Grace, who was sitting by the fire, staring into the flames.

'Grace?' he said.

She jumped at the sound of her name.

'Has something happened?'

'I saw him again today,' Grace said. 'That fella. I was in Simpson's shopping for some fabric, and he was there. He knew I'd seen him 'cos he smiled at me. Gave me a little wave like it was all great larks.'

'When was this?'

'Earlier. Around four o'clock?'

Albert glanced at the mantel clock. 'It's nearly ten, Grace. What have you been doing since?'

She huddled closer to the fire. 'Just been walking around. Didn't wanna go home 'cos I didn't want Ma and Pa to see how upset I was. Didn't know what to do with myself, and then I thought of you. Only you weren't here. Your housekeeper made me a cuppa, which was kind, weren't it?' She turned her gaze to Albert, her eyes filled with tears. 'I don't know what I'm gonna do, Albert. He ain't gonna leave me alone, is he?'

For the second time that evening, a young woman was crying in his house. This time, Albert provided a clean handkerchief and rang for more tea from Mrs Byrne.

'I don't suppose you got a better look at him this time?' Albert asked when the tea had been poured and Grace looked like she was starting to defrost a little.

She shook her head. 'He's clever, ain't he? He was in Simpson's, no real distance from me, but far enough that I couldn't get a decent look at him.'

'I know a young lad, Bobby. He was there the night we nearly caught this fella. I'll see if I can get him to escort you, so you've always got someone beside you when you're not at home.'

Grace gave a weak smile. 'D'you think that'll keep him away?'

'I don't know, Grace.' He wished he had a better answer to give her, but just like his earlier discussions with Minnie, he wasn't sure he could see a clear way forward.

TWENTY-FOUR

Minnie wasn't sure when she finally drifted off. She remembered hearing a clock chime four and knew she hadn't slept up until that point. As the first grey fingers of dawn started creeping round her curtains, she gave up on any further attempts. She needed to deliver the letter Charlotte had given her at Summerland, but it was still too early. There was someone she needed to speak to, and now was as good a time as any.

Ida Watkins handed her a cuppa as soon as she came through the door. There was always a pot of tea on the go at Ida's, although occasionally it would have been sitting for too long and resemble something closer to beef stew than tea. Fortunately, this one tasted like it had only recently been made.

Ida's kitchen table was completely buried under mounds of muslin, crepe and gauze cut into petal and leaf shapes. Minnie remembered being enchanted the first time she had seen the materials needed to make artificial flowers; the different fabrics, the vast array of colours. Then, over the years, she'd witnessed the hours of repetitive work Ida undertook, the paltry financial returns for all her labour. Recently, Minnie had tried offering her money to ease the strain, but Ida would have none of it.

Minnie took a seat facing her across the table, placing her tea at a safe distance from the fabric. Then, as was their way whenever they met, both women set to work, the movement of their hands somehow freeing up their tongues, enabling them to talk about whatever was troubling them the most. It was how they'd survived Rose's murder and all the horrors that came after it. Minnie pressed the fabric leaves into moulds, imprinting them with veins, while Ida took on the more skilled work of shaping individual flower petals.

They worked quietly for a few minutes, then Ida broke the silence.

'So?' she said. 'It's seven o'clock in the morning, and you keep theatre hours, Min. What's troubling you?'

Minnie recounted the argument with Albert, trying hard not to embellish it too much. It would be easy to position herself as the rightfully aggrieved, to polish her words to Albert, tweaking his responses just enough to cast him in a negative light. She didn't need to do that, she reminded herself. He was in the wrong.

When she'd finished she leaned back in her seat and stared pointedly at Ida. The other woman said nothing, instead lighting a spirit lamp and carefully heating a tool with a round metal ball on the end. When it was hot enough, she used the tool to shape each petal. When she'd completed a couple of dozen she looked up at Minnie.

'Well,' she said, 'you know what my first thoughts on this are.'

'That it was Rose, communicating from the afterlife.'

'Exactly. And that's the nice, simple explanation to my way of thinking. No one to get annoyed with, no one to be suspicious about. But I didn't think you believed in any of that, Min. You were very sweet and understanding when I was going to all them séances after Rose died, but it struck me you thought I was wasting my time and money.'

'Maybe back then, but lately I ain't so sure.' She held back from telling Ida about the spirit photograph. It felt like it might reopen wounds that had barely healed.

'But if we take Albert's side on this,' Ida continued, 'someone must have talked about what happened to you all those years ago, and one way or another that wound its way back to this Lizzie Spinks woman. So, my first question is: why didn't you think that person was me?'

'It wasn't, was it?'

Ida shook her head dismissively and rose slowly to refill the pot of tea. 'Of course it weren't. But why did you not think for a moment it might be?'

''Cos I know you.'

'Exactly. And you know Albert. And Mrs Byrne.'

'Well, if it weren't you, and it weren't Albert or Mrs Byrne, who are we left with?'

'Rose, of course. Either while she was alive or from beyond the grave, I'm not in any position to say which of the two, but God rest her soul, she was a bit of a tattle-basket. Particularly if she'd had a drink or two.'

Minnie shook her head defiantly. 'It weren't her, Ida. I know it weren't. And I can't believe you'd think it was.'

'Like Albert said, people ain't saints. She's gone and I miss her every day' – her voice broke slightly, and she lifted her eyes upwards to stem the tears that came all too readily when she spoke of Rose – 'but that weren't to say she didn't have her faults. And I've got to be honest, she loved a bit of gossip.'

Minnie shook her head again. 'No. She knew what all that business did to me. She wouldn't have ever said anything.'

Ida shrugged, and refilled Minnie's cup before resuming her task with the spirit lamp and the petals. 'You think what you want, Min,' she said. 'All I know is that you owe Albert one heck of an apology.'

'You think I was wrong? About Albert maybe telling more than just Mrs B?'

'Of course you were wrong. And you know it. That man would no more go round blabbing casually about what you told him than he'd fly to the moon in a horse and carriage.'

Anger flared in Minnie's chest. 'Why're you siding with him? You're supposed to be *my* friend,' she said, her voice high and whiny, the words making her sound about five years old. And feeling much the same, to tell the truth.

'I'm more than your friend, Min. I'm the closest thing you've got to a mother, and well you know it. And if your dear ma were still here, she'd say exactly what I've said to you. Albert has not betrayed you, and you know he hasn't. He talked to someone close to him, to figure out if there was a way to help the two of you move forward after what happened with Beresford. And you need to ask yourself why you're so quick to believe ill of him.'

'Meaning?'

'Meaning, how much more has that man got to do to prove his worth to you? What happened with Beresford – it was *years* ago, Min. But it's like your life stopped with that cab ride. Yes, yes,' she said, holding up her hand to ward off Minnie's interruption, 'you've made a success of your work at the Palace and now this detective business. But you've never let another fella come close to you. So it strikes me that Beresford's won, ain't he?'

'How can you say that?'

'Well, I'm assuming he's married now. Probably knocked out a few kiddies. Living a very nice life for himself, most likely with a bit of totty on the side. Whereas you – you live like a bleedin' nun. In fact, from what I read in the papers, the nuns are probably having more fun than you are.'

'That's not fair, Ida, and you know it.'

'I don't know about fair, but it's the truth. And so what if people know? You ain't the only girl who's ever got in a spot of bother over a fella, Min. What d'you think's gonna happen if people find out? You reckon Tansie's gonna stop speaking to you? Or they're gonna lock the doors at the Palace and not let you back in? The only person who might be a little bit bothered about what happened is Albert, and he already knows and the only reason he cares at all is 'cos of how much you're letting it bother you. Start living, Minnie. There's this lovely man standing right in front of you who loves you with all his heart. There is not another man on God's green earth who is more perfect for you than Albert. He would lay down his life for you. In fact, as memory serves, he took a bullet for you once. Then he *bought* you the Palace, Minnie. He bought it for you. When he could have been out spending his money on top hats and racehorses and Savile Row suits. Most fellas I know would have expected a little something in return for that kind of generosity. A little tit for tat. But not Albert. When he handed you the Palace he gave you the chance to live completely independently. The chance to walk away from him and every other man in the world and do just fine for yourself. That's what I call love, Min. And you won't let him in. Not even the tiniest little bit.'

Minnie faltered, all her anger replaced by simple pain. 'I can't, Ida. You know why I can't.'

'Because you can't have kids? But Albert knows that, don't he?'

'He does. He says he doesn't mind. But of course he does. Any man would.'

'Maybe he'd rather have a life with you, whatever strings are attached, than a life with anyone else.'

'That's what he says. Now. But what about in ten, twenty years' time, when he looks around him and realises all he's given up to be with me. What if he can't forgive me?'

Ida rose slowly, went to the back door and threw the dregs of tea out into the yard before refilling the kettle. 'Only Albert can answer that question, Min,' she said, turning back into the kitchen. 'And I think you have to start believing whatever it is he tells you.'

Minnie had visited Charlotte's mother but she wasn't in, would be back later that day. A servant who looked like she was in the middle of blacking the grates and most certainly shouldn't have been opening the front door had offered to take the letter, but Minnie knew it needed to be delivered directly to Mrs Sykes. So, now she had some time to kill. She didn't want to go home to her empty rooms, and she certainly wasn't going to see Albert again until the dust had settled. There was really only one place to go.

She opened the door to Tansie's office. He was ironing a shirt, wearing nothing but his vest and underpants. The monkey was sitting in his tiny deckchair, casually peeling a banana.

'Christ, Tanse,' she said, covering her eyes, 'you could give a girl a bit of warning.'

'I could say the same to you. What are you doing walking into my office like you own it? I'm the manager here again, remember?'

'Can't you at least find somewhere more private to do that?' she asked, gesturing at the flat-iron in his hand.

'And where would you suggest? My own private dressing room, what I don't possess? Or shall I get my valet to do the job?'

'Won't Barbara in Wardrobe do it for you?'

Tansie sniffed. 'Babs and I have had a bit of a falling-out. According to her' – and here he adopted the high-pitched voice he used for all women – 'it ain't her job to make clothes for a bleedin' monkey.' He gestured towards the monkey, who was sporting his fez and what looked like a baby's napkin. 'Which is all well and good, but he's getting through them modesty bloomers at a rate of knots and my sewing skills ain't up to it. You wouldn't, by any chance——?' He left the question hanging.

'No,' Minnie said flatly. 'I wouldn't. By *any* chance.'

By now, Tansie had put on his ironed shirt and had started on his trousers. Minnie grunted and left him to it.

In the Palace auditorium, she made her way to the bar and poured herself a large gin. From the shadows, someone coughed self-consciously to announce their presence, and Bernard emerged from the darkness.

'A touch early, wouldn't you say, dearest one?'

'The sun's over the yardarm somewhere in the world, Bernard.' She waved the bottle at him, but he shook his head, although he took a seat on the other side of the bar.

'There are only two people who can make you look like that, Minerva. You've only been here five minutes, which would be a record even for Tansie, so I take it this has something to do with the lovely Albert.'

Minnie drained her glass and poured another. 'The *lovely* Albert,' she muttered, but said nothing further. Explaining her upset would involve telling Bernard far more about her past than she was willing to share. 'I caught Tansie in his underpants just now,' she said, eager to change the subject.

Bernard gave a theatrical shudder. 'I'm aware that beauty is in the eye of the beholder and all that nonsense, but that man's success with the fairer sex is – I must confess – an enigma. And yet, for all that, there's no one to iron his clothes for him. Or there hasn't been for some time.'

The memory of Cora hovered in the air between them.

'Rumour has it that may be about to change,' he said, casting a questioning look at Minnie from underneath his lashes. 'Mrs Lawrence?'

Minnie scowled.

'Might I ask why you object to her quite so strongly?' Bernard asked. 'It strikes me as nothing short of a miracle that such a specimen would turn her gaze on Tansie. The woman is a goddess. Or is that the problem?'

'It ain't that,' Minnie said. 'To be jealous, I'd have to want Tansie for myself, wouldn't I? And if you're suggesting that, I think you might need a quick trip to Colney Hatch, get your napper seen to.'

'Your interest may not be romantic, but you care about Tansie. Might you be a little fearful of – losing him?'

'I don't think I could ever lose Tansie. God knows, I've tried to often enough.'

'So, why the objection to Dorothy? You've witnessed plenty of his romantic entanglements in the past quite happily.'

She fell silent, turning over his words. Finally, she spoke, the name catching in her throat even as she said it. 'It's Cora. You saw the mess Tansie was in after she died. How long it took to get back just a little of his sparkle. What if it happens again? Not that I think Dorothy's gonna drop the cue any time soon, but my worry is that she'll hurt him. Break his heart.'

'What if he breaks hers? He's broken one or two along the way.'

'Dorothy's different though, ain't she. I've seen the way Tansie looks at her when he don't reckon anyone's watching. This is the real thing. It's what he had with Cora, only ... more. Stronger. Him and Cora, they might have fizzled out given enough time. I can't see that happening with Dorothy. She's the kind of woman you don't walk away from.'

'She is, indeed, formidable. The kind of woman a man could make a life with. And you may fear that will leave *you* – out in the cold, perhaps?'

Minnie drained her glass. All the alcohol was doing was making her headache even worse. 'Last time I looked she didn't know how to run a music hall.'

'Last time I looked, neither did you. If memory serves, you nearly rendered us bankrupt.'

'You really know how to cheer a girl up, Bernard.'

He smiled, reached across the bar and gently patted her hand, while pointedly offering no apology for his words.

'I don't know what it is about her,' Minnie said. 'I mean, I like her. I think she does genuinely care for Tansie. And if Tansie can land her he'll be punching well above his weight. It's just – she makes me feel invisible. When she's in a room, with that hair and those curves, and those *gorgeous* clothes—' She broke off, lost in thoughts of Dorothy's wardrobe.

Bernard came round to Minnie's side of the bar and screwed the cork back into the gin bottle. 'At some point in the past, not long after the lovely Albert came into our lives, I described you to him as "a wench of excellent discourse; pretty and witty, wild and yet, too, gentle".'

Minnie laughed sarcastically. 'And what did Albert have to say to that?'

'He offered not a word of disagreement, dearest one. Not one word. Might I suggest you kindly remember that next time Mrs Lawrence is in the room.'

Minnie retraced her steps back to Charlotte's family home in Mayfair. The house, double-fronted with pillars and immaculate paintwork, made perfect sense. Wentworth wasn't going to be interested in Charlotte unless she had money.

The butler was back on duty, a pinch-faced individual who flinched when Minnie opened her mouth to introduce herself.

'The servants' entrance is to the rear of the building,' the butler said, taking stock of Minnie's clothes and clearly not liking what he saw.

'I've got a letter for Mrs Sykes,' Minnie said, waving the envelope at the man, 'from Charlotte.'

The butler went to take it from her, but Minnie snatched back her hand. 'To be delivered in person,' she said.

The man sniffed dismissively and gestured for her to follow him to a morning room, immaculately furnished but lacking any character. Seated at a walnut escritoire was a middle-aged woman, so rigidly bound it seemed one hasty movement might cause her to spring apart and unravel. Her corset looked like it was laced far too tightly and her neckline was buttoned right up to beneath her chin.

'A Miss Minnie Ward to see you, madam,' the butler said, somehow managing to make Minnie's name sound like the equivalent of something unsavoury you'd find on the bottom of your shoe. 'She has correspondence from Miss Charlotte.'

At the mention of Charlotte's name, Mrs Sykes's head shot up. 'You've heard from her?' she said, easing herself uncomfortably from behind the desk and ushering Minnie over to one of two armchairs by the fireplace. 'Where in heaven's name is she? Tell me everything you know.'

Mrs Sykes and Ida Watkins were a world apart in terms of wealth, but Minnie saw reflections of Ida in this woman's concern for her daughter. All the money in the world couldn't buy you peace of mind if something was amiss with your loved ones.

Minnie recounted the reason for her visit to Summerland and her brief conversation with Charlotte.

'I knew it,' Mrs Sykes said. 'I knew they had her, I just didn't know where they'd taken her.' She took the envelope from Minnie and tore it open, scanning the letter inside and then groaning. She passed the letter to Minnie without a word. The writing was crabbed and scrawled, as if written in a hurry.

Dearest Mother,

I have made the most dreadful error, I think, in coming to this house. I wish to leave, but I have no means of effecting my escape. As I write this letter, I have no certainty that it will ever reach you. These people are not who I thought they were. I am fearful, Mother. And so very, very sorry for ever having gone against your wishes. Please come and get me before—

Minnie turned the page, but there was nothing more to read. It looked as if Charlotte had been interrupted before she could complete the letter.

'Did you say you were a private detective?' Mrs Sykes asked, as Minnie passed the letter back to her.

'I am.'

Mrs Sykes frowned but decided to let the matter pass. 'And you're investigating these people?' she said, waving the letter.

Minnie gave a brief explanation of what had led her to the Spirit Sisterhood, and their possible involvement in the deaths of Gwendolen Harper and Henry Lawrence.

'Then you must, must go back to that house and get my daughter out of there,' Mrs Sykes said. 'Whatever it takes.'

'How did she end up there in the first place?' Minnie asked.

'In any other woman I would say it was an act of wilfulness and folly. But Charlotte is not like other women. From birth, she has been' – Mrs Sykes struggled to find the right word – 'a *gentle* soul who sees the good in everyone and never imagines anyone could wish her harm. My husband, before he died, declared her "simple" and wanted to place her in an institution. I fought him, Miss Ward.'

'And you won?'

'I did, but at great cost to our marital accord.' She waved her hand, as if discussion of her marriage were irrelevant. 'Charlotte is not insane. She is not incompetent. But I would argue that she is trusting to the point of gullibility. Which makes her vulnerable. She has always had an unhealthy interest in the whimsical. Fairies, when she was a child. Spirits from beyond the veil, now she is older. Three months ago she started attending séances run by the Spirit Sisterhood. None of which would be of any great significance, other than that she is due to inherit a substantial sum of money when she turns twenty-five.'

'Is she planning on giving that money to the Sisterhood?' Minnie asked.

'I believe so, although my solicitor informs me she hasn't amended her will. Two months ago she went to stay with them, but refused to give me the address. I've heard nothing from her since, until this correspondence. She's clearly changed her mind about the Sisterhood. You need to get her out of there, Miss Ward. I will pay you whatever you ask. Just bring my daughter back to me.'

TWENTY-FIVE

Albert spent the morning alternately sorting through paperwork and getting under Mrs Byrne's feet. By lunchtime she'd had enough.

'You're like a bear with a sore head, Albert, and it's obviously about Minnie. I'd suggest you find her and sort it out. At the very least, get some fresh air. Preferably for an hour or two. Maybe three.'

Albert did as she suggested, although he had no intention of finding Minnie. Let her find him and apologise.

Passing the Queen's Head just round the corner from his house, he decided to pop in for a swift one, picking up a newspaper on the way. He grabbed a table in a quiet corner and enjoyed the first few gulps of beer, glancing at the newspaper headlines with disinterest. He flicked forward a few pages, scanning the articles, then came to an abrupt full stop. Tucked away at the bottom of page four was a small piece.

FORMER CHILD PHENOMENON GOES MISSING

Miss Grace Hardy, who once enjoyed considerable renown as the Pocket Chanteuse, has been reported missing from her home in Stepney. Miss Hardy, now twenty years old, was recently the victim of an abduction which resulted in her finding herself abandoned on the banks of the Thames, with no idea how she had got there. Sources close to Miss Hardy expressed their grave concern for her safety.

Abandoning his half-drunk pint, Albert quickly made his way home. He'd just let himself into the house when Mrs Byrne appeared, the same newspaper in her hand. 'That's our girl, isn't it?' she said, pointing at the article.

'It is,' Albert said. 'And it's a very worrying development.'

They both jumped at a loud hammering at the front door. Mrs Byrne answered it and was nearly knocked over by a middle-aged couple who forced their way past her. Reginald and Martha Hardy.

'She's gone, Mr Easterbrook,' Reginald said, his breath coming in quick gasps.

'Gone?' Martha said. 'She's been taken, more like. Kidnapped.'

'That's right,' Reginald said. 'Kidnapped. And it strikes me you've done precious little to keep our Gracie safe.'

Albert ushered them into the drawing room and offered them both a seat, which Reginald refused, instead pacing the floor as an accompaniment to his words.

'She's gone,' he repeated. 'She left the house yesterday afternoon and she ain't come back.'

'She was here last night,' Albert said. 'Around ten o'clock.'

'Why'd she visit you?' Reginald said. 'Had something else happened?'

'She saw the man again. In Simpson's, yesterday afternoon.'

'Did he do anything?' Martha said, her face puckered with concern. She'd obviously been crying, her eyes swollen and red.

'No. He just smiled and waved at her. And then he was gone, just like every other time.'

'He's taken her again, ain't he?' Martha said.

'We went to the river, didn't we?' Reginald said to his wife, as if he'd forgotten Albert was even in the room. 'Went to the spot he left her last time. Not a sign of her.'

'But the tides, Mr Easterbrook—' Martha broke off, suppressing a sob. She didn't need to explain further. If Grace had been left on the banks of the Thames, one high tide could have carried her miles away.

'Have you been to the police?' Albert asked, trying to gain some control over the conversation and calm the pair down a little.

'Police?' Martha said, her contempt evident in the two syllables. 'What bleedin' use are they? We tried, mind. Went to them first thing this morning. Reminded them of what happened last time and told them about the fella who'd been watching the house, the one you took off after the other night. Young fella it was we spoke to, looked barely old enough to be out of short trousers. He started yawning as he was writing it down. Yawning, Mr Easterbrook. Can you believe it? Told us he'd look into it, but it looked to me like he was off for a kip as soon as we left the station.'

'And the hospitals?' Albert asked.

'Been to every one,' Reginald said. 'Not a sign of her.'

'You need to find her, Mr Easterbrook,' Martha said.

Her voice was gentle, desperate. Albert glanced at Reginald. The man's anger seemed to have dissipated, and he looked at Albert pleadingly.

'And there's no possibility that Grace has simply stayed out with friends?' Albert asked.

'What, *all night*?' Reginald said, as if Albert had suggested their daughter had sprouted wings. 'Our Gracie's a good girl, Mr Easterbrook. Never been no trouble. Always lets us know where she's going. Particularly recently, with that fella hanging around. No,' he said firmly, finally sitting down and crossing his arms as if this was the final word on the matter, 'he's taken her. And you need to find her.'

'I'll do my best, but I have to tell you I haven't had any success with finding the man who's been watching your house. And it doesn't help matters, speaking to the press.' He waved the newspaper in his hand.

'We didn't,' Reginald said.

'So, you're not the "sources close to Miss Hardy"?'

'We most certainly ain't. Wherever that story came from, it weren't from us. We're no lovers of the newspapers after how they treated Gracie last time.'

'So, how did they get hold of the story?' Albert said.

'It'll be that young copper we spoke to, I reckon,' Reginald said. 'They're all up to it, ain't they? Feeding stories to the press for a baksheesh.'

Albert couldn't deny the truth of this. He'd certainly encountered it often enough when he was a police officer. But there wouldn't have been time for the lad to have passed on the story and it be in today's newspaper, even with a late edition.

'I'll try her agent again,' Albert said. 'He might know more than he's letting on.'

'Do what you have to,' Martha said. 'Just find her.'

'I wondered when you'd turn up,' Artie Buckley said, offering Albert another of his excellent cigars. 'She ain't here, Mr Easterbrook, in case you were wondering.'

'I assumed as much. But I'm drawing a blank and thought you might know something.'

'About her mystery assailant? That I do not. If I knew anything, believe me, I'd have told the police quick smart. I've had half the girls on my books in here since the story broke, worrying they'll be next.'

'And there's nothing you can think of? No one she ever spoke about? Anyone who showed an interest in her beyond what you'd expect?'

Artie drew on his cigar, realised it had gone out and relit it. He leaned back in his chair and closed his eyes. 'There was one fella,' he said after a minute or so. 'Months ago, this was. An admirer, you might say, but a bit more than that.'

'How do you mean?'

'Grace said there was something strange about him. He was there every night, waiting for her, regular as clockwork. Wanted to walk her home but she always said no. Gracie said he gave her the shivers. Then, one night, he was just gone. She never saw him again.'

'How long ago was this?'

'Grace was at the Albion.' Artie reached forward and flicked through a small box of cards. 'Here we are. The Albion, six weeks last year. Fourteenth October to twenty-fifth November. She didn't say nothing about it while she was there. Only told me about him after that incident down by the river.'

'Why didn't she say anything at the time?'

Artie shrugged. 'Young girls like Grace attract a lot of attention, Mr Easterbrook. Not always of the desirable kind. If they came running to me each time it happened, my every waking moment would be spent fending off lowlives. The girls just get on with it.'

'And Grace never saw this man again?'

'Not that I heard of. And before you ask, no, I don't happen to have his name and address about my person. Or any description of him for that matter. She was very close to her parents, was our Gracie. There's a chance they'll know a bit more about him.'

Albert took his leave, trying not to dwell on the fact that Artie was already speaking about Grace in the past tense.

Half an hour later, the cab dropped Albert outside the Hardy residence on Nelson Street. Martha opened the front door and was at his side before Albert had finished paying the cabbie.

'Any news?' she said, her voice breathless with worry.

'Possibly,' Albert said, leading her into the house as if it were his own.

Reginald stood in the hallway, his arms stiff by his sides, braced for something bad.

'I've learned nothing specific,' Albert said, 'but Mr Buckley mentioned a young man who was bothering Grace when she was at the Albion late last year.'

'Bothering?' Reginald said, his hands slowly forming into fists. 'What d'you mean, "bothering"?'

'At the stage door, wanting to walk her home,' Albert said. 'Nothing more than that, according to Artie. But Grace said this man made her feel uncomfortable.'

'There was a fella who was sweet on her when she was at the Albion,' Martha said. 'But she didn't say nothing about him making her feel uncomfortable. Quite the reverse, I would have said. I thought maybe she was sweet on him too for a while.'

'Why's this the first I'm hearing about him?' Reginald asked.

'There was nothing to hear, Reg. And you know what you're like. So protective of her, you'd likely have turned up at the stage door and decked him one just for showing an interest in her.'

'Did she tell you anything more about him?' Albert asked.

'If we're talking about the same fella, he told her his name was Denny,' Martha said. 'Not sure if that was his first name or his surname, but that's the only name he ever gave her. She said he was from Manchester originally. He'd come to London for a better life, but after a few weeks he stopped turning up at the Albion so Gracie figured he'd gone back home. I've gotta say though, Albert, she never said nothing about him bothering her. Why would she have said that to Artie and not to us?'

'Maybe she didn't want to worry you,' Albert said, glancing at Reginald, whose fists were only now uncurling. 'Maybe she thought she could take care of herself. Manchester's a big city, Martha. I don't suppose she said anything else about him?'

Martha frowned. 'There was something about his ear, I seem to remember. He was missing a bit, that was it. He got it caught in some machinery when he was a nipper. And I think she said he worked in a cotton factory? That's not very helpful, is it?'

Albert groaned. Manchester. Cottonopolis. Everyone worked in a cotton factory. 'Any chance he told her what part of Manchester he came from?'

'Ancoats, I think she said. Is that a part of Manchester?'

One of the more notorious parts, Albert thought, but said nothing. He thanked Martha and Reginald and made his way out.

Manchester was, indeed, a big city, with a lot of cotton factories. And there was no guarantee that's where Denny had taken Gracie. Or even if he'd taken her at all. On top of that, Albert knew he was supposed to be investigating the deaths of Henry Lawrence and Gwendolen Harper and whether or not the Spirit Sisterhood were involved with either one. The sensible thing to do would be to stay put and maybe see if Tom could nip up to Manchester for him.

But Grace was in trouble. And right now, Albert didn't feel like being sensible. Right now he felt like getting as far away from London and Minnie as he could. Manchester was a good place to start.

TWENTY-SIX

Minnie threw the last of her clothes into the suitcase and fastened it shut. Ruth Warren had sent word that someone could meet her at Sudbury station if she caught the early train. She glanced at her pocket watch. She didn't have long. Which was good, because given time to think about it, Minnie wasn't sure she'd have the courage to go to Summerland. Whatever the details, something strange had happened to Gwendolen Harper in that house, and Henry Lawrence had been killed during his investigation into her death. But if Minnie followed her gut and stayed well clear of the house, how were they going to get to the bottom of what had happened?

And then there was the matter of Rose. The spirit photograph, the message with its knowledge of Minnie's past. Rose was dead, there was no mistaking it. But maybe Lizzie Spinks offered a chance to make contact with her. And although the idea filled her with a quiet fear, it wasn't a chance she felt she could pass up.

She drew paper and envelopes from the desk drawer and wrote two brief notes: one to Albert, one to Tansie, telling them she was going to stay at Summerland and would probably be there for a few days. If they needed to get hold of her, any correspondence must be addressed to Mary Butler or they would blow her cover. She wrote a third note to Dorothy, outlining her conviction that the house in Suffolk held the answer to Henry's death.

On the way to the station, she dropped the three letters in the nearest postbox and ran the last five hundred yards to the train.

Once seated on the train, Minnie turned over the events of her last visit to Summerland. Albert had been right: if Lizzie – and Wentworth by extension – knew about Rose, they'd more than likely know who Minnie really was. If either of them was implicated in Gwendolen or Henry's deaths, Minnie would be placing herself in harm's way going to Summerland. But why invite her back if they knew what she was up to? Surely it would make more sense to keep her at arm's length?

Exactly as promised, the pony and cart was waiting for her at Sudbury, with Aggie Meadows holding the reins again. They were at Summerland half an hour later, and the welcoming committee was almost the same as before. Except Charlotte Sykes was missing.

Jessica, the enthusiastic young woman who had been excited by her arrival, hurried forward and took her bags. 'Miss Butler,' she gushed, 'we're so happy to have you here again.'

'Please, call me Mary,' Minnie said. 'And I'm delighted to be back.'

Jessica led the way upstairs, stopping halfway down a long corridor and opening a door. 'This,' she announced with a theatrical flourish, 'is where you'll be sleeping.'

The room was small and modestly furnished. A narrow single bed, a worn runner, an upright closet in need of a lick of paint. A window overlooking the grounds.

Minnie forced a smile. 'How – charming.'

'Now, Mary, be honest,' Jessica said, 'it's not what we're used to, but Mr Wentworth says the absence of earthly luxuries facilitates access to a higher realm.'

How very convenient, Minnie thought. 'Does everyone sleep on this corridor?' she asked.

Jessica nodded.

'So there are only' – she counted the doors – 'nine people staying here?' Somehow she'd imagined more. If the women were here to be fleeced by Wentworth, why didn't he invite as many as possible?

'Only four of us at the moment,' Jessica said, 'plus Mr Wentworth, Lizzie and Ruth, of course. Mr Wentworth is very particular about who he invites to the house, or the "inner circle", as I like to think of it. The London séances are open to everyone and we've had several day visitors here, but you're the first person in months who's been invited for a longer stay. "Many are called, but few are chosen" – that's what Mr Wentworth always tells us.' The pride was evident in her voice.

'And how does Mr Wentworth decide who stays?' Minnie asked.

'Devotion to the cause,' Jessica said simply, as if the answer were obvious. 'Those with the most open hearts.'

And most open bank accounts, Minnie thought. 'You mentioned four of us "at the moment",' she said. 'Were there more women staying here before?'

A shadow passed across Jessica's face. 'Gwendolen sadly returned to London. I miss her a great deal, but this life isn't for everyone.'

Gwendolen Harper was dead. Harriet West had seen the death certificate. Her body had been disinterred. And yet Jessica believed she was still alive, as did Ruth. Why had her death been kept from the women if there was nothing suspicious about it?

'There was another young woman here when I last visited,' Minnie said to Jessica. 'Charlotte, I believe her name was. A most pleasant young lady. I didn't see her when I arrived.'

Jessica gave a tight smile. 'Charlotte Sykes? Oh, I was so fond of Charlotte. But sadly she left us. The day after your last visit, in fact. Very suddenly. She didn't even say goodbye.'

The day after her first visit, Minnie had visited Charlotte's mother, who had begged her to return to Summerland and bring her daughter home. Surely if Charlotte had arrived home that day, no matter how late the hour, her mother would have informed Minnie that there was no need to rescue her daughter? So now there were two women who had apparently made swift departures from Summerland. One of them was dead. Minnie hoped the same wasn't true for Charlotte.

She thought of Mrs Sykes, her desperate plea for Minnie to bring her daughter home.

'I'm surprised,' Minnie said. 'Charlotte seemed so happy here when I spoke to her.'

'It doesn't work out for everyone,' Jessica said.

'And your friend Gwendolen, did she leave without saying goodbye?'

'Mr Wentworth tells us that if life here at Summerland is not to your liking, it is wisest to make a swift departure. It can be distressing for those of us left behind, to wake up and discover one of our friends is no longer with us, but Mr Wentworth says that is merely our unhealthy attachment to the corporeal world.'

Minnie wondered if Jessica had any thoughts of her own, or if her job was simply to parrot Wentworth's apparent wisdom.

Jessica placed Minnie's suitcase on the bed. 'I'll leave you to freshen up, and then see you downstairs in the dining room.'

After she'd gone, Minnie looked round the room more carefully. The iron-framed bed was made up with rough blankets and sheets which felt like they didn't have much life left in them. Beside the bed was an upright closet with hooks to hang clothes from and two white dresses, identical to the ones the other women wore.

She made use of the facilities, then went back down the corridor, trying each door along the way. If anyone found her, she could simply say she'd got lost and was looking for the lavatory. Five of the rooms were replicas of her own, and she guessed these were the young women's bedrooms. The other rooms were less sparsely furnished and contained what looked like more personal items: photographs, ornaments, a set of watercolours and an easel. Minnie guessed these were Wentworth's, Ruth's and Lizzie's rooms, although it was difficult to determine the occupant from such a cursory examination. She made a mental note to explore in more detail at an appropriate time. There was a linen cupboard and, at the end of the corridor, a locked door, which Minnie guessed was another cupboard. As she descended the stairs, she noted that the carpet was worn bare in several places, with some stairs missing rods. If the Spirit Sisterhood were making any money, they certainly weren't spending it on carpet.

After lunch, Minnie had anticipated some time to herself, but this was not to be the case. Ruth Warren ushered her into an office facing out onto the tennis court. The gentle thwack of a tennis ball accompanied their conversation.

'Firstly, let me say how delighted we are to have you join us for an extended stay,' Ruth said. She didn't look particularly delighted, but Minnie was starting to wonder if Ruth ever looked pleased about anything. 'You said in your communication that you were unsure how long you might be with us, but be that as it may, you still need to be aware we follow certain rules here at Summerland.'

Minnie braced herself and Ruth seemed to register her concern. 'You need have no worries, Mary. There is nothing punitive or restrictive. Indeed, to call them rules may be a little misleading. Guidance might be a wiser word.'

Minnie gave a half-smile and nodded her head for Ruth to continue.

'While you're with us, we expect you to wear the white dress adopted by all the women. The household tasks are shared amongst us. That includes cooking, cleaning, laundry. Maintenance of the grounds is carried out by a groundsman whom we employ. I draw up a task rota each week, which you will find in the kitchen. As you are not yet a full member of the Sisterhood, you will have a reduced workload.'

Minnie nodded. So far, so good.

'Mr Wentworth is – naturally – exempt from any of this work.'

'Why "naturally"?' Minnie asked.

A small frown creased Ruth's brow. Clearly any questioning of Wentworth's actions was not encouraged. 'Mr Wentworth's time is taken up with the management of the Sisterhood and the promulgation of our message. He operates on a higher plane than the rest of us.'

'And Miss Spinks?' Minnie asked.

'Lizzie helps out as and when. If the spirits are particularly active her time is, naturally, spent with them. And after any such communication she is often very fatigued. But if they are quiet – which is sometimes the case – Lizzie is an enthusiastic and able member of our community. Trusting that arrangement is satisfactory for you, Mary, there is one other matter to draw your attention to. For the duration of your stay with us, there is to be no communication with the world beyond the boundaries of Summerland.'

Charlotte had hinted as much in her letter to her mother, but the confirmation that she wouldn't be able to get word to Albert was worrying. She did her best to hide her concern, but Ruth seemed to have been anticipating it. 'It is the one directive that can, on occasion, cause a little alarm for our new recruits, so please allow me to explain the thinking behind it.' She rose from behind the desk and walked to the doors overlooking the tennis court, her back to Minnie. 'Your time here at Summerland will be immersive. Your days will be filled with honest labour, designed to foster a harmonious community, and with a timetable of activities intended to enhance your spiritualism. Each day there will be periods of prayer, communication with the spirits, gentle exercise and talks from our dear leader.' A softness entered her voice as she spoke of Wentworth. 'We have found that our programme is most effective, elevates you most speedily to the higher realm, when there are no outside interferences. No letters, no venturing beyond the bounds of Summerland. You have everything you need here to fill your days and fill your heart. Those outside of our work – men, in particular – are threatened by what we do here. They wish to place restraints on us, to shackle us to the conventions society imposes upon women. And it is not always easy to resist their influence.'

Minnie waited for Ruth to return to her seat. She needed to examine the other woman's face as she said the next words.

'But – my brother,' Minnie faltered. 'When I left home, I told him I was uncertain of my length of stay here at Summerland. What if he should need to contact me? Or I him?'

If they knew she wasn't Mary Butler, they'd presumably know that there was no Jonathan Butler. Minnie scanned Ruth's face carefully. Either she was an excellent poker player, or Ruth had no knowledge of Minnie's real identity.

'Why should you need to contact him?' Ruth asked, her words benign but her stare fixed and, again, that slight frown. 'If you were to fall ill, we can care for you here. Or there is a hospital close by in Sudbury. And if you should decide to leave us we will arrange your transport back to London and inform your brother of your arrival. As to your brother contacting you here, we cannot, of course, prevent that. But Mr Wentworth will read his letters first. I appreciate,' she said, holding up a hand to stall Minnie's objections, 'that this can seem intrusive. But family members often misunderstand our work. In the early days of our community, we had women contacted by their fathers, brothers, sweethearts, and the tone and content of those letters was most disruptive to our work here. Most disruptive.'

'I am very fond of walking,' Minnie said. 'Is there any objection to my wandering into the nearest village?'

Ruth gave a brief shake of her head. 'We have an estate of forty acres here. Plenty of room for walking. And we keep the gates locked at all times. Not to keep you in, you understand, but the locals have been a little – curious, let's say. The presence of young women has provoked a more unsavoury element.'

'I don't remember the gates being locked when I arrived,' Minnie said.

'We knew you were coming,' Ruth said simply. 'If anything I have said is of concern, Mary, you are, of course, free to leave now. We don't want you to think you're being kept prisoner here. But, should you choose to leave, we would be unable to readmit you to our community. An unwillingness to conform to our guidelines has – experience has shown us – proved harmful in the long term.'

Minnie reminded herself of the look on Dorothy's face when she'd seen Henry's body, her distress over the loss of such a dear friend. The desperate note in Mrs Sykes's voice when she asked for Minnie's help. And Harriet West's conviction that Gwendolen Harper's death had been no accident. If she wasn't here at Summerland, the chance of getting to the bottom of any of those puzzles was pretty much non-existent. At the very least, she needed to find out what, if anything, had happened to Charlotte Sykes.

'Very well,' Minnie said. 'Things are not quite what I anticipated, but I am willing to follow your guidance if it will afford me the spiritual help I seek.' She paused, as if choosing her words carefully. 'There was a most delightful woman here when I last visited. Charlotte?'

Ruth gave a knowing nod. 'Charlotte is no longer with us. Her decision to leave was somewhat unexpected, but when a sister has chosen to return to the outside world, her departure is best facilitated with all haste. It proves less of a disruption that way.'

Ruth rose from her seat. The meeting was clearly at an end, and Minnie felt it would be unwise to ask any more questions about Charlotte Sykes. Jessica might be a few slices short of a loaf, but the same certainly couldn't be said of Ruth, and Minnie didn't want to arouse her suspicions.

'Feel free to explore the grounds,' Ruth said, showing Minnie out of the office. 'We encourage all forms of physical exercise here at Summerland. Oh, and Mr Wentworth would like to speak to you tomorrow morning at eleven. To welcome you.'

Minnie thanked her and made her way out of the house. In the distance she could see the walls surrounding the estate, twelve feet high at least, with broken glass studding the tops. The only break in the walls was the gates, securely padlocked. There was no getting away from it. She was trapped.

Dinner was disappointing, to put it mildly. Two small potatoes, a couple of spoonfuls of cabbage, a carrot so small it barely registered as a vegetable and one slice of bread and lard. All swilled down with generous quantities of tea, at least. It didn't taste like London tea, but they were out in the sticks. Nothing was quite as good outside of London.

With the plates cleared away, everyone moved towards the living room for the nightly séance. Wentworth stood before the group. 'Welcome all to our communion with the spirits, and a particularly warm welcome to our new sister, Mary' – here he gestured towards Minnie, and there were murmured greetings from the women in the room. 'Mary, I truly believe you'll be happy here. It can take a little while to become accustomed to our ways, but I think you will soon find you have no desire to leave us. And now, our sister Lizzie will lead the proceedings.'

There was a palpable excitement amongst the women and Minnie realised this must be the highlight of their day. This particular séance was slightly different from those conducted in London for public consumption. There was no singing and the lamps, although lowered, were not fully extinguished, so all the proceedings took place in a gentle half-light.

After the revelations during her walk with Lizzie the other day, Minnie was anxious about what would be communicated during the séance. But she had no cause to be. The spirits on this occasion focused exclusively on the other women, and there was none of the drama of the London séances. No apparitions, no rappings. Pooky, in particular, was notable by his absence. The spirits informed Lizzie that Jessica had entertained thoughts of returning home and this would be a grave error when she was so close to attaining direct communication with the spirit world. Maud, a tall, willowy young woman, was worried about her mother's health, but with no good cause. All the communications had a single purpose: to keep the young women at Summerland and ease any concerns they might have about the outside world.

So, what had happened with Charlotte Sykes that had made her so determined to leave?

Minnie woke with a start, uncertain of what had roused her, or even where she was. Slowly, the realisation dawned that she was in her bedroom at Summerland. The room was pitch black, the heavy curtains drawn across the window not admitting a single chink of moonlight. A sound had woken her. And whatever it was, it had scared her. She could feel her heart thumping in her ears, her breath coming quickly.

She sat up in bed, pulled the bed clothes up around her neck and tried to calm herself. There was nothing to be afraid of. Just a noise, like old houses make in the quiet of the night. She took one or two deep breaths, and then she smelled something. Sweet and aromatic, somehow familiar. She inhaled deeply again. A cigar. Someone was smoking a cigar nearby.

Minnie got out of bed and crossed to the window, parting the curtains and looking down onto the terrace below. Maybe Wentworth was having a late-night smoke. She wouldn't put it past Ruth, either, to have the odd cheroot. It was difficult to make anything out on the terrace, but there didn't seem to be anyone there and there was no glowing tip of a cigar. She opened the window and leaned out. The cigar smoke was not coming from outside. She closed the window and drew the curtains, padding carefully back to bed and taking care not to bump into anything in the darkness. The smell grew stronger as she got closer to her bed. She leaned over and sniffed the sheets and blankets, the pillows, realising how ludicrous she must look, sniffing her bed in the middle of the night. But the bedlinen only smelled of soap. She lit the candle beside her bed, shielding the flame with one hand. Slowly, she surveyed the room. Nothing.

And then she heard it. A woman's voice screaming in the distance. Somewhere out in those forty acres Ruth was so proud of.

She froze, listening intently. There it was again. And then again. And again. A sharp cry piercing the night. Her thoughts immediately flew to Charlotte Sykes and her mysterious exit from Summerland. What if the woman were being held somewhere in the grounds against her will?

Candle in hand, Minnie went to the door, turning the handle as quietly as possible and making her way out into the corridor. No light was visible from any of the other rooms. She walked carefully up to each bedroom door and placed her ear against it. No sound from within. And no smell of cigar smoke emanating from any of the rooms. Slowly she descended the stairs to the ground floor.

Minnie had never been afraid of the dark, but night-time in the countryside was completely different to what she was used to back home. In London, there were always street noises at any time of day or night, noises that comforted her, letting her know she wasn't alone. Here, moving through the ground-floor rooms, she could hear the sound of her own breath, the blood gently thrumming in her ears. And, with the curtains drawn across all the doors, the darkness was so dense, as if a heavy cloak had been thrown over the house.

She padded quietly along the corridor, to the rear door that led out into the grounds. It was locked. Minnie cursed the fact that she'd taken her hair down at bedtime and her hairpins were all lying upstairs on the table next to her bed. She couldn't be certain she'd be able to pick the lock but she'd be willing to give it a try. Reversing her steps, she tried the front door with the same outcome. She remembered the French doors leading from the library. And then she heard the unmistakeable creak of a footstep behind her.

She turned. Ruth stood halfway down the stairs, candle in one hand, the other holding closed a wrap she was wearing over her nightclothes.

'What on earth are you doing, Mary?' Ruth asked.

'I heard a noise,' Minnie said. 'A woman screaming. Somewhere out in the grounds.'

'Don't be so ridiculous,' Ruth hissed, keeping her voice low and quiet to not wake anyone else. 'How on earth could you have heard anything of the kind? It was a bad dream, nothing more.'

Minnie knew what bad dreams were. She'd had plenty of them since Rose's death. And this had been no dream. But she couldn't get any further in her explorations and, with Ruth now awake, her chances were even more limited.

Reluctantly, she followed Ruth back to the dormitory. She would investigate further in the morning.

TWENTY-SEVEN

Conversations with Grace's friends and work colleagues had drawn a blank. The journalist at the newspaper had, unsurprisingly, refused to reveal how he'd got hold of the story. No one knew where Grace was and no one was able to offer any more information about Denny than Grace's parents had done. Albert had obtained one of Grace's *cartes de visite* from Martha and he showed it to staff at the station while he waited for his train. No one remembered seeing her in recent days. More convinced than ever that this was a wild goose chase, he mounted the train and took his seat.

Albert had never been to Manchester. He'd never really felt the need, believing that London held everything he could ever want. He'd read about the city, of course. Knew of its reputation. And even though he'd spent most of his adult life in the world's busiest metropolis, he still wasn't quite prepared for what faced him when the train pulled into Manchester London Road station.

The factory noise was what struck him first, and then the relative darkness, with smoke choking off the light, and tall buildings louring on every side. In the midst of it all, the sheer number of people hurrying through the streets, intent on getting to their place of work, or home. He wondered if visitors to London were affected in the same way, whether it was just that he was used to London and had stopped noticing the relentless din, the throngs of people, the dirt and smoke and filth. And yet, somehow, Manchester felt like a completely alien environment.

His hotel was near the station, so he dropped off his bags and then walked to Ancoats. He figured if that was where Denny lived, he'd likely work close by and the area was full of cotton mills, so it seemed as good a place to start as any.

Three hours later Albert's head was throbbing, his feet were sore, and he'd got no closer to finding Denny than when he first arrived in the city. He tried to recall the different mills he'd visited, but after the first, they all seemed to merge into one giant, homogenous building. Towering frontages, dull bricks, multiple windows. Inside, a minimum of six storeys, each storey a vast room filled with industry and at times unbearable heat. Not to mention the noise. Dear God, the noise. It was thunderous, unrelenting. One supervisor he spoke to told him the factory hands had learned to lip-read so they could converse with each other above the cacophony. In one mill, Albert had looked out across the men, women and children – some as young as four years old – all of whom seemed to be as one with the machines they operated, dressed in blue gowns and jackets, all humanity or individuality lost in the relentless process of cotton production.

He'd achieved nothing. No one he spoke to had a worker named Denny, or fitting Denny's description, on their books. Hardly surprising, given he was looking for someone whose name might or might not be Denny, who was of average height and build and might have recently returned from a stint in London. Even if they did know him, no one was willing to tell him. As soon as he started to speak, he saw the shutters come down behind their eyes. Not for the first time, he wished Minnie was with him. She'd have known how to talk to these men, the women and children too. She wouldn't have aroused their suspicions as soon as she opened her mouth. At each mill, he'd left details of where he was staying in the vain hope that someone would remember something.

As Albert turned back to his hotel he brushed the cotton particles from his clothes. He could feel the fibres on his lungs even after just a few hours' exposure, and wondered how anyone coped with it day in, day out. He passed a news vendor and grabbed a paper. Grace had made it to the front page.

KIDNAPPER'S SHOCKING DEMANDS

Following the recent abduction of former child singing sensation Miss Grace Hardy, aged just twenty, the kidnapper has now issued a statement to this publication, requesting the astronomical sum of one thousand guineas to secure Miss Hardy's release. The ransom note was delivered with what is believed to be a lock of Miss Hardy's hair. The *Daily Herald* can exclusively reveal the kidnapper's devilish plans, but we would warn that those of a sensitive disposition should read no further. The abductor has said if his demands are not met, he will start removing Miss Hardy's fingers, posting them one at a time to the editor of this esteemed publication. The whereabouts of Miss Hardy have been unknown since her parents reported her missing two days ago. Police investigating the incident have said they have no leads as yet. If you have any information relating to the missing young woman, please contact us here at the *Daily Herald*.

Albert thought for a moment how delighted Grace Hardy would be to find herself headline news – if it weren't for the fact the story was about her own abduction. Two days had passed and Grace remained unfound. And now the kidnapper had issued this demand for a ludicrous sum of money, accompanied by the ghoulish threat. Albert prayed the man wouldn't follow through on that threat, but he wasn't willing to take the chance.

He passed a man crying out mournfully, the empty left sleeve of his jacket pinned to the lapel. 'Lost my arm, I did. Terrible explosion in a coal mine. Lost my arm. Wife and kiddies at home. Anything you can spare.'

He gave Albert a pitiful look, but Albert knew better. If he gave something to this man, dozens more would appear, all equally desperate.

At his hotel reception he checked for post and any messages. A letter from Mrs Byrne informed him that she'd seen neither hide nor hair of Minnie since the day of the argument. Did Albert want her to go to the Palace and see if she was hiding out there? *No*, Albert thought. *I don't want her thinking I'm looking for her, I just want to know that she's well and whether there's any progress on Henry Lawrence's death. If, indeed, she's doing anything and not simply riding around on her high horse, feeling morally superior to everyone.* He wrote a brief note to Mrs Byrne telling her not to worry about it and popped it in the postbox as he left the hotel.

On the corner nearby he'd spotted a music hall, the World of Wonders. He needed to rest, for a brief period at least – he was starving hungry, and he had no desire to eat in his hotel, a poky affair where every room somehow smelled of cabbage. He paid the entrance fee and took a seat near the bar at the rear of the auditorium, hailing a waiter to bring him a pint and a steak and kidney pie. Propping up the bar was the man he'd seen begging earlier, his left arm now miraculously restored and holding a pint.

Never had a place been more wrongly named than the World of Wonders. The place hadn't seen a lick of paint in how long. The beer was so thin he'd have had more of a chance getting drunk on water, and the pie had made only a passing acquaintance with anything that might qualify as beef. Both the audience and the performers had an air of quiet desperation about them that made the Variety Palace look like the Adelphi.

But Albert was tired, and he needed to gather his thoughts. He'd managed to visit a dozen or so mills but there were dozens, maybe hundreds more within the confines of the city alone. Even if he could find the elusive Denny, he had no evidence that the man was involved in Grace's disappearance. For all Albert knew, she might still be in London, albeit hidden away in someone's basement or a lock-up somewhere in the East End. His anger with Minnie, his desire to put some distance between the two of them, had led him here, on a wild goose chase that felt like it was doing no one any good. And he'd completely neglected the hunt for Henry Lawrence's killer. Memories of Dorothy's distress flooded his mind, swiftly followed by the image of Grace's parents, desperate for his help. It felt like he was in the wrong, no matter what he did. But he was here now, in Manchester. He'd stay a few days longer, see if the local constabulary knew anything about Grace's disappearance, visit some more mills, ask around in the pubs. Maybe he'd have some luck. If not, he'd have to head back to London and face the wrath of Reginald Hardy.

He sat through the trick cyclists, the jugglers and the acrobats, all of which only served to remind him of the Palace. And thinking of the Palace meant his thoughts turned, inevitably, to Minnie. He drained his beer and was about to leave when the headline act was announced, a 'singing sensation' by the name of Florrie Wilmore. She took to the stage to what amounted to rapturous applause from this particular audience; she was clearly a favourite, in her early twenties, tall and willowy with a beautiful head of hair. Her voice was passable, nothing to write home about, but it was her way with the audience that clearly marked her out from other performers. She was charming, funny, persuasive. When she sang of waving her loved one off to war, there was barely a dry eye in the house. But her next turn was a comic number, playing an old woman who'd bumped off her husband and was answering police questions with increasing ineptitude. The audience loved it, roaring with laughter. Whatever persona she adopted, she had them eating out of her hand.

One of Albert's great regrets was that he'd never seen Minnie perform. Her days treading the boards as a singer and mimic had been brought to an abrupt end by James Beresford and his casual seduction and betrayal, which had left her paralysed by stage fright. But Albert knew from listening to Tansie that Minnie had had a similar magnetism to Florrie Wilmore. She must have been quite the performer, he thought.

Albert sat and watched Florrie till the end of her act, which was marked by enthusiastic applause. He was grateful to leave the World of Wonders on a high.

As he walked through the cold Manchester streets, he thought once again of Grace Hardy and the man he'd pursued who'd been watching her house. He ran over the chase again in his mind, trying desperately to recall some detail, however small, that might provide a clue as to the man's identity. There was something there, he was sure of it, something that would distinguish him from all the other men of average height trudging the streets of Manchester. Albert remembered how he had leapt onto the bus, reaching forward with his hand to grab hold. His left hand. He had led with his left hand. A southpaw, then. Which narrowed things down slightly, but not nearly enough.

As Albert neared his hotel a figure emerged from the shadows. A man, narrow-faced and close-shaven with eyes sunk deep in his head. Instinctively Albert reached for the life-preserver in his pocket.

'Mr Easterbrook,' the man said, his voice thin and reedy. 'We spoke earlier. At Murray's.'

Albert couldn't remember him. Couldn't even be sure Murray's had been amongst the mills he'd visited. But the man seemed to know him.

'Do you have some information for me?' Albert asked.

The man sniffed, casting his eyes anxiously up and down the busy street as if fearful he was being watched. 'That Denny fella you're looking for. I know where he might be.'

'Why didn't you tell me earlier, when I was at the mill?'

'Couldn't remember him then. But I do now. Or at least I think I do.' The man stopped and looked pointedly at Albert, who reached into his pocket and handed over a few shillings.

'Fella going by that name lives in Angel Meadow. 27 Charter Street. Can't swear it's the bloke you're looking for, but it's a start.'

'How far is Angel Meadow from here?' Albert asked, looking at his watch.

'No more than a mile. I can give you directions, although most people round here know of Angel Meadow.'

The man laughed grimly, triggering a coughing fit that looked like it might see him off for good. Albert guessed Angel Meadow was notorious for all the wrong reasons, and it would be growing dark soon. Much wiser to pay a visit in the morning. But Grace was missing, and right now this was the only lead he had.

As soon as he entered the district of Angel Meadow, Albert concluded that if the angels had ever visited this part of the city, they'd deserted it long ago. He walked quickly towards 27 Charter Street, a house indistinguishable from the others around it, all of them marked by abject poverty.

The front of the house was filthy with soot. Every window was broken, stuffed with anything that had come to hand: hats, bits of fabric, old newspapers. The front door was open and Albert entered cautiously, taking care not to touch the walls and looking closely at where he placed his feet. He walked down a short corridor to a room filled with men and women.

Albert had visited many houses in his time as a police officer, most of them peopled by the destitute and the desperate, but what lay before him was the worst he'd ever seen. People wrote about the East End of London like it was some hellish underworld, but it was nothing compared to what lay in this dingy back room.

The smell was the first thing that hit him, a mixture of stale tobacco, sweat and what he guessed was faeces, whether human or from the dogs who roamed the room he wouldn't care to guess. Some of the men were seated on broken-backed chairs, others on dilapidated stools ranged around a filthy table, eating some kind of awful-looking mess that Albert didn't want to think about, washed down with quantities of beer. Running along one side of the room was a bench, men seated on every square inch of it, smoking and drinking. Before the fire, a young woman was kneeling, frying a single slice of bacon. She was dressed in rags which barely covered her modesty. Nobody seemed to notice. Crouched either side of her were two similarly dressed women, their faces swollen and dark with bruising. Albert wondered if one of the men in the room had delivered the punishment, and what it had been for.

On the mantelpiece above the fire stood a large white earthenware dog with a brown tail. Clearly the piece had no value, or it would have been sold long ago. And yet, serving as the sole piece of decoration in this hellish environment, it was the single most valuable item he had ever laid eyes on.

A few individuals raised their heads at the sight of Albert.

'I'm looking for a man called Denny,' he said. 'I was told I might find him here.'

Wordlessly, one of the men gestured upstairs with his eyes.

Albert went back along the corridor and ascended the narrow stairway. There was barely any wall still covered with plaster, and he had to tread carefully in case his foot went through one of the worn stairs. Upstairs was a single room filled with beds, the stained straw-filled mattresses covered with men and women of all ages, including children and babies. The oldest looking was a woman who appeared to be well into her eighties, but who Albert guessed was probably significantly younger. Just like downstairs, the smell was almost unbearable: dirty clothes, filthy mattresses, foul breath and, once again, the underlying stench of faeces.

A young woman raised her head, her glazed expression suggesting she'd scraped together a few coins for something to obliterate the horror. Living like this, every bodily function performed in front of other people, Albert could understand her desire to escape to the privacy of her own mind, if only for a few hours.

'Is there anyone called Denny here?' Albert asked. 'A young man?'

The woman glanced over Albert's shoulder. He went to turn, but too late. Something hard struck him on the back of the head and darkness descended.

TWENTY-EIGHT

After her run-in with Ruth, Minnie had gone back to bed and used a trick her ma had taught her, knocking her head on the pillow six times, to make herself wake at six in the morning. Her plan had been to get up ahead of the other women, explore the house and grounds in peace and see if she could fathom out what she'd heard the night before. When she woke, she could hear voices in the rooms below her. The trick hadn't worked.

She entered the dining room and everyone, with the exception of Ruth, looked delighted to see her. 'We thought we'd let you sleep in,' Jessica said, pulling out the chair next to her and patting the seat. 'As it was your first morning.'

Minnie forced a smile and gratefully accepted a large mug of tea. She was hoping for some kippers, or, at the very least, a few slices of bacon to get the day started. A bowl of food was placed before her. It looked like something you'd chuck at the pigeons in Trafalgar Square.

'It's a delicious combination of porridge oats, nuts and seeds,' Jessica offered, as if she were reading from a script. 'Very good for the digestion, so Mr Wentworth tells us. You have it with milk.'

Minnie glanced behind her at the sideboard. Nothing. It was the bird food or starvation. She added some milk and ate a mouthful. It was even worse than she'd anticipated.

'Did any of you hear something in the night?' she asked, after the second mouthful of the bird food convinced her she'd rather starve.

'I know this sounds a little extreme, but I could have sworn I heard a woman screaming.'

'Screaming?' said Jessica, almost jumping in her seat. 'Who on earth would have been screaming?'

'I told you last night, Mary. It was a nightmare and nothing more,' Ruth said dismissively. 'Someone had a bad dream and cried out in their sleep.'

'I don't think so,' Minnie said. 'It happened four times in a row. The exact same sound. A scream that sounded as if someone were shouting for help.'

Lizzie shared a conspiratorial glance with Ruth and laughed. 'Remember, Ruth? I was just the same my first night here.' She turned to Minnie. 'It was foxes, Mary. When the vixen screams it sounds just like someone's being murdered. You get used to it.'

Foxes, my arse, Minnie thought. She had to admit she'd never heard a fox's cry, but she had difficulty believing it made a sound exactly like a woman calling out. And even if it were true, it didn't explain the smell of cigar smoke.

'They might have been yelling at the dogs,' Jessica volunteered.

'What dogs?' Minnie asked.

'We have two dogs that we release into the grounds at night,' Ruth said. 'There were instances of locals finding their way onto the estate after dark. Young men who had an unhealthy interest in our work here. We needed a deterrent and the beasts have proved most effective. It's why we lock all the doors at night. We wouldn't want anyone wandering outside.' She gave Minnie a pointed look.

If the locals had made their way into the grounds, that meant there was a way in. Minnie just needed to find it.

Promptly at eleven, Minnie was admitted to Wentworth's study. Unlike every other room she'd been in, his was lavishly appointed, with a substantial mahogany desk, a large leather Chesterfield and an assortment of comfortable armchairs. A fire burned brightly in the grate.

'Miss Butler,' Wentworth said, gesturing towards an empty armchair. 'Or may I call you Mary?'

There was nothing about the way he spoke to her to suggest he doubted her identity.

'Of course,' Minnie said demurely.

'I trust that Ruth has made you comfortable and informed you of our ways?'

Minnie nodded. She'd forgotten Wentworth's habit of fixing you pointedly with a stare. Perplexing enough in a room full of people, but there was no one else for him to train his gaze on and it was making her uncomfortable.

'I have regular communication with all our sisters,' Wentworth said. 'I am a busy man, but I feel it is important to establish each individual's personal happiness. Remind me again what has brought you to us.'

Minnie knew full well Wentworth didn't need any reminding. Attending the first séance in London, she'd 'accidentally' let slip that she was in receipt of a substantial – although unspecified – inheritance and that was, she presumed, the sole reason for the invitation to stay at Summerland. 'I was impressed by Miss Spinks at the séances I attended and by the work of the Sisterhood as a whole,' she said. 'If I can make contact with my mother I am hoping she will provide me with some guidance as to my next steps in life.'

He smiled benignly. 'I am honoured that your gaze has rested on us. I understand from Ruth that you have a brother? Does he have some say in your future? I should hate for you to spend time with us, grow accustomed to our ways, find peace here, only to discover your sibling has other plans for you.'

'My mother was a most forward-thinking individual, William,' Minnie said. She'd noticed that, while everyone else was referred to by their first names, Wentworth appeared to be an exception. He winced visibly at her use of his name, but she carried on as if she hadn't noticed. 'Her will stipulated that my share of the estate was for me to dispose of as I wished. My brother has his own inheritance, which I believe he intends to invest in stocks and shares. He is decidedly more conventional than myself.'

'Indeed, indeed,' Wentworth said. 'My experience is that female energy is more exploratory, creative, less tied to the conventions of the world. Hence the work of the Sisterhood is targeted almost exclusively at women. We aim to nurture that energy within a peaceful, calm environment.'

'There were some men at your séances,' Minnie offered.

'At the séances, yes. We can hardly turn them away if they seek solace. But here at Summerland, we focus on the female spirit.'

'Apart from yourself, William,' Minnie said.

He winced again at her use of his first name, less pointedly this time, but it was still there. 'I deal largely with the administration of the Sisterhood and with promoting our message. It is a sad fact of life that most people would rather work with a man on such matters. Besides, it leaves the women free to explore the metaphysical realm without having to concern themselves with the mundane.'

Aside from cooking, cleaning and other household chores, Minnie thought. Wentworth's name was noticeably absent from the rota of tasks.

'I have a question,' Minnie ventured.

'Of course.'

'My friend, Gwendolen Harper, was the first person to mention the Sisterhood to me. And I was puzzled by something Ruth said the other day. She said Gwendolen left here and returned to London. Is she unaware of Gwen's passing?'

'She is. As are all the women here. For our work to thrive, I need to create an atmosphere of complete calm. The women would have been most distressed to learn of Gwendolen's death, so I kept it from them.'

'Why would it distress them? Surely they, more than anyone else, know it is merely the thinnest of veils between this life and the next.'

Wentworth nodded appreciatively, as if he admired her answer. 'You've met the women, Mary. Jessica, Maud, Amelia – their previous lives protected them from any vagaries or hardships. I like to think of them as the most rare and delicate of flowers. I made the decision to keep it from them. Perhaps I was wrong?'

'No, no. Not at all. I completely understand. You may rely on my discretion.'

Wentworth removed a bunch of keys from his pocket, selected one and locked his desk drawers. 'Well, Mary,' he said, rising from his chair and leading her towards the door. 'I trust your stay will be a happy and productive one. Oh, and one final thing,' he said, opening the door, 'please address me as Mr Wentworth, not William.'

'Oh,' Minnie said, 'I thought we all went by first names here.'

'That is true for the women. It invites a free and harmonious communication. And, in the early days of our society, I followed the same practice. But it proved problematic. Some of the women found it too intimate. It led to some – confusion. Since then it has been deemed wisest to maintain a respectful distance in nomenclature. I trust you have no problem with that?'

'None at all, Mr Wentworth,' Minnie said, taking her exit, Wentworth following close behind.

After lunch – another disappointment, consisting of a single hard-boiled egg – Lizzie approached her and suggested they take a turn in the grounds. What Minnie really wanted was some time alone to explore the house and garden, see if she could find any evidence of what had happened to Gwendolen, Henry and Charlotte. But Lizzie might provide some useful information. And Minnie remembered her cover: as Mary Butler she would be more than happy to spend time with Lizzie.

'And how are you finding us?' Lizzie asked as they passed the henhouse.

'Intriguing,' Minnie said, deciding honesty might be a more useful policy than the mindless enthusiasm shown by Jessica.

'How so?'

'The food. There isn't much of it, and what there is—'

Lizzie smiled. 'We practice vegetarianism here at Summerland. And reduced sugar.'

So, no chance of a few rashers of bacon any time soon. Or a slice of cake to top it off.

'And Mr Wentworth believes that overeating hinders the spirits' communication,' Lizzie continued.

'So a single egg for lunch is normal, then?'

Lizzie nodded. 'You're used to more, I take it.'

Minnie thought mournfully of the slabs of cake at Brown's, oysters for supper, kippers for breakfast. She loved her grub.

'I am,' she said.

'You get used to it,' Lizzie said, taking Minnie's arm. 'The women sometimes say they are hungry for the first week or so, but then they grow accustomed to the portion sizes. And I do believe it aids our communication with those who have gone before. On the rare occasion when I have overindulged I find Pooky and the other guides very unforthcoming. Although you're lucky with the timing of your stay. It's Mr Wentworth's birthday tomorrow and we always have some sort of treat.'

Minnie hated to think what would constitute a treat at Summerland. Maybe when she was on cooking duties she could sneak a few extra slices of bread into her pockets.

Passing by the tennis court, they wandered down to a large lake with a pontoon in the centre, where half a dozen ducks had taken up residence.

'Has my mother made any communication?' Minnie asked.

'She's there. I can feel her. But something is preventing her breaking through.'

'Is that – my fault?'

'Nobody's fault, Mary. It's just that sometimes the noise of the earthly realm takes longer to diminish. Staying here will help that.'

'When did you first make contact with the spirits?' Minnie asked.

'About three years ago.'

'And how did you come to work with Mr Wentworth?'

'We've been working together for eight years, since I was ten,' Lizzie said.

Minnie was surprised to learn that Lizzie was only eighteen. Although she looked younger, she had the maturity and self-possession of an older woman.

'Ten?' Minnie said. 'That's awfully young.'

'Not in the world I came from, Mary. If someone offers you a job you take it, no matter what age you are.'

'So, what was the job?'

'You might say what we did at first was similar to what we do now, but it was like the difference between night and day.'

'In what way?'

'What we did before Pooky first visited me? It was trickery. Magic. Deception. Putting it simply, we lied to people.'

Minnie was surprised that Lizzie was being so forthcoming, and her confusion must have shown in her face.

'Ever since Pooky and the other spirits entered my life,' Lizzie said, 'I swore I'd tell the truth about what we did before. To show the difference.'

'What kind of thing did you do?' Minnie asked.

'Mind-reading, mainly. Or the pretence of mind-reading. You give everyone in the audience a small card and an envelope. They write the question on the card, seal it in the envelope. I collect in the cards and place them on a table in full view of the audience. Then I take up one of the envelopes, hold it against my forehead and say, "This card asks what will the price of flour be in June. Who wrote that?" Someone in the audience says, "That was my question". I open the envelope and read aloud "What will the price of flour be in June?" showing I got the question right.'

Minnie knew this trick. She'd seen it done a million times at different music halls over the years. But she remembered she was supposed to be Mary Butler, a woman with no knowledge of the halls, so she let Lizzie continue.

'I then take up the next envelope, hold it to my forehead, predict what the question is. Someone in the audience acknowledges they wrote it. And so on, until we get to the end. With all the questions correctly predicted.'

'How on earth did you do it?' Minnie said, feigning an ignorance she didn't possess. 'You said it was trickery, but how could it be? The envelopes were sealed.'

'The first question about the price of flour, that's a dummy. The man in the audience who says that was his question, he's working with me and Mr Wentworth. When I open the envelope and apparently confirm it's the question about the flour, I'm actually reading a completely different question. Which I then pretend I've predicted by holding the next envelope to my forehead. And so on. Each time I open an envelope, I'm reading the next question I'm going to predict.'

'And nobody ever questioned what was on the cards?'

'Never. People want to believe, Mary. If they didn't want to, they wouldn't be at a séance or a mind-reading in the first place. And they're more likely to believe a child. That's why Mr Wentworth offered me the job in the first place.'

Minnie looked at Lizzie. With her white-blonde hair and pale skin, she was a striking-looking adult. At only ten she must have looked like she'd come straight from the spirit world.

'After a while we needed to expand our act. People won't pay money to see the exact same thing every time. So we did a trick with palming questions. I give you a small square of paper, you write on it the name of a deceased loved one and a question you want to ask them. You fold up the paper very small. I've got a similar piece of paper, folded in the same way, but I've palmed it between my index and middle finger.' Lizzie pulled a leaf from a tree and palmed it in the way she'd described: the leaf disappeared completely. 'I take your piece of paper and appear to raise it to my forehead, but what I've actually done is drop it into my lap and I'm holding the blank piece up instead. With a bit of misdirection, I open your piece of paper and read your question, all the time making it look as if your question is still firmly folded up.'

This was a new one on Minnie. She'd have to tell Tansie about it when she got back to the Palace.

'When did Pooky first contact you?' she asked.

'About three years ago. One night we were doing the trick with the folded paper and I heard this voice in my head. Urgent, it was. Desperate to talk to me. From that moment on, I never went back to the old trickery.'

They had circled the lake and were now heading back towards the house.

'What you said to me the last time I was here,' Minnie ventured, 'it shocked me, truth be told.'

Lizzie nodded sagely. 'The spirits have a habit of doing that. What was it exactly that shocked you?'

'The person you said had communicated it to you—'

'The spirit's name was Rose, wasn't it?' Lizzie interrupted.

Minnie nodded. 'I was just – surprised that she would have shared that information with anyone. It was very personal, something only three people know about, Rose being one of them. I find it difficult to believe she would have told anyone about it.'

'You're worried one of the other people you told has betrayed your secret?'

Minnie hid her surprise at Lizzie's perceptiveness. 'I am,' she said.

'I can assure you that my knowledge of your past came from the spirit called Rose and no one else. Mr Wentworth says,' and here

Lizzie seemed to be recalling his words exactly, 'the afterlife affords the dead a laxity or licence they might not have enjoyed on earth.' She shrugged. 'Sometimes they say surprising things. Quite often they're – bold, rude even.'

'And do you pass that on to their loved ones?'

'It depends. If they're not long dead, or if I think their living relative is a little frail, I'll interpret what the spirits say. Soften it a little.'

'Did you do that with Rose?' Minnie found she was desperate to know the answer. If nothing else, it might eliminate the nagging worry that someone, somewhere, had shared the secret of her past.

Lizzie stopped walking for a moment, clearly recalling what Rose had told her. 'No. She presented me with images, no words.'

'Did she tell you anything else about me?' Minnie asked.

'She did. I didn't say anything at the time because it was sensitive. I had no idea if I was ever going to see you again and I didn't want to cause any further distress. But you're here now, wanting to become one of us, I hope. You got rid of a baby, didn't you?' Lizzie asked, but there was no judgement in her voice, only understanding.

Minnie nodded, horrified that she was discussing this with anyone, the secret she had kept hidden from nearly everyone who knew her.

'It was the right thing to do,' Lizzie said. 'Rose wants you to know that.'

Minnie raised her eyes skyward, trying to fight back the tears.

'But it left a scar,' Lizzie continued, taking Minnie's other hand in hers. 'You can't have any more children, can you?'

Minnie said nothing, the tears now falling freely. Lizzie pulled her closer, Minnie registering the scent of jasmine she'd noticed on their first meeting before surrendering to the other woman's embrace. For what felt like the first time since it had all happened, Minnie allowed herself to grieve for the loss of what might have been. A life with Albert, children. The future she'd been denied by Beresford's careless affections, and the brutal actions of an unfeeling doctor.

Lizzie simply held her, saying nothing while Minnie cried. After a few minutes, Minnie pulled away, extracting a handkerchief from her sleeve to dry her tears.

'You shouldn't be ashamed,' Lizzie said. 'You had no choice.'

'I'm not ashamed,' Minnie said, surprising herself with her answer. It was true. She wasn't sure how long she'd felt it for, exactly when the shame had turned to something else. It had something to do with Albert, that much was certain.

'I'm not ashamed,' she repeated. 'I'm just sad. For the person I was. For how that man changed me.'

Lizzie took her hand and, as if by an unspoken agreement, the two women turned in silence and walked slowly back to the house.

Lizzie had been kept awake half the night with the spirits, so she left Minnie after their walk to grab a bit of shut-eye. Minnie finally had some time alone before supper. She took a book from the library and slowly pushed open the door to Wentworth's study, her nose apparently buried in the book. Glancing up, she saw that the room was empty. For how long, she couldn't be sure, so she needed to work quickly.

She hadn't got much of a look at the key Wentworth used to lock his desk drawer, but it seemed fairly straightforward. Withdrawing a hairpin from her hair, she crossed the room to the desk, inserted the hairpin in the lock and gave it a sharp turn. With a satisfying clunk, the drawer opened. Inside were piles of papers, the kind of thing Dorothy would be able to decipher with barely a glance. But Dorothy wasn't here, and Wentworth might walk in at any moment.

Quickly, she scanned each sheet of paper. Receipts for various household items. Bills from the local greengrocers. And a butcher, Minnie noted. Somebody wasn't sticking to the vegetarian diet, and she had a pretty good guess who it was. Aside from catching

Wentworth out in a fairly harmless lie, there was nothing significant. Nothing to tie the Spirit Sisterhood to Henry's or Gwendolen's deaths. Nothing to explain Charlotte's absence.

Buried beneath the papers was a ledger. Minnie turned the pages; entries for sums of money received from, presumably, women duped into the Sisterhood. Small amounts, five or ten pounds at widely spaced intervals. Then significantly larger numbers from women whose names weren't familiar to Minnie. The ledger had a flap inside the back cover. Minnie withdrew a letter from Ravenscroft Bank. A bank statement dated a month ago for Mr William Wentworth, showing his account was significantly in the black. Minnie did some quick totting up in her head. The amount in Wentworth's personal account was very close to the sum of the moneys received from the various women.

Minnie hadn't made much of a fist of running the Variety Palace. But she knew that any money they made didn't go straight into Tansie's or her personal bank account. The Palace had its own account and all finances went through that. Wentworth was siphoning off most of the money these poor, gullible women were entrusting to the Sisterhood. It explained the threadbare carpets and the measly rations.

Minnie recalled the notes they'd found in Henry's papers of what looked like financial dealings. Had he discovered what Wentworth was up to? Not for the first time, she wished desperately she could get word to Albert. Send him details of what she'd found in the ledger and see if it tallied with Henry's notes.

The tap of footsteps in the hall outside pulled her out of her thoughts. Quickly she rammed everything back in the desk and locked the drawer. She grabbed the book she was supposed to be reading and was nearly at the door when it slowly opened. If it was Wentworth or Ruth, she was fairly certain they weren't going to believe a word she said.

'Why, Mary,' Jessica said, 'what on earth are you doing in here?'

'I got lost,' Minnie said, making every effort to keep her voice calm and steady. 'I thought this was the library. I was returning this.' She held up the book by way of explanation.

Jessica giggled. 'Just as well it was me who found you. Mr Wentworth sent me in here to find his glasses. Come on, I'll show you where the library is and then it'll be supper.'

The evening routine was a repeat of the night before. Dreadful dinner then an uneventful séance and bed. Vixens, Minnie thought, as she started to fall asleep. Just vixens.

Except when she woke again in the darkness, it wasn't to the sound of a woman screaming. It was the echo of a dream that woke her. The memory of Madame Ivanova singing, the edge of a dream that slipped from her grasp as she tried to catch it.

Seizing the opportunity to explore the house, Minnie got out of bed, slipped on her robe and slippers, took her candle and opened the door. She crept downstairs, past the dining room and the library. She'd noticed a door at the rear of the house earlier that day, one that hadn't been explored on the tour. She turned the handle, slowly pushing the door open.

She peered around in the gloom, her candle casting long shadows. She could make no sense of what she saw. Three large benches about seven feet long were spaced out at regular intervals down one side of the room, facing a large chair positioned next to an upright piano. On each bench was a large ball of string.

Minnie looked carefully under each of the benches, scanned all four walls. There was nothing else in the room, except this puzzling arrangement of items. Eventually, unable to fathom what purpose the room might serve, Minnie retraced her steps and slowly climbed the stairs back up to her bedroom, turning the same questions over and over in her mind. What was the room for, and why had Ruth kept it hidden from her?

TWENTY-NINE

Someone was screaming.

Loud, piercing, persistent. The kind of scream you couldn't help but respond to. Yet Albert was unable to move. Or rather, when he tried to move, it felt like his head might just explode.

Slowly, he opened an eye. Even his eyelids were hurting. His tongue was thick in his mouth, and he could taste stale alcohol. In front of him, he saw a pair of legs. Other legs, some seated, some standing. And still the screaming.

As he stirred into full consciousness, he registered that the voice was a woman's. And judging by what he could understand, she was very unhappy. Unhappy and unfairly treated. According to her guttural wailing, she'd done nothing, it wasn't her, the coppers had it all wrong.

With a jolt, he realised where he was. In a police cell. He forced himself to open his eyes fully and then slowly raised himself into a seated position, all the while trying not to vomit from the violent throbbing in his head. Tentatively, he reached a hand round to the back of his skull and found a lump the size of a golf ball. Dimly, as if he was struggling against the world's worst hangover, he recalled his visit to the house in Angel Meadow, the blow to the head.

So, how had he ended up in a police cell?

Avoiding any eye contact with the other men he was incarcerated with, he crossed to the bars and called for some assistance. After a very long time, during which the screaming woman was abruptly silenced by what sounded like a sharp slap, presumably from someone sharing the cell with her, a weary-looking police officer made his way to Albert's cell. The officer raised one quizzical eyebrow.

'My name is Albert Easterbrook. Might I ask why I'm being held?'

The officer looked at him blankly then turned and walked away. A few minutes later he returned. 'Drunk and disorderly. Assaulting a prostitute,' he said.

'What?' Albert said. 'I did no such thing. I was attacked in a house in Angel Meadow.'

'That's not what it says on the charge sheet,' the officer said. He couldn't have sounded more disinterested if he tried. 'You consorted with a prostitute, refused to pay her for her services, and then gave her a black eye when she protested.'

Albert thought back to the downstairs room in Charter Street, the women whose faces were a tapestry of bruises. He'd obviously been set up, but why? What could anyone gain from making false charges against him? Unless they wanted him out of the way.

'My name is Albert Easterbrook,' he repeated. 'I'm a former Metropolitan Police detective. Who's the officer in charge at this station?'

'Inspector Jerome.'

Albert knew Jerome by reputation and was hopeful the knowledge would work both ways.

'Please,' he said to the officer, 'tell Inspector Jerome who I am and that I'm being held in the cells for a crime I haven't committed.'

The officer looked less than willing to comply. Albert reached for his money. Of course. They'd taken it. And his watch.

The officer lowered his head and gave Albert a long look. 'Don't tell me. The prostitute you didn't assault took all your money.'

'Look,' Albert said, 'please just talk to Inspector Jerome. I'm begging you.'

The officer grunted and turned away without saying another word.

Further down the corridor the shrieking resumed.

It felt like several hours before the police officer reappeared. Unlocking the cell door, he nodded at Albert and gestured for him to follow.

'Am I free to go?' Albert said.

'Inspector Jerome wants a word. Don't ask me what about, 'cos I don't know.'

Jerome was waiting for them in his office. Albert knew something of his dogged reputation and his persistence in the face of seemingly impossible odds. His most celebrated case had been the murder of an elderly gentleman, found dead in a cab, with no witnesses and no apparent motive. Within two weeks, Jerome had found the killer.

Given his fearsome reputation, Jerome had a surprisingly gentle appearance, particularly his eyes, which were kind and thoughtful and made him look more like a university professor than a police inspector. He rose as Albert was admitted to the room.

'Mr Easterbrook. Please, take a seat.'

Albert did as requested. Jerome laid to one side the papers he'd been examining, and steepled his fingers under his chin.

'My apologies for your arrest and incarceration. They did a good number on you. Poured enough whisky down you to sink a battleship and then screamed blue murder. Why on earth were you in Angel Meadow of all places?'

Albert explained about the disappearance of Grace Hardy, the elusive Denny of the mangled ear and the visit to the house. 'It was a set-up, right from the word go. But what did they hope to gain from the woman's accusation? I understand what they achieved by knocking me out. They have my money and watch. But why accuse me of the assault?'

'It's a common enough scam in these parts, Mr Easterbrook, and I regret to say it's often committed with the collusion of the police. The prostitute says she was attacked and not paid. The alleged perpetrator is arrested but told the whole matter will be dismissed if he pays the prostitute what she says he owes her, plus a little bit on top for the assault.'

'And the little bit on top goes in the police officer's pocket, I assume?'

'Indeed. It's a practice I have no time for in my station, but the officer who arrested you is new and took the woman's word at face value. You were targeted, as you say, right from the moment you set foot in Angel Meadow. This Denny fella you're looking for, did he spend some time in London at the tail-end of last year?'

'He did. Do you know him?'

'If we're talking about the same chap, I do. Minor criminal. Bits of thieving and the like. I know where you might find him. But first I have a favour to ask.' He rooted in his desk drawer and handed Albert a pocket watch and a handful of coins. 'You'll need these.'

After his release Albert nipped back to his hotel, washed and changed his clothes. As he left the hotel he bent down to tie his shoelace. A young man who'd been gazing with interest into the nearby shop windows ambled over. He was a pleasant-looking fellow, with an open face and a ready smile.

'Could I trouble you for the time of day, sir?' he asked.

Albert straightened up and glanced at his pocket watch. 'Two o'clock.'

The man carried on walking in the same direction as Albert, close enough to appear friends. Ahead of them sauntered two other men and, further along, a man was on his knees shuffling a pack of cards.

'Ladies, gentlemen,' the man on his knees said, his voice cutting through the street noise, 'pay close attention. Three cards, see? Seven of diamonds, two of clubs, and the lovely queen of spades. All you have to do is find the lady and you'll earn yourself the easiest money you'll ever make. I'll take it nice and slow, so you can keep an eye on her. Can't play fairer than that, now can I?'

The two men in front slowed as they approached the man with the cards, and appeared to show an interest in what he was doing. Albert's new friend nudged him. 'Here, let's have a look,' he said.

The man with the cards, a sallow-skinned individual, was moving the three cards with impressive dexterity but slowly enough that it was reasonably easy to determine the location of the queen of spades. A crowd quickly formed, and the first few players were successful. Albert glanced round him. A crowd like this was perfect for pickpockets.

'I'm good at this,' Albert's new friend said. 'Tuppence says I find her.'

'Tuppence it is,' Card Man said, flexing and slicing the cards.

The money changed hands and Albert's friend successfully spotted the queen.

'Now you,' he said, nudging Albert. ''s only tuppence. And I'll tell you where she is.'

Albert fished in his pocket and drew out two pennies. With the assistance of his new friend, he successfully found the queen. He pocketed his winnings and turned to go, but a delighted cheer from his friend made him turn back again.

'A shilling!' his friend said, showing Albert the shiny coin. He leaned in closer to Albert, dropping his voice to a whisper. 'It's money for old rope, my friend. Stick with me and we'll make enough for a slap-up meal at Delmonico's.'

Albert placed a shilling and won again.

And that's where it all started to go wrong. No matter how confidently his friend identified the location of the queen of spades, every time she eluded them. Eventually, Albert turned out his pockets. Not a penny left.

His friend pulled him to one side. 'I've figured out what he's doing,' he whispered. 'One more bet, and we'll win back everything we've lost. I'm sure of it.'

'You haven't been very successful up until now,' Albert said. 'Besides, I've got nothing left to bet.'

His friend pointed to Albert's pocket watch.

'That was my grandfather's watch,' Albert said. 'I can't lose it.'

'And you won't,' his friend said insistently. 'Trust me, we'll win it all back and then some.'

Albert hesitated, then reluctantly handed over the timepiece. Card Man showed them each of the three cards, shuffled them for the last time and placed them face down on the pavement. Albert's friend pointed towards the middle card. 'No,' he said quickly. 'Not that one. This one.'

The card was turned over. The two of clubs.

Albert dropped his head into his hands and groaned. Even Card Man looked pained, as if he shared in Albert's loss. He appeared to undergo some inner struggle, then said, 'Tell you what, you meet me in the lobby of this hotel in half an hour with twenty pounds and I'll give you back your watch. You can bring your friend with you, in case you don't trust me. Now, I can't say fairer than that, can I?'

'That's the pair who were walking ahead of me,' Albert said. He and Jerome were positioned in an uninhabited cellar opposite the Grand Hotel on Thomas Street which, half an hour earlier, had been the scene of Albert's humiliating losses.

Jerome nodded. 'We've arrested that pair more times than I've had hot dinners. It's Walker – the fella who befriended you – and Sinclair, the one with the cards, who've eluded us. We can never get anyone to admit they've been conned.'

'Embarrassed by their own gullibility, I imagine,' Albert said. He understood the feeling. Even though he'd enjoyed the sting, he'd had a fleeting moment of vulnerability, helplessness even, placing himself in the power of a con artist. He thought of Minnie seated opposite Potts, being humiliated by him, handing him an envelope of cash to buy his silence for her supposed misdemeanours.

A brief scuffle on the pavement, and Walker and Sinclair's accomplices were arrested. Jerome and Albert ran out of the cellar and crossed the road to the hotel, Jerome slipping round the back. Albert had agreed to meet his new friend inside the lobby and, sure enough, Walker was seated on a leather button-back chair. He was deep in conversation with Sinclair and didn't notice Albert at first. When he did, he sprang to his feet and rushed over to grab Albert's hand. 'My dear friend,' he said, 'I was just trying to convince this chap that twenty pounds is a little steep. He won't be moved, unfortunately.'

Albert glanced over the man's shoulder. Jerome had just emerged from the hotel kitchen and was bearing down on Sinclair. Walker followed Albert's gaze and sprang backwards, fists clenched, squaring up to Albert. He feinted with a few jabs, but Albert knew the man was no match for him. With Walker raising his arms high to protect his face, Albert delivered one swift blow to his opponent's stomach, bringing him to his knees. Jerome appeared at Albert's side, whipping a pair of handcuffs out of his pocket and securing Walker. Albert fished in the man's pockets and extracted the cheap tin watch Jerome had given him.

'Excellent work, Mr Easterbrook,' Jerome said, panting slightly as Walker struggled ineffectually to free himself from the cuffs. 'That fella you're looking for. Try Cavendish Street. Number 34.'

Compared to the house in Angel Meadow, 34 Cavendish Street looked positively palatial. Only two of the windows were missing their glass, the front door was actually closed and it looked like someone might have swept the step sometime in the last month.

A young woman answered the door and gestured towards the stairs when Albert asked after Denny. 'Upstairs,' she said. 'The room at the front.'

Albert mounted the stairs and pushed open the door. A young man was dozing on the bed, waking slowly as he became aware of Albert's presence.

Albert couldn't have sworn this was the man who'd been spying on Grace's house; it had been dark, and he'd never got a decent look at him. But judging by the expression on the young man's face, he clearly recognised Albert.

He leapt from the bed and barrelled towards Albert, trying to force his way past. Albert pushed him back onto the bed with ease and then grabbed a chair, placing it against the door and sitting on it. Denny wasn't going anywhere.

Albert took a closer look at him. Denny was younger than Albert had imagined, probably not much older than Grace. He was very fair, his eyebrows and eyelashes almost white, with full lips that seemed wasted on a lad. Just as Martha Hardy had said, he was missing a sizeable chunk from his left ear. He cowered back against the wall, as if fearful Albert might land a blow.

'It weren't me,' he said, before Albert had the chance to say anything. 'I've been reading about it in the papers. It weren't me.'

'What wasn't you?' Albert asked.

'Gracie,' Denny said, as if Albert were an idiot to even ask. 'It's obvious, ain't it? You were doing something, working for Gracie or her ma and pa that night when you chased me. She goes missing and suddenly you're here. You think it's me wot took her, don't you? But I wouldn't. I didn't, I swear.'

'You call her Gracie,' Albert said.

'So? What of it? It's her name.'

'She refers to herself as Grace. Only her parents and her agent call her Gracie.'

'Well, I know her, don't I? She's Gracie to me. We became friends when I was in London.'

'Not according to her, you didn't. She told her agent you were a nuisance, wouldn't leave her alone. Hanging round the stage door every night, not taking no for an answer.'

Denny looked confused, deflated. 'She said that?'

Albert nodded.

'It weren't like that,' Denny said, his voice gentle now. 'I was sweet on her. Thought maybe she was sweet on me too.'

'So why did you leave London last November if you were sweet on her?'

'My little brother sent word he was poorly. I had to come home and look after him.'

'And then you went back to London recently? Started spying on Grace's house? Why? If you thought she was sweet on you, why not just court her like a normal person? And where did you get the money to be travelling back and forth between London and Manchester?'

Denny shifted uncomfortably on the bed, then seemed to find a defiant core within him. 'That's none of your business,' he said, tilting his chin upwards as if the action would give him the courage he was lacking. 'And you ain't a copper so I don't have to answer none of your questions. All I'm saying is that I didn't take her. And I don't know where she is. Now sling your hook, or else there'll be trouble.' This last was obviously an empty threat. Albert could have taken the lad with one hand behind his back, and they both knew it.

But Albert had learned when it was wisest to walk away. And he had seen something that confirmed his suspicion that Denny was involved in Grace's disappearance. He stood up from the chair and removed it from the doorway. 'Thanks for your time,' he said, leaving an astonished Denny gaping after him.

Out on Cavendish Street Albert found a narrow alleyway on the opposite side of the road to Denny's room. He'd be able to hide there and keep an eye on Denny's comings and goings. At some point, the lad would lead him to Grace, he was certain of that now. Denny wasn't the neatest of people. The top drawer in a chest of drawers had been open, items of clothing spilling out of it, including a scarf with a pattern of roses and lilies of the valley that was the double of one Grace had been wearing the first time Albert had met her. Obviously, the girl wasn't anywhere in Denny's room, and if he tried to push things too far there was a chance the lad would go quiet on him and refuse to reveal where he'd got Grace hidden.

So, for now, all Albert could do was wait.

Three hours later, Albert was still waiting. And by now he was very hungry. Not for the first time he regretted undertaking this mission on his own. With Minnie present, they could have shared theories, split tasks, followed up different leads. At the very least, he'd have been able to grab a bite to eat without abandoning the surveillance of Denny's room.

It was a risk, but he needed food. He'd passed a pie shop on the corner of Cavendish Street. With any luck, he could be back in position in five minutes.

Albert passed a news vendor calling out the evening's headlines. The man's strangled vowels made him impossible to understand at first, but finally Albert made sense of what he was hearing.

Murder.

He threw a penny at the vendor and took a copy of the paper. Blazoned across the front page was the news that the body of a young woman had been found earlier that day in an old mill left vacant for the last couple of years. The description of the woman matched Grace Hardy to a tee.

THIRTY

The next morning Minnie managed to wake early and wrote a letter to Albert, filling him in on what she'd learned so far: the lack of communication with the outside world, some suspicious-looking financial records and the fact that the women were in total ignorance of Gwendolen's death. Now she just needed to find someone to post the letter for her. Aggie was the obvious choice, but there'd been no sign of her since she'd dropped Minnie off two days ago. The groundsman might prove willing, but every time she got near him, one of the women swooped in for a walk or a chat or a task they needed help with.

After breakfast Lizzie suggested they take another walk.

'I wanted to ask you about the spirit photographs in Mrs Turner's house,' Minnie said, as they passed the lake and pontoon.

'Fascinating, aren't they?'

'They are. I was wondering – the spirits who appear in them, are they known to the subjects of the photographs? Relatives or loved ones who've passed on?'

'Not always. Sometimes the spirits who appear are complete strangers to the sitters; sometimes they know each other intimately. Why do you ask?'

'I thought I recognised someone in one of them. A friend of mine who died a few years ago.'

'And did you know the sitters?' Lizzie asked.

'No. And my friend was poor. I can't imagine anyone in her family would have had the money for a photograph.'

'So, like I said, she may have been a stranger to them. But not to you.'

Minnie said nothing, her mind filled with thoughts of Rose. How had she appeared in that photograph? Was it just as Albert had speculated, some trickery used to give the illusion of a ghostly appearance?

'Any more screaming women last night?' Lizzie teased.

'No, but something else.' Minnie recounted the events of the night before, the discovery of the strangely appointed room with the piano and the balls of string.

The briefest of shadows crossed Lizzie's face. 'You weren't supposed to see that. Not yet, at least. But, seeing as you have—' She turned and strode back towards the house, Minnie hurrying to keep up with her.

They entered the house by the back door, and Lizzie led the way to the puzzling room. It was just as Minnie remembered it. Three large benches, a piano, the balls of string.

'This,' Lizzie said, 'is our waiting mortuary.'

'A waiting what?' Minnie said.

'A waiting mortuary,' Lizzie said, as if it was the most natural thing in the world to find in a country house. She registered the look of confusion on Minnie's face. 'And your face is precisely why we don't tell anyone about it when they first arrive here. I've grown so used to our ways, I forget we might appear a little unconventional at first.' She moved towards one of the benches, which Minnie suddenly realised was about the size needed to take a human body. 'From what Pooky and the other spirit guides have told us, there is a short period after death when the spirit may return to the body and be restored to life. In our modern world, bodies are either stored in cold rooms, or buried very quickly. Too quickly in some cases.'

'Too quickly?' Minnie said.

'There have been accounts in the newspapers of individuals still alive when their bodies were interred,' Lizzie said casually. 'The spirit may only have departed temporarily, with the intention of returning at some point. Imagine the horror of reinhabiting your body, only to find it buried deep within the ground, and no means of escape.'

Minnie shivered. The idea of being buried alive was something she'd feared since childhood. She'd even considered purchasing one of the safety coffins she'd seen advertised in the newspapers, with their elaborate system of ropes and bells that enabled you to alert the living if you'd accidentally been buried before you'd fully expired. But then the practicalities of keeping a coffin in a small set of rooms had dawned on her and she'd abandoned the idea.

'This period of time when the body might be restored to life – how long are we talking?' Minnie asked.

Lizzie grimaced. 'Pooky is, sadly, a little vague on the exact length of that period, but he has suggested it is anything between one and thirty days.'

'So, this is where you would—'

'—keep the bodies, yes,' Lizzie said briskly, as if it were the most commonplace occurrence to store a body for a month after death. 'Obviously no one among our number has died yet. Our community is very young, Ruth and Mr Wentworth excepted. The life we live here promotes health. So far, we have lost none of our members, and we don't anticipate that being the case for many years to come, but in the event of such a circumstance, we are prepared.'

'And the string?' Minnie said, pointing towards the large ball of twine that lay on each bench.

'The aim is for one of the living to sit with the body at all times' – Lizzie gestured towards the large chair facing the benches. 'But that may not always be possible.'

Or advisable, Minnie thought, given the smell that was likely to set in after a day or two.

'The string will be tied to the fingers and toes of those whose return we await. The other end of the string will then be connected to the piano' – Lizzie motioned towards the musical instrument.

'The moment the spirit returns to the body and the individual awakes, their movements will pull on the string, the piano will play and the noise will inform everyone of the joyous event. So when the individual reaches full consciousness, we will all be present to welcome them back.'

There was very little that truly flummoxed Minnie. She'd grown up on the streets of Seven Dials, entered the world of the Palace when she was fourteen and her work with Albert had unearthed some bizarre practices. But this time she found herself genuinely lost for words. She imagined waking in the night to hear the piano's ghostly notes, with the knowledge that behind the door lay someone – some-*thing*, surely, by that point – who might have been dead for as long as a month and was now awaiting a joyous reception.

Minnie couldn't help herself. 'What about the smell? I mean, if Pooky's right and it could take a month for someone to return, it's gonna whiff a bit, ain't it?' Too late she realised she'd allowed her accent to slip a little, but Lizzie didn't seem to have noticed.

'We have considered that. We will have pomanders and pot-pourri in various areas around the room. This room also faces north, so it is the coolest space in the house. But Pooky has informed us that the body does not decay during this waiting period. It is simply held in stasis. No – whiff, as you so delicately put it.'

Minnie wasn't sure she'd feel confident in taking Pooky's word for it. A few dried flowers would be no match for the stench of death. Still, assuming no one died at Summerland in the next few days, it wasn't something she needed to worry about.

'This was your idea?' Minnie asked.

Lizzie shook her head. 'Ruth's. Her brother died during the Indian Rebellion and was buried out there. She got this idea in her head that he'd been buried alive, became obsessed with it for a while. Mr Wentworth has told her if our numbers grow we'll have to sacrifice this room for sleeping quarters. But for now, it stays as it is. It's not doing anyone any harm.'

After lunch, Lizzie left for communion with the spirits and Minnie had some free time. The letter to Albert was still burning a hole in her pocket but the groundsman was nowhere in sight, so she decided to take the opportunity to explore the grounds a bit further. Forty acres was a great deal bigger than Minnie had thought and it was taking a while to explore it systematically, particularly as she didn't want to draw attention to what she was doing. So far, she'd examined the two sheds by the smallholding and a dilapidated barn that was on its last legs. No sign of Henry Lawrence having been there. No sign of Charlotte Sykes. Nothing untoward at all.

In the far reaches of Summerland's grounds was a stretch of woodland, and Minnie turned that way. The trees were densely planted and reminded her of something from a fairy tale. Hopefully there was no witch's cottage in the heart of this particular forest.

Making her way towards the dark canopy of trees, she saw two people in the distance walking around the perimeter of the forest. Given the height and gait, one of them was definitely a man. The other was a woman. They were a good way ahead of her. There was something strange about the woman's movements. She was walking without any real purpose, her head lifted to the sky as she swayed forward. As Minnie watched, she stumbled and fell to the ground, lying there without moving. There was no alcohol allowed at Summerland, or Minnie would have sworn the woman was drunk.

The man was more purposeful, raising the woman to her feet and grabbing hold of her arm, dragging her onward. Carrying across the breeze, Minnie could hear the stumbling woman's voice, a thin, reedy wail. She sounded unhappy, but Minnie couldn't catch what she was saying. With her back to Minnie, it was impossible to identify who she was.

Minnie moved forward more quickly. She stood on a fallen

branch, and the sharp crack reverberated through the air. The man turned. Wentworth.

Unless his eyesight was remarkably poor, he must have seen Minnie. He pulled on the stumbling woman's arm and said something to her, dragging her forward as if desperate to put further distance between the two of them and Minnie. Wentworth and the woman turned sharply into the darkness of the woodland. Minnie picked up speed, taking care not to trip over her skirts as she broke into a trot. When she entered the canopy of trees, the temperature cooled almost instantly, and the ground underneath was a little boggy. Minnie's eyes took a moment to readjust to the gloom, as if she were entering a heavily curtained room after being in bright sunshine. She peered in the direction Wentworth and the woman had been heading and thought she spotted the merest glimpse of white through the shadows. Picking her way carefully over protruding tree roots that rose up on all sides as if to thwart her progress, Minnie followed the occasional flash of white. But as she drew closer, she realised it was a shrub of some sort, blowsy with tiny pale-coloured flowers. She looked all around her, listening intently for sounds of footsteps or movement through the trees.

Wentworth and the woman had disappeared. Minnie was left with nothing but the rustle of the wind above her.

An hour later, Minnie had explored every inch of the woodland and found no trace of Wentworth or the stumbling woman. She figured they must have either left the forest from the other side and returned to the house or maybe doubled back and exited the grounds through the main gates. As she entered the house, Wentworth came out of his office.

'Have you had a pleasant afternoon, Mary?' he asked.

'I have,' Minnie said. 'A lovely walk down by the woodland. And you?'

'Oh, no chance of any recreation for me. I've been holed up in the office since breakfast, seeing to the books.'

'No chance of even a little fresh air?' Minnie said, disingenuously.

'Perhaps later,' Wentworth said. 'Now, if you need to freshen up, it's not long until supper. Where there will, I believe, be a small celebration.'

Minnie looked blank.

'My birthday,' Wentworth said coyly. 'The women insist.'

Taking her cue, Minnie took the stairs to her room. She sat on her bed and thought about the afternoon's events. Was the stumbling woman Charlotte Sykes? Her hair had been covered, and she'd had her back to Minnie the whole time and been at some distance. Even if she'd turned, Minnie had only met Charlotte once, and would be hard pushed to remember exactly what she looked like. She couldn't be confident about who she'd seen with Wentworth, but there'd been something not right about the woman, that was for certain. And where had they gone when they'd entered the woodland? The trees were densely planted but still, surely she'd have seen them, particularly if the woman was dressed in white. She'd entered the wood not long after them, but they'd completely disappeared. And now Wentworth was acting as if he hadn't been out of the house all afternoon. More than ever, Minnie was convinced that Charlotte Sykes had never left Summerland. The question was, where were they keeping her? And for what purpose?

Supper was the usual disappointment, but the women were excited and giggling for much of the meal, sharing glances and whispering to each other. As they were clearing away the plates, Minnie remembered why. Wentworth's birthday.

Jessica hurried from the room and reappeared with a cake covered in icing. 'Now I know you hate a fuss, Mr Wentworth,' she said, smiling so hard Minnie wondered if her face would split open, 'but this is a day of such joy for us here we cannot let it pass unobserved.'

She handed him the cake and everyone burst into applause. Wentworth was making a decent fist of looking embarrassed but was clearly loving every minute. Jessica reverently took the cake from his hands as if it were a precious artefact. She disappeared with it into the kitchen, emerging a few seconds later with slices on plates.

'Do we celebrate everyone's birthdays?' Minnie asked Lizzie.

'No,' Lizzie said, her face hard to read. 'Just Mr Wentworth's.'

Minnie held back for a few minutes, allowing everyone else time to tuck in. There was a chance they might have slipped something in the cake, although she couldn't think why. But everyone attacked the treat with relish, so Minnie took her lead from them.

It was delicious. Possibly the best she'd ever had. And she'd had some excellent cake over the years.

Later that evening, Minnie was readying herself for bed when a movement out of the side of her eye caught her attention. A flash of white in the corner of her room. She turned her head, but there was nothing there. And then another movement, the same thing, but this time outside in the grounds. She rose and went to the window, moonlight illuminating the garden.

There she was again, the stumbling woman Minnie had seen earlier. Although, on closer examination, not the same woman, Minnie was sure of it. She stood in the centre of the lawn, staring up at Minnie's window. Slowly, she raised her hand in salute. And with that simple movement, Minnie knew her.

Rose.

Minnie knew she should be afraid. Rose was dead. Minnie had identified her body in the morgue, traced the ligature marks on her wrists and ankles. She'd kissed her forehead, the skin cold beneath her lips. So she could not be standing in the garden at Summerland. And yet she was.

Transfixed, Minnie raised her own hand and pressed it to the windowpane, registering the cold of the glass. Instinctively, she knew that if she moved too quickly, or went downstairs, Rose would be gone.

She tried the latch on the window, thinking she could call down, ask her why she was there. But it was sealed tight.

She looked down again. Rose was gone.

Minnie turned away. And then, as if someone had instantly blown out all the lights, the room was plunged into darkness.

She knew the moonlight should still be illuminating the room. It couldn't be this dark. And yet it was.

But something was glowing in the corner of the room. A pale shape, larger, more defined than the flash of white she'd noticed earlier. Her heart caught in her throat. A woman, standing by the window, her eyes fixed on the grounds outside.

'Rose?' Minnie said, her voice catching.

Compelled by something she no longer understood, Minnie took a tentative step towards the woman. She looked down. She wasn't wearing any shoes. The worn runner felt rough beneath her feet. She registered the cold, so cold her breath misted in the air in front of her. How had it got so cold?

She moved hesitantly towards the woman until she was within arm's reach of her.

'Rose?' she said again.

With a sudden, sharp movement, like an automaton, the woman swung away from the window towards Minnie. It was Rose. Her eyes were black in her head, her lips blue, the tongue peeping out between them. She swayed, and Minnie realised with a sickening lurch that Rose's feet were not touching the ground. She was hanging from the ceiling, a noose around her neck, her feet kicking and twitching, her hands grasping at the noose.

Minnie grabbed hold of her, trying to take her weight, to lift her up long enough to stop the noose doing its job. Minnie cried out, but her voice made no sound at all. She shouted again, louder this time, screaming for help. Rose twitched and writhed in her arms, even though Minnie was holding her up to save her. Minnie hitched her higher, but there was something wrong. No matter what she did, the noose was tightening. Rose was dying.

She screamed again, and this time she made a noise, a brutal, inchoate sound from somewhere deep within her. Surely someone would hear her before it was too late?

Desperate, she let go of Rose and ran to the door to seek help. She turned the handle but the door was locked. She hammered against the wood, screaming until her throat was raw. Where was everyone? Why could no one hear her?

Minnie turned back towards Rose, but she was no longer hanging from the beam. She had somehow freed herself and was walking with calm deliberation towards Minnie, her head hanging at a sickening, unnatural angle. As Rose drew closer, Minnie slid to the floor. Terror engulfed her. She felt Rose's hand on her shoulder, her voice whispering in her ear. Strange words that made no sense. Rose inserted her hand under Minnie's chin, lifting her head, forcing Minnie to look at her.

And then Minnie was falling. Falling into a deep darkness from which there was no escape.

Minnie woke. She looked towards the window. No Rose. But something had roused her.

She looked around the room. Her bedroom door was wide open. And then she heard it. Distant at first, tentative even, but then growing louder. The notes discordant and fragmented. Her blood chilled in her veins. She knew that sound.

A piano.

And there was only one place it could be coming from.

The waiting mortuary.

Minnie whimpered with fear, then told herself it couldn't be. No one had died at Summerland since she'd arrived. There were no bodies in the waiting mortuary. But she had seen Rose. Rose, who she knew was dead.

And someone – something – was playing the piano.

She pressed her hand to her mouth to stop herself crying out in fear. Taking several deep breaths, she reminded herself she'd faced worse than this. She'd been brave a hundred times, and she could be brave again. But always, in those previous times, there had been someone close by. Billy, that time in the ice house. And, more times than she cared to remember, Albert. Always there to watch her back. To save her.

Only Albert wasn't here now. She was completely alone.

One hand holding her candle, the other tightly gripping the banister, she forced herself to descend the stairs. The sound of the piano grew slightly louder as she approached the waiting mortuary, and the air was filled with a heady scent. Jasmine. The smell she associated with Lizzie. As she neared the door the scent grew stronger.

She turned the handle, opened the door. The room was dark. The sound of the piano ceased abruptly. In the darkness, she peered towards the instrument, trying to fathom who or what had been playing. She could just make out a shape seated in front of the piano, a shadow of someone. The shape rose from the seat, turning slowly towards her. Its movements were juddering, erratic, as if it were somehow not used to walking. Minnie told herself to remain calm. This was some trickery. But the thing lurched towards her, its gait clumsy and uncertain, reaching out a hand towards her.

She stumbled backwards and somebody grabbed her round the waist, placing their hand over her mouth. She felt their breath, hot against her face. Hands on her body. The arm around her waist loosened and, for a moment, she thought she could get away. Then she felt a piercing pain in her neck. A needle. Everything went dark.

THIRTY-ONE

The assistant at Manchester Infirmary took Albert down a long, tiled corridor, opening the door at the end leading into the mortuary. They all smelled the same, Albert thought, the sharpness of chemicals that never quite managed to cover the slightly sweet, cloying odour of decay. And inside the room, the rows of bodies on trolleys, loosely covered with sheets that always looked like the merest breeze would blow them off. His mind was thrown back to the previous year when Tom had gone missing and he'd visited a mortuary almost identical to this one. Thankfully, it hadn't been Tom, but how much longer could his luck hold?

Albert introduced himself to the coroner, a weary-seeming individual who looked as though nothing could shock him.

'This one,' the man said, gesturing towards the trolley furthest from the door. With no warning or ceremony, he pulled back the sheet.

Albert was never ready for this. He'd seen countless dead bodies in his time on the force, and too many since he'd become a private detective, but he was always unprepared. The emotion that engulfed him wasn't horror or disgust but overwhelming sadness. A life, with all its hopes and aspirations, its sorrows and joys, all gone. All reduced to a body on a trolley and a disaffected man holding a sheet and hoping for a speedy identification.

The body was the right size. The clothes were unlike anything Albert had seen Grace wearing, but that didn't mean anything.

'She was killed by a single knife wound to the chest,' the coroner said.

'And the beating?' Albert asked.

'Before the knife wound.'

Albert felt numb. This young woman's face was all but obliterated, and this had happened to her while she was still alive. He forced himself to look more closely. If this was Grace Hardy, he needed to be sure.

The hair was the same dark colour as Grace's, but there was something not quite right about it. The roots were a mousy brown, the rest of it dark, a harsh black that didn't look natural. The woman's hair had been dyed long enough ago for the roots to be showing through. It wasn't Grace.

Dawn was breaking as Albert left the hospital. And while he was relieved the body on the slab hadn't been Grace's, nothing could remove the terrible sadness of seeing a young life so brutally brought to a close. The police had no idea who she was but figured she was maybe fifteen or sixteen, probably a streetwalker, given her clothes. No one had seen it happen. There was little chance the police would catch the killer. They might not even bother looking.

Albert knew he needed to go back to the hotel and grab some sleep, but witnessing that young woman's body and realising it could have been Grace made him want to redouble his efforts to find her. He'd continue his surveillance of Denny's room until exhaustion took hold.

He traced his way back to Cavendish Street and took up position. The street was busy at this early hour with mill workers setting off for their shifts. Albert scanned the faces that passed, hopeful that one of them would be Denny's, leading him to Grace.

With a jolt, he recognised a figure moving through the crowds. Tripping along with purpose, a paper bag under her arm that he suspected contained a loaf of bread. Not afraid. Not restrained. And clearly not the victim of a kidnapping.

Albert stepped out of his hiding place and crossed the road, reaching number 34 just before Grace. There was a split second where she looked at him and failed to register who he was. Then realisation dawned, and he witnessed the calculations behind her eyes, wondering how she could explain herself.

'Mr Easterbrook!' Grace said, clumsily trying to hide the loaf behind her back. 'Oh, thank God you're here!'

'Don't, Gracie,' Albert said. 'Please don't. I know what you've been up to.'

'What on earth do you mean?' she said.

You had to hand it to her, she was determined. But Albert was exhausted; he'd spent the night braced for the identification of her body, and he hadn't the energy for games. He gave her a long look and she visibly slumped.

Wordlessly he took her hand and walked to the end of the street. He found a small teahouse and ordered them both a large mug of tea and a warm bread roll. They ate and drank in silence for a few minutes.

'Before you start,' Albert said eventually, 'I need to get word to your parents.'

Grace shook her head. 'I sent them a telegram last night. They know I'm safe.'

'Were they in on it?'

'No. Neither of them knew a thing about it.'

'They've been desperate with worry, Grace. They thought you were dead.'

Grace dropped her head. Tears fell into her lap. 'I've messed everything up,' she said eventually. 'Hurt the people I love the most. And it weren't even worth it in the end.'

Albert nodded at the waitress to bring them more tea and passed his handkerchief to Grace. 'So,' he said gently, 'do you want to explain what's been going on?'

'I reckon you've figured it all out, ain't you?'

'Most of it, but I'm puzzled as to why you did it in the first place.'

She sighed, glancing round the tea room. Once again, Albert was reminded of how young she was, despite the bravado and performance.

'I'm gonna have to go back a ways,' she said.

Albert nodded.

'I'm guessing you heard about what happened when I was eleven? The performance at the Swan?'

'I spoke to Artie Buckley. He mentioned it.'

'D'you know, I don't remember any of it. One minute I was in the wings, waiting my turn, and the next thing I was coming off to boos.'

Albert recalled Minnie telling him about her own stage fright, the paralysis that had engulfed her and brought about an end to her career as a performer.

'Did something happen before you went on stage?'

She shot him a sharp glance. 'How'd you know that?'

Albert shrugged. 'A guess. You'd had years of flawless performances and then, suddenly, you freeze. I'm assuming there was a reason for it.'

Slowly she nodded her head. 'There was.' She gave him a sideways look, clearly weighing up how much she should tell him.

Albert said nothing.

Eventually she spoke. 'I ain't never told anyone, Albert. Not even Ma and Pa. I mean, they knew something was up 'cos I refused to go back on stage for a month, but they didn't know what caused it.' She took a sip of her tea. 'There was this fella. A hypnotist he was. Stage name was Mesmer the Magnificent and that's what he called himself all the time, like it was his actual name. We called him Harry Haw-Haw, 'cos he was a bit of a toff. Not as much of a one as you, but nicely spoken and such. No one really understood how he'd ended up in the halls. When I started at the Swan I heard the older girls talking about him, saying he used to accidentally walk in when they were changing, that kind of thing. Which happens all the time in the theatre, you can forget about privacy, but most of the fellas pay no mind. And half of them ain't interested in girls anyway, so you could have everything out on display and they wouldn't bat an eyelid. But Harry was different. He'd hang around, sneak looks at the girls, rub himself up against them in the corridor when there was plenty of room for him to get by. You know the kind of thing. Or no – you probably don't.'

'I've met his type.'

'And he always seemed to know stuff about us. Just bits of gossip and tales that he couldn't have overheard. But he knew it somehow.'

'What kind of thing?'

She shrugged. 'The usual. Girls having trouble with their fellas, arguing with their parents. One time this dancer, Maisie I think her name was, she'd been going on for weeks to the girls about this hat she wanted and couldn't afford. Nothing special it was, but she was mad for it. Every time we were in the dressing room, she'd start on again about this hat. Starving herself so she'd have enough to buy it. One night we come in, she opens her locker and screams. There's the hat, sitting in her locker. Note pinned to it saying "With love and admiration from Mesmer the Magnificent". Maisie couldn't figure out how he'd known. Didn't want the hat any more after she knew he'd bought it.'

Grace pulled her scarf tighter around her neck and took another sip of her tea. Albert had the feeling she was playing for time.

'Anyway,' she said after a few minutes, 'this one time I'm in the girls' dressing room on my own, putting on the slap ready to go on. And I don't know what made me do it, maybe there was a noise or something, but I turned my head and right next to me, carved in the wall, there was a little hole, about so wide.' She held her fingers apart about an inch. 'I'd never noticed it before, and I can't tell you what made me do it, but I reached forward to take a closer look. And looking right back at me was an eye.'

She pulled a piece off her bread roll but left it uneaten. 'I knew it was him. Just knew it. He comes racing round from the props cupboard, which is where he'd been hiding all this time, looking at us girls, listening in on our conversations. He's sweating, frantic, wants me to say nothing. Promises me money, anything I want. Swears he'll seal up the hole, never do it again. But I knew he was lying. I might only have been eleven, but I'd seen a lot of the world, Albert. I knew what people were capable of. And I knew when they were lying. So I told him I weren't having none of it. Said I was going to tell everyone what he'd been up to. He'd never get another job in the halls. Not in London, for certain. And who wants to work in the regionals? You might as well be dead.'

She picked at the breadcrumbs on her plate, her voice growing quieter, her body shrinking into itself.

'He changed. You could see it in his face. One minute he was begging me, desperate. And then it was like something shifted in him and I knew he was gonna do something awful to me. I just didn't know what. But it became clear pretty quickly.' She broke off. Albert took her hand in his and they sat in silence until she was ready to speak again.

'I always thought I'd fight, y'know? I heard about it happening to other girls and I always figured it wouldn't happen to me. I'd scratch his eyes out, knee him in the nuggins, scream bloody murder. But it weren't like that. I just – I couldn't move, Albert. I just couldn't move.'

'You were eleven, Grace. You shouldn't even have known that such things existed.'

She gave him such a sad and knowing look, it felt as if Albert were the younger of the two. And, for the first time, he saw the grit in her, the hard core that she'd had to cultivate in order simply to survive. It was a grit he recognised, having seen it in Minnie's face the first time he met her, and on numerous occasions since.

'Maybe in your world, Albert, an eleven-year-old is still a child. I certainly weren't. And all the time he's – y'know – there's this song running through my head. "Strolling Along the Strand". You know it?'

Albert nodded.

'It kept playing in my head. Over and over. Just the chorus. I can't stand to hear it no more. First time I heard it after – I was walking down the Strand and some street performer was singing it. I threw up. Right there on the street. Anyways,' she said, rousing herself, 'he didn't get the chance to see it through. Not right to the end, although that don't make much difference does it? The runner knocked on the door, gave me the five-minute call and Harry pulled himself off me. I sorted out my clothes, stumbled out of there, went on stage like I did every night. But this time it was different. I just went blank. Couldn't remember a single word. Couldn't even have told you my name if you'd asked me. It was like I was rooted to the spot. The stage manager had to drag me off. A month later, Ma fell ill. Something with her stomach that was gonna cost a lot of money. Which we didn't have 'cos we spent it as soon as I earned it. So I made myself go back. Struggled to breathe the closer I got to the theatre, thought I was dying. But I made myself go through with it. Only they didn't want me back. Said I was unreliable. And, while I'd been away, Dolly Carter had appeared on the scene. Even younger than me, even smaller. Everything had changed in just a month. But that's the theatre for you. A week on the stage is like a year anywhere else, I reckon.' She chased the remaining crumbs around her plate. 'Imagine knowing the best days of your life are already behind you, Albert. And you're only eleven.'

'There's more to life than performing.'

'Said the man who's never set foot on a stage. It gets into your blood, Albert. Nothing else is quite as – real. Sounds daft, don't it? Make-believe is more real than real life. But that's what it's like. You can't let it go.'

'But you didn't need to, did you? I mean, you're still able to perform. Training for the opera?'

She gave him a look so weighted with sadness and bitter knowl-edge it almost broke his heart. 'I thought opera was just squealing a bit and pretending you were singing in German, but there's a lot more to it than that, Albert. You'd be surprised. And it turns out I ain't as good at it as I thought I was, and everyone knows it.'

'But you could still get work in the halls, surely? Singing? A bit of dancing?'

'Maybe. But where would I be on the billing? That's what counts, Albert. When you've been the headline act, it's like torture to go on before Millie the Dancing Dog and Elastico the Rubber Band Man.'

'So that's when you decided on the Thames incident?'

She nodded. 'I figured if I could get myself some publicity it would push me up the billing. Only no one took it that seriously. They thought I was just acting up again, which was true – only I hadn't been acting up the first time. That time, it had been real. When the Thames thing didn't work, I roped Denny in. Wrote to him and asked him to come back to London and help me.'

'To watch the house,' Albert said.

'He agreed to stand outside the house a few times, make him-self noticed. It was him you chased after that night. He's a sweet boy,' she added, as if talking about someone decades younger than her.

'And I'm assuming it was you feeding the story to the newspapers. The ransom note? The lock of hair?'

'All me. It'd be really helpful if you could go along with it, Albert. "Missing Gracie found by famous detective", that sort of thing. It'd do wonders for your reputation.'

'I can't do that, Grace. I'm quite happy with my reputation just as it is. And I'm not overly fond of lying.'

She nodded, as if she'd expected this answer all along but was nonetheless disappointed with Albert's response.

'One more thing,' Albert said. 'Why did you hire me in the first place? There was no mystery abductor leaving you on the banks of the Thames, no stranger watching the house. You must have known I was going to work that out.'

'I hired you 'cos you'd done that job for Madame Ivanova and you caught Lord Linton, didn't you? You're quite famous, Albert,' she said, as if this might be news to him. 'I thought some of that fame might rub off on me.'

'But you knew I'd solved those other crimes. Did it never cross your mind I'd solve this one too?'

'I thought I was cleverer than you, Albert. Turns out I was wrong.'

Albert paid the waitress and pushed back his chair. 'Let's get your things together and catch the next train back to London.'

Albert managed to sleep for an hour or so on the train. As they neared home, he gazed out of the window at the houses clustered near the train tracks. Innocuous domestic spaces that told nothing of the lives of their inhabitants, the secrets they were keeping, the lies they were telling themselves and others.

'What happened to the man?' he asked. 'The peeping Tom.'

'By the time I went back to the Swan he'd moved on,' Grace said. 'Worked at the Canterbury for a while and that was the last I heard of him.'

'He should be made to pay, Grace. For what he did to you.'

She sighed and patted his hand, as if he were a child and she was having to tell him the truth about Father Christmas. 'Fellas like that never have to pay, Albert. They do what they like and then they just move on to the next girl.'

'And you never knew his real name?'

She frowned, then shook her head. 'He was always just Harry.'

After Albert had deposited Grace with her parents he caught a cab to Artie Buckley's office. Artie was positioned behind his desk, almost as if he hadn't moved since Albert had last seen him.

'Do we have reason to celebrate?' Artie asked.

'We do. Grace Hardy has been returned to the bosom of her family.'

'Unharmed?' Artie asked, his concern showing beneath the bravado.

'Entirely.' Albert explained everything to Artie.

'I've got to hand it to her,' Artie said, lighting a cigar and passing one to Albert, 'the girl's got chutzpah. I might be tempted to try that little ruse myself, if one of my artistes suffers from a falling off.'

'Please don't,' Albert said. 'Or at least, don't involve me.'

'Oh, I have other plans for you,' Artie said, puffing contentedly on his cigar. 'Now, something about the cut of your jib suggests to me you have a little favour to ask.'

'I do. The man who did that to Grace should be made to pay. She never knew his real name. I'm thinking perhaps you do.'

'I do, as a matter of fact. And I heartily agree that the fella should be made to pay. But a little quid pro quo wouldn't go amiss here.'

'How much do you want?' Albert said, reaching into his pocket.

Artie winced. 'Please, Albert, what are we? Philistines? I was thinking more in the way of performance.'

Albert said nothing, fairly certain he knew what was coming.

'One night. And it ain't for a few weeks yet. The Playhouse. No lines. And you'll be swaddled in bandages so your own mother wouldn't recognise you.'

'Very well,' Albert said, so impatient to get the information out of Artie he'd have agreed to anything.

Artie gave a broad grin. 'I knew you wouldn't be able to resist. And I am confident, Albert, that this will be the start of your life on the boards.'

'I doubt that very much,' Albert said. 'The name?'

'Ah, yes. Mesmer the Magnificent. No longer in the entertainment line, at least not directly so. Last I heard he went into the spiritualism business. Lots of hypnotists and magicians go down that route. Easy pickings. His name is Wentworth. William Wentworth.'

At eight o'clock, the Palace was thrumming with activity, performers rushing around backstage or waiting in the wings to take their turn. Albert made his way to Tansie's office, where Minnie could often be found, but it was locked. From the auditorium he could hear the introduction for the next performer. He moved on to Wardrobe, hoping to find her there. The room was empty, except for Bernard, who appeared to be taking an inventory of all the costumes.

'You haven't seen Minnie, have you?' Albert asked.

'Neither sight nor sound for the past few days, dearest one,' Bernard said. '"Melted into air".' He looked questioningly at Albert, but Albert had no time for Bernard's game.

'When was she last here?' Albert asked.

Bernard thought for a moment. 'Four – no, five days ago. She stormed in, caught Tansie in his underpants and then she was gone. I don't believe the two events are linked, but one can never be sure.'

'And no one's seen her since?' Albert asked. He couldn't think of a single day when she didn't pop into the Palace at some point. Never mind five days.

Bernard shook his head. 'Should we be concerned, dear boy?'

'I hope not,' Albert said. 'Is Tansie in? Maybe he's heard from her.'

'It's his night off, dearest one. I suspect he's with the lovely Mrs Lawrence, but I couldn't tell you where.'

Having no luck catching a cab, Albert ran to Minnie's lodgings, but her landlady hadn't seen her in nearly a week. 'I think she was getting a train somewhere,' the woman said. 'Left with a suitcase, I know that much.'

Albert didn't like the sound of this. The two of them had argued and Minnie had disappeared. Where could she be?

He hurried back to his house and was greeted by Mrs Byrne at the door.

'Did you find her?' Mrs Byrne asked.

Albert shook his head.

'Oh, her poor parents,' Mrs Byrne said. 'They must be going out of their minds.'

Albert looked blank for a moment, then uncrossed the wires. 'I found Grace Hardy,' he said. 'Long story, which I'll tell you later, but you haven't seen Minnie, have you?'

Mrs Byrne shook her head. Albert grabbed the stack of correspondence waiting on the hall table and quickly leafed through it. Near the bottom of the pile was an envelope addressed to him in what looked like Minnie's handwriting. He ripped it open and scanned the brief note inside.

She'd gone to Summerland. She was still there now.

With William Wentworth.

THIRTY-TWO

The journey the following morning seemed to take an age, but finally Albert alighted at Sudbury. There wasn't a cab in sight and the stationmaster laughed at the mere thought of it.

'You heading out to where all the young ladies live, are you?' he said, with no attempt to disguise a lascivious leer. 'If you are, Matty's heading out that way' – he gestured towards a young man seated on a horse and cart. 'You'll have to sit on the coal sacks, mind, but it's a long walk otherwise.'

Thirty torturous minutes later, Matty pulled up at the gates to Summerland. Albert had never given a great deal of thought to the comfort levels of a sack of coal, but it made his Aunt Ann's chair seem positively luxurious. Soon all thoughts of his painful rear end were forgotten. The gates to Summerland were securely fastened with padlock and chain. Through the gates, a long drive curved away into the distance, the house completely hidden from view behind a large bank of trees.

'Yous got no chance of making yourself heard,' Matty said behind him, clearly enjoying the spectacle of a 'fancy gentleman from London', as he'd earlier termed Albert, frustrated in his efforts to gain access to the house. 'House is set right back. They'll never hear you, no matter how hard you yell.'

'Any suggestions?' Albert asked.

'Well,' Matty said, metaphorically chewing a hay-stalk as he leaned back against the trap seat, clearly savouring his one brief moment of power, 'yous could try that there bell.' He pointed a few feet along to the right of the gates where, buried within an overgrown privet bush, was the pulley for a bell. 'Can't guarantee it'll bring anyone anytime soon, mind,' Matty said. 'They keeps themselves to themselves, that lot.'

Albert jerked the pulley. Not a sound. He could only hope that somehow the lever was connected to a bell inside the house. They waited in silence.

'Haven't you got somewhere to be?' Albert said to Matty, who had settled himself comfortably into the seat of his trap and looked like he was happy to stay all day.

'I 'ave, as it 'appens,' Matty said. 'But if they won't let you in – which is more'n likely, given what I know of 'em – you've got a long walk back to the station. Happen you might be grateful I stayed.'

Albert couldn't ignore the logic of the argument. He strode over to the privet bush and rang the bell a second time, but clearly his first attempt had been successful: a woman had just appeared, rounding the curve in the drive. As she drew nearer Albert recognised her as Ruth Warren, the formidable doorkeeper at the séance in London.

'Yes?' she said curtly as she reached the gates.

'My name is Jonathan Butler. I wish to see my sister, Mary Butler,' Albert said. 'It's Miss Warren, is it not? I believe we met a few weeks ago at the séance at Mrs Turner's house.'

Ruth surveyed him calmly. 'I remember you,' she said. 'Why do you wish to see our sister, Mary?'

Inwardly, Albert breathed a sigh of relief. It seemed that Minnie's cover hadn't been blown.

'Our aunt Matilda has fallen gravely ill,' he said. 'I tried to send word to Mary but have received no response. It is vital that I speak to her.'

'I don't remember her mentioning any correspondence from you,' Ruth said. Albert had a suspicion that any letters entering Summerland were vetted. But Ruth was hardly likely to want to admit that to him. So they were bluffing each other, and he imagined Ruth knew that was the case.

'Be that as it may, Miss Warren, I must insist that I be allowed to see my sister.'

Behind them, Matty suppressed a snicker. He was clearly enjoying the spectacle a great deal, and Albert could imagine his retelling of events over a few pints later that evening.

Ruth surveyed Albert calmly, completely ignoring Matty. 'I'm afraid you've had a wasted journey, Mr Butler. Your sister left us this morning to go back to London.'

'Why did I receive no word from her?'

'She reached her decision last night and left this morning. I imagine you'll find word when you return home.'

'Did you speak to her before she left?'

'Mr Wentworth did.'

'Then I want to speak to Mr Wentworth.'

'Of course. But he' – and here she gestured towards Matty – 'is not setting foot inside these gates.'

'What makes you think I'd want to,' grunted Matty. 'I'll be back here in half an hour, and I'm happy to take you back to the station. I shan't imagine you'll be wanting to stay much longer than that.' He clicked the reins and turned the horse away.

Ruth led the way up the drive. As they turned the corner, the house opened itself up to them. It was impressive at first glance. But as they drew closer, Albert could see it was badly in need of a coat of paint and weeds were sprouting through the gravel drive.

Ruth showed them into the house and gestured to a room just to the right of the front door. 'If you wait in here, I'll fetch Mr Wentworth for you.'

The room she left him in looked to be some sort of library. As with the house's exterior, this showed signs of neglect, with a threadbare carpet and curtains that looked like they'd disintegrate with a gentle tug.

After a few minutes, Wentworth entered the room. He exuded an air of preternatural calm that Albert found immensely irritating.

'Mr Butler, I understand you wish to know more about your sister's decision to leave us.'

'I do.'

Wentworth gestured towards a seat, but Albert remained standing.

'Mary was uncertain of her decision to join us from her first day here,' Wentworth said. 'Lizzie was having difficulty making contact with your mother, and Mary grew increasingly frustrated. Late last night, she decided to leave. I took her to the station myself this morning and put her on the eight o'clock train to London.'

'It all seems very sudden,' Albert said.

'Experience has taught us, Mr Butler, that when one of our women grows unhappy with her lot here at Summerland, a swift exit is the wisest move. Less unsettling for the other women.'

'Mary spoke to me of a young woman she felt an affinity with when she first visited you. Charlotte, I believe her name was. Could I speak to her?'

'Charlotte, too, left us a little under a week ago. That might explain the affinity your sister felt. A mutual restlessness, perhaps? Discontent, even.'

'You're not having much success, are you?' Albert said. 'Keeping the women here?'

'We do not "keep" them, Mr Butler. All our sisters are here of their own desire. If they are happy, they stay. If the reverse proves to be the case, they leave.'

There was a possibility that Minnie had, indeed, left the house that morning. Their trains might have passed each other and she was, even now, firmly ensconced back at the Palace. But Albert had his doubts.

'Might I look round the house?' he asked. 'And speak to the other inhabitants?'

'Why?' Wentworth said, a benign smile failing to hide a flicker of irritation.

'Because I'm not convinced my sister is back in London. I don't share her belief in spiritualism, Mr Wentworth. I think you're all a bunch of liars and charlatans. And I'm not entirely sure she isn't still here, and you're spinning me a tale to get me to leave.'

Wentworth went to the door and opened it. 'Be my guest,' he said. 'The other women are about their daily chores, but I will gather them together in the kitchen.'

Albert started with the upstairs rooms, but they were all empty. Downstairs was the same story. In the kitchen, the women were waiting for him: Ruth, Lizzie, whom he recognised from the séance, and three others who introduced themselves as Amelia, Jessica and Maud.

'I fail to understand why you need to speak to us,' Ruth said, bristling with a quiet anger. 'Mr Wentworth has informed you of what happened.'

'And I have my doubts,' Albert said. He turned to Amelia. 'When did you last see my sister?'

'Last night,' Amelia said. 'We had the evening séance and then departed for bed. In the morning, when we came down for breakfast, Ruth informed us that Mary had left.'

Albert looked at the other women, who all nodded their agreement. 'And you didn't think it strange that she just upped and left without saying goodbye?' he asked.

'Mr Wentworth says a swift departure is always wisest,' Jessica said, as if parroting a much-repeated phrase.

He wasn't going to get any further with them. Whatever lies Wentworth was spinning, they all believed him.

Wentworth showed Albert out of the house. As they walked down the path to the front gate, Albert surveyed the grounds.

'Forty acres,' Wentworth said, following Albert's gaze. 'You're free to explore them if you wish.'

Not now, Albert thought. *Later.*

THIRTY-THREE

Minnie woke in a gloomy half-darkness, long shadows cast by the light of a single candle beside her. Her head was throbbing and she reached up a hand to the side of her neck, remembering with a sickening lurch somebody's hands grabbing her, plunging in something that had felt like a needle.

She was lying on her side, on a bed, she guessed. Facing her was another bed with the shape of a body on it. She tried to sit up but a wave of nausea swept through her, so she lay back down again for a minute or two until the sickness had passed. Much more slowly this time, she righted herself to a seated position and looked round her.

'Hallo?' she called out tentatively. Her voice felt rusty, as if she hadn't spoken in a while. How long had she been here?

A head lifted from the occupied bed and turned towards her. In the semi-darkness Minnie saw enough to realise who it was.

Charlotte Sykes. Although not as Minnie had last seen her. The woman's skin had a dullish pallor with a coating of sweat. Her eyes were having difficulty focusing and she smelled sour, like milk left too long in the sun. She was dressed in just her chemise, drawers and corset, her legs bare.

'I've been waiting for you to wake up,' Charlotte said, moving slowly across the room to sit on Minnie's bed. 'It's Mary, isn't it? Did you get the letter to my mother?'

'I did,' Minnie said. 'She sent me to bring you home, but they told me you'd left. How long have I been here?'

Charlotte shrugged. 'A while? I don't have a watch. He took it away from me.'

Minnie checked her pocket. Her watch was also missing. 'Wentworth?'

Charlotte nodded.

'And you've been here—'

'Since the day after you first visited,' Charlotte said. 'He saw me talking to you. So now I'm being purified.'

'Purified?'

'That's what he calls it. Made better. So I can return to the Sisterhood and find my rightful place.' Charlotte repeated the words as if they were a litany she had been taught to recite.

'Where are we, Charlotte?'

'I don't know. I think we might be somewhere underground, but I wasn't awake when he first brought me here. I think he moves me sometimes. I fall asleep in one room and wake up in another.'

Minnie raised her hand to the sore spot on her neck. 'Does he drug you?'

'I think so. I have these dreams – nightmares. When I wake up I don't know how long I've been asleep, or if I've been asleep at all.'

'I think I saw you yesterday – maybe the day before that. You were walking near the woods with Wentworth.'

'Was I?' Charlotte shook her head as if the action might restore her memory. 'I don't remember, Mary. Are you sure it was me? I think he has other women—'

'Other *women*?' Minnie interrupted. 'How many?'

'I don't know. I haven't seen anyone else, but look' – she pointed to the wall alongside Minnie's bed. Carved into the wooden beams was a set of initials. GH. Gwendolen Harper?

The space they were in felt damp and smelled of soil. 'Could we be somewhere in the woods?' Minnie asked.

'Maybe.'

'You said Wentworth is purifying you. What exactly does that involve, other than keeping you locked up here?' Minnie was afraid of what the answer might be.

Charlotte held her gaze for a moment, then lowered her eyes and turned away, her voice dropping to a whisper. 'He says it's part of the purification. That I have to embrace the earthly realm if I am to make contact with the world beyond the veil. I think sometimes he does it when I'm asleep. I wake up and I feel – sore.'

Minnie wanted to cry, but that was a waste of time and energy. She'd faced worse than this, the memory of a gruesome discovery in Teddy Linton's house springing to mind. But Albert had been there to save her. There was no one now. Charlotte might be here in the room with her, but she suspected Charlotte wouldn't be any match for Wentworth, particularly if he was armed with a syringe. And, Minnie thought, she'd brought all this on herself by refusing to trust in the one person who would never hurt her. Distancing herself from Albert, from everyone else. Flouncing off to Summerland, convinced she was best on her own, that she didn't need anyone. When she'd needed all of them, all this time. Despite her best efforts, a sob erupted from her throat, and she angrily wiped tears from her eyes.

'Does he have a routine?' she asked Charlotte. 'Does he come here at certain times of day? Or night?'

Charlotte shook her head. 'I've got no idea what day it is, Mary. Whether it's day or night. He appears, brings food and drink. Sometimes he – does things. Sometimes not.'

So she had no way of knowing how much time she had before he appeared again. Minnie scanned the room. Four beds, a table with a pitcher of water and a bowl. A bucket in the corner of the room. She stood quickly, then grabbed the bedpost as a wave of nausea overtook her. Taking a few deep breaths, she forced herself to straighten up.

She went to one of the walls and hammered on it, shouting for help. Her voice sounded dull and flat.

'There's no point,' Charlotte said. 'I've tried it. No one ever comes. Or no one you want.'

'Only ever Wentworth?'

'I think one time there was someone else. A woman, maybe? I was barely awake and I saw a figure looking down at me. Or maybe it was just a dream.' Her eyelids were drooping. 'I'm so tired, Mary. I think I need to lie down for a little while.'

'No!' Minnie shouted. 'Don't sleep. Don't leave me here alone.'

'Just for a little while,' Charlotte said, crossing to her bed. 'I promise.'

Within minutes Charlotte was snoring gently. Minnie ran her fingers over every inch of wall, desperately hoping for some means of escape. Nothing.

She crossed to her bed and sat down. Albert knew she was at Summerland. He'd have read her letter and, when she didn't return to London, he'd come and find her, surely. But if he did come for her, how was he going to find her here, wherever 'here' was?

Another sob erupted from her throat. She knew why. She'd wronged him so terribly, accused him of such awful betrayal. How could she ever have imagined he would harm her? She knew that if Albert didn't find her, she would die here. Or worse.

She lay down on the bed and the sobs racked her body. She cried herself into quietness, like a child after a tantrum and, despite her determination to stay awake, she slept.

Sometime later, she woke with a start. A figure loomed above her, blocking out the light from Charlotte's candle.

'Why, hallo, Miss Butler,' Wentworth said. 'Or should I say – Miss Ward?'

THIRTY-FOUR

The telegrams to Mrs Byrne and Tansie had confirmed what Albert had feared. Minnie wasn't in London. He emerged from the post office and spotted Matty straight away, lounging beside his cart. This time he was actually chewing a stalk of grass. A lazy smile spread across his face.

'Well, if it ain't Mr Butler,' he said.

'I'm wondering if you can help me again,' Albert said.

'That depends,' Matty said.

Albert reached into his pocket and withdrew his purse, handing a few coins to Matty. 'It strikes me that you know rather more about the layout of that house than you're letting on.'

'I might do,' Matty said, never taking his eyes off Albert's coin purse.

Albert handed over some more coins. Matty gave him a pointed look. Clearly the man wasn't quite the fool Albert had taken him for. Albert handed over yet more money.

'What do you need?' Matty asked, pocketing the coins.

'I need to get inside,' Albert said. 'Tonight. I need a plan of the house and any other information about the grounds, and the habits of the people who live there.'

'They're all tucked up in bed by ten at the latest,' Matty said. 'And fast asleep five minutes later.'

Albert didn't want to think about how Matty knew this. The man had obviously been inside the house, possibly more than once.

'They keep the gates locked all the time,' Matty continued, 'but there's a gap in the wall along to the right of the gates. Might be a bit of a squeeze for you, mind,' he said, taking in Albert's girth.

'And the layout of the house?' Albert asked.

Matty reached up to the seat of his cart and grabbed a paper bag and a stub of pencil. Within a few minutes he'd drawn a remarkably detailed map of the house, with all the rooms labelled. 'You can get in here' – he pointed to the doors leading from the rear of the house to the garden. 'They lock the doors, but it's easy enough to get in through the window.'

Albert took the map. 'How often did you break in?' he asked, not sure he wanted to know the answer.

'Only a couple of times. I weren't thieving or being snouty or nothing,' Matty said. 'I just liked to watch them sleeping. Made me feel very peaceful, like. You know the kind of thing.'

Albert had to admit he didn't, but he kept the thought to himself. He thanked Matty for his help and asked him if he knew of anywhere he could book a room for the night.

Matty pointed to a double-fronted house next to the station. 'Mrs Webb might let you have a room. Tell her I sent you.' He winked conspiratorially, then returned to the ruminative chewing of the grass stalk, considerably richer than he'd been ten minutes ago.

Mrs Webb had proved most obliging, offering him a very pleasant room for what Albert guessed was about three times what she usually charged. His suspicions must have shown on his face, as she offered to throw in dinner as well. But Albert refused. He had no appetite.

After another punishing exchange of money, Matty had taken Albert out to Summerland earlier that day, shown him the hole in the wall and promised to drive Albert back to the house later that night. If Albert had weighed a few more pounds he wasn't sure he could have squeezed through the hole, but he just about managed it. All there was to do after that was to return to his room at Mrs Webb's and wait until dark.

The minutes ticked by slowly until finally it was just gone ten o'clock. Albert patted down his pockets, felt the reassuring bulk of the gun. He didn't normally carry it, but he'd had a feeling it might come in useful tonight. He also had some candles and a box of matches. He had no clear idea of what he was going to do when he got to the house. Matty's map was detailed and comprehensive but of course it didn't tell him which room Minnie might now be in. If she was even in the house, which she hadn't been earlier in the day.

He slipped out, deflecting Mrs Webb's questions by telling her he was just taking a walk. As he approached Matty waiting by the cart, he felt a hand on his shoulder.

'And where might you be off to at this time of night, sir?'

Albert turned. The glow of the lamps from Mrs Webb's living room revealed Inspector John Price.

'What on earth are you doing here?' Albert asked, although he had to admit he felt immense relief.

'Popped by the Palace and heard you'd taken yourself off to Sudbury. It weren't too difficult to find you. The village idiot' – he nodded towards Matty – 'seems to have taken up residence at the train station and will tell you anything for a shilling.'

'Only a shilling?' Albert said, reflecting mournfully on his empty pockets, 'I think it's me who's the idiot. If you're here to help, John, I'd advise you to go back home. What I'm about to do isn't strictly legal.'

'Then best you have someone to lend a hand.'

THIRTY-FIVE

Wentworth settled comfortably on Minnie's bed. She edged herself up against the wall, as far away from him as possible. On the other bed, Charlotte looked like she'd shrunk into herself; she sat, eyes focused intently on the ground, afraid to look at Wentworth for fear of what he might do.

'I'm so glad you're awake, Miss Ward,' Wentworth said. 'Or I suppose I should call you Minnie, given our fondness for first names here at Summerland.'

'When did you find out?'

'I've known all along. From the moment you attended that first séance at Margaret Turner's house I've known who you are. You and your colleague, Mr Easterbrook.'

'How?'

He shrugged. 'I have my ways, Minnie. You'd be surprised by the things I know.'

'Why invite me here?' Minnie asked. 'If you knew who I was.'

He reached a hand towards her across the blanket and she shrank even further back against the wall. Wentworth laughed, and left his hand positioned between them.

'I learned that you were investigating Gwendolen Harper's death, and your reputation preceded you as quite a tenacious individual. I thought if I brought you to the house, I could find out what you knew – or thought you knew. Plus, I figured we might have some fun, you and I. We have had fun, haven't we? And we've barely started.' He leaned back a little, surveying her carefully, and then he smiled. 'You haven't worked it all out yet, have you? And you, such a clever girl.'

'I think I have,' Minnie said. 'I know I was drugged with that birthday cake, although I'm not sure what was in it. Chloral? Laudanum?'

'Something more exotic that's readily available if you know who to ask. It's called puerta, which I understand is Spanish for doorway. It expands the mind. The results are not always predictable.' A shadow crossed his face.

'Meaning?'

'Meaning never you mind. Everyone who joins us here at Summerland receives a very small dose initially, just enough to relax them and make them receptive to what we're trying to achieve here.'

'Fleecing women of their money,' Minnie said.

'Freeing women of the shackles of expectation and conformity. Offering them joy and independence. Enabling them to dispose of their wealth in a meaningful way.'

'Like I said. Fleecing them.'

Wentworth looked genuinely pained. 'From your conversations with Lizzie, I thought you'd started to understand us a little. Maybe some more time in here with Charlotte will clarify your thinking. Enable you to piece together the whole puzzle. Charlotte has found her time alone most edifying, haven't you, Charlotte?'

Charlotte flinched as the question was directed towards her. 'Yes,' she murmured, her voice barely audible.

'Charlotte has undergone a purification, which has *almost* cured her of her chattiness. I say "almost". We have a little way to go yet, don't we, Charlotte?'

A sob escaped Charlotte's throat and she pulled her knees up to her chest.

'Now you, Minnie, have another fault that is most unbecoming in a woman and is not conducive to our collective happiness here at Summerland. You have the fault of curiosity, and we all know what kind of trouble that lands women in, don't we? Pandora. Bluebeard's wife. You could argue it all goes back to Eve. We'd still be in Paradise if it wasn't for women and their nosy little ways. So, that is something we need to cure you of. I suspect it will take some time.'

He reached out a hand and tried to tuck a stray lock of hair behind Minnie's ear. She batted his hand away. With no warning, so quickly she had no time to see it coming, Wentworth slapped her hard across the face. Her ears rang with the force of it. He leaned in close, so close she could smell his breath, feel the heat of it on her skin. 'We'll have none of that,' he said, his voice low and measured. 'You belong to me now, Minnie. And I shall do with you just as I please.'

He reached into his pocket and extracted a syringe.

'No!' Minnie shouted, scrabbling backwards across the bed, although there was nowhere to go. 'You ain't doing that. You get your filthy hands off me!'

Wentworth grabbed her by the neck, slamming her head back against the wall. She was struggling to breathe, gasping for air, her arms flailing wildly. Wentworth pressed harder and harder, and she felt her body go limp. So, this is it, she thought. This is how I die. Alone. Without even a hand to hold. Without Albert.

The pressure eased on her throat, the thrumming in her ears lessened. She opened her eyes.

'I want you awake,' Wentworth said, putting the syringe back in his pocket. 'I want you to feel everything. And now – for a while – I want you to lie here in the darkness and think about what we will do together when I return.'

And with that, he climbed off the bed and went to a corner of the darkened space. There was a ladder, which Minnie hadn't noticed. He climbed it and pushed open some sort of hatch, which admitted no light into the room. He pulled the ladder up behind him and was gone.

Immediately, Minnie cursed herself for not having tackled him, tried to overwhelm him in some way so she and Charlotte could escape. But he had the syringe. And, much as she might like to think otherwise, there was no way she could overwhelm a man of Wentworth's height and build. She'd need help.

Minnie leapt out of bed and started to explore the room. The walls seemed to be carved out of the earth, with wooden struts at different intervals. There wasn't even a chink of light coming from outside the space, and the whole room smelled earthy and musty.

'Are we underground?' Minnie asked Charlotte. 'I know I've asked you that already, but can you remember anything – anything at all – about the times Wentworth has moved you?'

Charlotte shook her head. She looked terrified. And who could blame her, given what Wentworth had subjected her to.

Minnie crossed the room and sat on Charlotte's bed, taking both her hands. 'Charlotte,' she said, 'look at me.'

Charlotte raised her head. Her eyes flitted from side to side, as if afraid to make contact.

'What he's done to you,' Minnie said, 'he's going to pay for it, I promise you.'

'How?' Charlotte said dully. 'He's never going to let us out of here, is he?'

'No,' Minnie said. 'He's not going to let us out. I think he killed a woman he kept down here, and he killed the fella who was looking into her death. So, he ain't gonna let us walk away from here any time soon. But we are going to get out of here, nonetheless. We're going to find a way. But I can't do it on my own. I need you to help me.'

'I don't know anything, I've already told you,' Charlotte said, her voice high and whiny. 'I'm never awake – or barely awake – when he moves me. I don't know if we're underground. I don't know if we're in the house. Or somewhere else. All I know is that, at some point, he's going to come back.'

'Then we need to be ready for him.'

THIRTY-SIX

They pulled up at the gates to Summerland just before eleven o'clock at night. Matty jumped down from the bench and tied the horse to the railings.

'Thought I might come in with you, part of the way at least,' he said. 'I ain't breaking in again, mind. My sister's hitched to a copper, and she says what I did before was illegal. Can't see why. I didn't touch them or nothing. Still, best to be on the safe side. It'll be easy enough to get in if they haven't locked the window, but if they have, I know another way. Once you're inside, I'll come back here and wait for you.'

'I don't know how long we'll be,' Albert said. 'If we're not back by daybreak, can you get word to—'

Albert was unsure of where to seek help. It was normally John or Minnie in situations like this. But John was sitting next to him, and it was Minnie they were going to rescue.

'—Inspector Napier of Marylebone police station,' John offered.

Matty nodded his head once, as if he were entirely used to this kind of assignment and was on first-name terms with Inspector Napier. Albert hadn't spent much time in Sudbury. Maybe this kind of thing went on all the time.

They scanned the high wall surrounding the house. Albert directed John to where the gap was. Thankfully John was much slimmer than Albert. He'd have no trouble squeezing through. Nor would Matty.

It was a beautiful night, a full moon lighting up the landscape around them. A night that would warrant a gentle stroll and an appreciation of the starlit sky, if they didn't have a job to do. Once they'd squeezed through the hole under the wall, they looked round quickly, appraising where they were in relation to the house.

And then they heard the dogs. More importantly, they *saw* the dogs. Running towards them. At speed. Judging by the language coming from Matty, the dogs were a recent addition, and one he hadn't been expecting.

The moon illuminated them perfectly, even at a distance. Two dogs. Huge, fast and unhappy. Albert knew they had no chance of outrunning the creatures, and there were no convenient trees close at hand for them to climb. He cursed himself for not bringing a stick to ward them off with. There was no other solution: they were going to have to go back the way they'd come. Then he remembered his gun.

Just as he reached into his pocket, a sharp crack pierced the quiet of the night followed by a fleeting whimper, then another crack. John had a pistol in his hand, his arm raised to take aim again if needed. But there was no need.

'Did you kill them?' Albert said.

'Not sure and don't care,' John said. 'Dead or alive, they ain't gonna be bothering us any time soon.'

Albert ran towards the dogs. Neither of them appeared to be breathing. Which was a blessing, he supposed. Their end had been swift. He looked up at John, the horror clearly evident on his face.

'Well, what other bright ideas did you have?' John said defiantly. 'They'd have killed us, Albert. At the very least, taken a few nasty bites out of us. We're here to get Minnie, remember? And there's no way we'd have managed it with that pair around. My only worry is that the noise of the gun will have woken the household.'

Albert was forced to agree with him, although it didn't make him feel any better about what had just happened. He looked up at the house, the dark mass of it looming ominously. There were no lights visible. Maybe they'd got away with it.

Praying that there were no other dogs loose in the grounds, they ran swiftly towards the house, and then round to the rear. Albert had memorised the layout from the map Matty had drawn for him. He knew that the study lay on the left-hand side.

Matty ran ahead and peered at the sash window. 'You're in luck,' he whispered. 'They haven't locked it. Just push the lower window upwards with the palms of your hands.'

Albert did as directed. Matty was right. It was surprisingly easy. He nodded his thanks to Matty, who headed back towards the gates.

Once they were inside the house, John took a candle from his pocket, lit it and surveyed the empty room. Albert did the same and they quietly made their way out into the corridor. The house was deathly still, like all houses in the dead of night. Except it was only just gone eleven o'clock. A noise pierced the quiet, an unearthly scream that had terrified Albert as a child. Foxes. Nothing to worry about.

Taking care to tread quietly, turning each door handle with almost painful slowness, they investigated each of the downstairs rooms. Albert's first impression of the house was confirmed. Whatever money was coming into the organisation, it wasn't being spent on luxuries or even basic maintenance.

The staircase loomed before them in the dark. Given Matty's assertion that everyone in the house was asleep by ten, upstairs was where they would find Minnie if she was there.

They took the stairs and opened the first door they came to. In the darkness Albert could make out a bed, the shape of a body outlined by the blankets and sheets.

He turned to look at John. Wordlessly, with an ease that reminded him of their days together on the force, he communicated that he'd check if any of the women in the bedrooms were Minnie while John explored the other rooms. John nodded, pulling a set of lock picks from his pocket.

Turning back into the room, Albert tried hard to push aside the image of Matty creeping in to look at the women as they lay sleeping. This wasn't the same thing, but he still couldn't shake his discomfort as he moved slowly towards the bed, the quiet pierced by gentle snoring. Albert eased back the covers, just far enough to see the woman's face. Not Minnie.

He went back out into the corridor to explore the other bedrooms.

'You need to see this,' John whispered. He led Albert to an open door at the far end of the corridor. 'You go in, I'll stand guard.'

Holding his candle before him to illuminate the pitch darkness, Albert took a tentative step forward. He was in a narrow corridor, no more than a couple of feet wide. Rough brickwork was on his left, which he figured must be the outside wall of the house. On his right were wooden lathes.

He moved forward slowly, completely bewildered as to where he was and what might lie ahead. The ground underfoot, which he'd expected to be dusty and dirty, was surprisingly clean. As if somebody had recently swept this narrow passageway that must surely lead to nowhere. Except at the end of the passageway, where he'd expected to be faced with a brick wall, he reached a sharp bend, the corridor now stretching away to his right.

Albert realised where he was. In the walls of the house, in a passageway running between the outside wall and the inner walls of the rooms. Rapidly configuring the layout of the house in his head, he moved forward, slightly quicker this time, estimating the distance with his footsteps. After twenty steps, he figured he was on the other side of the bedroom he'd just been in.

And there, in this tiny space, was a chair lying on its side.

He inched closer to the overturned chair and righted it, taking care not to make a sound. He seated himself and moved the candle along the wall in front of him, the wall of the bedroom. A few inches above his head, he spotted something. He held up the candle to examine it more closely. A small hole, just wide enough for an eye to peer through. Looking straight into the bedroom and the sleeping woman.

He moved further along the narrow passageway. Positioned at the same height, looking into each of the bedrooms, a spy-hole.

Someone had sat here, watching and listening. And given the height of the spy-hole it would have had to be someone tall.

Wentworth.

Listening in on the women's conversations, just as he'd done at the Swan with Grace and her fellow performers.

But there was something else at play here. The chair was what worried Albert more than anything else. Wentworth wasn't just using the space to learn the women's secrets. Without any proof, but somewhere deep in his gut, Albert knew that Wentworth had sat here in the quiet of the night, watching the women as they slept. He could watch them as they awoke, roused themselves, dressed, undressed. Who knew what else he had planned? A night-time visitation from a spirit in corporeal form? With a rush of horror, he thought again of Grace Hardy's assault.

Albert turned and crept quietly back down the passageway, turning left at the bottom and making his way out onto the corridor where John waited for him. And then, with the full force of his lungs, he shouted Minnie's name.

THIRTY-SEVEN

Minnie couldn't tell how much time had passed or when Wentworth was likely to return. It was a clever game, she had to give him that. The expectation of something awful hanging over you, but no understanding of when it was likely to happen. Or of exactly what it was likely to be. Given what Wentworth had done to Charlotte, it didn't take a genius to guess what his plans were for her. It was what came afterwards that really frightened her. He wasn't going to let her go, was he? Not with all she now knew.

Still, his absence had given her time to prepare. She didn't know if it was going to work. And she had only one chance. He'd be armed with that syringe, she was pretty certain of that, and once he realised what she had planned he'd be able to overcome her in an instant.

She lay in the semi-darkness, watching as the final candle burned lower.

'Do you think we should blow it out?' Charlotte asked. 'When we hear him? It might be easier to do it in the darkness, he won't see what's coming.'

'I dunno,' Minnie said. 'It's a good idea, but—'

'I know,' Charlotte said.

The thought of lying in the darkness, hearing Wentworth move towards her, waiting for that first touch of his hand on her flesh.

'No,' Minnie said, 'leave the candle. It might have burned out anyway, by the time he gets here.'

'What if it doesn't work?' Charlotte said, voicing the thought that had preoccupied Minnie since she'd come up with the plan.

'It will,' Minnie said, with a bravado she didn't feel. 'And if anything does go wrong, you get up that ladder and go for help. He'll be busy with me. He might not even notice what you're up to. You go straight to the house and make enough noise to raise the dead.'

Charlotte nodded and silence descended upon the room. There were faint rustling sounds in the corners of the room which Minnie guessed were mice or rats. She hadn't bothered to investigate. Didn't want to know. Normally, the thought of being trapped in an underground room with rats would have terrified her. Turned out there were worse things. Much worse things.

Minnie turned onto her side and forced her mind to think of other things. She recalled her first meeting with Albert, when he'd been sporting a black eye and had charged Ida a fraction of his normal costs out of the kindness of his heart. The night she'd sat by his bed, willing him back to health. How he'd held her after she told him about her past and said he would wait for as long as it took. His arms around her when she had cried for all those poor dead girls. And then, lastly, the look on his face when they had argued, his features distorted with pain and anger.

Albert. As thoughts of him flooded her mind she realised it was his name she was whispering to herself. Over and over. But totally, utterly pointlessly. Albert couldn't save her.

Charlotte gasped. 'He's here,' she whispered.

There was a scraping sound from the roof above them, then the noise of the hatch opening and the ladder being placed in position. Minnie's heart was thundering in her ears, and she forced herself to slow her breathing.

Footsteps told her Wentworth was descending the ladder. She lay in the bed, the blanket pulled up to her neck, her eyes closed. Wentworth's breath was laboured, whether from activity or expectation, it was impossible to tell. He stopped by Charlotte's bed and for a sickening moment Minnie thought he was going to start with Charlotte. But he must only have been checking she was asleep, and he crossed the few feet to Minnie's bed. He stood beside it. She could feel his eyes on her. Then his hand on her head, brushing the hair from her eyes, as if he were the tenderest of lovers waking her from sleep.

He pushed back the covers and slid into bed next to her. His hand was on her thigh, pushing up her skirts. His breathing grew heavier, and this time there was no confusion over what was causing it. She felt his lips on her face, his breath hot and sickly on her skin.

Minnie gripped the steel stay from Charlotte's corset tightly in her right hand, raised it and plunged it deep into Wentworth's eye. He screamed, a brutal, animal, guttural shout like nothing Minnie had ever heard. She pushed him from her and he fell to the floor, his hands tightly grasping his face. Even by the light of a single candle, she could see that blood was pouring from his eye, and some other clear fluid. The corset stay was still protruding from it, and she thought she would be sick but told herself there was no time. Charlotte was sitting up in bed, her face frozen in horror as she looked at Wentworth, heard the noises emitting from his mouth.

Minnie grabbed Charlotte's hand, hauled her to her feet and pushed her towards the ladder. The woman was like a dead weight.

'Move,' Minnie shouted. 'We ain't got much time.'

Charlotte stumbled towards the bottom of the ladder, and then froze. 'I can't,' she said faintly. 'I—'

'You bleedin' well can,' Minnie hissed.

She looked behind her. Wentworth was still making the awful sound, but he was on all fours now, struggling to stand. If Charlotte didn't shift herself he'd be on them.

'Charlotte!' Minnie shouted. 'He's coming!'

Charlotte remained rooted to the spot. Minnie slapped her hard across the face. 'Get up that bleedin' ladder right now,' she said, 'or I will, and I'll leave you down here with him.'

The threat and the slap stirred Charlotte into action. She grabbed the ladder and ascended, Minnie just behind her. Charlotte pushed open the trapdoor in the roof and pulled herself out. She turned, grasped Minnie's hand and hauled her out. Minnie slammed the door shut behind her. The two women took deep lungfuls of air. They were outside, but they had no idea where they were. It was night, and the darkness was intensified by the heavy canopy of the trees.

'We're in the woods,' Minnie said. 'We ain't far from the house.'

Which was true, but which way should they turn in the near-total darkness?

'Look,' Charlotte said, pointing ahead of her. 'There's lights. It must be Summerland.'

What Minnie couldn't figure out was why there were any lights coming from Summerland. Judging by the darkness all around them, it was the middle of the night. Who was awake in the house?

Pushing these worries aside, she grabbed Charlotte's hand, and the two of them ran towards the house, taking care to avoid stumbling over tree roots and holes. Finally they were clear of the woods and crossing the expansive lawn. On the first floor of the house, candlelight seemed to flicker at every window. Why was everyone awake?

'Look,' Charlotte said, pointing to the open window at the rear of the house. They climbed through it. From upstairs, Minnie heard raised voices. And through them all, a single voice, a great roar of anguish. And in the heart of that roar was one word. Her name.

Albert.

Hoicking her skirts with one hand, she took the stairs two at a time and was on the landing in moments. There were bodies, voices; confusion and anger. She pushed her way through the women until she found him. Fleetingly, she registered John's presence. Then she was in Albert's arms, her head against his chest, breathing in the smell of him, folding herself into his solidity.

'Minnie,' he whispered into her hair.

She lifted her head and her lips found his. Everything around them seemed to fall away, time slowed, voices receded into the distance, the only sound her heart beating. Or was it his? She raised both hands and locked them around his neck, pulling him closer to her, as if she couldn't get enough of him, as if she were finally awake after years spent half-asleep.

Reluctantly, she pulled herself away from him. 'Wentworth,' she said.

Albert nodded and she took hold of his hand, leading him down the stairs and out the rear of the house.

'He's in the woods,' she said, pointing to the dark shadows ahead of them as she dragged him forward. 'There's an underground room where he kept Charlotte. Gwendolen too, I think.'

Within minutes they had entered the forest. Minnie faltered, afraid she'd lose her way, but she needn't have worried. Fifty yards away was the faint glimmer of the open trapdoor.

And, with a terrible realisation, Minnie knew what she'd done wrong. 'I didn't take the ladder away,' she said. 'We were so desperate to get out of there, I didn't think. I should have taken the ladder. He'll be gone, Albert.'

Albert had reached the hatch and disappeared down it. Within moments, he emerged. 'You're right, he's gone. Is he injured?'

'I stabbed him in the eye with a stay from Charlotte's corset.'

'You did *what* – no, don't tell me again. Once was enough. With an injury like that, I can't imagine he'll have got far.'

THIRTY-EIGHT

Matty agreed to take John to the police station at Sudbury, although in all probability the police would wait until daybreak to start looking for Wentworth. He was unlikely to get far with such a horrific injury, and no one had any desire to traipse through the woods in the darkness in the hope of finding him.

Back at the house, Minnie passed the tea round to the women and Albert. It was a poor substitute for the large brandy she felt they all deserved, but she'd searched every cupboard and found not a trace of alcohol.

John said he'd send word to Jessica, Maud, Charlotte and Amelia's families and they'd likely be arriving the next day to take the women home. For now, an eerie quiet had descended on the house, as if they were all holding themselves still, waiting for some fresh horror to reveal itself.

The women had decamped to the library, ranged in seats along the walls and staring into the distance. They had reacted with shock and disbelief to the news of what Wentworth had been up to. Even with Charlotte to confirm Minnie's account, they still couldn't countenance how far Wentworth had betrayed them.

Minnie and Albert had settled themselves in the kitchen. Every ten minutes or so one or the other of them went to check on the women, but there was no movement, no conversation from the other room.

Lizzie was missing. In the mêlée of Minnie and Charlotte's arrival back at the house, she'd disappeared.

'She's gone to find him, I reckon,' Minnie said.

'You sound disappointed,' Albert said.

'I am. I thought she was one of the good ones.'

Albert refilled Minnie's cup and took a seat next to her. 'There's something I need to tell you.'

'I'm not sure I can take anything more, Albert, to be quite honest.'

'I'm not sure I want to tell you, but I think you need to know.'

Minnie nodded her head.

'Wentworth was spying on you. You and the other women. He had a hiding place, in between the walls of the house. There were spy-holes in the walls, looking directly into the bedrooms.'

'That explains the cigar smoke,' Minnie said. 'The first night I stayed here, I woke up and I could smell cigar smoke. He was watching me, weren't he?'

'I believe so,' Albert said.

Minnie turned away, trying to navigate her way through this knowledge. Remembering the ease with which she had lived in the house, dressing, undressing, moving freely. And all the time Wentworth had been watching her.

'That's not all,' Albert said. 'Grace Hardy was raped by Wentworth. Years ago, when he worked in the halls. It's what put an end to her career.'

Minnie lowered her head, fought back the tears. They could come later, when Wentworth was caught and made to pay for what he'd done.

'Grace. Charlotte. Henry,' she said. 'Gwendolen. I saw her initials in that underground room. I reckon he had her down there and realised he couldn't just let her go. So he killed her. Probably with that drug he told me about. Which would explain why the autopsy didn't show anything. They didn't know to look for it.'

'Somehow Henry found out Wentworth had killed Gwendolen, so Wentworth poisoned Henry.'

They sat in silence for a while, contemplating the enormity of Wentworth's actions. Minnie's thoughts were with Gwendolen and the horror of dying alone in that underground room. She'd come close to it herself, she knew that now.

'They gave it to me, too,' Minnie said. 'The drug. We had cake for Wentworth's birthday. A few hours later, I saw Rose. In the grounds and then in the room with me. I thought she was real, Albert.'

It had all been a trick of her mind. All smoke and mirrors. Rose had never been there. Minnie had never held her, never smelled her skin, her hair, felt her heart beating. Never tried to save her. And even though, deep down, she had known Rose couldn't be real, Minnie felt the loss of her all over again, as raw and painful as the day she'd heard of her death.

She roused herself from her thoughts. 'I still don't get it,' she said. 'He kills Gwendolen two months before she's due to inherit. Why not wait, get her to change her will, and then kill her?'

'And why imprison Charlotte?' Albert asked. 'With what he was doing to her in that underground room, he could never let her go free. So he was going to have to kill her – again, before she inherited. And what about Lizzie Spinks?' Albert asked. 'What was her part in it all?'

'I dunno exactly. But she's missing, ain't she? Why would she run if she weren't in on it? She must have helped Wentworth lure the women out to this house with stories of spirits and voices from the afterlife. She had me fooled for a while.'

Before Minnie had a chance to say anything further, a voice spoke from the doorway.

'That's not how it happened at all,' Jessica said quietly. She stood, her face calm, a gentle smile playing about her lips.

THIRTY-NINE

'You've got it all wrong,' Jessica said.

'Have we?' Minnie said. 'I don't suppose you'd like to tell us what really happened?'

'Well, firstly, I don't know why you think Lizzie had anything to do with it. She's a sweet girl, but not exactly the brightest spark.'

'Not like you?' Minnie ventured.

'Exactly,' Jessica said, bowing her head to exhibit a modesty she clearly didn't feel.

'You certainly had me fooled,' Minnie said, guessing that flattery would be the quickest way to Jessica's heart. 'So how did you do it all?'

'Before I tell you, you need to understand my life with William,' she said, her face glowing with a quiet fervour when she said his name. 'When I first came to Summerland, I was William's favourite. He called me his sweet pet. His darling. We did things together he swore he had never done with anyone else. Things that would enable me to access a higher realm, to facilitate my communication with the spirit world. Things that would make me pure.

'And then Gwendolen arrived,' Jessica continued, a bitter note entering her voice. 'William told me Gwendolen needed a great deal of help on her spirit journey. He said he would have to work closely with her. Just the two of them. Alone.' Her voice faltered for a moment, then she gave herself a little shake and carried on. 'I was jealous, I have to confess. William said my jealousy was one of the blocks to my communicating with those beyond the veil. It was something I needed to overcome, particularly when there was no reason for it. He swore I was still his sweet pet, but Gwendolen was riddled with sin and there was only one way to expel it. So I tried – very hard – to fill my heart with love for Gwendolen. And it was working. Until he took her away.'

'To the underground room,' Minnie said.

Jessica nodded. 'William told us Gwendolen had gone home, but I saw him one day walking in the woods and I followed him. I found the entrance to the room, and I went back later that day when I knew he was busy with other matters. I found Gwendolen. She said such things about William – wicked, wicked things.' Jessica clapped her hands over her ears as if to drown out the memory of Gwendolen's words. 'William was right, she was riddled with sin, and I knew nothing could save her. I feared what she might do to William, what she might tell the world about him. So I got a syringe full of puerta and I went back the following day and I gave it to Gwendolen. She was already drowsy with what William had given her, so it was easy.'

'Did you mean to kill her?' Albert asked.

'Oh yes,' Jessica said calmly. 'There was no other option. I had to protect William from her lies.'

'Did Wentworth know it was you who killed Gwendolen?' Minnie asked.

'We never spoke of it. But he must have known it was me.'

Minnie recalled the shadow crossing Wentworth's face when he had talked about the temperamental nature of puerta. 'He thought it was an accident,' she said. 'He reckoned he'd given her too much of the drug, and that's why she died. Which would explain why he didn't wait until she got her inheritance.'

A gasp escaped from Jessica's throat and for the first time she looked genuinely distressed. 'That was never my intention,' she said. 'Oh, poor William, to be carrying such a heavy burden all this time.'

'He did trap her underground, pump her full of drugs and rape her,' Minnie said. 'He's hardly blameless.'

Jessica glanced quickly at Minnie then looked away, as if dismissing her words. 'I open all the post that comes to the house, deal with what I can and pass anything important on to William. So when Henry Lawrence wrote to William I realised it was the perfect opportunity to prove my devotion yet again. To deal with this matter before William even became aware of it. I wrote back to Henry Lawrence, pretending to be William, saying I'd come to his house on the Friday night after the London séance.

'And then it was easy,' Jessica continued. 'So easy, as if the spirits were guiding me the whole way. Henry Lawrence's servants weren't home; they'd gone to a wedding, I believe. I told him William was on his way and asked for a glass of water. When his back was turned I stabbed him in the neck with the syringe. He struggled, lashed out at me, but within seconds he was as helpless as a baby. I gave him a second dose in his arm. Within minutes he'd crossed to the other side. Problem solved.'

'Except there never was a problem,' Albert said. 'Gwendolen's aunt had her body exhumed and there was no evidence of her having died under suspicious circumstances. Lady Harriet continued to have her suspicions, and Henry might have been investigating Gwendolen's death, but he wasn't going to find anything. Your killing Henry was pointless. And it just led us to your door. If you'd done nothing, Henry would still be alive, and you'd be living out your days here in Summerland.'

'And the photographs?' Minnie said. 'There were mucky photographs left near Henry's body. Where did you get them?'

'Not long after I joined the Sisterhood,' Jessica said, 'William asked me for a gift. A *special* gift. Something he could look at whenever he chose. Something to keep me always in his thoughts.'

'So he took dirty photographs of you,' Minnie asked. And she realised why she'd recognised Charlotte the first time she'd met her. She'd been in one of the photographs left by Henry's body.

'I can't say I'm fond of your way of describing it, although I'll confess that is how I first thought of it. But then William explained to me how this was a gift, given willingly out of love. He said it would be a demonstration of my faith in him, that I would trust him with something I would never share with anyone else. Our special secret.'

'But did you know he was taking photographs of the other women,' Minnie asked, 'not just you?'

Jessica blinked rapidly. 'Not until I found the photographs in his drawer.'

'And that didn't bother you?' Minnie asked. 'Realising you weren't that special after all?'

Jessica bridled. 'I was unhappy for a short while, but then William explained it was just my jealousy distracting me from my higher purpose yet again. He said the other women loved him so much, they wanted to give him something precious. He'd accepted their gifts, but mine was still the most important.'

Jessica's belief in Wentworth was unwavering, Minnie thought. There was nothing the man could do that would convince her of his venality.

Minnie recalled Charlotte's vague memory of a woman visiting her when she was held prisoner. 'Did you visit Charlotte when she was trapped underground?'

'I did. William said she'd gone back home unexpectedly, and I remembered that was the story he told us about Gwendolen. I went to the woods and there was Charlotte.'

'Would you have killed her too?' Albert asked.

'I think I would,' Jessica said, unnerving Minnie with her honesty and calm, 'but I had no puerta with me, and then – then *you* arrived, and everything became more complicated.'

She stood, stretching her arms high above her head and yawning before turning to Minnie and smiling. 'Well, that's me done,' she said, 'you can call off the hunt for William and Lizzie. It's clear he's done nothing wrong.'

'You'll need to speak to the police when they get here,' Minnie said.

Jessica looked puzzled. 'Why?'

'People will want to hear your story. They'll want to know everything you did for William. How you saved him. And what a special man he is,' Minnie said, surprised by the ease with which she lied.

Jessica's face lit up at the thought of sharing her knowledge of Wentworth. 'Best I get some sleep, then,' she said.

She left the room and Minnie followed, nipping into the library to get the room keys from Ruth.

After a few minutes, Minnie returned. 'I've put her in Wentworth's room. She was delighted. I'm not sure she even noticed I'd locked her in.' She lifted the teapot and went towards the stove, then stopped, as if struck by the futility of making tea in the face of what they'd just heard. 'Why on earth did she confess?' Minnie said. 'We were convinced Wentworth had done it all. It never even crossed my mind—'

'She's proud of what she did,' Albert said quietly. 'In her mind, she's proved her devotion to William. And she believes she's saved him from the noose.'

'Not if we've got any say in it,' Minnie said.

FORTY

Two days later Minnie and Albert were back in Brown's tea room. Minnie had ordered the largest slice of cake they had for sale and was demolishing it with impressive speed.

'No sugar, Albert,' she said in between mouthfuls. 'I could maybe have learned to live without meat, but no sugar?'

Albert let her eat in silence, smiling to himself as she visibly relished every mouthful. When she had wiped up the last of the crumbs with her finger, she leaned back in her chair.

'What?' she asked.

'Nothing,' Albert said. 'I'm just… wondering.'

'About?'

'Us.'

A shadow fell across Minnie's face. 'You've changed your mind. I knew it—'

'—no,' Albert interrupted her train of thought before it spiralled out of control. 'I have not changed my mind. I'm just checking you haven't.'

'Why would I?'

'Because you've spent three years saying no, and nothing has changed recently. Other than the fact you came close to dying at Summerland.'

'And you're worrying that might be the reason I planted a smacker on you?'

'Yes.'

'That weren't the reason. I'll talk to you about it soon, I promise. But, trust me,' she broke off, staring out of the window at the crowds passing by on the pavement outside Brown's, then turned her gaze back to Albert. 'This don't come easy, Albert. All that lovey-dovey stuff. But you don't need to worry about me. Not one little bit. I'm your girl. Always will be.'

He reached for her hand across the table.

'But what about you?' Minnie asked. 'I still can't have children, that ain't changed. You sure you want a life where you'll never be a father?'

'I'm sure,' he said, raising her hand to his lips.

They sat in silence for a while, both lost in their unexpected happiness and the vision of a future life together.

'Any news on Lizzie?' Minnie asked eventually.

Albert shook his head. 'I think when they find Wentworth, they'll find Lizzie.'

Minnie sighed. 'I can't bear the thought that she was in on it all along.'

'Why else would she run?'

'I dunno. Fear? Panic? She's been with Wentworth for years. She might not know how to be without him. I just... trusted her, I suppose.' She fell silent again.

'What is it?' Albert asked.

'I saw things. At Summerland. Things that don't make any sense to me. And I think only Lizzie can provide the answers.'

He squeezed her hand again. 'They'll find her, don't you worry.'

'And Jessica's trial?' Minnie asked.

'Next week, apparently.'

'Blimey, that's fast.'

'She's not denying anything. And it's become a very public case, which calls for a swift resolution. The wheels of the legal system can move with remarkable speed when they need to.'

'C'mon,' Minnie said, gesturing to one of the waitresses for their bill. 'Let's swing by Marylebone and see if John's got any news.'

As they left the tearoom, Minnie slid her hand into Albert's, as naturally as if they'd been doing it all their lives.

The trial was over quickly. A blessing maybe, given the verdict was never in doubt. A morning's worth of witnesses, thirty minutes' deliberation and the judge donned his square of black cloth. Jessica Mortmain was to be hanged by the neck until she was dead. In two days' time.

Minnie couldn't have said why she felt the need to be present in court, but she turned up nonetheless. She'd asked Albert to stay away from the trial, but he was waiting for her as she exited the courtroom, taking her hand without saying a word. They walked in silence back to the Palace, where Tansie and Dorothy were expecting her. One look at Minnie's face and they knew the outcome.

'I know I should be glad that Henry's killer has been brought to justice,' Dorothy said, 'but it doesn't seem enough. Wentworth should hang as well.'

'They need to catch him first,' Albert said. 'Although, even then, there's a chance he'll escape the noose. Jessica made it very clear that Wentworth played no part in Henry's murder, or Gwendolen's, and there's no evidence linking him to either crime.'

'But he concealed the cause of Gwendolen's death from her family, bribed the doctor to sign the death certificate,' Dorothy said.

'A clever barrister might convince a jury that was all done in a misguided effort to protect Jessica,' Albert said.

'Could you and Min give a statement to the police?' Tansie said. 'Tell them about what Wentworth did to those women?'

'We've already done it,' Albert said, looking across at Minnie. 'Charlotte too. Whether or not the judge will pay any mind, who can say?'

Minnie took the gin Tansie offered her and slumped into a chair. She closed her eyes. Jessica's face was there, as she'd appeared in court earlier today, gloriously defiant, flushed with joy in the belief that she'd saved Wentworth. Minnie felt her mind wander as the tiredness from the day's proceedings set in. Would they cut Jessica's hair, she wondered, before they hanged her? If she'd got a prison sentence, they'd have cut it then. Minnie had heard that women prisoners kept their hair in a box of their belongings awaiting their release. She imagined how it might feel to serve years in Newgate or the like, to be released twenty, thirty years later and open the box of your possessions to find that long hank of hair, belonging to a much younger woman …

'Minnie?' Albert said loudly.

She'd been lost in her thoughts. She raised her head slowly and gave him a weak smile. 'I'm here,' she said.

'Tansie wondered if we might all go for supper,' Albert said. 'If you feel up to it.'

Minnie thought about it and realised she was ravenous. She nodded.

The next day Minnie stood silently at the entrance to Newgate, the grey, imposing façade looming above her. She had asked Albert not to come, but now she was regretting that decision.

She made her way round to the governor's house and was ushered into a tiny office with windows looking out on the Old Bailey, where she was asked to wait. Minnie glanced round the room. A shelf ran around it, with plaster heads positioned all the way along, accompanied by the occasional plaster hand.

She moved forward and read the inscriptions carved into the clay beneath each head. Greenacre. Good. Müller. The names needed no further explanation. Everyone had heard of Daniel Greenacre, James Good, Franz Müller. Notorious for all the worst reasons.

A small, brisk-looking woman entered, her broad smile somehow incongruous in this room of death. She was dressed entirely in black with a huge ring of keys at her belt. 'I am Mrs Jeffries, one of the wardresses here. I see you've been looking at the death masks of our more notorious inmates. Perhaps one day you'll provide us with some additions.'

Minnie gave her a blank stare.

'With someone you catch, Miss Ward,' she said. 'Your reputation precedes you. It would be quite the coup to have Lord Linton as part of our little collection, but he is seeing out his sentence in Broadmoor, I understand.'

'I'm here to see Jessica Mortmain,' Minnie said. She'd had to call in a few favours and grease a few palms to secure this meeting with Jessica. She didn't want to waste any of the precious time available to her.

'Of course, of course,' Mrs Jeffries said. 'If I might trouble you first to sign our visitors' book?' She gestured towards a large journal, which Minnie dutifully signed while Mrs Jeffries disconnected the ring of keys from her belt.

Within the first minute of leaving the small office, Minnie had lost track of where she was. The smell was the first thing she noticed: sweat and dirt and food. And overlying it all, something else. It seemed too poetic to say it smelled of despair, but that was the best way to describe it. They passed through what felt like an endless number of heavy oak doors, each one needing to be unlocked and relocked behind them, leading to narrow stone passages that looked just like the ones they had left behind, then further doors, further locking and unlocking.

Mrs Jeffries spoke over her shoulder. 'On my first day here I was convinced I'd never find my way back out. I entertained the strangest fancies that I might end up being mistaken for a prisoner and find myself incarcerated at the end of the day. But you learn your way round remarkably quickly. For a start-off, this is the women's wing of the prison. Then each corridor, each door, has its own little idiosyncrasies. See, the nails on this door are in a slightly different pattern to the one we've just passed through. The different wards form a square. One side abuts the Old Bailey, another what used to be the College of Physicians, and so on.'

'And that?' Minnie said, gesturing through yet another door to a narrow yard, where about twenty women were passing to and fro.

'Where our prisoners take their exercise,' Mrs Jeffries said. 'See that iron enclosure?' she pointed towards something that looked more like a cage to Minnie's eyes, about six feet high with a roof and iron bars at the front. 'That is where friends and family of the prisoners may communicate with them at certain hours of the day.'

Minnie stopped for a moment. Standing within the visitors' cage was an old woman, holding a small baby in her arms. The woman's skin was almost yellow, and she wore a tattered gown that might once have been black but was now faded to an indeterminate grey. On her head, the remains of a straw bonnet. She was talking earnestly, her fingers stretched between the bars to touch the hand of a young prisoner who looked to be about Minnie's age, but was possibly much younger. Minnie knew how poverty could age you, and she wondered what the young woman was imprisoned for. She thought of asking Mrs Jeffries, but guessed the answer would only make her feel more disheartened than she already did. Petty theft, most likely, a chicken or a handful of eggs to feed herself and her child.

Other women stood at the grating, talking to friends or family, but the majority of the prisoners had no visitors. Minnie wasn't sure which was worse: no one to speak to, or a few snatched moments and then having to watch your loved one turn their back and walk away.

Eventually they reached a cell door exactly like all the others and Mrs Jeffries unlocked it.

Minnie hadn't known what to expect, but the word 'dungeon' sprang to mind. The room was about six feet square, with a table and chair and a narrow bed. There was barely room to move. On the table a Bible, and beneath the bed a privy bowl. An iron candlestick was fixed to the wall, its candle unlit, but Minnie guessed it would barely illuminate the gloom when darkness fell. A single, small window was placed so high up the wall it was impossible to see out of it, even if you stood on the table. Minnie recalled her visit to Teddy Linton the year before, the relative luxury of his cell in Broadmoor, equipped with rugs and cosy blankets, numerous books and writing materials. Windows he could look out of at any point.

Jessica was seated on the solitary chair by the end wall but rose immediately when she saw who it was. A shadow of disappointment crossed her face, and Minnie knew she'd been hoping it was Wentworth.

Minnie had thought the knowledge of her impending death would bring about a change in the young woman, but she seemed no different. She offered Minnie the seat, positioning herself on the edge of her bed.

'If you've come to gloat,' Jessica said, defiantly tilting her chin upwards, 'you've wasted your time. I'm not afraid of what's to come. And I'm not ashamed of what I did. William is a remarkable – an exceptional – man. My actions saved him from the wickedness of others. I'd do it again tomorrow.'

'I ain't here to gloat,' Minnie said. 'I'm hoping you can give me some answers. Or at least confirm what I think I already know.'

Jessica held her gaze.

'The servant girl who let Dr Venables into Summerland?' Minnie asked.

'That was me.'

'And the person playing the piano in the waiting mortuary?'

'Me again. I had some fun with that one, walking towards you like I was a creature from beyond the veil. You should have seen your face.' She smiled at the memory.

'I smelt jasmine that night. Lizzie's scent.'

'I can't imagine why that was. Lizzie played no part in it.'

Perhaps it had just been an association, Minnie thought. She'd been shown the waiting mortuary by Lizzie and then she'd heard the piano playing and somehow connected it to Lizzie.

'The night of Wentworth's birthday, when we all had cake,' Minnie said. 'He put puerta in my slice, I'm assuming.'

'He did. The cake was already cut, if you remember.'

'But why poison me?'

'You'd seen him in the woods with Charlotte. We knew you were getting closer to the truth and we needed to do something to get you off the scent. William wanted to put more in the cake, but I told him you might notice the taste and get wise to what we were doing. So we gave you enough to confuse you, make you suggestible. Then I lured you downstairs with the piano and William drugged you again.'

'Why didn't the other women wake up at the sound of the piano?'

'They might have done, but William and I locked them all in their rooms so they couldn't do anything even if they'd heard it. We opened your door, if you remember, so you'd hear it more clearly.'

'And that underground room – I'm right in thinking you or Wentworth were going to kill me?'

'We never discussed it, but I think I'd have killed you, yes,' Jessica said calmly, as if they were discussing the weather.

Minnie rose from the seat. 'That's all I need, thanks,' she said, adopting an indifference she did not feel.

Jessica looked disappointed. 'You've come all that way, just for those few questions? You're sure you don't want to know anything more?'

'I've got what I needed,' Minnie said.

She knocked on the cell door. Mrs Jeffries slid back the observation hatch and called through the door, 'Stand in the far corner, Mortmain. Hands where I can see them.'

Jessica did as instructed and the heavy key turned in the lock.

'One thing,' Jessica said, as Minnie started to leave the cell. 'Have they found him?' And for the first time, her voice wavered with emotion.

'This morning,' Minnie said. 'He was caught at Dover, trying to leave the country. He'll go on trial within a few weeks, I should think.'

'But he won't hang,' Jessica said, her voice rigid with defiance. 'They've nothing to hang him for.'

'We'll see about that,' Minnie said.

She took her skirts in her hand and swept out of the cell.

FORTY-ONE

When Minnie got back to the Palace Tansie was hovering in the alley by the stage door.

'What's wrong?' Minnie said.

'Lizzie Spinks is here to see you,' Tansie said. 'I've sent for Albert. What about the police?'

'No need. Is she alone?'

'She is. I've put her out in the auditorium. Kippy and Bobby are working out there, so you'll have someone if you need them. But I'm thinking you should wait here until Albert arrives.'

Minnie shook her head and made her way through to the auditorium. She knew she had nothing to fear from Lizzie. Jessica's answers in Newgate had confirmed what Minnie had suspected all along. Lizzie was seated on a chair near the stage, her long white-blonde plait pulled forward over her shoulder. She did not rise from the seat at Minnie's approach. She still possessed the unnatural calmness that she'd shown at Summerland.

Close to the stage, Kippy and Bobby were painting a set of scenery flats, a job they would normally have undertaken in Kippy's workroom. Their quiet conversation was a comforting backdrop. Periodically they glanced over, and Minnie knew they were ready to spring at any moment. Tansie hovered in the wings.

'Why did you run?' Minnie asked, pulling up another seat and asking the question as if they were just resuming a recently interrupted conversation.

'I'm not entirely sure. I had thoughts of killing him, but I knew I'd never be able to do it. Maybe I just wanted to find him. Ask him why he'd done what he'd done.' Lizzie looked round her at the auditorium. 'This is where I first met you.'

And with those words, it was as if a veil fell from Minnie's eyes and she saw clearly for the first time in weeks. 'So Wentworth knew who I was because of—'

'Me, yes. It was me who recognised you at that first séance.'

'But we didn't know each other – did we?'

'Not as such,' Lizzie said. 'Years ago, when I was only ten, eleven, and William and I were first starting out, we appeared at the Palace a couple of times. You were performing then, topping the bill most nights. You had the audience eating out of the palm of your hand.'

'Why don't I remember you?' Minnie asked.

'There were a lot of acts, coming and going. And, like I said, we were only there once or twice. I was younger. William made me wear a dark wig for a while. Said it made me look more mysterious.'

'So, if you worked at the Palace, that's how you knew Rose.'

'I met her first when we were both at the Star. We were great friends for a little while, in that way that happens when you work together.'

'And it was Rose who told you,' Minnie said.

'About what happened to you? Yes. But I don't want you to think she just blurted it out, mind. We were talking about fellas, and I was spouting some romantic nonsense about true love, and Rose said you couldn't trust any man. That's when she told me about you. By way of a cautionary tale.'

Albert and Ida had been right all along. Rose had shared the most intimate details of her life. She wished Rose were still alive so she could give her a right bullyragging for what she'd done. And then hug her afterwards in forgiveness. For what did it matter, after all. She no longer felt ashamed of what had happened. And Ida had been right. The one person whose opinion mattered more than anyone else's already knew about Beresford. Knew and didn't care, other than for the pain it had caused her.

'And the spirit photograph?' Minnie asked.

'A bit of a lark. And a way of making money. William set it all up and we did well out of it for a while. But Rose didn't like it. Said her ma believed in it all and it felt like we were conning people.'

Minnie remembered her finger tracing the outline of Rose's face, her knowledge that it couldn't be Rose and yet the overwhelming hope that it could be. A flash of anger twisted in her gut.

'You're saying you weren't involved in what Wentworth was up to, but you must have told him who I was. Set me up to believe Rose was speaking to you. Got me out to Summerland. What was all that, if it weren't helping him?'

Lizzie gave a bitter laugh. 'I've grown so used to doing what William asked of me over the years, I didn't think to question him about this. Or anything else. He knew you were a detective 'cos of the newspapers writing about you and Albert. Said he didn't know what you were after, but you were going under a false name so you must be investigating the Sisterhood, and the best way of finding out was to invite you to Summerland. Once we got you there, I swear I didn't know anything more about what went on.'

'The puerta?'

A shadow crossed Lizzie's face. 'I think he was giving it to me for years without me knowing. The first few days after I left Summerland I thought I was gonna die. Terrible headache, like my head was gonna split open. Heart racing. Sweating buckets. And then I slowly started to feel better. Except—' She broke off, fishing in her sleeve for a handkerchief. 'I don't hear the spirits any more. They've gone. All of them.'

'It was the drug?'

'It must have been. All those years I believed in it, and it was just another one of his wicked lies.'

Minnie's anger subsided as swiftly as it had arisen. She reached forward and took Lizzie's hand while the girl sobbed quietly. Kippy and Bobby had abandoned any pretence of painting the flats and had moved closer, drawn in by Lizzie's words.

'I need to tell you something, Minnie,' Lizzie said, breathing deeply and drying her eyes. 'I've kept it a secret all these years, but if it will help to put him in prison, I want people to know.'

Minnie dreaded what Lizzie was about to tell her. Her heart was so heavy with what she'd learned and witnessed in recent weeks. Gwendolen's terrible, lonely death. Lady Harriet's grief and blame. Dorothy's vacant stare when she considered the loss of Henry. She wanted to hold up a hand, to stop Lizzie telling her anything more. To put an end to all this sorrow and wickedness and loss.

But she couldn't do that, could she? Lizzie needed to tell her story, and Minnie needed to listen.

'I was ten,' Lizzie said, her voice wavering and so quiet that Minnie had to lean forward to hear her. 'My brother, Ralph, he was seven. It was just me, Ralphie and Ma, living in a filthy, tiny room in Southwark. My pa?' she shrugged. 'No idea where he was. He left just before Ralph was born.' She looked up at Minnie. 'I'd love for you to meet my brother,' she said, the pride evident in her voice. 'Smart as a whip. Proper clever. He uses words I've never heard of. Feel like I need to carry a dictionary with me every time I see him, just so I can figure out what he's saying. 'Course, some of that is his schooling, but he was clever before he ever set foot in school. You need to understand that.'

Minnie nodded.

'So, I was ten, Ralphie was seven. And we didn't have two farthings to rub together. Ma was working all the hours God sent just to put some food on the table. She went hungry more times than I can mention, just to make sure Ralph and I were fed. It was desperate.'

Minnie nodded again, this time with genuine understanding. She knew what it was to go hungry. And what the options might be for a young girl to put money on the table.

'Ralph made a few pennies as a crossing sweeper, but he was little and young, and he never stood a chance when some older cove wanted to muscle in on his pitch. I did all the piecework I could lay my hands on, but it was rough work. I weren't good enough with my needle to do any of the fancy stuff that makes more money. Ma did the same when she got home from her cleaning jobs and factory work. But we weren't doing well. And that's when William entered the picture.

'He took the rooms on the floor above us, and he got chatting to Ma one day. Said he was an experienced practitioner in the art of spiritualism. Turned out later, that was a lie. He was only just starting out. He'd worked in the halls as a mesmerist for a while, but he said he'd got tired of it and that was when the spirits drew him to them.'

'He raped a girl the year before,' Minnie said. 'When he worked in the halls, he spied on the women, just like he did at Summerland. He raped a woman called Grace Hardy. She was a girl at the time. Eleven years old. That's why he abandoned his mesmerist act. I'm assuming he changed his appearance in some way when he went back into the halls with you.'

'I didn't know that, about the other girl,' Lizzie said. 'If I'd known that—' She broke off and rose from her seat, moving into the darkness of the auditorium, her long plait of hair almost glowing. 'Anyway,' she continued, 'he told Ma he was in need of an assistant. He said I gave off a forceful energy, and he reckoned that with a bit of training, I'd be able to channel the spirits. If Ma had been a different kind of woman, she might have told him to sling his hook. But she believed in it all. Her parents were Irish and Ma reckoned she had the gift of the sight. And here was this fella, all charm and flash, saying that I had the gift as well. He spoke like a toff, or enough of a toff to fool Ma and me, and we fell for it. There was money in it. He said he'd pay for Ralph's education. Send him to a really good school, where they'd appreciate how clever he was. I wanted it, too,' she said, 'I don't want you thinking Ma forced me into it. She didn't. I was just as charmed by him as she was.'

'But you were ten,' Minnie said. 'And it was your ma's job to look after you.'

Tears filled Lizzie's eyes. 'She thought she *was* looking after me. And I never told her the whole story.'

'Why not?' Minnie asked, although she already knew the answer. Lizzie hadn't told her ma – hadn't told anyone, she guessed – because nobody would have believed her. And it wouldn't have undone what Wentworth had already done.

'I couldn't tell her,' Lizzie said. 'She'd have tortured herself with guilt. And what good would that have been for anyone?'

'When did it start?' Minnie said.

'Straight away,' Lizzie said, her matter-of-fact tone making Minnie want to cry. 'The very first time I was left alone with him. He was so – bold. So sure he could do whatever he pleased and I'd say nothing. And I couldn't, could I? Ralph was about to start at his new school. Said he wanted to become a teacher one day. Or maybe even a doctor. He was so full of hope. And if I said anything all that hope would be gone, wouldn't it.' Her hands moved in front of her, like a magician palming a card. 'I had nothing to gain from saying anything and everything to lose. It was all over for me the minute William first laid his hands on me.'

She started to cry again. Minnie stood up and took Lizzie into her arms. After a few minutes, Lizzie pulled away from her, dabbing her eyes with a handkerchief. 'You must let me finish,' she said. 'This isn't the whole story. Not yet. And if I don't tell it now, I never will.

'So that was the start of my new life. William taught me some tricks like I told you, Minnie, palming and the like, and we set ourselves up as spiritualists. We made some money, enough to keep Ralph in school and Ma out of the workhouse. But it weren't enough.

William always wanted more. Said we needed a completely new act, a way of making a spirit materialise.'

'That's where Pooky arrived on the scene, I take it?'

'Pooky was already talking to me as part of our act. But William said it weren't enough, that we needed people to *see* Pooky. *Feel* him the way I did. Or thought I did, at least. That was the way to make real money.'

'But it's you, isn't it? When Pooky is at the séances, moving among the audience, that's you,' Minnie said.

'It is. But we had to come up with a few tricks. The luminous stuff on Pooky's clothes, you drop the heads of a load of matches into a bottle of water. When you let a little air into the bottle it glows, and you sprinkle the liquid on some cotton or muslin.'

'And you have some means of freeing yourself from the rope bindings,' Minnie said.

Lizzie nodded. 'I sit well forward on my chair when I'm being tied to the back of it, so there's a bit of slack. Then it's usually just a few twists of my hands, and I'm out. No one's ever much cop at tying knots, particularly when there's a pretty girl involved. Once I was free, I'd slip a luminous sheet over my head and move among the audience. And it was a huge success. Bigger than we could ever have imagined. We made a lot of money. I never knew how much, exactly, 'cos William looked after that side of things. That's when he got the idea of the Spirit Sisterhood. Said we could set ourselves up in the countryside. Make some serious money.'

'That's something I don't understand,' Minnie said. 'Wentworth was getting young, rich women out to Summerland with the view to taking their money. Why not fill the house with women? Why so few of you?'

'Women can be troublesome, William always said. They like to talk. With only a handful of us there, he could supervise what we were doing, thinking. And I wonder now if the money was just a side issue. What he really wanted was the chance to spy on us, control us.'

'Moving there, encouraging young women to join you, did you not worry he'd—' Minnie said.

Lizzie looked blank.

'—do to another girl what he'd done to you?' Minnie continued.

Lizzie laughed, but there was no joy in her laughter. 'Not at the time. William said I was special. Said he wanted no one but me.' She faltered, as if facing all over again the level of Wentworth's deceit. A shadow of great sorrow crossed her face. 'He said we had this special bond. That the spirits had brought us together, so that made it all right. What we did together. But that I was to tell no one, 'cos the spirits would be angry and they'd cut off all communication.'

It was evident from the way Lizzie spoke about Wentworth that she had believed everything he told her. Loved him, perhaps, no matter how little he felt for her.

The stage door slammed in the distance, and moments later Albert rushed into the auditorium. He looked as though he'd run all the way from his house. Probably had, knowing Albert.

Minnie held up a hand. 'S'alright. I'm fine. Lizzie's not fine, but she ain't gonna hurt anyone. She played no part in it all.'

Albert bent over, hands on his thighs, and took several deep breaths. 'Tansie said—'

'I know what Tansie said. But we can call off the cavalry.' Minnie grabbed another chair, took Albert's hand and forced him to sit down. She nodded at Lizzie to continue.

'When he told me to encourage you out to Summerland, I didn't question it, Minnie, and I should have. But he said our work would be threatened with you nosing around. That you might discredit us and then the money would dry up. I just wanted everything to stay exactly as it was. For the next few years at least, until Ralph was schooled and out in the world. 'Course that's all over now. He won't hang, will he?' she said, echoing Jessica's words but with a very different intent.

'He will if we've got anything to do with it,' Minnie said. 'Albert and I have given statements to the police. Charlotte too. And you, if you're happy to do so.'

Lizzie gave a tired smile. 'Like I said, he won't hang. His family have money, you know. That much was true.'

'How on earth did he end up working in the halls?'

'He never said. I think it was to get him closer to young girls. Girls he could exploit.'

Minnie fought back the tears. All those girls and women. Starting with Rose – but, no, starting long before Rose. Exploited and used, tossed aside when they'd reached the end of their usefulness or entertainment. Sometimes it felt like a tidal wave, her and Albert fighting against it, making tiny steps of progress, thinking they were making a difference. But then the tide surged forward again, pulling them under. One day, she thought. One day we'll stop the tide.

But not today.

FORTY-TWO

A few months later, on a beautiful late summer's evening with the heat of the day still lingering in the air, Minnie and Albert entered the Cremorne Gardens. The daytime visitors were leaving, children sleepy in their parents' arms, young men and women kissed by the sun, older couples walking in companionable silence. In an hour or so, when the sun had fully set, the more unsavoury of the Cremorne's clientele would arrive, the darkness affording them a licence for acts usually carried out in the privacy of a bedroom. But Minnie didn't want to think about that now. Tonight, for a few hours, it was just her and Albert.

He helped her into the woven basket, following close behind. A gun was fired, the ropes were loosened and the enormous balloon, filled with gas, ascended into the air. Or, Minnie thought, it would be fairer to say the earth seemed to suddenly fall away beneath them, a sea of upturned faces gazing upwards, hundreds of outstretched hands waving goodbye.

'It's like the stage at the Adelphi,' she said to Albert. 'You can lower it. Tansie's desperate for us to get something similar at the Palace, but after the disaster with the water tank I'm putting my foot down.'

'A lot of good that'll do you,' Albert said. 'You know what he's like. He'll probably have it installed by the time we get back.'

'Albert, are you sure about this? What if the wind takes us and we're swept away?'

He pointed to beneath the basket. The ropes were still tethered to the ground, but they'd been let out, allowing the illusion of freedom.

The balloon rose gently above the trees and below them lay the road outside the Gardens, with groups of tiny little figures and the occasional cry of 'Look, the balloon!' reaching them through the still evening air.

Albert opened a picnic basket which lay on the floor of the balloon and produced a bottle of champagne and two glasses. 'Happy birthday, Miss Ward,' he said, popping the cork with a flourish.

'How'd you know?' Minnie said, narrowing her eyes. 'No one knows when my birthday is.'

'And that is precisely why they call me *Detective* Easterbrook.'

Minnie looked over the high side of the basket. It didn't feel like they were moving at all, more as if the earth below them was slowly unfurling like a diorama laid flat on the ground. She'd expected it to be noisy but it was completely quiet, just the hum of voices and trains and carriages from below. Like the faint buzzing of hundreds of tiny bees.

'What changed?' Albert said, handing her a glass filled with champagne.

'About what?'

'Us. This,' Albert said, taking her hand.

'I was chatting to Lizzie one day at Summerland. She said the spirits were telling me not to feel ashamed any more. Of what Beresford did to me. And I realised I hadn't been ashamed for a long time. 'Cos of you.'

'It was nothing to do with me.'

'Well, that's just where you're wrong, Albert, 'cos it had everything to do with you. Tansie and Bernard and Ida and everyone else – I knew they loved me, cared about me. And keeping busy at the Palace made me feel important. Like the place couldn't run without me—'

'Which it couldn't,' Albert interrupted, 'despite what Tansie says.'

'Dorothy and Bernard might disagree with you there. Anyway, I'm trying to say something nice here, and you keep interrupting.'

Albert placed a finger to his lips.

'You made me – more myself,' Minnie continued. 'The person I became after Beresford, that person had always been a little – toned down.'

'Good God,' Albert said, 'I'd hate to imagine you toned up. I'd only known you about five minutes and you told me I was wound up tighter than a cat's arse, as I remember.'

Minnie gave him a thump on the arm. 'Will you shut up?'

'Not another word,' Albert said. 'I swear.'

'Maybe "toned down" is the wrong way of putting it,' she said. 'I just never felt I could let my guard down. Never felt I could allow myself to really care for someone. 'Cos what happened with Beresford meant I didn't deserve to. Or be cared for in return. But you changed all that. And when I saw Rose – or thought I saw Rose—' She broke off, unsure of how to formulate her feelings. Darkness was descending, and the lamps on the streets below looked like tiny Christmas lights. 'When I saw Rose,' Minnie continued, 'it felt like she was pulling me back towards the past. And I realised I'd been hankering after that ever since she died. Wanting to go back to who I was before all that happened. But when I saw her, when it felt like she was offering me that chance, to undo everything that's happened in the last few years, I knew I didn't want to go back any more. I want to go forward, Albert. With you. With whatever life might throw at us. Mind you, it weren't exactly how I imagined it would be.'

'What wasn't?'

'Us. This. Our first kiss.'

'So you *did* imagine it then?'

'Maybe once or twice,' she said, smiling to herself.

'And that once or twice – how was it?'

'Well, a little more conventional. A nice supper somewhere on the Strand. Maybe a glass or two of fizz. Me wearing a nice frock.

You walking me home under a moonlit sky. That sort of thing. Not me bursting into a room full of people, red and sweaty from running through the woods, having just poked out a fella's eye.'

'You looked beautiful, Minnie.'

'Like I've said before, you need to get your peepers seen to.'

Minnie looked out at the vista before them. They were floating effortlessly, soundlessly above the earth, the sky above them the deepest blue and studded with hundreds of thousands of stars. Below them, too, a sea of lights. Immeasurable. Endless. They said nothing for a while.

'I hear Ralph Spinks is thriving at school,' Albert said eventually.

Minnie gave a gentle smile. 'So Lizzie tells me. Mrs Sykes's very generous payment went to good use.'

'And Grace?'

'Even better. She might not have a career in opera, but she'll do nicely for the Palace. Not top billing, but not far off. Artie must be happy.'

'He is. He's even happier about my forthcoming performance at the Playhouse. The man's convinced it will be the first step in my glittering theatrical career. His enthusiasm is unrelenting.'

'Just what you need in a manager,' Minnie said, emptying her glass and holding it out to Albert for a refill. 'And so nice of Tanse to shut the Palace that night so we can all go.'

'Any further developments with Tansie and Dorothy?' Albert asked, deliberately ignoring her last comment.

'Tansie and Dorothy are – well, they're Tansie and Dorothy. It makes no sense to me. An intelligent, beautiful woman perfectly capable of making her own way in life falls for a short, foul-mouthed, tight-fisted bumble puppy like Tansie. There's no oddsing it. Still, there's one upside.'

'Which is?'

'The monkey's gonna make a lovely pageboy.'

CODA

The man is tall, his nose flattened and crooked, fists like plates. The woman is a great deal shorter. There is a liveliness about her, an asymmetry to her face that some would say holds her back from true beauty. But that is not how the man sees her at all.

His arm slips round her waist, his hand broad and strong, the fingers warm, so warm she swears she can feel their heat on her skin.

He holds her hand. They laugh about how it's like she's holding hands with a bear, her slender paw enveloped in his.

They walk together like this, talking of nonsense as their heads incline towards one another.

He helps her into the basket and, with a single shot of a gun, the balloon ascends.

They are watched. Not by Wendall Potts. He is firmly ensconced in prison for extortion, and a few other offences thrown in for good measure. His days of watching Minnie and Albert are firmly behind him.

This time, the watcher is a woman. A tiny woman, probably no more than four and a half feet. Like a little doll, with a rosebud mouth and large brown eyes. Her skin is tanned, but not from an English summer. She is trim, with a nervous energy about her, dark eyes glinting in a face that looks like it would fall easily into a smile. She sports sparkling rings on every finger and her wrists are wreathed with what look, at first glance, to be gold bracelets. And why would anyone look closely enough to question the authenticity of how she presents herself?

If she were to speak, her voice would prove surprisingly deep for such a tiny frame, her accent straight from the streets of Whitechapel.

And buried within the folds of her hair, a star-shaped hairpin. Seven points to the star and a large green gem at the centre, encircled by clear stones.

Edie Bennett watches as Albert and Minnie ascend into the air, as they lean over the side of the basket and marvel at the wonders below them. A smile spreads slowly across Edie's face.

Perfect, she thinks.

Just perfect.

ACKNOWLEDGEMENTS

This book has undergone a bit of a journey, starting out with one publisher and entering the world with another. My thanks go to Joe Harper, Claire Handscombe, Polly Mackintosh, Lucy Ramsey and to everyone at Pushkin Vertigo who generously offered me a home.

Huge thanks to the following: my beloved Micky, whose razor-sharp editorial eye brooks no nonsense; Isobel Dixon and Sian Ellis-Martin at Blake Friedmann, without whom I'd be adrift; and my support network of Sara Bayat, Caroline Birks, Maria Butcher, Emily Coutts, Antony Dunford, Jayne Farnworth, Ben Hunt, Natasha Hutcheson, Louise Mangos and Emma Styles – love you, one and all. Massive thanks to the crime writing community, the kindest, most openhearted and generous bunch you'll ever hope to meet; I won't even attempt to list all the wonderful people I've met in the last few years, but you know who you are!

And lastly, but most importantly, all the booksellers, bloggers, librarians, reviewers, crime fiction aficionados and readers who have welcomed Minnie and Albert into their hearts and made all those solitary hours tapping away at a keyboard worthwhile.